THE LAWYER'S TALE

THE LAWYER'S TALE

D. Kincaid

Turtle Bay Books

A Division of Random House

New York

1 9 9 2

Library of Congress Cataloging-in-Publication Data
Kincaid, D.
The lawyer's tale / D. Kincaid.—1st ed.
p.   cm.
ISBN 0-679-40772-3
I. Title.
PS3561.I424L39   1992
813'.54—dc20   92-15628

Manufactured in the United States of America
9 8 7 6 5 4 3 2
First Edition

For B.

THE
LAWYER'S
TALE

1

Harry Cain set his watch on L.A. time, kicked off his Gucci loafers, and eased back into the big first-class seat. It was only five o'clock in New York, but the January afternoon had already faded into evening. He could barely make out the hard-packed snow that lined the runway.

Harry smiled up at the tall blond stewardess offering champagne. In a broad southwestern drawl, she announced that she was "Dalma." She stood, model-like, one foot posed behind the other, her tight black skirt accentuating the lush curve of her hips and her long, well-shaped legs. Very nice, he thought, as she moved up the aisle. He wondered if Dalma might like a ride home when they got to L.A. He pictured his hand on her silken thigh as they sped across the city in a moonlit limousine. And then . . .

His fantasy was interrupted by the booming voice of the captain. "Sorry, folks, but it looks like we'll be delayed awhile awaiting clearance to take off. Please remain in your seats with your seat belt fastened. The good news is we still anticipate an on-time arrival in Los Angeles."

Harry peered through the window, straining to see the wing. It was very cold outside. Would they be in the plane too long before takeoff? Would the wings ice up? He imagined the huge plane thundering down the runway, struggling to rise, failing, the panic of his fellow passengers, the obliterating moment of impact.

The news would be a shock. "Cut down in his prime," they'd say. Maybe it was trite, he thought; but it was true. It *was* his prime.

4

There'd be a memorial service, of course. Friends would want to speak. Actors, authors, at least one senator. For the finish, Sinatra's "My Way" would tear their hearts out. He could picture the crowd moving slowly up the aisles, some fighting back tears, others weeping openly.

He hummed softly as the words sounded in his mind, ". . . and more, much more than this, I did it my way."

By God, I did, he thought. I always did it my way. He looked up to see Dalma coming toward him down the aisle. She was carrying a newspaper and smiling broadly. The memorial service gone from his mind, Harry focused on her fluid, sensual walk. She stopped at his seat and handed him the *Daily News*.

"Some picture of you, huh, Mr. Cain?"

"What picture?"

"Right there . . . see?" she pointed to the front page of the tabloid. SULTAN AND SUPERLAWYER FIGHT OVER GIRL screamed the headline.

Below it was a huge picture of Harry, his coat sleeve torn, lunging toward the camera. A tall, dark-haired woman stood behind him, looking beautiful and frightened. Between them was a small, rotund man, his face smeared with what appeared to be blood.

The story on the second page described a fistfight in front of "New York's lavish Ritz-Carlton Hotel between legendary California lawyer Harry Cain, often called the 'Sunset Bomber,' and the sultan of Bandar, the fifth wealthiest man in the world."

According to the story, neither man would comment on the cause of the fracas, but it appeared to involve "beautiful musician Alla Van Meer, reportedly a constant companion of Mr. Cain on his frequent trips to New York."

"Holy shit!" said Harry under his breath.

"Did you ask for something, Mr. Cain?", said the stewardess, smiling down at him.

"No, but I'll have a vodka on the rocks—make it a double."

There was no way this story wasn't going to reach his wife—hadn't reached her already. He leaned back and closed his eyes. He had to think of a way to explain it. Only six months ago, a "good friend" had told Nancy she'd seen Harry kissing and fondling a tall, dark girl in the doorway of a San Francisco hotel room. He'd sworn that it was just a drunken one-night stand—a crazy mistake. He'd promised it would never happen again and pleaded for forgiveness.

For two days, Nancy had shut herself up in their bedroom, not saying a word and not eating. When she finally emerged, she forgave him, but told him it had to be the last time. She couldn't take any more. The pain was too great.

What would she say now? What would she do? He was afraid he knew.

Nancy Cabot Cain was his center, the person who shared his life. She'd been that since they first met in Harvard Square so many years before, Harry, the superachieving "A" student, the *Law Review* editor, bursting with energy and ambition, and Nancy, the dark, patrician Radcliffe girl, so feminine, so warm, so quietly intelligent. They'd fallen deeply in love and spent every available moment together, delighting in a physical relationship that changed their lives.

Before Nancy, girls had been "the enemy," a prey on whom to use any tactic leading to bed, where he savored the victory as much as the pleasure. Nancy showed him that making love and being in love were intertwined . . . wonderfully so. She was on his side. More than that, she *was* his side. They were like one person, as they laughed and played and loved in those long Cambridge nights.

To them, this was "forever." Both knew it with a fierce certainty. When law school was over, Nancy had defied her parents, had gone with Harry to live in California. He'd grown up there as an orphan, hardened by his forced independence, and it was there he'd felt his roots.

They'd married and had a daughter, Gail, who almost died at birth. Gradually, employing his intelligence and energy in an endless round of fifteen-hour days, Harry had risen to the top of his profession. He'd won case after case, and the cases grew in importance as the years went by. The facts might be against him . . . or the law . . . or both, but, somehow, he'd found a way to win. He'd had to. And he did. Ultimately, he'd become the litigator of choice in every major case. Slim and darkly handsome, with a quotable wit, he'd developed into a media favorite. He was dubbed the "Sunset Bomber" for his unbroken string of courtroom victories and his lavish offices on

6

Sunset Boulevard. He had arrived. He was becoming a legend. And he loved it.

Meanwhile, Nancy, having made a lovely, beautifully organized home for him, began to wonder about her own life. Not one for self-pity and having been a *summa* in art history, she'd thrown herself into the complexities and politics of the art world. Ultimately, the force of her intelligence and the scope of her knowledge led her to become chairman of the Arts Council, and then the governor's advisor on fine arts. Her life began to work well again, to have a loving, pleasant harmony.

One problem slashed at that harmony like an obsidian blade—Harry's women. Orphaned as a child, Harry had battled loneliness by reading, submerging himself in a world of fantasy, lust, and high adventure. Suddenly, finding himself a young adult with mounting responsibilities, practicing law and providing for his family, he yearned for the romance and excitement promised by the novels he'd read as a boy. He was a bright, attractive man, as sensitive and bold, he felt, as the characters in those books. Shouldn't he live with the same dramatic intensity—experience the exciting things he'd read? It was life imitating art. Giving little thought to its impact on Nancy or anyone else, he became involved in a series of brief but intense affairs.

But never—never—had he considered leaving Nancy. She was his life and he was hers. They were still "forever" as far as he was concerned. But would she feel that way when she read the *News*?

He looked around and saw that they were in the air. He hadn't even noticed the takeoff. He barely paid attention to Dalma as she set down his drink. All he could think of was the pain Nancy would suffer when she saw this lurid story. And for what? How could he hurt her with someone like Alla? Why did he go on doing this? Jesus, what a cretin he was! He slammed his hand down on the armrest, spilling vodka into his lap.

Once he'd dried himself, he settled back in his seat and turned to the rest of the *Daily News*. It was a relief just to stop looking at himself lunging across the front page. Almost immediately he sat forward again. The words FORTY MILLION DOLLAR FILM STOLEN leapt out at him. What is this? he thought. Harry Cain Day in the *News*? The brief story reported that the work print of Consolidated Studios' big budget picture *The Last Battle*, directed by Academy Award–winner Joseph Miletti and starring Rod Townsend, had apparently been taken from the editing rooms where it had been stored. The New York sheriff's office was investigating the matter, and the studio was asking for the FBI's assistance.

Only the FBI? Harry thought. Why not the marines? Given the political and financial power Consolidated would bring to bear, he should have an interesting week just trying to keep himself out of jail. Had he gone too far this time? Put himself and his career in jeopardy? Well, there's one thing; he smiled to himself sarcastically. I did it my way.

He sighed and sipped what was left of his drink. Then he closed his eyes and began to review the events that had put his foot in this personal and professional quicksand.

The snow fell heavily, silhouetted against the darkening sky. You could see it from the bed. The room was dark, too. And silent, except for a high, keening sound and the soft *rish-roosh* of silk. After a time, there were small movements, a low moan, a creaking of the large wooden bed. Then a voice, feverish, verging on hysteria:

"My God, don't do that! I'm your sister . . . your sister." Ignoring her pleas, the man began to move with a slow, powerful rhythm. "No, no, we shouldn't. We can't! Dad'll hear us. He'll kill us." Her words trailed off as he continued the relentless motion. Silently, she began to move with him, matching him thrust for thrust. "Oh, no . . . No . . .Oh, Buddy . . .Oh, yes, *yes* . . .*Yes!*" She hissed the word out like a giant female cat, arching her back, pressing herself up against him until she was swept into the throes of a vibrant, shuddering climax.

Hungrily, she wrapped her arms around him, staring up with huge green eyes. For a moment it seemed she should be serious. Then came her low, erotic laugh.

"Oh God, when you're my brother, I can't resist you."

"Better than when I'm the chauffeur?"

"Absolutely. When you're my brother, I'm gone thirty seconds after we begin." She released his grip, stretched luxuriously, and reached for her cigarettes.

Harry got off the bed, walked to the window and stared out over

8

Central Park, blanketed white with snow. He heard her voice behind him.

"I wish you didn't have to go back tomorrow. The trouble with my living in New York is I don't get enough of you."

"Not enough?" he asked, without turning from the window. "If I came more often, you'd cripple me."

"Yes," she said, in a low, throaty voice. "I would. Why not give up that hotshot California law practice and stay here . . . with me? We'll live on love." She walked over to stand beside him. Silent, they watched the snow swirl and dance above the park, muting the lights of the distant buildings.

Harry had known Alla Van Meer for almost a year. Tall, full-figured, with long dark hair, she was half Dutch, half Balinese. Their relationship had started on the coast, where Alla had played the flute with the L.A. Chamber Orchestra. It had continued after she moved to New York to take a job with the New York Philharmonic. She was beautiful and graceful, a complex, often surprising person. A Juilliard graduate, she was an intensely serious musician. Yet, she had the mouth of a dockworker, a volatile temper, and a powerful and imaginative sexuality. She was wanton with Harry, hungering for his lovemaking, which she enhanced by her insistence on playing out her fantasies . . . brother and sister, housewife and traffic cop, heiress and chauffeur. Each of their sexual minidramas seemed to excite Alla more than the last. Each new bizarre or perverse relationship sent her into even faster and more intense waves of erotic pleasure.

Alla had long ago concluded that Harry would never leave his wife. Yes, she could make his body respond. Yes, he was loving, affectionate, and appreciative. And they could discuss anything . . . anything. But it was obvious that Harry felt something for Nancy Cain that went far beyond all that; it was as if they were bonded for life, two aspects of the same person. This was something Alla couldn't comprehend, but she knew it was a barrier she'd never cross, a land she'd never enter. That was why she'd taken the New York job.

Now, sharing his last evening in New York, Alla smiled wistfully, unable to keep her thoughts to herself.

"Harry?"

"Yeah."

"What's going to happen to us?"

"Oh, you'll marry a handsome prince, and I'll win the Nobel Prize, and be knighted and . . ."

"You know what I mean, *us*. Will things ever be different? Are we? . . . Oh, fuck it! In all the time I've known you, you've always avoided coming right out and saying 'I'm never going to be with you permanently—*never*' or 'You don't cut it compared to Nancy' or even 'Your ass is too big.' If I ask you, you won't lie; but you don't ever speak up and tell me where I fit in your life, and my guess is it's probably nowhere."

Harry said nothing. He'd heard speeches like that before, from other women. They could be dangerous. There was no safe reply. Silence was best.

Alla took a long pull on her Gauloise and slowly exhaled.

"I'm sure it was the same with all your women. I used to think it was cowardice. But I changed my mind. It's a kind of love. Misguided and arrogant, but still love. You love women. You hate to hurt them, want them to be happy . . . even at the risk of letting them build false hope.

"On the other hand," she continued, "there's a schlock poem from a pseudo-Chaucerian collection of poems written in the twenties about different people in the city. It's called 'The Lawyer's Tale' and it's about a lawyer who lives behind a mask of self-confidence and rectitude. But what's really there is very different. The author says we'll never see behind the mask or know what's in this lawyer's heart. Maybe that's you."

Still saying nothing, Harry pulled her closer and tenderly kissed her.

"Oh no, you're not going to shut me up with a patronizing kiss on the cheek. I know all your tricks."

But she was smiling now. She threw her head back, and Harry sensed that the danger was past. She stubbed out her cigarette and took him by the shoulders. "Okay, you didn't come here for a lecture. I'll tell you what, let's be the countess and the bellboy." She paused, thinking. "Yes, I'm swathed in sable and jewels and you've just carried my bags to the room."

He turned to her with a grin. "Why do you always get the good parts and the best costumes?"

10

She laughed. "You're just kidding. But you've got a great idea there. Would you consider doing it? Playing the countess, I mean? You'd love it, I promise. I'm the slim young bellboy. I slowly help you off with your furs. Then, before you realize what I'm doing, I'm unzipping your dress, letting it slide to the floor, running my eager hands over your soft body . . ."

"Jesus, Alla. What's next? The gym coach and the fat little boy? The farmer and the chicken?"

"Oh, Harry, don't be such a stiffo. Sometimes you're very square, you know? I enjoy our little games. They excite me, and what's wrong with being excited, *however* you get there? Besides, they let me be someone other than myself, and that's good too."

She leaned closer and stared into Harry's dark eyes.

"Do you think I'm crazy? Perverted? Evil?"

He reached out, taking her hands in his.

"None of those things, Alla. None of them." He pulled her close, holding her to him, looking over her shoulder at the falling snow. "Anyway, we'd better get dressed if you're going to make your eight o'clock concert."

She drew back and looked into his eyes.

"And when you come back to New York?"

"When I come back, we'll play the bellboy and the countess. But, goddamn it, I'm the bellboy!"

They descended in the small mirrored elevator, their images reflected a hundred times.

In the lobby, Alla paused.

"One second, Harry. Hold my flute while I get something from the hotel kitchen."

"What, for Christ's sake? You're going to be late."

"It'll just take a minute. I need the stuff they use to decorate cakes. It's the concertmaster's birthday, and I've got him a spectacular devil's food."

She handed Harry her black instrument case and disappeared into the Jockey Club, returning moments later clutching a spray can of icing.

"Got it. They insisted I take it as a present. But it's orange. I wanted pink." She looked at her watch. "Oh, my God. I am late. Give me my flute and let's find a cab."

The snow was falling even more heavily as they left the lobby. Alla pushed forward to the doorman just as a white stretch limo pulled up to the curb. A large man in a dark suit leapt out and opened the door for a tiny rotund man with a Vandyke beard.

Alla tugged at the doorman's sleeve, distracting his attention.

"Can you get me a taxi? I'm very late."

As the doorman started for the street, the short man seized his arm.

"Excuse me. You must unload my car now!" he commanded in a thick Middle-Eastern accent. "My associates are waiting."

As he spoke, a second car sped to the curb. The car doors flew open and three men rushed out, loaded with photographic equipment. They began shooting pictures of the diminutive foreigner.

"Go on! Get me a cab!" cried Alla to the confused doorman.

"Forget this woman!" bellowed the man. "I need my things *now*!"

Harry saw something in Alla's eyes—something dangerous that impelled him to reach for her.

Too late. She tucked her flute under one arm, raised the spray can, and, moving her hand back and forth in graceful strokes, covered the small man's face with orange icing. Then, with deliberate precision, she decorated his hair, his tie, and his shirt.

Orange stalactites hung from the man's nose and beard. He tried to clear his eyes of the gooey mess, while strobe lights flashed over and over again in a news-photo frenzy.

"You arrogant little worm," cried Alla, bending to spray his shoes.

"Little?" he wailed, "*Little?*"—as if "arrogant" and "worm" carried no insult.

By this time the large dark-suited man had reached Alla, was shoving her roughly away from his orange-faced employer. Her flute flew from under her arm, sliding across the icy sidewalk.

"Hey!" cried Harry. "Get your goddamn hands off her."

"Fuck off, you kike asshole," the big man snarled at Harry, giving Alla another shove with his massive hands.

Harry dove at her assailant, and the two men went down grappling, grunting, trying to punch each other as they rolled in the snow. Alla screamed. The strobe lights continued flashing.

12

Two hotel security men appeared from nowhere, and, with the aid of the doorman, separated the combatants. In a blind rage, Harry kept trying to pull away from the security man, who pinned his arms behind him. Struggling to free himself, he attempted to get at his opponent, who, with his associates, was quickly and firmly escorted into the Ritz-Carlton lobby. When they had gone, the security man handed Alla her flute, put her in a cab and politely guided Harry to the elevator.

"You're lucky you didn't get killed, Mr. Cain. That's the sultan of Bandar; and that big body guard of his is no one to mess with." As Harry rode back to the nineteenth floor he noticed that the sleeve of his jacket was ripped and he had a smear of blood on his shirt. He could find no cuts or bruises. He looked at himself in the mirror and grinned. The blood wasn't his.

Georgine's, Harry's favorite New York restaurant, is a rose-colored, candlelit room in the East Seventies, where Georgine, a tall, striking woman, invariably dressed in black, gives quiet attention to the needs of serious New York diners who know the magic of her kitchen.

Harry was dining there with Anne and Mel Brooks, old friends, who were also in New York for a short stay. Laughing at his own clumsy role, he described the scuffle earlier that night at the Ritz-Carlton. He left out Alla's visit to his suite, describing her as a "friend of a friend" he'd met in the lobby—a "nice lady, who, it's clear, doesn't like waiting for a cab."

Actually, he didn't need to lie. Anne and Mel were loyal to the core. They wanted only the best for both of the Cains. If they found Harry in bed with another woman, they'd say nothing—ever. But he wouldn't put them in that position. Besides, he'd known the Brooks for years and considered their marriage rock solid. Pride itself made Harry hide the flaw in his own.

They were sharing a succulent risotto with baby asparagus and prosciutto; and, as he piled a heaping spoonful on his plate, Mel asked what kind of a case had brought Harry to New York.

"Consolidated Studios wants to seize Joe Miletti's new film and recut it. I'm representing Joe."

Anne leaned forward, intrigued by the issue.

"Can they do that?"

"We'll see tomorrow. Joe's contract says he has 'final cut.' That means he controls the final form of the picture, and the studio can't re-edit what he gives them. So Joe should win. But you never know."

"Miletti's made some great films. Why would the studio ever *want* to recut his work?"

Harry put down his fork and smiled. "You don't know Yank Slutsky. He's got control of the studio now and he's using it—every day in every way. He likes a happy ending, and Joe's picture doesn't have one. Besides, all studios hate giving up the right of final cut. When they hire a world-class director like Joe, they usually have to. But they still hate it."

"Can you argue the case here in New York?"

"I can, but I'm not going to. We're using a New York lawyer, Andy Goodwin."

The conversation turned back to the hotly debated issue of who should determine the content of a film or play . . . the question of "final cut." Mel remarked that no one seemed to have thought much about the issue until the early eighties, when Warren Beatty battled Paramount over *Reds*. Harry disagreed, arguing that the issue had been around for centuries. He cited *The Merchant of Venice* as an example, pointing out the strange contrast between what sounded like twentieth-century humanism in Shylock's "If you prick us, do we not bleed?" speech and what seemed crass pandering to the bigotry of the Elizabethan crowd at the end of the trial scene.

"Maybe Shakespeare—whoever *that* was—wrote a different trial scene, maybe he didn't have final cut, so the theater owner said 'Hey Bill, the play's okay, but that scene's gotta go.' "

The waiter brought their second dish, capellini con vongole. As they were served, Anne leaned forward, poking her fork at Harry. As always, she had a strongly held opinion. "What do you mean 'whoever that was'? There's no reason to think the plays were written by anybody but Shakespeare himself. You're too smart to buy that nonsense about Bacon or Queen Elizabeth secretly writing them."

Harry's eyes flashed in the candlelight. Along with many other aspects of English history, he loved the Shakespeare controversy.

"Look," he argued, shaking red-pepper flakes on his pasta, "Shakespeare was tight as hell, absolutely obsessed with money and property. He was so picky when writing his will that he even left his wife his 'second-best bed.' But the will says nothing about any literary property, and his unpublished plays would have been an extremely valuable asset . . . if he really wrote them. I don't buy the Bacon cryptogram theory any more than you do. I'd love to think it was the queen, but I see no evidence of it, and there's a strong argument against her . . . based on *Richard the Second*. You can make a good case for the Earl of Oxford though, and also for Marlowe."

"That's one I'd like to hear," said Anne skeptically, grinning at her friend's enthusiasm.

"Well, to begin with, Marlowe was a fine writer, and he supposedly died in a whorehouse brawl that sounds like a complete fake to me. Marlowe was in trouble with the Crown—probably thought he was going to be arrested, maybe burned. So he visits a sort of private brothel, has some drinks, and supposedly gets killed there in a fight with a guy who just happens to work for Marlowe's patron, a guy who's been Marlowe's buddy for years. And Shakespeare's plays were only published after Marlowe supposedly died."

"You're kidding, counselor," Mel said, twisting capellini against his spoon.

"I'm not. I think the fight and Marlowe's death were phony, staged to get him off the hook. Of course, that doesn't prove he wrote Shakespeare's plays, but I think I could sell the theory to a jury."

"Harry Cain! Am I glad to see *you*."

Harry looked up. A pale, lightly freckled redhead in an ankle-length chinchilla coat stood beside the table. She was in her early forties and faint signs of age were just beginning to appear in her otherwise lovely face. Harry rose to greet her.

"Well, Pat. How are you?" Without waiting for an answer, he turned to the others. "Pat, this is Mel and Anne Brooks. Pat Campbell, Mrs. Ewing Campbell."

Ewing Campbell, a magazine publisher and philanthropist, was one of L.A.'s richest and most influential citizens. At seventy-eight, he had married Pat Somerset, a former model turned television executive, and a formidable lady in her own right.

Mel stood to greet her, taking one of her outstretched hands.

"Harry, I won't disturb you now, but I'd like very much to see you back in town. When do you fly home?"

"Tomorrow afternoon, Pat. Why don't you call me?"

"I will, Harry."

"Well, I'll let you get back to your dinner. Please excuse my interruption." Giving them a gracious smile and a "nice meeting you," Pat Campbell swept out of the restaurant with two other women who had been waiting for her near the door.

Harry was intrigued. Why would Pat Campbell want to see him? It wouldn't be an ordinary legal problem. The Campbells were clients of a large downtown law firm. Divorce? It seemed unlikely. Despite the enormous difference in their ages, the Campbells' marriage seemed to be hugely successful. But you could never tell about a marriage from the surface, from what two complicated people allowed the world to see.

Harry knew that better than most.

The next morning was the coldest of the year. Down in Foley Square, grimy snow piled high against the old stone courthouse. An icy wind blew it in drifts across the worn marble steps. Lawyers, judges, and litigants hurried up and down, huddled into their coats, faces drawn, grimacing. The wind's howl drowned out the incessant noise of the New York traffic.

Inside, in the second-floor hallway, it was warm and quiet. Courts were already in session behind a long row of closed, padded doors. Here and there, lawyers sat on heavy wooden benches in silent perusal of files and briefs, waiting for their cases to be called.

Two judges, black robes billowing behind them, walked briskly down the corridor, heads close together, speaking in low, murmuring tones. As they rounded the corner, the area returned to orderly, contemplative silence.

Somewhere, a clock was ticking. There was a low muffled cough. Pages were turned. Then, once again, quiet.

Suddenly, the swinging doors of a courtroom burst open. Harry Cain strode into the corridor, his face tight with anger. A pudgy, balding lawyer came through the doorway behind him, carrying a heavy briefcase. Harry's voice boomed down the corridor, shattering the silence.

"Justice? Are you kidding? That wasn't justice and that was no fucking judge! That two-bit political hack!" From the hallway benches, lawyers looked up, startled at the tirade.

"All that asshole cared about was which side could do more for him, and the answer to *that* was obvious . . . Consolidated Studios."

The nearest courtroom doors swung open and a heavy-faced bailiff peered out with a scowl, seeking the source of the loud and impermissible noise.

Harry stopped and put his hand on his companion's arm. He went on in a quieter tone. "Don't feel bad, Andy. It's not your fault. You argued it well, but, with that dirt bag on the bench, there was no way you were going to win. Just no way."

A television camera crew came around the corner as he finished speaking. Spotting Harry, they ran forward, cameras raised, strobe lights flashing. A microphone was thrust in his face as he turned away from the harsh glare. "Mr. Cain! WCBS, Mr. Cain. Any comment on the court's order to turn Miletti's film over to the studio?"

"No comment."

"Will the studio recut *The Last Battle* now that the court's given it to them?"

"No comment."

"Mr. Cain, you've become a legend out on the coast. Would *you* have won if you'd argued the motion yourself?"

"No comment" was Harry's irritated response. Then he saw the hurt look in his companion's eyes. "No. I *will* comment on that. Mr. Goodwin here did a fine job. I could have done no more. The decision was simply wrong and unfair."

"Is it true Joe Miletti spent three years working on *The Last Battle?*"

"Yes, that's true."

"Doesn't that seem a very long time?"

"Not to someone who knows anything about the process of making a serious film."

"Will Miletti appeal?"

"We're discussing that now, so if you gentlemen will excuse us . . ." He took Goodwin's arm, steering him down the corridor away from the lights and the reporters, who were huddled together discussing their story.

"Sometimes the press gives me a pain in the ass, Andy, you know that?"

"I can imagine, Harry; but, listen, an appeal's not out of the question here. I think we can turn this thing around in the Appellate Division."

"There's no time for that, Andy. Once the studio gets their hands on the film, they'll recut it and release their own ridiculous version, and everything Joe Miletti's worked for over the last three years will be down the drain."

Harry paused, staring at the tile floor. He seemed deeply troubled. His jaw muscles tightened, his fists clenched. After a moment he looked up, his dark eyes flashing with anger.

"I'll tell you something, Andy. I'm not going to sit back and take this. If they want to forget the rules, use a perjured affidavit, and a judge who's crooked or incompetent, or both, then . . ." He didn't finish the sentence.

"Listen," he said impatiently, "I've got some calls to make. Where can I get change?"

"At the newsstand over there. But why not use your credit card, or just charge the calls to your office phone?"

"I can't. These calls are special."

Harry gave no further explanation. He looked warily down the corridor, then turned back to his companion. "So okay, Andy, I'll call you later." With a mock salute, he moved toward the newsstand, still looking angry, but determined.

Five minutes later, Harry stood at the bank of pay phones, his fingers drumming nervously on one of the black-and-chrome boxes. "Mr. Matsuoka, please. This is Mr. Cain. No, forget my messages for now, just get me Mr. Matsuoka." There was a brief pause, then Harry heard his partner's familiar voice.

"Harry, how'd it go?"

"Terrible, John, a disaster. It wasn't really a 'hearing' at all. The fucker just ignored the record and ordered the film turned over to the studio. It was absolutely unbelievable. If I can't stop 'em somehow, they'll pick up the film today and Joe Miletti can kiss his picture good-bye. In ten days, it'll be Yank Slutsky's idiotic version, happy ending and all."

"But, Harry, the contract gave Joe final cut. They *can't* change the picture after he's cut it. The judge had to see *that.*"

"Sure, John, but he ruled that Joe lost his right to final cut because he didn't finish by February first."

"That's crazy! Sid Serlin told Joe he could have until May. He's the senior vice president of the studio, for Christ's sake. So how could the judge rule Joe was late?"

"He couldn't, but he did. Serlin filed an affidavit that just left out the extension he gave Joe. Didn't deny it—simply left it out . . . just said the written contract required delivery of the film by February first, and it wasn't delivered by then, so the studio can take it away from Joe and recut it. Just a goddamned lie! Andy Goodwin put in two affidavits proving that Serlin said a May delivery was okay; but that little motherfucker of a judge just ignored the evidence and said that according to the contract Joe was late delivering the film and so lost his cutting rights. And because of that, the asshole ordered the film turned over to the studio 'forthwith.' "

"Maybe you should have argued it yourself, Harry—New York or not."

"I don't think it would have made any difference, John. Andy did his best. He kept screaming about Serlin's extension of time; but the judge wouldn't read the file. This wasn't a legal decision. It was Kafka—a nightmare. I think Slutsky bought the guy. Maybe not directly, with money, but, somehow . . . with influence, promises, a blow job, who knows? Anyway, John, I'm not going to sit by and let this happen. I'll tell you that. They didn't play by the rules and, for once, they can't expect *me* to. Fuck *them*!"

"What are you going to do?"

Harry paused. Should he involve his partner? He decided. "I don't know yet, John, but I'll think of something."

Minutes later, Harry was on his third telephone call. "I know Mr. Miletti's in the cutting room, but this is Harry Cain. I've got to speak to him right now. It's important!" There was a brief pause, than a click on the line and an excited voice.

"Harry! What happened? What'd he decide?"

"Never mind about that, Joe. There's no time to talk. I want you to do exactly what I say and ask no questions. Okay?"

The voice on the line became quiet, subdued. "Okay, Harry. Sure."

"Joe, I want you to tell your staff you're going to put off any more work on the film until you hear what the court decides. Give them the rest of the day off and get them out of there right now. Okay?"

"Okay, Harry."

"Fine. Here's what else I want you to do. Listen carefully. Get out of there yourself—right now. You like to gamble—go to Atlantic City. Book a room, come back in the morning. Okay?"

"Sure, Harry, but does this mean we lost, that Slutsky can take over my picture, recut it?"

"We've got no time to talk about that, Joe. I haven't even said the hearing's over. I want you to get your staff out of there and get yourself to Atlantic City . . . *now*!"

"Okay, Harry, if you say so."

"I do say so, Joe. Listen, I'm going back to the coast this afternoon. I'll call you from there tomorrow. And, if you get any calls from the press about *anything,* the answer is 'no comment.' Now I gotta run." He hung up and, reaching for one of the quarters stacked in front of him, began the next of his calls.

Harry was awakened by the amplified voice of the stewardess.

"We are making our final approach to landing at Los Angeles International Airport. Please fasten your seat belts, make sure your tray tables are secure, your seats returned to their upright position and all carry-on bags stowed under a seat or in an overhead compartment. We should be on the ground in approximately fifteen minutes."

Putting aside his empty glass, he folded the *Daily News* and jammed it in his briefcase. He didn't even want it lying around the plane. He wished he could have kept it from Nancy, but there was no chance. She'd be bombarded by "good friends" anxious to tell her the news, to read her the lurid details. She'd be devastated at the report of his having a street fight over another woman, at the thought of that woman being his "constant companion," at the whole bloody mess. She might really leave this time. He couldn't let that happen. Somehow he'd convince her. He had to.

"That's the way they sell newspapers, Nance . . . you know that. They'll say anything that smacks of sex, drugs, or corruption. They're not afraid of libel anymore. Almost no one sues them, and besides, they're covered by insurance and protected by the First Amendment privilege. So instead of just reporting what happened, they have to juice it up, talk about my 'constant companion' and stuff like that. But it's all bullshit, believe me. This girl's just a friend of Dan Melnick." Nancy leaned back on the moss-green velvet sofa and sipped her wine. She looked silently at Harry, weighing his words, trying to gauge his sincerity.

"She was leaving the hotel when I was," Harry continued. "Hundreds of people come and go at the Ritz every day. She gets into an argument over a cab. Some goon pushes her. I push him, and they make it a sex scandal. Complete bullshit. They didn't even get the scuffle right. That shows you how inaccurate they are, how careless with the truth. I didn't touch the sultan, or whatever the hell he is. I just tried to stop his bodyguard from manhandling Dan's friend. But SULTAN FIGHTS LAWYER IN LOVE NEST sells more papers. So the hell with the truth. Nance, I don't even know the girl's name. I swear to God."

The light of the fireplace flickered across Nancy's face illuminating the deep line that etched her brow when she was angry or troubled. Tonight she was both. But Harry had talked virtually nonstop for half an hour, explaining, persuading, using every device he knew to reassure her, calm her anger, soften her fear. After all, he was a pro, and he had no reluctance about using his skill at home, just as he would in court. It was working. He could tell.

Harry told himself this was one situation in which lies were morally justified. The truth would wound, would kill. Lies—even half-believed lies—allowed Nancy hope and dignity and the ability to go on with a relationship the truth would render impossible. And the lies, the skilled rhetoric, were working once again. Wanting to believe, Nancy was believing. She reached out her hand, taking Harry's.

"Look, your record's not great, my love. But you knew how important, how really vital this is to me. I don't think you'd do it again. Besides, the paper said the affair had been going on for a long time, and I'd *know* if that were the case. I'd know."

She paused for another sip of wine. A Mozart flute concerto played softly in the background.

"And I realize the press—particularly those New York tabloids—distort the facts to sell papers. I've seen it before. So, okay then, let's forget this whole thing and go to bed. I've got my annual checkup tomorrow afternoon, and Phil Cohen says it'll take two, three hours to complete. You know, blood, urine, stress test—all that nonsense. . . . Ugh!"

"I hate 'em too. But I'll tell you what: Suppose I pick you up at the doctor's when you're done. We'll go out for a drink. Maybe we'll drive out to Geoffrey's, catch the sunset in Malibu."

"I'd love that, Harry. But you've just come back from New York. Can you spare the time?"

"Sure I can, Nance. Sure I can."

He couldn't. But, under the circumstances, it was the least he could do.

Harry arrived at his Sunset Boulevard office early the next morning. He was in a fine mood. The art-deco furnishings, their pale gray tones reflected in smoky mirrors and softly lit by filtered sunshine, heightened his sense of well-being.

He eased himself into the gray corduroy armchair and, reaching behind him, switched on Vivaldi's *Four Seasons*. The trade papers, *Daily Variety* and *The Hollywood Reporter*, were on his desk along with *The New York Times* and *The Wall Street Journal*. He unfolded *Variety*. Its banner headline was CONSOL PIC STOLEN. Like the *Daily News*, it reported the theft of *The Last Battle*, Consolidated Studios' forty-million-dollar antiwar epic, directed by Joe Miletti and starring Rod Townsend. It detailed how a sheriff's deputy had gone to Miletti's office to pick up the work print, only to find that it had already been taken by "persons unknown." A studio representative announced that no duplicate print existed, but that he was sure the film would be located and finished in time for its scheduled release the following month. A "person close to the studio" was quoted as speculating that it was being held for ransom by political extremists.

The intercom buzzed just as Harry reached for *The Hollywood Reporter*.

"Mr. Slutsky calling, Mr. Cain."

"Okay, Carol, put him through."

Yank Slutsky was Consolidated Studios' largest shareholder and had recently become its chairman. Fat, irascible, and very rich, he used the studio's president, Aaron Fernbach, as a solid, presentable front for his own iron-fisted control of studio affairs.

"Cain?"

Harry knew it was going to be an angry call from Slutsky's use of his last name. Normally, he was "pal" or "babe" or at least "Harry." But Slutsky's temper was legendary, and this morning he had much to be angry about. Harry tried what he thought was a tone of good-natured innocence.

"Good morning, Yank. You're in early."

"I'm still at home. I didn't go to bed last night. Because of you, you shyster fuck!"

"Hey, what's eating *you*?"

"Don't gimme that innocent shit, motherfucker. Just tell me where it is—before I do something I'm sorry for."

"Where *what* is, Yank?"

"My film, you whorehouse towel; my film! I've got forty million bucks in that turkey—ten million alone for fucking Rod Townsend—

and it's gone, and your pals got it . . . or *you* do—and if you do, you're a dead man—you hear me? A *dead man*!"

Slutsky's rage always moved Harry to laughter or, worse, to sarcasm, a reaction that invariably increased his fury.

"Hold on, Yank, the trade papers say it's the work of political extremists. It's probably the Hezbollah or . . ."

"Listen, cock-bite. I don't wanna hear that shit. You think I'm as stupid as your guinea client? I *know* you and that asshole Miletti took my film, and I'll tell you this, it better come back right now—today— *this morning*—cuz if it don't, then I'll tell you, Cain, you and your buddies are gonna feel pain and I mean real ball-tearing, eye-gouging *pain*!"

The phone went dead. Harry looked at the buzzing instrument in his hand and smiled. It didn't sound like the FBI was coming in on the case, and he'd certainly rather face Slutsky's ranting threats than a federal investigation. He felt better—a little scared, but definitely better.

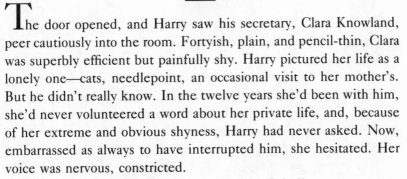

The door opened, and Harry saw his secretary, Clara Knowland, peer cautiously into the room. Fortyish, plain, and pencil-thin, Clara was superbly efficient but painfully shy. Harry pictured her life as a lonely one—cats, needlepoint, an occasional visit to her mother's. But he didn't really know. In the twelve years she'd been with him, she'd never volunteered a word about her private life, and, because of her extreme and obvious shyness, Harry had never asked. Now, embarrassed as always to have interrupted him, she hesitated. Her voice was nervous, constricted.

"Mr. Putnam would like to see you, Mr. Cain."

"Mr. Putnam?"

"The new office manager you hired. The one from Stockton and Morris. He's been working in the office for two or three days."

Clara blushed as if she had just made some startling erotic disclosure.

Now Harry recalled the man she was describing. A banker friend had convinced him he needed a law office manager. And Harry had to agree. His income was well over a million dollars a year, but it came in irregularly, and his expenses were huge and completely uncontrolled. When his friend made the suggestion, Harry had thought a little management might be a good thing. And, after reading Milo Putnam's impressive résumé, he'd hired the veteran law officer manager with only the briefest of interviews. Now he was here, ready to start managing.

"Okay, Clara, send Mr. Putnam in."

Clara turned and gestured down the hallway. Into the room came a thin, long-faced man of about fifty, with light-brown, thinning hair, a long, aquiline nose and pale hazel eyes. He wore a tan polyester suit, a starched white shirt, and a beige-and-brown striped tie of a heavy woven fabric. His expression was serious, almost mournful.

Harry remembered Putnam as being a little more relaxed, a little less funereal. But then, he had no one to blame but himself for hiring someone after a ten-minute interview. As Harry extended his hand, Putnam began shaking his head and making clucking noises.

"Mr. Cain, what are we going to do with you?"

"What do you mean, Mr. Putnam?"

"I mean I've been going over the accounts, and we have to change our thinking. This is not an eleemosynary institution, Mr. Cain, but it's being run like one."

"Well, I know I'm not a good manager, but is it really that bad?"

"It is, Mr. Cain, believe me." The tiny eyes bored into Harry's with surprising intensity. "Do you know you've receivables of seven hundred and fifty thousand dollars, most of which are over ninety days old?"

"Well, no, I . . ."

"I'm preparing a list for you. We'll talk about each client and what to do about them."

"Do about them?"

"Absolutely. 'A lawyer's time and advice are his stock-in-trade,' Mr. Cain. Lincoln said that. Your time is very valuable. We can't afford to have you waste it on those who can't or won't pay."

"Well, let me have a look at the list, and we'll discuss it. Anything else?"

"Did you know that your secretaries are sending all written communications by special messenger at an annual cost in excess of sixty thousand?"

"Well, yes, the mail is so slow and unreliable that . . ."

"But, Mr. Cain, messengers to refuse dinner invitations? To pay the phone bill? To return a Bar Association questionnaire?"

"I see. That does seem excessive, Mr. Putnam; but it's entirely my fault. One day, I'd just had it with the mail. Always late, often lost. I just said 'no more mail—never—not for anything' and . . . well, they're simply following that order."

"I'm sure they are, Mr. Cain; but that's all over now. We're going to run a tight ship here, and we will not be sending your annual donations to the Red Cross by messenger."

"Well, I'll try to help all I can, Mr. Putnam. And now, I hope you'll excuse me. I've got lots of work to do."

He rose, extending his hand.

"I wish you luck, Mr. Putnam. I suppose you'll need it."

"It will not be luck, Mr. Cain. It will be policy. Sound fiscal policy. No more giveaways, right?"

"Uh . . . right," said Harry, somewhat uncertainly.

Putnam rose and took Harry's hand, then nodded and backed from the room as if leaving royalty.

The moment Putnam had left Harry's intercom buzzed.

"Mrs. Campbell's calling. She's on the line now."

"Okay, put her through."

Harry heard the phone click.

"Harry?"

"Yes, hi, Pat. How's Ewing?"

"Uh . . . he's fine, Harry, but I'm not. As I said in New York, I've got a rather unique problem—a personal matter. Actually, I'd prefer not to discuss it on the phone. Could we get together, say for lunch? As soon as you can, Harry, please."

Pat Campbell was not one to cry wolf, and Harry could hear the stress in her voice. He consulted his calendar. "How about today, Pat? I had a lunch meeting canceled; but I've got to pick up Nancy at four."

"Oh, we'll be through long before that, and lunch would be ideal. I'll be at a gallery near the beach. But I can meet you anywhere you like."

"No. The beach is fine. I'll be in court this morning in Santa Monica. How about Seventy-two Market Street at one o'clock?"

"Perfect, Harry. I really appreciate it."

"That's okay, Pat, but listen. You and Ewing have used O'Melveny and Meyers for years. I'm sure they can handle whatever this is. Why not take it up with them?"

"I can't do that, Harry. They can't even know about this. I need my own independent lawyer, someone as unique and special as this problem is, and, from what I've seen over the years, that's you. In fact, it's probably *only* you. Anyway, let's discuss it at lunch."

"Fine, Pat. I'll see you at one." Harry put down the phone. He was intrigued.

Later that morning, Harry drove his silver Bentley along the curves of Sunset Boulevard toward Santa Monica. He reviewed the unusual argument he'd make that morning on Section One of the Sherman Act, actually speaking aloud his response to a critical question he was sure the judge would ask. As he spoke and gestured, he noticed that a man driving in the next lane was pointing Harry out to the woman beside him. Both began to laugh.

Embarrassed, Harry picked up the car phone and dialed his office.

His only calls were from Joe Miletti and Jeffrey Katzenberg. He was involved with a dispute with Katzenberg's studio, and he wanted no angry shouting match with the bright but combative executive to disturb his concentration on the way to this important hearing. He punched in Miletti's preprogrammed number, and as the Bentley moved regally through the lush gardens of Holmby Hills, the director's hoarse, feisty voice came on the line.

"Holy Christ, Harry. What the fuck did you do? They're goin' crazy. That's the only work print, and the shot book's missing too. That leaves 'em nothing but a million strips of unorganized negative. The picture's opening in a few weeks; and even with a team of editors, it'll take 'em a year to assemble another usable print . . . if they *ever* can."

"I know, Joe. I got a call this morning from Yank."

"Me too, and I'll bet it was the same call."

"What did you tell him, Joe?"

"The truth. That I had no goddamn idea where the film was. He didn't believe me—said I'd be hangin' on a meat hook—stuff like that."

"I know. That's Yank. But I wouldn't worry about anything like that."

"Why not for Christ's sake?—he's sore enough!"

"That's true. Yank likes to talk, but I don't think he'd ever *do* anything. I think it's mostly an act. Besides, the lawyers will convince him they can squeeze us legally—jail us for contempt, force us to tell where the film is."

"But I don't *know* where the film is."

"I know that, Joe. Which is why we might be okay."

"Well, I hope *you* know where it is. I mean it *is* forty million bucks worth of film, and . . ."

"I don't want to discuss this stuff over the car phone, Joe. Anyone might hear—and anyway, for all you guys out there listening in on scanners, I don't know dick about that film."

"Well if you *do* know, and they haul us into court, you'd have to lie under oath. That's serious shit, man. You've always said you'd never do that."

"And I won't, Joe, believe me. I've got a plan and it doesn't involve *anybody* lying under oath—especially not me. So don't talk to anyone about the situation, just get on with your business."

"My business? Listen, my 'business' is hidden out there, somewhere, by someone—maybe you—and that's great; but there's not much I can do till I get it back."

"Well, then, go fishing, Joe—you know, that's a good idea. Go fishing."

Two hours later, Harry stood on the courthouse steps. His motion had been granted, and he was elated. It wasn't easy to get a state court judge to make a ruling based on a complex federal statute. He'd tried it, and it had worked.

He breathed deeply, savoring the morning air fresh from the sea. Nothing—absolutely nothing—compared with the high of winning.

Opening a news-vending machine, he picked up the late edition of the L.A. *Times*. In the corner of the front page was a story headed $40 MILLION FILM VANISHES. Like the coverage in the trade papers, the *Times* story told how Consolidated Studios had obtained a court order for possession of the film, how the New York sheriff's office had failed to locate it, and how neither the studio nor Miletti had any idea where it was.

The story added that the studio believed it knew who was behind the theft and planned to take "prompt and decisive action." Harry knew the other shoe had to drop very soon. The studio had to attack. He was ready for them, he thought. He'd have to be.

72 Market Street is at the beach in Venice, California. In the twenties Venice was linked by canals like its Italian namesake. Some of the canals still exist, but the gaudily painted gondolas, built in a vain attempt to promote the seaside tracts, have long since disappeared. The hippies who had flooded the Venice area in the sixties had disappeared like some vanished Indian tribe. Gradually, they were replaced by more successful artists and young professionals. Expensive condos and chic restaurants appeared among the old frame houses, and, decades too late, Venice began to fulfill its developer's

dream. One of those "in" restaurants was at 72 Market Street, its address having become its name.

Harry and Pat Campbell sat at a corner table enjoying the informal crowd and listening to the soft piano music in the background.

They ordered—oysters, chili, and grilled lime chicken. Then they began to talk about everything but Pat Campbell's problem. Their conversation ranged from the future of the L.A. *Times* to who was in and who was out at the major studios, to how the huge new Oriental population was affecting the city's tastes in art and music, as it already had in food.

Their oysters arrived, plump and fresh, with a subtle taste of the sea. As they were finishing them, a serious, well-dressed man in his early forties approached the table.

"You know Jeff Berg, don't you, Pat?"

"Of course, who doesn't in my business?"

Berg was the chairman of ICM, one of the largest of the talent agencies. Harry liked him. A sensitive, well-read man, his formal, sometimes unbending persona could not disguise a combative nature and a keen mind. He was Joe Miletti's agent, and, today, he seemed particularly ill at ease.

"Harry, could I talk to you for just a second, alone?"

"Sure, Jeff. Excuse me, Pat."

Harry rose and joined Berg a few feet from the table. The agent spoke in a low, confidential tone.

"Harry, this is strictly between us?"

"Of course, Jeff."

"The studios are not going to take what's gone down here with Joe's picture. Joe—and you too—are in big trouble. I can't go into it any more than that. I don't even *know* more than that. But be careful for Joe will you? . . . and for yourself too. Call me if I can help." He squeezed Harry's arm and moved toward the door.

Harry spoke to his back. "Thanks, Jeff, I appreciate it."

Berg turned, a slight smile on his usually serious face. "You'll find a way, Harry. You always do."

Harry went back to the table, where Pat was waiting patiently. Their main courses had already been served.

"Trouble?"

"Not really."

"Does your face know it?"

Harry laughed and changed the subject. He gestured with a spoon toward the large bowls before them.

"Taste that chili, Pat, it's absolutely the best in town."

Pat took a spoonful of the thick, reddish-brown stew.

"Mmm, that really is good. Cumin, I think."

"That's what I think too, but Tony won't tell me."

"I'll find out for you, Harry. We don't get here often. It's too far from San Marino. But Ewing and I own a bit of this place. The recipe can be part of your fee. Speaking of which, we'd better get down to my problem. We'll never get me out of trouble gossiping about Ray Stark and Mike Eisner."

"Trouble, Pat?"

"You bet, Harry. One thing that's plain about my situation is that I'm in trouble, big trouble."

"Look, when we're through, we'll take a walk and discuss it. Meanwhile, let's enjoy lunch."

"That's okay with me, Harry. I've got all afternoon."

Half an hour later they left the restaurant and turned onto the boardwalk heading north. They could see the distant hills of Malibu, a shadowed purple rising from the bright azure bay. Immediately, they were surrounded by a vast, unplanned carnival. Music, an infinite variety of music, came at them from every direction. A circle of roller skaters were break-dancing to a portable radio blasting hard rock. A few steps up the boardwalk, three Mexican guitarists were solemnly harmonizing to "Gloria Eres Tú." Further on, a slim black man leaned against a synagogue wall, his eyes closed, his clarinet casting a bittersweet spell with "Sophisticated Lady," while nearby, an elderly blind man played honky-tonk jazz on a battered upright piano. His back was to the sea, and a hand-lettered sign identified him as DANNY O'DOUL, THE TOAST OF BROADWAY. A stand-up comic passed the hat after finishing his routine, his impromptu audience already drifting away in the direction of a mime, who was starting his own act a few feet away. Five different types of massage were offered by turbaned Sikhs, barrel-chested Slavs, and wiry Japanese in white medical uniforms, each with a cot on the beach. Finger cymbals and ankle bells rang as a troupe of Asian dancers performed nearby.

Vendors were hawking Persian rugs, cotton candy, yakitori, T-shirts, oil paintings, crystals, Zuni fetishes, and a huge variety of unrelated articles. A crowd of every race, age, and type was walking, skating, dancing, eating, or just sitting and enjoying the sunny day, the sea air, and the rich and varied spectacle.

Harry led Pat to a bench facing the ocean, somewhat removed from the crowd. When they were seated, he turned and faced her.

"Okay, Pat. Time to talk. What's this all about?" He saw a quick and surprising look of fear in her eyes. She turned away, gazing out to sea. After a moment, she began.

"I've got a real problem, Harry. A serious one. One that threatens me and threatens my marriage, which, by the way, means a lot to me. I love Ewing very much."

"What kind of problem?"

"I'd call it blackmail, Harry, although that's probably not the correct legal term."

"Blackmail? Who's blackmailing you and why? With what?"

"You do get to the point, Harry," she said turning back to him with a smile.

"Got to, Pat, that's my job."

"Okay then, the blackmailer is Tommy Bowers."

"Tommy Bowers?"

"That's right, America's favorite TV star. The hard-boiled, soft-hearted tough guy. Well he's not so goddamn softhearted, I can tell you, and he's being very, very hard-boiled."

Bowers had been the hero of a long-running, top-rated television series about a stocky, streetwise private detective. The series, produced by Pat Campbell's company, had run eight years and made millions for Pat and the network; but Bowers had been publicly grumbling that it hadn't made enough money for him.

Pat described her plan to satisfy Bowers and keep him in tow until she could find a new series for him. She'd formed a production company, giving Bowers a third of the stock, keeping 51 percent for herself and handing over the balance to her long-time business manager, Terry Winfield. Four months later, Pat had found herself in a dispute with Winfield over his handling of the company's finances, particularly his approving outlandish expenses for Tommy Bowers—rental payments for a 100-foot yacht, a full-time limo and driver,

$20,000 dinner parties. It was crazy. Yet Winfield had given the okay to all these items without a murmur. When Pat found out, she fired Winfield and started an audit. It showed $425,000 of obviously improper expenditures for Bowers, all approved by Winfield.

Pat called a meeting—just the three of them. She told Winfield and Bowers that the company was going out of business, that she was suing both of them for the $425,000. When she finished, Bowers simply sat there, a strange smile on his face. Winfield looked down, embarrassed. Bowers put his feet on the desk and leaned back in his chair. In a smirking, arrogant tone, he announced that Pat was in no position to sue anyone. On the contrary, he said, they were going to sue *her*. Her personal conduct had damaged the company; and, in settlement of their claims, he wanted her to transfer all of her stock to them and pay $5 million to the corporation in damages, which would, of course, be for their benefit as the new owners of the company.

"What 'personal conduct'? Damages for what?" Harry asked impatiently.

"For nothing. To pay them off."

"Pay them off for what?"

"To keep them from disclosing things about me."

"What things?"

"Just things." She looked down at her hands, embarrassed. "My diary."

"Your diary?"

"Yes."

"How'd they get it?"

"I assume Terry took it from my bedroom. He always had the run of the house."

Harry put his fingers under Pat's chin and lifted her face so he could look into her eyes. "What's in it, Pat? You've got to level with me."

She sighed and, shielding her eyes from the sun, looked back out to sea. Harry could see the anxiety in her face. After a long pause, she spoke in a voice so low he had to bend closer to hear.

"Harry, I've been married to Ewing for twelve years now. He's more than thirty years older than I; and, as I've said, I love him dearly. I don't want to lose him. I . . . ."

"Why would you lose him?"

"When we were first married I was under a lot of stress. I was much younger and far less mature. I did some very foolish things, things that would hurt Ewing terribly, make it impossible for him to go on with our marriage."

"Maybe you're exaggerating the effect of those 'things,' Pat. Ewing's a sophisticated, understanding man."

"I'm not exaggerating them, Harry. I assure you, I know Ewing well. If this comes out, he'd have to divorce me. Believe me, he'd not think twice. Inwardly, he might not want to, but his pride and, more important, his position would require a divorce. There'd be no other way, no other choice."

"Tell me about these 'things,' Pat. I need to know what's in the diary."

"That's part of the problem, Harry. I'm not sure."

"You don't know what you wrote?"

"No. These things happened nine, ten years ago. That's all over now. I can't recall what I put down and what I didn't. At times I wrote everything. Thoughts, inner feelings, everything. Other times, I didn't. I just don't know."

Harry sat forward on the bench, turning to look at Pat. "I don't see how they can use the diary in litigation with you. I don't see what it has to do with your case against them or their case against you. And if they're just threatening you with exposure, that's garden-variety extortion. They can go to jail for it."

Pat Campbell leaned forward excitedly. "Christ, if only you could put them there. Maybe that's the solution."

"I'm afraid it's not, Pat. It's probably the *last* thing you should do."

"Why?"

"The trial of Tommy Bowers for extortion would be the media event of the decade. He's still a major star, and, since the diary would be a significant element in an extortion case, there'd be no way to keep it out of the papers."

"But can't we ask for a closed hearing?"

"Not in a criminal case, Pat. That would violate Bowers' constitutional rights."

Again her face fell. She looked frightened, vulnerable. "Is there anything I can do short of giving them my stock and paying them five million?"

"There might be, Pat. Let me think about it."

"You have an idea?"

"Well, I'm starting on one. Give me a little time to let it cook. I want to meet with them first, get a better feel for what they're thinking. Besides, I'd like to see the diary or at least a copy."

She blushed. "You'd have to see it, I suppose."

"Of course I have to see it." He paused, rising from the bench and helping Pat to her feet. "It's that bad?"

"I think it's that bad, Harry. I really do."

7

Driving back from lunch, Harry tried to focus on how he could best help Pat Campbell, what tactics could put Bowers in check. As the big car swept through the Ocean Park underpass, his attention was diverted to the boldly painted murals on the concrete walls. On one side, blue whales were leaping and diving in foamy waves. On the other, carousel horses were breaking loose and running free against a desert sky. Who painted these wonderful things all over the city? Who were these talented people that spent months turning gray concrete into magic? Sometime, he'd like to . . . his thoughts were interrupted by the warble of the car phone.

"Mr. Cain, Michael Ovitz is calling you. He says it's urgent. Can I patch him through?"

Mike Ovitz was the most powerful agent in town. A forceful, energetic man, he had fought his way to the top of his highly competitive profession and enjoyed close personal relationships with every studio head. His broad array of famous clients gave him unparalleled clout, and even the powerful men who ran the major studios needed Mike far more than he needed them.

Years before, when Harry was a young lawyer and Mike was just starting his own agency, he'd handed Harry a dollar, calling it a retainer, so Harry could never sue him. Harry had grinned, treating it as a joke . . . and a compliment. Every year since then, Ovitz had sent him another dollar, and Harry had never sued his agency. They'd had their battles, gone through periods of cool hostility, but, generally, had remained cordial friends. Occasionally, each exerting his own special kind of influence had helped the other through difficult situations. Mike liked Harry, even though he sometimes found him an uncontrollable factor in a world Mike could otherwise control. Harry liked Mike too. Mike was bright and he made Harry smile. That was something in itself.

Now the superagent's voice came booming over the car speaker phone. "Listen, asshole, you've really done it this time."

"Done what?"

"You know what. Jesus! Who's your career counselor, Icarus? Even *I* can't get you out of this one."

"Did I ask your help?"

"No, but you need it. You need the U.S. Marines, pal."

"How come?"

" 'How come,' is they're going to *get* you. It's not cute this time, Harry. There was a big meeting this morning—Yank, Jeffrey, Sid, Bob—all of them. The meeting was about Miletti's film, and they had their lawyers there too. They're not going to take this, Harry. They can't. They're going for your balls. All the way. The whole Association."

"So? I'll keep my legs crossed."

"It's not funny, Harry—they're going to come down on you like an avalanche. So be ready. That's all I can say now. And, listen, we never had this conversation . . . okay?"

"Okay. Mike, thanks."

"So long."

The phone went dead.

Mike was inclined to dramatic expressions—no doubt about that. But first Berg, then Ovitz—there must be *something* to it—or at least the studio wanted him to think there was.

Harry smiled to himself. But he was just a little scared.

Dr. Phillip Cohen came into his reception room still wearing his white lab coat. A dark, stocky man, he was a brilliant internist and had been Harry's friend and physician for many years. Harry breathed a sigh of relief. Never good at waiting, he'd read two magazines and outlined an appellate brief on the back of an envelope. Now, finally, he and Nancy could get out to the beach before sundown. Cohen extended his hand, and Harry felt the surprisingly firm grip.

"You planning to be in town for a while?"

"Come on, Phil. You've been talking about having 'that lunch' for three years now. You'll never get around to it. You're even busier than I am. Anyway, I'm leaving for London on Friday."

Cohen removed his glasses and peered at Harry. Then he spoke quietly.

"This is not about lunch, Harry. And I'm afraid you're not going to London. I don't like what we found. Not at all."

"What do you mean, Phil? What did you find?"

"Well, based on what I saw on Nancy's X-rays, I sent her next door for a bronchoscopy. What we found, Harry, was lumbar carcinoma . . . cancer. Both lungs involved. Almost certainly metastasized—gone into the lymph system and the bloodstream."

Harry felt as if the floor were moving beneath his feet. He felt dizzy, clammy. He fought for control.

"Does Nancy know?"

"Yes. I've told her."

"Can you operate?"

"We don't think so, Harry. But we'll fight it other ways. We've got some pretty effective chemotherapy now. And radiation treatment is improving every day."

"How long does she have, Phil?"

"It's early to talk like that, Harry. And besides, we don't know. Too many variables, too many imponderables. In some cases, the tumors are totally arrested by chemotherapy or radiation. In other cases, they're slowed. Some don't seem to respond at all. We've got a lot of tests to do before I can give you any kind of prognosis."

"Come on, Phil. You're my friend. Based on what you found, what you know, what's the average life expectancy?"

"As I say, it varies enormously with many factors, including the effectiveness of the chemo or the radiation. And there are a number of new experimental programs out there, like interferon and TNF— tumor necrosis factor. The TNF program at Harvard has been getting some promising results. You should talk to Karen Lloyd. She's the deputy head of the President's Commission on Cancer. If anyone can work Nancy into that program, it's Karen. And Nancy could be one of the lucky ones."

"But the average, Phil, the average. Don't bullshit me. What's the average?"

The pudgy doctor nervously cleaned his glasses with his tie, then looked up at Harry. His large, dark eyes were moist.

"Given what I saw this morning, Harry, the average would be six to eight months, just six to eight months."

They were both in a state of shock. They drove to Malibu and sat on the garden terrace at Geoffrey's, high above the beach. Both drank martinis as if they were a miracle cure. They touched each other often as they spoke.

Gulls wheeled and cried above them, as the setting sun cast a rose-gold light on the sea. They didn't notice.

"Nancy, it's like anything else. Some will make it, some won't. You'll be one who does. I talked to Karen from the doctor's office while you were getting dressed. She's going to work on this Harvard program right away. Their TNF program is supposed to be very effective, and there are other programs too. Look, we know some people beat cancer. We also know that, all over the world, they're working on new treatments. They're gonna find a cure, and we'll hold on 'til they do. We'll fight this thing, Nance. We'll find a way to beat it."

Nancy reached out, stroking his face.

"Oh, my sweet warrior. If a nuclear bomb were falling on us, you'd rush out to fight it. But Harry, there are some things you can't fight. Not even you. Some things are just too big, too explosive."

"Don't talk like that, Nance. Don't give in to it. You know some people think a positive mental state has a great deal to do with who makes it and who doesn't."

"Maybe, Harry, maybe. Look, I'll try. I really will."

He took her hands in his and looked into her dark, frightened eyes.

"Nance, do you want me to quit work, so we can just be together?"

She smiled, but he saw her eyes moisten.

"No, Harry, I want us to have as normal a life as we can, for as long as we have. As much as possible, I want to live like a person, not a cancer patient. If you stopped work, that would be harder to do."

Harry tried not to show the relief he felt—was ashamed of feeling. He wondered if he'd really meant the offer. He hoped so, but he wasn't sure.

Nancy sipped her drink and looked out at the setting sun spreading its red-purple glow across the sky.

"You know the worst thing about the idea of dying, Harry? It's that I won't be with you any more. That's the thing I dread, the thing I hate most about it, that I'd never see you again."

The next morning Harry was unable to focus on his work. Over and over again, his mind wandered to Nancy. He knew they were starting a long battle with a deadly foe, and that the stakes were so high he dared not dwell on the consequences of losing. But he also knew that if he was to be effective in that battle, he had to preserve the other part of his life—had to keep practicing law. He'd have to find a way to do both, to do both well. After all, what hadn't he done well once he'd put his mind to it?

He continued to stare through the window at the city spread out below. Then, sighing, he turned to the unanswered telephone messages stacked neatly on his desk. The first message was marked "urgent." It was from the Fujiwara Company, one of Harry's favorite clients. He represented the powerful Japanese film organization in the United States, and sometimes in Europe and Latin America. Harry enjoyed his Fujiwara cases. They were generally interesting and highly lucrative, and he had developed a relationship of mutual respect and trust with Isamu Morita, the company's local representative.

"Ohayo gozaimas, Cain-san."

"Ohayo gozaimas, Morita-san. How are you?"

"I'm fine, thank you. How is Nancy-san?"

For a moment Harry was at a loss for an appropriate reply. But his relationship with Japanese clients tended to be formal and polite. He decided Morita would be embarrassed to be told of his personal problems.

"She's fine, thank you. It's kind of you to ask."

"She is a rare woman, Cain-san. Since we were all together in Rome, she has often been in the thoughts of Fujiwara-san and his son, and, of course, in my own." Harry felt even worse. A wave of anxiety swept over him as his thoughts returned to the sentence Phil Cohen had seemingly passed on Nancy. He forced his mind back to the conversation.

"Thank you, Morita-san, and please tell Fujiwara-san and Kami that I appreciate their thinking of us."

Masao Fujiwara was the founder of the company, a man still brilliant and vigorous, though in his seventies. Although Harry had never asked Fujiwara directly, he had joked with Nancy that the crusty old man had probably commanded a Japanese aircraft carrier during the war. Kami, his charming, Yale-educated son, was slowly taking over the company management.

"Cain-san, there is, in Los Angeles, a young lady who is a friend of Kami . . . of Kami's wife to be more precise. Both of this lady's parents are dead, and Kami thought perhaps you could be of assistance to her."

"I'd be delighted. How can I help?"

"If Cain-san would meet with me about this young lady, both Kami and Fujiwara-san would be most grateful."

"Of course I will." Harry knew his schedule was heavy over the next few days and he wanted to leave time for a quick flight to Harvard with Nancy if it could be arranged. The new TNF program was about to begin and Harry was determined Nancy would be there. "Perhaps we could meet next week, say Thursday morning?"

"I hope Cain-san will forgive me. I am aware of his busy schedule, but is tonight impossible? As you sometimes say, 'Time is of the essence.' I know Kami would appreciate it."

Harry became curious. The Fujiwaras had never made such a request before. Still, he didn't want to be away from Nancy.

"I must be at home this evening, Morita-san. Could we meet there?"

"Yes, certainly. Perhaps at jujihan . . . half-past ten?"

"Well, ten—juji—would be better. Is that okay?"

"Fine. I will be there at juji."

"Good, Morita-san. You remember the house?"

"Certainly I do. It is a rare place, reflecting you and Nancy-san. There is no place like it."

"Domo arigato, Morita-san. I'll see you at juji tonight."

"Hai, Cain-san. Sayonara."

"Sayonara."

Harry wondered what trouble had befallen Kami's friend, why "time was of the essence," and why the young lady wasn't coming herself. He knew from experience that his Japanese clients were often reluctant to disclose the depth and seriousness of their problems. To them, it was an intrusion on Harry's peace of mind and an embarrassment on their part. It was considerate, even charming in a way, but it made them difficult to represent in a lawsuit. There was always some damaging contract or letter that you weren't told about because "We didn't want to upset Cain-san." Harry hoped this time, when all the news came out, it wouldn't be too bad; that it wouldn't, at least, be irreversible.

Harry continued leafing through his messages. He had no heart for returning the calls, for the fighting, the persuading, the reassuring that was the stuff of his usual day. Well, he'd have to do it, would have to focus, to . . . He was interrupted by the intercom.

"Ms. Lloyd calling, Mr. Cain."

"I'll pick up, Clara."

Karen Lloyd was a skilled and experienced motion-picture producer, perhaps the most successful female in a business that historically places little value on female skills other than acting, singing, or ice-skating. In addition, as Phil Cohen had pointed out, Karen was assistant to the head of the President's Commission on Cancer. The commission handed out the federal research grants, and she was vigorously wooed by every university medic who was trying desperately to be the one to beat the dread disease . . . to be cancer's Dr. Salk. Most important, Karen was a longtime friend, the first of their friends to have been told about Nancy's condition.

"Hi, sweetie. How're you two holding up?"

"We're doing okay, Karen. Nancy's being very brave about it. Hasn't lost her sense of humor."

"That's good, Harry. If anyone can beat it, you two can. But listen. I've got some good news and some bad."

"Give me the good news first. I haven't had any for some time."

"Okay. They can make room for one more person in the Harvard program. Our preliminary reports show that TNF has a good success rate. If those reports hold up, this could be the cure, at least for some kinds of cancer. I'd love to see Nancy get in that program."

"What do you mean 'you'd love to see her there'? What stands in the way?"

"That's the bad news, Harry. When Armand Hammer died, the president appointed a new head of the Cancer Commission. It's

Maurice King—you know, the big construction honcho? My impression is you and King had some problem. Am I right?"

"I tried a case against him a few years ago—stopped him from stealing an old friend's building. It cost him a bundle, so I don't suppose he likes me very much. Why?"

"Well, he was rushing out of the office when I told him about Nancy, and how I was shoehorning her into the Harvard project. But he looked kind of grim and said not to do anything yet. That we'd have to talk about it. I wondered what was up."

"Well, he's a mean son of a bitch, all right. But I can't believe he'd hold it against Nancy that I beat him in court, or that he's even still that sore at me. It's been four or five years."

"I'm sure you're right, sweetie. Anyway, for now it's looking good. Tell Nancy I send my love."

"I will, Karen, and thanks. Thanks so much."

Harry had scheduled that first day so that he could leave early and spend the afternoon with Nancy. Normally, his work load wouldn't permit that, but he was determined to manage it whenever he could. As he prepared to leave the office, Milo Putnam caught his arm.

"May I have a brief word with you, Mr. Cain?"

Harry was in no mood for more of the prissy manager's suggestions, but he knew Putnam was trying to do his job, and it might just as well be now as later.

"Sure," he said, in a voice he tried to make cordial, "Come into my office." He led the manager to a seat opposite his desk, sat down in his gray corduroy desk chair, and leaned back, gesturing with his hands for Putnam to begin.

"Mr. Cain, I'll get right to the point. I've uncovered a series of mischarges among clients going back over the past five years."

"Mischarges?" The ugly word caught Harry's attention.

"Yes, one client charged for another's expenses."

"Give me an example."

Putnam picked up an accounting-style spread sheet and ran his long fingers down the first page.

"Well, we billed forty-five dollars' worth of photocopying to Apple Corps. Limited, when, in fact, it was done for Ray Stark."

"How many items are there?"

"Twenty-six."

"And what's the total over the five years?"

"Nine thousand, three hundred thirty-eight dollars and sixty-two cents."

"And we haven't received anything we shouldn't; that is, the error's just between clients?"

"That's right."

"And what's the most we've incorrectly charged to a single client?"

"Two hundred five dollars . . . to Joel Silver."

"Okay. What's the best way to handle the problem now, after all this time?"

Putnam smiled. "I'm glad you see the problem, sir. Too much time *has* passed. Nevertheless, my recommendation is that those clients who were undercharged be billed for the correct amount. We can bill it as if they were current costs. They'll never know it's for old items."

Harry's face darkened. "I don't like the sound of that at all. What about the clients who were overcharged?"

"Mr. Cain, you've consistently billed less than you should have, and you've spent your own money all too often on clients' expenses. My recommendation would be just to forget it. You'll simply look foolish trying to return money they paid us four or five years ago."

Suddenly irritated, Harry leaned forward, jabbing his finger at his manager across the desk.

"Now look, Mr. Putnam. If you're going to work here, we've got to understand each other. You're asking me to keep clients' money I'm not entitled to. I can't do that. I'll *never* do that."

"But, Mr. Cain, we'll seem grossly negligent billing and crediting now for erroneous charges we made years ago."

Harry paused, thinking. "You're right about that, but I'm still not going to keep clients' money. Here's what we'll do. We'll just forget about the clients who were undercharged and those who were overcharged will get a reduction in their next bill."

"But that means eating the entire nine thousand dollars yourself."

"Exactly."

Putnam's small eyes shone with emotion as he leaned toward Harry.

"Please, Mr. Cain, you mustn't do that! That's the kind of decision you've been making all along, and it is precisely why the bottom line hasn't been what it should."

Harry was growing more and more impatient. He stood up, indicating the interview was over.

"I'm sorry, Mr. Putnam, I can't give you more time on this now. I've got too much to do. Just do what I said, okay?"

"Of course, Mr. Cain. I realize that you have a busy schedule. We'll talk later."

"We can talk all you want, Mr. Putnam; but I want those bills reduced. I'm too old to start keeping money that doesn't belong to me."

Harry's study was a fine example of Nancy's taste and imagination. The floor-to-ceiling bookshelves and the ceiling itself were a highly polished deep red lacquer. Comfortable French armchairs were covered in handsome floral print of rose, scarlet, and beige. The floor was sable oak and on it lay two splendid Persian rugs; Nancy had hung a very old Chinese mirror, so that, as Harry sat at his antique mahogany desk, the soft lamplight reflected his guests in a comforting world of deep red, dark wood, and a thousand wellworn books.

The Japanese, who understood such things, appreciated the ambiance of his singular room and often commented on it. Tonight, however, the soothing effect of the library was quickly dissipated.

"Murder, Morita-san? You say she's accused of murder?"

"Yes."

"And who is she accused of murdering?"

"Her husband, Hiraiko Masami."

"The head of Nippon Motors?"

"The same, Cain-san."

"When did this happen?"

"He was found early this morning in his bedroom at the Beverly Wilshire Hotel."

"And Mrs. Masami?"

"She was there in her own bedroom in the same suite. She is now in prison."

"I see. And you want me to defend her?"

"It is the wish of the Fujiwara family, Cain-san, and, of course, my own wish as well."

"You know I'm not basically a criminal lawyer. I did a lot of that kind of work when I was young, but for many years now my cases have been primarily civil; business disputes, sometimes a divorce, and even fewer of those over the past years. Not much criminal law."

"We know this, Cain-san, but, in our view, you are the ichiban— number one—bengoshi—lawyer in America, and, most important, you are the only one the Fujiwaras trust. The entire family wishes you to defend their friend. No one else, only you."

"Well, I'm honored, Morita-san, and I will, of course, defend her. Now tell me what happened."

For the next half hour Morita told Harry of Mrs. Fujiwara's gentle, loving friend Fumiko, and of the brutal drunkard she had married, a man who humiliated her unlike any other husband, who beat her and made her life hell. It was unusual for a Japanese to be so candid about such a personal problem, but Morita was a man of intelligence and business experience and he understood that Harry needed the facts. He described how Masami and Fumiko had been at the Beverly Wilshire for a few days, and how, every night, Masami, roaring, boisterous, crazy drunk, had brought whores to his suite, forcing Fumiko to stand and watch him perform with two or three women a night. This much Morita had been able to find out through his own inquiries. He also knew that when they found Masami dead in the morning, Fumiko had a black eye and severe bruises on her neck and arms.

"Then perhaps, Morita-san, the killing was self-defense. Perhaps he came at her and she had to kill him to save her life."

"Perhaps, Cain-san, but I think that this would be a difficult defense even for a bengoshi as skilled as yourself."

"Why is that?"

"Hiraiko Masami died of poisoning."

"Poisoning?"

"Yes, and I am told that the phial of poison was found in Fumiko's purse, still half full."

It was 8:30 A.M. Harry's gaze kept wandering to the misty gray morning outside his office windows. He found it hard to concentrate on the two men seated across from his desk trying to explain their elaborate tax-oriented plan for investment in a wind-generated energy field, thousands of giant motor-powered windmills placed in the deserts as an alternative to hydroelectric power. Harry had wanted to cancel the meeting after it was arranged. He was anxious to prepare for the meeting he'd scheduled with Tommy Bowers later that day, and he had little interest in the intricacies of wind-generated power.

But Milo Putnam had urged him to take the matter on and to keep the appointment, arguing that it could lead to very sizeable fees. As the two men unfolded still another four-color chart, the intercom buzzed. This concerned Harry, since his instructions were not to interrupt meetings unless something was urgent or unless it was Nancy. Quickly, he reached for the phone.

"Mr. Cain, Karen Lloyd's here. She says she has to see you right away."

"Okay, Clara, show her into my conference room."

He turned to the two promoters. "Gentlemen, please excuse me, I have to see someone for a few moments on an urgent matter." Without waiting for their reply, he swept from the office into his adjoining conference room. He closed the door and waited. He noticed that his hands were shaking.

In a moment, the door opened and Karen, a tall, statuesque brunette, entered. Taking off her dark aviator glasses, she gave Harry a fierce hug.

"That cocksucker. That miserable cocksucker."

"Who, Karen, who?"

"Maurice King. He's actually blocking Nancy's admission to the Harvard TNF program. He doesn't even use an excuse like it's too crowded or something. He wants you to know it's your fault. 'Tell Mr. Cain it's payback time,' he said. What a prick! I threatened to resign. I threatened to punch him out. I think I will punch him out. I'll certainly resign. I . . ."

"Slow down, Karen, and listen. It's not your fault. There's nothing you can do. Your resignation won't help. Neither will slugging him. It's up to me now. I've got to find a way. How much time do we have?"

"She'd have to get to Harvard in time for the first round of treatment. That's in three weeks."

"Okay, Karen. After all you've done, somehow, someway, we'll be there. That's a promise."

After walking Karen to the elevator, Harry returned to his own office. The two promoters looked up from their charts and spread sheets. He had no heart for further conversation about energy grids and kilowatt hours. Besides, he had something to do . . . something urgent.

"Gentlemen, I'm terribly sorry, but I've got an emergency on my hands. I've got to prepare an application for an injunction to be filed downtown before noon. I'm going to have to reschedule our meeting for another time. Please forgive me."

"Of course, Mr. Cain. We understand. That's one of the risks of dealing with a famous attorney."

The two began gathering their papers and charts. Not willing to wait, Harry promised to make another appointment and quickly re-entered his conference room. He closed the door and immediately picked up the phone.

"Carol, ask Skip Corrigan to come by as soon as possible. I need to see him this morning—wherever he is, whatever he's doing. It's urgent."

Harry stood for a moment gazing out the window at the traffic on

48

Sunset Boulevard. He had to make this work. Had to! Nancy was depending on him. Nancy was his client now. And the stakes weren't money this time. The stakes were her life.

Forty minutes later, Harry sat facing Skip Corrigan, an ex–New York cop and highly successful, highly paid private investigator. Harry would be late for his meeting with Tommy Bowers, but it couldn't be helped. This came first.

Corrigan's real first name was not Skip. It was Cipriano. He was half Italian, half Irish, a short, wiry man with light-brown, thinning hair, a long straight nose, and a high-cheekboned Tuscan face. He was always immaculately dressed and soft-spoken. But he was dangerous. Although he never mentioned his connections with the Mafia, they were close and reliable, as were his contacts with the FBI and with the police forces in most major cities. He was a karate black belt, and had also mastered the ancient Oriental art of using any object as a deadly weapon. A shoelace, a rolled-up newspaper, or a pocket comb, in his skilled hands, could cause mortal damage. It was said that he'd once killed a Colombian hit man by driving a pencil through his heart. Harry believed it. But aside from one or two instances when he'd used Corrigan to protect threatened clients, Harry relied more on the investigator's fact-finding ability than his physical prowess.

Now Corrigan, having heard that Maurice King was blocking Nancy from the Harvard program, was uncharacteristically allowing his emotions to show.

"Let me talk to him, Harry. He'll let her in, I guarantee it."

"What do you mean, talk to him?"

"You know fuckin' A what I mean. Me and two friends . . . men of respect . . . will persuade him to change his mind and, if he doesn't, he won't be there to block Nancy any more. Capice? I know you don't like that stuff, Harry, but just this once, you can't afford to be a candy ass. The stakes are too high. Besides, it'll never come to anything rough. We'll persuade him. I guarantee it, and I won't charge you a dime. This one's just for friendship."

"I appreciate it, Skip, and maybe we'll have to get to that. But try it my way first. Call everybody this guy knows, his doctors, his accountants, his friends, his household help—and leave big footprints. Let him know we're investigating him. At the same time, really get me every goddamn fact you can on the guy. Everything. Then we'll see. And I've got to have it done in just three or four days. I'll pay whatever costs you have, no matter what, and a fee too. You're no charitable institution."

"Forget that. You're my friend, and you're in trouble. Friends don't charge for that kind of help. Besides, I hate that son of a bitch, and you know I love Nancy. It'll be a pleasure to do the job."

" '**A**n *affair?*' You think she just had 'an affair'? Oh my God, that's marvelous."

Tommy Bowers's raucous laugh boomed from deep inside his barrel chest. He rocked back and forth in his chair, making explosive snorting sounds. Then, as quickly as his mirth had started, it stopped. He leaned forward, fixing Harry with the coldest of ice-blue eyes. His big hands were on the table clenched into formidable fists. He was short, muscular and built like a steel vault. A former Golden Gloves champion, Bowers was famous for picking fights at parties, in bars, in any social situation. He would publicly insult, even slap another man, until the man was forced to fight or seem the most abject of cowards. Then Bowers would slowly disfigure his opponent, careful not to knock him out until he'd broken a nose, splintered a cheekbone, dislodged teeth. He loved to inflict pain and humiliation, and he had the skill and determination to do it well. Now he was trying a new and different game that was just as vicious.

"I don't have to let you see the diary, Cain. I don't have to give you jack shit. But I might let you have just a taste. I'll think about it."

Harry detested the man. He slowly lifted his face until his eyes bored directly into Bowers's. "While you're thinking about that, star, you better think about how you'll get the diary in evidence if you file your lawsuit. Because, offhand, I don't see its relevance, and I'll bet a thousand to one it never gets before the jury."

"You just might have a bet, counselor," snapped Bowers. "Explain it, Leo." He turned to a fleshy, moon-faced man seated beside him wearing a double-breasted blue suit, a Masonic pin, and a diamond pinkie ring.

Leo Hartstein was no great shakes as a lawyer, but he was not stupid. He had some political connections and an undeserved reputation for being tough. To Harry he had neither the standards or the skill to be a topflight lawyer but, like any opponent of reasonable intelligence, he was not to be underestimated. Hartstein played nervously with the legal papers before him.

"Harry, I'll level with you. We've got the complaint all prepared in draft form. It's right here." He patted the papers. "We can file, and we *will* file, if we don't get the stock and the five million in a couple more weeks."

"But, Leo, your damages couldn't possibly be anything like that."

"Maybe not, but it'll take that to settle . . . given the existence of the diary."

"Come on, Leo, you've got to get the diary in evidence. Can you tell me how the diary's relevant to any corporate claim against Mrs. Campbell? How are you going to get it before the jury?"

"Oh, it's relevant all right, Harry. Firstly, we claim her wild conduct and loose morals have damaged the company; and we've also got Terry Winfield's claim for wrongful termination, that the lady fired Terry *because* he'd seen her diary and knew what was in it, so she trumped up her charges of phony expenses after she'd approved those very same payments herself. Besides, I don't need to get the diary in *evidence*, Harry. A choice sample is attached as an exhibit to the complaint. All I have to do is file the complaint, and it'll be on every front page in the world."

Harry was shaken, but tried not to show it. He sought to play for time, to get as much free information as he could. "Well, from what you say, Leo, that's only a small part of the diary. To get it all in, you'll have to show its relevance and you'll have to do better than what you just said. For example, how will you ever explain—"

Bowers interrupted. "Don't bother arguing with this asshole, Leo. This is no legal debate." He glanced at Harry. "I don't give a shit what we get in evidence. Once we file this complaint, I'll just call a press conference on the courthouse steps and hand out copies of the whole diary. We'll see how Mrs. E. Fucking Campbell likes that. It's not libel, cuz it's all true. She wrote it herself. So don't waste my time. Just have your client pay the five million . . . and fast. I don't like to be kept waiting."

"Are you saying you'll make the diary public unless Pat Campbell pays you five million bucks?"

"You bet your ass I am, counselor."

"That's extortion."

"No shit? Listen, why don't you just go to the DA, instead of just talking through your pigeon-shit mouth. Huh?"

"I may, Tommy. I just may."

"Sure you will, dickhead. And every newspaper in the world will cover my trial and print daily excerpts from Pat Campbell's very juicy diary. I'll take my chances on that. You're not *that* stupid."

He was right, of course; but, again, Harry tried to look unruffled. He turned again to Leo Hartstein. "Want to give me a copy of the complaint, Leo?"

"Sure, Harry. I've got an extra right here." He shoved it across the table, his liquid brown eyes trying their best to convey sincerity and compassion. "Look, Harry, don't make this into an ego thing. We've all been in this spot. We've all had to cave now and then. Go over the complaint with your client. She'll want to settle. She's got so much money, five million'll mean nothing; and this will all be behind her. You've got my word. You'll get back the original diary and every single copy. I mean every one, Harry. For that, five million's not a bad settlement. It's *best* for her, Harry . . . really." He took a soiled handkerchief from his pocket and blew his nose loudly.

Harry stood, picking up the draft complaint. "Thanks, Leo, but without a copy of the entire diary, I just don't see how I can even consider your offer. Pat doesn't remember what she wrote nine, ten years ago and maybe you've only got the excerpts you've attached to the complaint. I haven't even read those yet."

Hartstein sat back and smiled. "First of all, Harry, it was only *three* years ago; and, as I told you, the sample will be enough. Read it. You'll see. Trust me, Harry, you'll see."

On the fifth floor of the county jail, Harry gave the guard his business card, signed the register, and was led to the retaining cell in which he was to meet Fumiko Masami. He was accompanied by Isamu Morita, who was to act as interpreter, since Fumiko spoke very little English.

A big female deputy led a slim Oriental woman in her early thirties into the grimy, ill-lit cell. Her high cheekbones and glossy black hair set off magnificent almond eyes. She was tall for a Japanese, but her body moved gracefully under the rough chambray shirt stenciled "L.A. County Jail." How out of place she seemed in that drab gray building smelling of overflowing toilets and jammed with crack addicts, gang-bangers, and whores.

When the deputy left, Morita took the woman's hand and spoke quietly to her in Japanese. Then he turned to Harry and bowed deeply from the waist.

"Cain-san, this is the Fujiwaras' dear friend, Fumiko Masami."

Harry turned to the lovely young woman and attempted to bow. He knew better than to make quick judgments based on appearance. But he also knew a jury would be reluctant to think this was a killer. It was an advantage he'd use.

"Hajime mashite," he murmured, "I am happy to meet you."

Smiling shyly, she bowed in return. Harry gestured to the cot and two chairs. "Please be seated," he said, surprised to find himself speaking so formally.

Morita and Fumiko each took a metal chair. Harry sat on the cot.

"All right, Fumiko, please tell me everything that happened beginning early on the evening of your husband's death."

Morita repeated Harry's words in rapid Japanese. The girl immediately replied, bowing her head slightly as she spoke.

"Fumiko will not speak of those events, Cain-san, or of any part of the crime of which she is accused."

Harry looked back at Morita, perplexed. "Morita-san, you know a lawyer can't defend his client without the facts. He simply can't succeed." Harry gestured toward Fumiko. "Please explain to her. Make her understand. Not speaking could cost her her life."

Again Morita spoke in rapid Japanese. Harry caught the words "bengoshi". . . lawyer. . . and "wakarimasu" . . . I understand . . . but nothing else. Fumiko replied with a long speech that seemed to cause her pain, but her expression reflected firm resolve.

"She will not discuss it, Cain-san. It is the Japanese way and, even more, it is Fumiko's way. We will not change her mind no matter what we say. I can only pray that, for the sake of the Fujiwara family and, of course, for the sake of Fumiko herself, you will continue as her bengoshi."

Harry looked over at the puzzling young woman. Although her eyelids were shyly lowered, her shoulders were squared and her back straight in the metal chair. She was a woman of contradictions and complexity, Harry thought. There was strength there and, of course, considerable beauty.

"I will take the case, Morita-san, but you must understand that without the basic information from my own client, it will be extremely difficult, probably impossible."

That night, alone in his study, Harry opened his briefcase and took out the photocopied pages of Pat Campbell's diary that Leo Hartstein had attached to his draft complaint. They were in a feminine hand that Harry assumed was Pat's. He poured himself a glass of Warre's Port and, sipping the dark, velvety wine, began to read.

Tuesday May 13th. Strange thing happened at Sidney's Market. There to get endive and other stuff for Wilson dinner (chef never selects greens right). Looking through herb section, squinting at cilantro. Suddenly a man's hand reaches from behind, cups my breast. Jesus! Look side to side, no one else in aisle. Start to scream. He puts other hand over mouth. Right there in market. I'm terrified but, damn it, feel nipple harden. He pulls me back against him. Hard, big. He takes hand from mouth, grabs my hand, puts it on him. Think I'll scream, but don't. He spins me around. New greengrocer, square-faced Italian type, balding black hair, dark beard. Dangerous. I pull away, look daggers at him. He's unconcerned by daggers. Frightening. Exciting? "If you want more," he grunts, "come back tomorrow afternoon. Wear something red." I turn on my heel and walk away as fast as I can, rush out to car, heart pounding. Forgot endive, but don't go back. Will change markets.

Harry took a sip of port, rubbed his eyes and continued reading.

May 14th. Garden in A.M. Think of market, disgusted. Grab lunch, read McLuhan, hard to follow. Deliberately obscure? Rest in bedroom, but no nap—tense, tense, tense. I shower, sprinkle with Joy, look in mirror. Body looks good, still young. How long? Put on clean denims, white shirt, black Mary Janes. Try McLuhan again. Can't get through one page. Thoughts of market break in, heart pounds, feel strange, like elevator dropping fast. Open drawer, grab red sweater, throw over shoulder and go to market . . . same one. Walk in, heart pounding in chest. What will he do? Never mind that, what will I do? Up one aisle, down next, looking, but trying not to look like I'm looking. No sight of him. Day off? Feel let down. Dare I ask? Stand in aisle looking at cilantro again. Becoming expert. Suddenly he's behind me again. Without a word, his hand goes inside denims, inside panties, his fingers serenade me. I feel floor rocking under me. I'm wet and slick. Fingers make me weak in knees. Again, he puts my hand on him. Huge, my God! "You're gonna feel that inside you, big and hot." That's the way he talks. "Are you ready?", he growls. Am I ready? Is the pope catholic? I nod weakly, say nothing. He takes my arm and leads me toward back of market. Can I walk? I can. We pass customer. He nods. What if Sidney sees me, or Mike, the butcher? I don't care. Feel like there's a sign on my shirt, "horny—about to be fucked," but nobody pays attention. We go to small room behind store. Cot, chair, boxes of lettuce along wall, terrible nude calendar. He locks door. Commands me to strip. This greasy tradesman commands me! I obey. I lie on filthy cot. He pulls off pants, leaves on shirt and shoes. A pig. He has his way with me . . . his way with me? Jesus! I'm talking like romantic novel. What he does is fuck me. I enjoy it, I love it. When he's done, he pulls on pants. "Anytime you want more," he says, "come on back in the afternoon. Wear something red." He leaves. I lie on the cot, still panting. Finally I pull on clothes. Think everyone in market must know. I slink out to car. Will Ewing see it in my face? He didn't."

Holy shit, Harry thought, as he turned off the light, and sat alone in the darkened study. Pat was right. Ewing Campbell will never forgive that. He can't. He's got to divorce her, and there's probably more in the diary. Given the sound of the real Pat Campbell, there's probably much more. And only three years ago, not nine or ten years, as Pat had said—not at the beginning of their marriage, when she was stressed and immature.

Still, she probably had her reasons. Things like this were never black or white. They were always gray—full of shadings, complexities, unseen causes. And besides, whatever she'd done couldn't justify what Bowers was doing. This man was a vicious bully, who was threatening to inflict the worst kind of pain on someone who'd turned to Harry for help and protection. He had to stop them from using the diary. But how? In law school they used to say "For every wrong there's a remedy." Nice words, but what's the remedy here? How could he stop Bowers from filing a lawsuit? Isn't that every citizen's right? It seemed impossible.

He vaguely remembered the communiqué Marshall Foch sent to the French General Staff when the Germans were threatening Paris. It was something like "Outnumbered on all sides. Enemy massing for assault. Situation hopeless. I will attack." That's got to be it, he thought. I will attack.

Over the next few days, Harry worked on the court papers he was preparing to file against Tommy Bowers and started to gather the facts he'd need to defend Fumiko Masami. He wanted to get that work done before he went back to Harvard for Nancy's first treatment . . . *if* he could get her in the program. He'd still had no report from Skip Corrigan.

On a rainy morning, he drove downtown to L.A.P.D. headquarters at Parker Center, where he was able to see the police report and the lab analysis of the poison. Hiraiko Masami had been found dead in his bedroom at the Regent Beverly Wilshire at 10:00 A.M. A chambermaid had discovered his body and called the assistant manager, who called the police. They found Fumiko reading in her own bedroom. Advised of her rights through a Japanese interpreter who worked at the hotel, she refused to discuss anything relating to her husband or his death. Her purse contained a large glass phial half full of a dark-brown liquid. Laboratory analysis identified it as antimony chloride, a poisonous substance fatal if ingested in any quantity. Half of the phial, or even a quarter of it, would have been more than enough to kill. A glass bearing traces of a dark-brown fluid was found on a nightstand beside the victim's bed. Laboratory analysis showed the fluid to have been a mixture of two very different things. One was Fernet Branca, a dark-brown Italian bitters used as a stomachic. The other was the poison, antimony chloride.

Employees of the hotel reported that, for the preceding four nights, Mr. Masami had been visited by two or three women who appeared to be prostitutes. From approximately ten each evening, Masami was extremely drunk, noisy, and abusive. Several times, other guests had complained. Room-service records showed that Masami ordered three or four bottles of Dewar's Scotch each night. On the last night of his life, he had also ordered a bottle of Fernet Branca.

Cursory observation of the accused, Fumiko Masami, showed a black eye and a number of dark contusions on her neck and arms. An autopsy showed the cause of the victim's death to be poisoning by ingestion of antimony chloride and the time of death to be between 3:00 and 4:00 A.M. Latent Prints reported that clear sets of the accused's fingerprints were on the phial of poison found in her purse. The phial contained no other prints. Fumiko Masami's prints were also on the bottle of Fernet Branca and on the glass that had contained the bitters and the poison. The only other prints on the glass and the bottle were those of the victim.

It looks clear enough, thought Harry. A really solid case . . . if you're the prosecutor.

Later that day, Harry sat in his office, sipping a cup of tea and watching a light rain falling on the city below. He was growing more and more anxious about getting Nancy into the Harvard program. Her condition was on his mind so much of the time now that he'd become concerned about his ability to concentrate on his work even for short periods.

Sighing, he leafed through the *Times* and read that the prosecutor in the *Masami* case would be his old adversary, Bailey J. Scuneo. A skilled, self-driven trial lawyer with a wide streak of meanness and a penchant for publicity, Scuneo had moved to the district attorney's staff after twenty years with the city attorney. The veteran prosecutor liked to be called "B.J." by lawyers and court officials; but, at least behind his back, he was more frequently called "Scumbag Scuneo" and, as Harry often remarked, it was more description than alliteration. The rumor was that Scuneo intended to run for district attorney himself. He was one of the few prosecutors well known to the public, and his record was superb—except against Harry. Twice before, Harry had beaten Scuneo in highly publicized cases, situations that had been humiliating for the proud, ambitious prosecutor. He cordially hated Harry and was obsessed with beating him in a trial. This time, with the evidence stacked against Fumiko Masami, he would have an excellent chance.

Harry read on. As usual, Scuneo was playing to the media. The *Times* quoted him as predicting a prompt conviction of this "cold-hearted woman who would find that the citizens of this country did not consider poison a recreational drug." When advised that Fumiko would be defended by Harry, Scuneo had responded, "It figures she'd get someone of that ilk."

"That ilk"?, thought Harry. What ilk is that, Scuneo? The ilk that kicks your butt?

He smiled at his own arrogance. If anyone's butt was about to be kicked in the *Masami* trial, it was not likely to be Scuneo's.

Harry put down the paper and leaned back, enjoying the quiet of his office, the gray art-deco furnishings, the soft light. It was one of the few places where he could retreat, find some moments of solitude and the opportunity to think.

Let Scuneo rant. Harry had seen many, many battles, and this was just another one. There were more important things in life—certainly *Nancy* was more important. Who gave a fuck about lawsuits? Then, after a moment, Harry smiled at himself again. Bullshit! he thought, you don't mean that. You're just as obsessed with winning as ever. Sure Nancy's important, but if you don't beat that asshole Scuneo, you'll never face yourself again.

He jammed the newspaper in his wastebasket, forced the *Masami* case from his mind, and picked up the brief he'd prepared to stop Tommy Bowers from terrorizing Pat Campbell.

He was proud of the brief and even more proud of the unique strategy he'd devised to prevent Bowers from carrying out his threat. His plan had problems. Its very novelty was a problem, so was its constitutionality. Still, he . . .

The shrill ring of the phone broke in on his thoughts.

"Neil Wegman calling from New York, Mr. Cain."

Harry recognized the name of the New York lawyer for Consolidated Studios.

"Okay, Carol, put him through."

"Cain?" The voice was harsh, angry.

"Yes."

"This is Neil Wegman of Tilling and Brown. I want to give you notice that the New York Supreme Court has set a contempt hearing in *Consolidated* v. *Miletti* for February twentieth at nine A.M. And I want to tell you one more thing, Cain. We know all about your role in the theft. We've amended the complaint to make you a defendant personally, along with Miletti—and it's not just Consolidated. The whole Producers Association is backing us, and you're finally going to get what you deserve. Now, will you accept service, or do I have to hunt you down with a process server?"

Harry ignored the man's extraordinary rudeness; he knew Wegman was seething. It had been his responsibility to pick up the film after the court order, and he'd been too slow about it . . . let it slip through his fingers. Harry could imagine how Yank Slutsky had treated Wegman when he found out, what choice invective Yank must have lavished on the poor lawyer, who had failed to act decisively enough, was outsmarted, and let $40 million worth of Slutsky's film get away.

Harry knew he could duck the contempt proceeding for a time; but he couldn't stay out of New York forever, and in any event, his plan for that case required an early hearing, while the studio lawyers were still off balance.

"Yes, I'll accept service, Mr. Wegman, and thank you so much for calling me."

"I intended no courtesy, Cain, and no favor. As far as I'm concerned, you're a thief, and I'm gonna nail you unless we get that film back. And I mean today."

"Oh, really?"

"Yes, really. You were there in court when the order was made, you heard it, you were bound by it and you violated it. We've talked to Miletti's office staff and we can prove you talked to him immediately after the order was made and just before the film disappeared. We also know that Rod Townsend, the star of the picture, who surely knows *something*, refused to talk to investigators because he said he didn't want to hurt his friend Harry Cain. He didn't just say he was protecting Miletti. He said he was protecting *you*. It's obvious you're in this thing up to your neck, Cain, and, like I said, I'm going to nail you. So unless you like prison stripes, you better get that film back pronto."

Smiling to himself, Harry kept his tone pleasant and chatty. "Well, thank you, Mr. Wegman, it was certainly a pleasure talking to you. Say, if you're ever out here on the coast, let's have lunch."

"Go fuck yourself, Cain."

"Phrasemaker," said Harry sweetly, as he heard the dial tone. He smiled to himself. Wegman had grabbed at every piece of bait Harry offered. His plan might just work.

Driving down Doheny, between rows of towering palms, Harry heard the insistent warble of his car phone. Nancy? he thought. He picked up the receiver. "Mr. Cain, it's Alla Van Meer from New York. She says it's important. Shall I connect her with you?" He was almost at his lunch meeting; but if Alla was in some kind of trouble . . . He told his receptionist to put the call through to his car.

"Hi. What's the problem?"

"The problem is I miss you, dickweed." The connection was bad, but the throaty voice was unmistakable. Harry sighed and made a left turn at Melrose. "Listen, the lady explorer is lying here in bed, almost asleep. It's dark in the jungle, and a perfect time for that huge hairy ape to come crashing through the window. How long will it take you to get here, my simian seducer? I can't wait much longer." Her low, resonant laugh vibrated through the phone.

Harry knew from Neil Wegman's call that he had to be in New York quite soon. He smiled to himself. It might be exciting to be with Alla again. Then he thought of Nancy and the struggle she was facing. Suddenly, he was overcome with the conviction that this was a critical point in his life, that arranging to see Alla in New York meant Nancy would die.

"Listen, Alla, Nancy's very sick."

"Sick? What do you mean?"

"It's cancer. We're fighting it; but her chances are not very good."

"Oh my God, Harry! I'm so sorry!"

"Thanks. Anyway, it just wouldn't be right, you know, for us to . . ." He left the sentence unfinished.

"Of course, Harry, I understand. Let me know if there's anything I can do?"

"Sure, Alla. I'll call you, okay?"

"Okay, Harry, 'bye."

He hung up the phone and breathed a deep sigh of relief. He felt better. Almost proud of himself. Then his intellect took over. What did he want, a medal? For what? For not fucking around on his wife—his wife, who might die any time. Christ, what an asshole he was!

It was a clear, sunny day and Pat Campbell looked cool and fresh in a white, gauzy Laize Adzer dress and wide-brimmed straw hat. Harry had booked a table for two on the small patio of the Ivy, one of his favorite restaurants. He ordered crab cakes and abalone, and as he poured himself a glass of Sonoma-Cutrer chardonnay, Benny, the maître d', came to their table to announce a phone call for Harry. Could it be Alla again? I'll kill her, he thought, making his way

through the maze of umbrellas, plants, and tables to the phone behind Benny's desk.

"Hello" he growled, sticking a finger in his free ear to cut out the
noise of six well-dressed matrons greeting each other with kisses and
shrill cries as they gathered to claim their table.

"Boy, do you sound pissed off." It was Joe Miletti.

"I'm sorry, Joe, you got me in the middle of lunch. Is everything
okay?"

"Is everything okay? Are you serious? My film's missing. Slutsky's
gonna hang me on a meat hook, and now I get served with a paper
called 'Order to Show Cause re Contempt.' What the fuck does that
mean?"

Harry explained quickly about the contempt hearing set for the
twentieth in New York. He added that he was also a defendant now
and that, if things went wrong, they could both end up in jail.

"Will you handle this one yourself, Harry? I mean this guy Goodwin may be okay, but he's not the fucking Sunset Bomber. You know
what I'm saying? You *will* do it yourself, won't you?"

"Yeah, Joe—given that my own neck's on the line, I think I'll do
it myself."

"That's great, Harry. I feel much better already."

"I'm glad, Joe. Now who's going to make *me* feel better? Listen,
I've got to get back to my table. I'll call you later, okay?"

"Okay, 'bye."

" 'Bye."

Harry put down the phone and rejoined Pat, who was well into her
soft-shell crabs and sipping a glass of chardonnay. "I should have
waited for you," she said, smiling, "but I was too hungry."

The waiter brought Harry's order. Pat's face had taken on a serious, troubled expression. "The reason I wanted this lunch, Harry,
was to apologize."

"Apologize?"

"Yes. I'm afraid I misled you. . . . Hell, I just plain lied to you."
She paused for another sip of wine. "That stuff in my diary?" He
nodded silently. "It didn't happen ten years ago as I told you. It was
more like three years ago—when I was going through a very bad
time. Because you knew Ewing and me as a couple, I was just
ashamed to tell you."

"I know."

"You know?"

"I had a talk with Bowers and his lawyer."

"My God. Did you get the diary?"

"I got this." From his coat pocket Harry pulled a copy of the diary excerpt that was Exhibit A to the complaint Bowers threatened to file. He handed it across the table. As she read it, a crimson flush rose to her cheeks. Then, as she looked back up at Harry, her color faded.

"Oh, my God," she whispered, "Oh, my God. How could I write such things? How could I *do* them? Nothing can help me now. I'm going to lose Ewing, I know it. And just when I've come to realize how much I love him." Her voice broke.

Harry reached out and took her hand. "Pat, we all do stupid, selfish things sometimes. And sometimes we suffer for them." He thought of Nancy and his own childish behavior. "You're suffering now; but I'm going to do my damnedest to keep you from suffering more—to keep you from losing Ewing . . . or five million bucks." He smiled, trying to comfort her, give her confidence.

"You've found a way to stop them?"

"I've got a plan."

"Will it work?"

He gave her a big grin. "Hey, do they call me 'the Sunset Bomber' for nothing?"

She took his hand in both of hers; and, with tears running down her cheeks, gave him a smile so glowing, so filled with relief and gratitude that he felt his own eyes begin to moisten.

Silently, he wished that he felt half the confidence he'd pretended. Now that he'd told her the plan would work, he'd have to make sure it did . . . somehow.

When Harry returned to his office, Skip Corrigan was waiting for him with a report on Maurice King. Grinning, he told Harry that King was already getting calls from all over the world to the effect that someone was out there investigating him. From what Skip could observe, King seemed to be very nervous and upset about it. Like a man with plenty to hide. For half an hour Skip read Harry his detailed notes about every aspect of the wealthy builder's life. When he finished, Harry leaned back in his chair and gazed up at the ceiling. After a moment, he looked back at the wiry detective.

"Good job, Skip. Two or three things we can really use. Tell me more about that girl, Maria whatsername."

"Sure. Supposedly she's a 'writer'; but she's really just a part-time hooker. Mostly B and D, I think. Got one of those black-leather bikini outfits with the chains, you know?, and a full-size inflatable rubber girl. Two or three guys a week come by and stay for an hour or so. I think they fuck the blow-up doll while she whips them. I can get all the specifics on that if you want, but here's what's interesting: Guess who pays the rent on the apartment?" Without waiting for an answer Skip nodded. "That's right. Maurice King. He comes over twice a week. I guess for a 'treatment.' And he calls her two or three times a day from his office phone in between sessions. Don't ask me how I know. You don't wanna know. Anyway, I think she's talking dirty to him over the phone and he gets off on it. How do you want me to handle it?"

Harry didn't want to threaten either the girl or King. He didn't want to commit extortion if he could avoid it. But, he had to get a message to King that would change his mind about the Harvard program.

"Tell the girl you think her story would make a terrific book. Tell her you'll pay her a twenty-thousand-dollar advance to write it. Go higher if you have to, maybe to fifty thousand. I mean it. I'll really buy the rights. Tell her that if it goes well, there could be more books, maybe a novel; but tell her she'll have to include details about King in the book. That's the stuff that'll sell. Tell her that it's Harry Cain who's buying the book, that we want her to be completely open about this. She should tell King what she's doing, that I'm involved; and she should ask if she can interview King's wife to find out what he's like at home. I want her to talk to King before she gets started on the book; and she doesn't get the advance until she has that conversation. Got it?"

"Sure. King will go crazy when he gets that call. It may do the job, but why not let *me* persuade him, too?"

"No, I don't think so, Skip. And it's not just my feeling about that kind of stuff. Any direct threat is extortion. King's tough and dangerous. If we commit extortion, he'll go right to the DA, and I'll be fighting a criminal charge when I need all my time and energy for Nancy. No, we can do it without making a single threat. Now tell me more about his Palm Beach project."

"Well, he's very heavily invested down there. Actually, much heavier than he can afford. It's a huge project, but he's had cash-flow problems, and he can't sell any units at all in this market. Meanwhile, the debt service is eating him up. If he can't refinance, he can lose everything. But he's working on it, and I think he's got a refinancing package almost in place."

"Whose money?"

"It's a consortium of British and European banks, about six hundred million dollars from the combine. The lead bank is Cudner-James."

"No shit. Cudner-James out of London?"

"Yeah. Powerful private bank. Without them, King's a dead man."

Harry stood, walked around the desk, and kissed Corrigan on the ear.

"Cipriano, you wonderful guinea bastard. You've done it again."

"What do you mean?"

"Four years ago, I handled a divorce case for Sir Hilary Cudner. Saved him a bundle. His wife was a twenty-six-year-old starlet. When she met him, she lived in a tiny Hollywood apartment. He moved her to a palace behind the Beverly Hills Hotel. Then he moved there himself. That was his mistake. The girl had a problem. She couldn't stay away from black musicians—was obsessed with black cock. After a year or so, they split; and, of course, this being a no-fault divorce state, she claimed Sir Hilary had converted all his assets into quasi-community property. She asked for a billion dollars. A billion, Skip, with a 'b.' Anyway, we had a long trial, and the judge gave her zip. Sir Hilary swore he owed me his life. We remained friends. I see him from time to time when I'm in London."

Harry looked at his watch. Then he turned and picked up the phone.

"Carol, get me Sir Hilary Cudner in London. If he's left his office, try him at his place in Surrey."

Minutes later Harry had explained the situation to the English banker, who, enraged at Maurice King's conduct, told him that Cudner-James would not deal with such a man. He pronounced King's refinancing dead. King would be told immediately.

"I appreciate your help, Hilary. You're a good friend indeed. But I want you to handle it differently, if you will."

"Anything, Harry, you know that."

"First, when you cut off King's loan, tell him why you're doing it. Second, if I call and ask you to—even though the man's a vicious animal—please reinstate the loan."

"*Reinstate* it? Do business with such a monster?"

"Yes, Hilary, please—do it for me; but only if I ask you to. I'll leave a code message at your office. It'll say 'forgive.' You'll know that means to reinstate King's loan."

Later Harry walked Skip Corrigan to the door, his arm around the detective.

"It's gonna work, Harry. I don't think you need to give the girl the book deal."

"Do it, Skip. We'll play both angles for insurance. As you said, the stakes are too high."

Later that day, as Harry was packing his briefcase to go home, he got a call from Karen Lloyd.

"Sweetie, it's a miracle. I can't believe it. Maurice King just called. He *wants* Nancy in the Harvard program. He said he's had a change of heart and didn't want to punish her for his dispute with you. Isn't that great? I could kiss him."

"Karen, that's wonderful news. I think you must have convinced him, and we really appreciate it. Thanks for telling me."

Five minutes later, Harry sent a fax to London. It was a one-word message to the office of Sir Hilary Cudner: "Forgive."

Nancy was resting in their bedroom when Harry brought her the news that she'd been accepted in the Harvard program. She rose and pulled him to her in a fierce hug. Almost immediately, he felt her tears on his cheek.

"Why are you crying?"

She pulled back, still holding his shoulders. She sniffed and took a deep breath, her dark eyes glistening.

"I'm crying with joy. But it's not just because I'm in the program. It's joy over you . . . having you on my side, having you in my life. I couldn't fight this thing without you, and, to a great extent, I'm fighting it *because* of you, because I want to keep on *being* with you . . . for a long time . . . and because you've taken this thing on as the fight of your life, and I don't want you to lose."

He pulled her close and kissed her, first tenderly, then with a growing passion. She felt her body respond through the thin silk robe. She pressed against him, her hands moving over his back and hips. They fell onto the bed, still clinging to each other. They kissed again, and he gently slid her robe apart. He moved above her and inside her, penetrating deeply, fully. Her hips rose to meet him and they began to move as one, clutching each other, crying out together, for the moment a single being, swept away with love.

Harry boarded the New York flight with only carry-on luggage. He'd just be in New York for the contempt hearing; and then, if he wasn't in jail, he'd meet Nancy in Boston for her TNF treatment.

A tall blond stewardess leaned over Harry and, putting her lips close to his ear, whispered in a husky voice, "Here's *Variety*." Gently, she laid the green-and-white trade paper in his lap.

He remembered getting the *Daily News* story of his New York fight from a stewardess who could be this one's twin. Did these girls all think he was hungry for news? And why *Variety?* Did he look *that* Hollywood? Maybe it was his tan, the white Reeboks he wore with his tweed jacket and jeans. She wasn't bad looking. Nice legs, he noticed, as she moved away reluctantly, smiling back over her shoulder.

He settled back into the huge first-class seat, sipping his Bloody Mary as he unfolded *Variety*. The headline was startling. MILETTI, CAIN FACE SLAMMER. The story reviewed the troubled history of *The Last Battle* and how the $40-million film had been taken by "persons unknown." It added that the lawyers for Consolidated Studios had charged director Joe Miletti and his lawyer Harry Cain, the legendary "Sunset Bomber," with taking the film in deliberate violation of a court order. It noted that a hearing was set for February twentieth in New York, with the Academy Award–winning director and his controversial lawyer facing possible prison terms.

A spokesman for the Motion Picture Producers Association was quoted as saying that if Harry and Joe were guilty as charged, they should lock them up and throw away the key, that no crime could be more serious. Harry was bemused, thinking of the tiny, pompous man who apparently ranked the theft of a film ahead of murder and rape. Still, Harry recognized the danger he faced. A great deal of power was ranged against him, and he'd need all his skill to make his plan work.

Throughout the trip the stewardess offered Harry magazines, drinks, and extra food, ignoring the elderly lady sitting beside him. Three times the girl had knelt in the aisle beside Harry, showing beautiful thighs, making intimate eye contact and speaking quietly and suggestively. The last time, just before the plane started its descent into Kennedy, she let her fingers trail along Harry's leg and asked pointedly where he was staying. She did this while Harry's elderly seatmate asked twice, in vain, for club soda.

Harry looked into the stewardess's eyes and smiled. It was tempting, but he'd promised himself he was out of the game. He owed that to Nancy. At least that. Was this the new Harry Cain, he wondered, Harry Cain, the adult? Maybe so. Still, he found it hard to reject the girl too harshly. There was no need to hurt her feelings.

"I'm staying with friends this time; but, look, I'll see you on the next flight. Okay? You know, I think this lady needs some club soda."

The contempt proceedings against Joseph Miletti and Harry Cain were called as the first case on the calendar of Judge Benjamin Mancuso of the New York Supreme Court. It pained Harry to be back in the same drab building in which Consolidated Studios had used a phony affidavit to obtain the order seizing Miletti's film. At least he had a different judge. Harry didn't know Judge Mancuso, but he liked his looks and demeanor, and Harry's New York friends had described him as bright and honest.

The gallery was packed, mostly with reporters. Film cases were something of a rarity in New York, and the word on the street was that there'd be celebrity witnesses. The bailiff quieted the reporters, who were still greeting each other while stuffing their overcoats under their seats and stamping snow from their shoes.

Consolidated's lawyer, Neil Wegman, was a short, stocky man, with jet-black hair and eyes and a square, florid face. Still angry and embarrassed by his original failure to collect the film before it disappeared, he stood at the counsel table like a small enraged bull. Invited by the court to begin, he plunged into his argument that Harry as well as Joe Miletti had deliberately violated the court's order to turn the film over to the studio.

"First, Your Honor," Wegman bellowed, "I'd like the record to show that the defendant, Harry Cain, was present in court on February third, when the order in question was made. This is shown by the court minutes of that day, of which this court may take judicial notice."

The judge looked courteously at Wegman. "All right, counsel, judicial notice is taken of the fact that the defendant Cain was present in court when the order of February third was made. Do the minutes show that the defendant Miletti was also present?"

"No, Your Honor; but there will be other evidence that Mr. Miletti was aware of the order."

The judge made a quick note on the pad before him and turned again to Wegman. "Very well, you may call your first witness."

"We call Deputy Eli Markowitz, Your Honor." A heavy-set, balding man in a tan uniform moved ponderously to the stand. He was sworn and gave his name.

Wegman moved away from the counsel table, closer to the witness. "Now, Deputy Markowitz, would you please tell the court what happened on February third of this year with reference to the motion picture *The Last Battle*?"

"Yes, sir." The officer consulted a small blue notepad, turning back the cover and reading from the first page. "On February third at eleven-thirty A.M. I received a copy of the court's order to pick up all negative and positive film footage of that motion picture and deliver it to the offices of Consolidated Studios. The order was directed to the offices of Joseph Miletti at 210 West Fifty-seventh Street in New York City and to any other place where said film might be located."

"All right, Deputy Markowitz, what happened next?"

Again the heavy man consulted his notebook. "I proceeded to 210 West Fifty-seventh Street where the film was supposedly located. I arrived there at twelve thirty-five P.M. on the third. No one was there, and the office was locked. I returned to the defendant's office at one-thirty P.M. The office was still locked and no one was present. I spoke to the super, who located an assistant editor, Sophie Plotkin, at her home. Ms. Plotkin came down at two-forty, and, after searching the premises, told me the film wasn't there—that it was missing. I reported that to my office at three-fifteen."

"Okay, Deputy Markowitz, please tell us the next event that occurred with reference to the film."

"The following morning, February fourth, I returned once again to defendant Miletti's office, arriving there at nine forty-five A.M. This time Mr. Miletti was present, and I spoke to him."

"What did you say?"

"I said I had a court order to pick up the film and deliver it to Consolidated Studios. I served him with a copy of the order, and I told him the film appeared to be missing."

"And what did he say?"

"He confirmed that it was missing. He said he had no idea where it was or who had it."

"Did he explain how the film could have been taken without his knowledge?"

"He said that the office had been closed most of the day on the third and that, when he arrived for work on the morning of the fourth, he was told that the film was gone. He showed me the film-storage locker where he had kept it. I examined it. It did not appear to have been broken into, but it was, like he said, empty. There was no film in the locker or anywhere else on the premises."

"Did you ascertain who had keys to this locker?"

"Yes, sir. Both Mr. Miletti and his office staff confirmed that Mr. Miletti and Rod Townsend, who was working with Mr. Miletti on the film, had the only keys to the storage locker."

"And did you interview Mr. Townsend?"

"No, sir, not at that time."

"Why not?"

"Well, I couldn't locate him until February fifth. When I did finally contact him, he told me he would testify if subpoenaed, but that Joe Miletti and Harry Cain were his good friends and he didn't want to participate voluntarily in any interview that might adversely affect them."

"Now let me understand this, Deputy Markowitz. Mr. Townsend

said that *Mr. Cain* was also his good friend and that he did not want to participate in a voluntary interview that could hurt Mr. Miletti *or Mr. Cain?*"

"Yes, that's correct."

"Did he explain why telling you what he knew about the missing film could hurt *Mr. Cain?*"

Wegman spat the word "Cain" each time he used it. He glared across the room at Harry, who was seated quietly at the counsel table.

"No, sir. He didn't."

"Have you attempted to locate the film, Deputy Markowitz?"

"Yes, sir."

"Have you been able to do so?"

"No, sir."

"So far as you know is it still missing?"

"Yes, sir."

Wegman turned on his heel, snapping. "Your witness."

Harry got to his feet slowly. "Deputy Markowitz, when you advised Mr. Miletti on February fourth that there was a court order to pick up the film, what did he say?"

The deputy consulted his notepad again, turning the pages, looking for the appropriate entry. Finally he located it. "Mr. Miletti said, and I quote, 'That goddamn judge must be crooked or crazy.'"

Laughter swept the gallery until Judge Mancuso angrily rapped for order. Harry continued.

"Did Mr. Miletti give any indication that he knew of the court order before you told him about it on February fourth?"

"No, sir."

"And, by that time, the film was already missing, right?"

"Right."

"Did Mr. Miletti tell you why the office had been closed on the third?"

"Yes, sir. He said there was no point working on the film any more until they heard what the court decided, so he gave everyone the day off and closed the office."

"And did he tell you where he was going after he closed the office?"

"Yes, he did. He said he was going to Atlantic City."

"And did you check his story out?"

"Yes, sir. He did register at the Sands. And, in fact, he did occupy his room that night."

"Thank you, Deputy Markowitz. That's all I have."

The judge turned to the other counsel table. "Any redirect?"

"No, Your Honor."

"All right, this witness may be excused. You may proceed, Mr. Wegman."

"We'll call the defendant, Joseph Miletti, as our next witness, Your Honor."

Harry got quickly to his feet, speaking as he rose.

"Your Honor, a contempt proceeding is quasi-criminal in nature. The defendant need not testify any more than he would have to in an ordinary criminal case."

"That sounds correct to me, counsel," said the judge, looking over at Wegman. "Any reply?"

"Well, sir . . . I . . . no, I suppose not; but, if Mr. Miletti really wants the truth to come out, then . . ."

Harry interrupted, speaking excitedly. "Your Honor, that's improper, and Mr. Wegman knows it! He knows he's not entitled to comment in this kind of a proceeding on a defendant's decision not to testify. That's fundamentally improper."

Down came the gavel. "All right, gentlemen, that's enough. Mr. Miletti, you need not testify in this matter, and, if you decline to do so, no comment will be made about your decision, nor will I draw any adverse inference from that decision."

"Mr. Miletti does decline to testify, Your Honor," said Harry quietly.

"Very well, you may resume your seat, Mr. Miletti. Mr. Wegman, please call your next witness."

"In that event, we'll call Mr. Cain, Your Honor."

Once again Harry stood. "Your Honor, I have also been named personally as a defendant; and I also decline to testify."

Wegman's face suffused with anger. "Your Honor! Mr. Cain can't refuse to testify and then proceed to argue the case. He's just trying to tell his story to court without taking an oath or being cross-examined. He simply can't . . ."

Down came the gavel again. "Enough, Mr. Wegman! Please don't use that tone in my court." He paused, then began again. "You adopted the unusual tactic of making opposing counsel a defendant in his personal capacity. Having done so, you must take the consequences; and one of the consequences, Mr. Murphy, is that Mr. Cain need not testify. At the same time, I know of nothing that prevents him from arguing the case."

"But, Your Honor, that's just a sharp tactic designed to . . ."

"No, Mr. Wegman!" boomed the judge, "I will not tolerate that! One more outburst, and you'll be in contempt yourself. Please proceed with your case. To this point, you've put on precious little evidence to support this very serious charge."

Wegman was enraged and fighting to control it. His hands, held behind his back, were balled into tight fists.

"We'll call Rod Townsend as our next witness," he announced, anger and frustration discernible in his almost surly tone.

A buzz went through the gallery. As far as action-adventure films were concerned, there was no bigger star than the internationally famous Rod Townsend. The bailiff quieted the crowd, and the actor came forward, was sworn, and took the stand. He was a tall, rugged-looking man in his late forties with a full head of unruly brown hair and large friendly eyes of the same chestnut color. Hand-tooled cowboy boots showed beneath the trousers of his well-tailored gray suit. He settled into the witness chair, nodded politely to the judge and looked over expectantly at Neil Wegman.

Townsend was not a defendant and could not decline to testify. He could refuse to answer individual questions on the ground that his testimony would tend to incriminate him. But this would be an unpopular position for a major film star to take, and something Harry hadn't asked of him.

Wegman, of course, knew that Townsend had the only other key to the film-storage locker; but Harry had guessed that he had lacked the courage to name a famous movie star as a co-defendant without more evidence to link him to the charge.

Once again Wegman stepped away from the counsel table to examine the witness.

"Mr. Townsend, you were the star of the motion picture *The Last Battle*, isn't that correct?"

"Yes, sir."

"In January and early February, you were working on the film with the director, Joseph Miletti. You were helping with the editing process, isn't that right?"

"Yes, sir, that's correct."

"And you had a key to Mr. Miletti's editing rooms, isn't that correct."

"Yes."

"And you also had a key to the film-storage locker where the only work print was kept, isn't that correct also?"

"Yes, sir, that's true."

"And the shot book was kept there too, isn't that so?"

"Yes."

"Would you explain to the court what the 'shot book' is?"

"It's the record of which shots have been printed and which printed shots have been selected for inclusion in the work print."

"And those shots are listed in the book by number?"

"Yes."

"And the strips of film are stored under those same numbers?"

"That's true."

"And there are millions of feet of film, right?"

"Right."

"Without the shot book, no one could find the right strips of film or put them together into a showable picture. Isn't that also true?"

"Well, it would be very hard. If it could be done, it would take a very long time."

"Thank you. Now, did anyone but you and Mr. Miletti have a key to the film-storage locker?"

"No. We had only two keys."

"Did you see the film-storage locker after the film was missing?"

"Yes, I did."

"Okay then, when you saw it, did it appear to have been broken into or forced in any way?"

"No, it appeared to be intact and not to have been tampered with."

"It appeared to have been opened with a key, isn't that correct?"

Joe Miletti looked over at Harry, expecting him to object. But Harry sat quietly listening.

"Yes, sir, it did."

"Well, Mr. Townsend, if there was no break-in and there were only two keys, either you took the film yourself, or it had to be taken by Mr. Miletti, isn't that right?"

Townsend paused before replying. He looked up toward the ceiling, pondering the question. He turned to the judge. "Your Honor, could I hear that question again, please?" The judge directed the court reporter to read it back. She pulled at the paper in her stenotype machine and then reread the question.

Townsend looked directly at Neil Wegman. "I think the answer to that question is 'yes.' "

Wegman seemed puzzled by the curious nature of Townsend's response.

"Is there some doubt in your mind as to what my question meant, Mr. Townsend?"

"No, sir. Now that I've heard it again, I believe I understand it and, as I've said, the answer is 'yes.' "

"Okay then, we've established that either you or Mr. Miletti took the film—and we know *you* didn't take it—right?"

Townsend frowned, as though this question too created a problem. Finally, he spoke.

"No, we *don't* know that, Mr. Wegman."

Again Wegman looked puzzled.

"Please explain, Mr. Townsend, why we can't eliminate you as the one who took the film?"

"Because I *was* the one."

There was another excited buzz from the gallery. One reporter bolted from the room, headed for a phone. The rest stayed, making hurried scratches in their notebooks. If it could be proved that Rod Townsend knew of the court order when he took the film, one of the world's biggest stars would almost surely be charged with contempt and would probably be jailed.

Judge Mancuso rapped for order.

On the trail of something even bigger than he'd hoped, Wegman eagerly pressed on.

"You took the film, Mr. Townsend?"

"Yes, sir, I took the film."

Again, there was an excited buzz from the gallery. Again, the judge rapped for order.

"And did you know at the time you took the film that there was a court order for it to be turned over to Consolidated Pictures?"

"Not at the time. I learned that two or three days later."

"I see. Now, if you didn't know there was a court order and you weren't trying to avoid that order, will you please explain to the court why, after months of editing the film at Mr. Miletti's office, you removed it from there on February third—the very day of the order?"

Every eye in the now silent courtroom was on Rod Townsend.

"Certainly, Mr. Wegman. A man called and told me . . ."

Harry was on his feet at once. "Objection, Your Honor. We are obviously about to get hearsay in the record. What this unidentified man may have said may be admissible just to show that the words were spoken, but the statement may not be received as evidence of the truth of what was said. That, of course, would be hearsay."

"Sustained. The remarks of the caller will be received only for the limited purpose of showing that the words were, in fact, uttered, but they are not received as evidence of their truth."

The judge nodded to Rod Townsend. "All right, the witness may proceed with his answer."

"Well, this man called me and told me that he was a friend of Joe Miletti's. He told me that they had a tip that Consolidated was going to grab the film that day—just physically take it—and that it was in Joe's best interests and the best interests of the film for me to go immediately to the office and take the film and the shot book out to a place in Connecticut that the man described."

"You took the shot book too?"

"Yes."

"Did this man give you his name?"

"No, he did not."

"Did you recognize his voice? I mean was it Mr. Miletti?"

"The answer to both questions is 'no.' The man had a very heavy French accent."

"And you just accepted this Frenchman's word that he was a friend of Miletti?" Disbelief was evident in Wegman's tone. "That his instructions should be followed to the point of taking forty million dollars' worth of film from the film-storage locker and hauling it out to somewhere in Connecticut?"

"Well, it sounded plausible to me, Mr. Wegman. I knew about Joe Miletti's problems with Consolidated. I was very anxious that the studio not recut the film the way they proposed, and I thought that, in light of the circumstances, they might well try to grab the film, just as this man said on the phone. At the time, what he was suggesting seemed like a good idea."

"And you ask the court to believe that you knew nothing of a court order directing that the film be turned over to the studio?"

"I knew nothing of that order. Not at that time. That's correct, sir."

"Did you check with Mr. Miletti before picking up his forty-million-dollar film on the instructions of some unidentified Frenchman?"

"I tried to. I called him twice, first from home and then again when I got to his office, but there was no answer either time, and the Frenchman had said that there was no time to spare, that the studio guys would be there to pick up the film any minute. So when Joe didn't answer I just took the film, loaded it in my car, and left."

"Did you check with Mr. Cain before you did that?"

"I called his office; but he wasn't in either."

"Just where did you take the film, Mr. Townsend?"

"Out to Darien, Connecticut, to the home of Professor Morris. That's where the Frenchman told me to take both the film and the shot book. He said Professor Morris was an old friend of Joe Miletti."

"And when you got there you gave the film and the book to the professor?"

"No, I gave them to the professor's wife. The professor was out of town."

"And where did she put the film?"

"In the garage, Mr. Wegman. I helped her unload it. She had also received a call that morning from the same Frenchman. He told her I would be bringing the film out and that she should store it in the garage and cover it with a tarp so that it would be dry and safe."

Relief showed on Wegman's face. He had finally located the film. Now, with his principal worry behind him, he would still try to nail Harry and Joe Miletti, and perhaps bloody Rod Townsend in the process.

"And so you and this lady put forty million dollars' worth of film out in her garage, is that it?"

"Yes, sir. That's what we did. That's what the Frenchman told us to do."

"And all this time you've left that highly valuable and delicate property just sitting out there in a Connecticut garage. Right?"

"No, sir, that's not right."

"What do you mean?"

"I mean it isn't there anymore."

Wegman looked anxious again. "Well, where is it now?"

"I don't know."

"You don't *know*?" Wegman bellowed, his face reddening.

"That's right, I don't know."

"Will you please explain to the court how you know the film is not in Professor Morris's garage, where you and Mrs. Morris put it?"

"Well, sir, two or three days after I took the film out to Connecticut, the Frenchman called again and told me there was a court order and that I should go out there and get the film and shot book and bring them back to New York. I agreed. After all, as you say, it was a very valuable piece of material, and, since there was now a court order, it seemed the right thing to do. I called Mrs. Morris; but when I told her I wanted to come out to pick up the film, she became extremely upset. She said a driver in a limo had just come to the house and told her I had sent him to get it. She believed him and gave it to him, and the shot book too. He just took them away."

Wegman looked stunned. "He took them away?"

"Yes, sir, that's what she said."

"Are you telling us that you did *not* send this man?"

"That's correct, sir. I did not send him."

"Did she get his name?"

"No, sir."

"Or his license number?"

"No, sir. I asked her that, but she said she hadn't looked. However, she did notice that the limo was black."

"Oh, *thank* you, Mr. Townsend," sneered Wegman, "that's really very helpful."

Harry could see the beads of sweat on Wegman's upper lip. His voice carried a note of desperation. "Do you have any information at all as to the identity of the man who picked up the film, Mr.

Townsend? And, before you answer, I remind you that you are under oath."

"No, sir. I have no such information."

"Do you own a limousine?"

"No, sir."

"Do you know anyone who does?"

"Oh, many people I know hire limos all the time, but the only person I know who actually owns one is Yank Slutsky . . . I suppose it's *possible* that he took his own film, but . . ."

An excited buzz swept the gallery.

"That's ridiculous!" snapped Wegman, fighting to keep his control. "Are you telling us that you have no idea at all where the film is today?"

"None whatsoever, Mr. Wegman. I have no idea who that driver was or who sent him or where he took the film. Maybe the same Frenchman, the one who called me and Mrs. Morris, arranged for the driver, but I don't know why he would. And, even though you say it's 'ridiculous,' it's just possible that Mr. Slutsky may have arranged the whole thing—just to make Joe look bad."

There was another murmur from the gallery and the bailiff stood up, putting his finger to his lips to indicate silence.

Wegman turned to the judge, his tone biting. "I move to strike the witness's personal speculations about what Mr. Slutsky may have done."

"It will be stricken. Anything further, Mr. Wegman?"

Wegman paused, looking at Townsend with disgust and frustration. Then, he turned back to the judge. "No, Your Honor, that's all I have of this witness . . . *for now.*"

"Any cross-examination, Mr. Cain?"

"None, Your Honor."

"Very well then, call your next witness, Mr. Wegman."

Wegman had remained standing. Now he addressed the court. "Your Honor, we'll need a short continuance of these proceedings to bring in Mrs. Morris and to check on her story and that of Mr. Townsend. Ten days should suffice."

Harry began speaking as he rose. "Your Honor, as I have said, these are quasi-criminal proceedings. They should not have been brought in the first place unless Mr. Wegman was prepared to prove them. If he had taken the trouble to prepare his case and ascertain the facts before bringing these charges, he would not be in this position. Nor should we be left with these very serious charges hanging over our heads. As Your Honor may know, I've flown in from California to attend this hearing. I have an active law practice there and a full trial calendar. A delay of ten days and the necessity to return would be not only inconvenient, but unfair and improper. Given the present situation, Your Honor, I move to dismiss these charges against both Mr. Miletti and me."

"Mr. Wegman?" asked the judge.

"Your Honor, first Mr. Cain won't even take the stand to testify under oath, to give the court the facts; and now he wants to argue that we shouldn't even have the opportunity to find out the truth. After all, I'm only asking for ten days, not a long period of delay, and millions of dollars are at stake here . . . as well as the integrity of a court order."

Harry sensed that the judge might be wavering. It was important that Wegman not get more time. He rose again. "Your Honor, I have a suggestion that might solve this problem. Let Mr. Wegman call Mrs. Morris from your chambers. She can be given the oath and testify by phone; and, if Your Honor has a speaker phone, we can all listen and even cross-examine her if necessary. Mr. Miletti and I will waive any objection to proceeding on that basis."

Judge Mancuso nodded thoughtfully, turning to Wegman. "Well, that seems a fair solution to me, Mr. Wegman. Any objection?"

"Yes, Your Honor, I'd like to go out and see this lady, interview her like any other witness before she testifies. Besides, I'll need the time to check out her story and do other investigation."

Harry began to reply, but the judge motioned him to remain silent. He looked over at Wegman once again. "Mr. Wegman, I'm inclined to agree with Mr. Cain here, that you should have investigated and prepared your case before you brought these serious charges, especially against a fellow attorney. I'm going to let you examine Mrs. Morris by telephone; and, if she comes up with some new fact that we haven't heard before, and it requires time to check, I'll reconsider your request for a continuance. But, as of right now, it's denied."

Judge Mancuso announced that additional testimony would be

taken in chambers. The reporters emitted a collective murmur of protest but were silenced by the gavel.

The lawyers filed into the judge's chambers, followed by the clerk and court reporter. A call was placed to Mrs. Morris on the speaker phone. When she came on the line, Judge Mancuso introduced himself and explained the situation. The clerk administered the oath, and Harry could hear the nervousness in the woman's voice even as she replied "I do."

Nervous or not, when Neil Wegman began to question her, pacing back and forth in front of the telephone speaker, she confirmed Rod Townsend's testimony in every respect.

"And so you simply accepted the word of this limousine driver you had never met before, and you gave him millions of dollars' worth of film, is that what you did?"

"Yes, that's what I did. I figured that if the driver knew the film was stored at our house, then he had to have spoken with Mr. Townsend and had to be telling the truth, that Mr. Townsend sent him to pick up the film and take it to some other safe place. It never occurred to me that he was simply making up a story and that he hadn't really come from Mr. Townsend at all. I *still* don't see how that was possible."

"The driver didn't indicate where he was taking the film?"

"Well, I *thought* he was taking it back to Mr. Townsend; but he didn't really say so."

"You didn't get his name or even his license number?"

"No, I didn't. But I do remember one thing: The limo was black."

"Yes, ma'am, we've already heard," said Wegman disgustedly. Then he shrugged. It was a dead end now, and he knew it. The film was gone. "No further questions," he muttered, slumping into a chair.

"Mr. Cain?"

"No questions, Your Honor."

"Very well then; thank you, Mrs. Morris. We appreciate your cooperation. Good day."

"Good-bye, judge." The amplified buzz of the dial tone filled the room until Judge Mancuso pushed the button, ending the connection.

"Your Honor," intoned Wegman, his tone almost pleading now,

"I must renew my motion for a continuance. It's obvious that we need more time here and no one can really be hurt by ten more days."

The judge rose and stood by his chair. "Denied. Has either side anything further to offer?"

"Nothing further, Your Honor," Harry replied, the crispness in his tone hinting at his determination to see this hearing end as quickly as possible.

Neil Wegman was less crisp. "Well, Your Honor, in light of the court's ruling on my request for a brief continuance, I have nothing further. But I certainly would have something further if given the time to check the facts."

Judge Mancuso glared for a moment at Wegman, then started for the door. "Very well, gentlemen, let's return to the courtroom for argument."

Neil Wegman wasn't giving up. Somehow, between leaving the judge's chambers and starting his argument, he'd found his natural combativeness again. His strident tone reflecting his anger and frustration, he listed the evidence that he insisted proved both defendants guilty of contempt. It was conceded, he said, that Harry Cain knew of the court's order. It was conceded that, shortly after the order, Cain called Joe Miletti, who had been in the cutting room working on the film. Obviously, Cain had something important to tell Miletti. It was also clear that, shortly after that telephone call from Harry Cain, the film was taken in violation of the court's order.

It was taken by Rod Townsend, an admitted friend of both Miletti and Cain; and it was hidden at the home of Professor Morris, another long-time friend of Miletti. And when Townsend was asked to relate what he knew, he said he didn't want to hurt Miletti or Cain. He didn't want to hurt those two by telling what happened.

Now Wegman spread his hands out in a gesture of appeal. "Your Honor, we don't just look at each separate fact. We put them together and draw inferences from them as to what *really* happened. The *only* rational inference from these facts is that Harry Cain called on the third to advise Joe Miletti of the court's order and to plan, with Miletti, how the film would be taken and hidden by Rod Townsend and how this court would be fooled and its order flouted." Wegman pounded the table, his booming voice filling the courtroom.

After a pause he proceeded in a quieter tone. "That, Your Honor, is contempt. That, Your Honor, is something this court—no court—should ever condone. I ask you not to allow it, Your Honor. I ask you to find these men guilty of contempt."

Wegman returned to his seat. Despite the quiet tone with which he had concluded his argument, Harry could see that he was still seething.

Harry rose slowly, and in a firm but polite voice began to address the court. "This is not a jury case, Your Honor, and I will not appeal to the court's emotions, but to its logic and to its knowledge of the law. This is a quasi-criminal proceeding, as I have already said. There must be clear and convincing evidence of guilt. *Evidence*, Your Honor, not theories, not speculation as to what might have happened.

"A finding of contempt requires evidence of two basic elements: number one, knowledge of the order, and number two, a deliberate, willful violation of that order.

"There is no such evidence here. Not as to *either* element so far as Joe Miletti is concerned; and not as to the second required element so far as my own guilt is concerned.

"What do we have in this record? We have the fact that I was present in court when the order was made and that I called Joe Miletti. These are facts we never denied, but they prove nothing. There is no evidence I told Mr. Miletti of the court's order. None. Common sense tells us it's not even *likely* that I did. I'm a lawyer. The court can infer my awareness of the widely known rule of law that Joe Miletti could not be found guilty of contempt unless he *knew* of the court order when the film was taken. If, as Mr. Wegman hypothesizes, I was planning the removal of the film, the last thing—the very *last* thing—I would do would be to put my client on notice of the court order about to be violated. On the contrary, I would try to *keep* him from knowing of that order, so that he would be in a better position to defend himself against just this kind of charge.

"And, Your Honor, we have the testimony of Deputy Markowitz that Mr. Miletti still appeared *not* to know of the court's order the following day, February fourth . . . the day *after* the film had already been taken. That was evident from Mr. Miletti's very open, although perhaps intemperate statement on the fourth, when he was told of the order—a statement completely inconsistent with the reaction of a man who had known about the order beforehand.

"So right there, Your Honor, without any further question, without even considering the fact that there isn't a hint, a scintilla of evidence that Mr. Miletti ever did anything to *violate* the court's order, his lack of knowledge of that order, in itself, demands a finding that *he* was not in contempt.

"Now let's turn to my own guilt. Unlike the case against Mr. Miletti, we have evidence that I *did* know of the court's order. It's never been denied. But there is no evidence—none—that I did any act or induced any other person to do any act that violated that order. Again, we have the fact that I called Joe Miletti the morning the order was issued. But there is no evidence in the record of what I said or that Mr. Miletti did anything to violate the court order, either as a result of what I said or otherwise. How can I be found guilty of inducing Mr. Miletti to violate the court's order, when there is no evidence whatsoever that he ever committed such a violation, when the only evidence indicates that, the day *after* I spoke to him, and the day *after* the film was taken, he still did not know of the court's order? And is there any evidence that I induced some *other* person to violate the order or that I directly violated it myself? Absolutely not. Not a shred. Surely Rod Townsend's statement that he didn't want to hurt my interests is not such evidence. There isn't any evidence in the record that I even spoke to Mr. Townsend during the period in question or, for that matter, at any other time. At the *most* Mr. Townsend's statement would be speculation on his part that I was somehow involved, and that would hardly be the kind of 'clear and convincing evidence' essential for a finding of contempt.

"So, if we consider the *evidence*, rather than Mr. Wegman's suspicions, the result is clear. Both of us are innocent of the charge. Thank you."

The judge nodded to Wegman. "Any reply?"

Wegman stood again. Harry could see a trickle of sweat being to run down the side of his face. It was getting away from him. He'd lost the film and now he could be losing the case. "Your Honor, we've just seen exactly what I predicted would happen in this case. Mr. Cain refuses to testify under oath and then he gets up and tries to tell us what happened here. It's simply . . ."

Judge Mancuso interrupted. "Mr. Wegman, I've already ruled that you are not to comment on the defendant's decision not to testify. Moreover, Mr. Cain has not attempted to tell us what he actually did or said, but simply to summarize the evidence in the record. Now, do you have anything further or shall I make my ruling?"

"I do have something more, Your Honor." He paused, his hands clasped tightly behind his back. "Your Honor, our courts cannot function if their orders are flouted. It is not only the right, but also the duty of every judge sitting on this court to see that such orders are obeyed, by enforcing them through the remedy of contempt. Especially, Your Honor, the orders of a brother judge. These men violated a court order here, the order of Judge Berman, entered after careful consideration of the evidence. I know they violated Judge Berman's order. They know it. Everyone in this room knows it. And this was no mere *technical* violation. It completely frustrated what Judge Berman intended the order to accomplish. If that can be done with impunity, no court order means a thing. Not the orders of this court or of Judge Berman or of any other court. Any court's order becomes a hollow mockery, if these two men are allowed to go free. I ask the court not to let that happen. Thank you."

Wegman resumed his seat, and both lawyers looked up at Judge Mancuso. The judge closed his notebook and glanced over to see if the court reporter was ready to take his ruling. She was, her fingers poised on the keys of the stenotype machine.

"Gentlemen, I agree with Mr. Wegman that court orders must be obeyed and must be rigorously enforced." Harry saw a look of worry cross Joe Miletti's face. He felt some concern himself at the judge's opening words.

"But," Judge Mancuso continued . . . and Harry, hearing that wonderful word, breathed more easily . . . "we live in a society that demands *proof* of guilt, not mere suspicion, no matter how profoundly believed and how widely held. That's essential to a free society. And it is that on which we must focus our analysis.

"On this record, gentlemen, the conclusion is inescapable that there is insufficient evidence of guilt. There is no real evidence at all from which a supportable inference of guilt on the part of either defendant could be drawn, much less the clear and convincing proof that the authorities tell us is required.

"Accordingly, the application to hold Joseph Miletti in contempt is denied. The application to hold Harry Cain in contempt is also denied. Thank you, gentlemen." The judge rose to leave the bench as the reporters scrambled for the hallway phones.

Neil Wegman slammed his briefcase shut and turned to Harry with a snarl. "You may think you've beaten this, Cain, but you'll still face a civil action for damages . . . more damages than even *you* can afford, hotshot."

"Oh, I don't think so," said Harry politely. "I'm more inclined to think Consolidated will sue you and your law firm for negligence in failing to collect the film before it disappeared. Fact is, I'm going to suggest it to their general counsel as soon as I get back home. And say, whenever you're out on the coast, let's do have that lunch."

Harry settled back into the plush upholstery of the limousine as it made its way slowly up Madison Avenue through a driving snowstorm. He felt fine. It was warm and comfortable inside the car and there was, as always, the incomparable high of winning.

Joe Miletti loosened his black knit tie and opened the collar of his blue chambray workshirt. He looked over at Harry and grinned. "Okay, counselor, you did it again. But how? And who the fuck's the Frenchman who made all those calls? And, by the way, where's the film?"

"Ah, monsieur, so you wondair who is zee, how you say, meesteerious Franshmaan, n'est-ce pas?"

"It was you?"

"Mais oui, mon ami . . . who else?"

"But shit, Harry, what if he'd made you testify? You said you wouldn't lie under oath."

"And I wouldn't have. But the strategy was to get Wegman to

name me as a defendant, so I wouldn't have to testify. That's why I told your secretary I was calling right after the hearing, so she'd tell the sheriff, and the sheriff would tell Wegman. That's why I told Townsend to say he wouldn't cooperate because he was *my* friend and didn't want to hurt me. I figured Wegman would be sure by then that I was involved and, being the vindictive, arrogant little prick he is, he'd name me personally as a co-defendant."

"But you told the judge you had nothing to do with taking the film."

"The hell I did! I'd never lie to a judge. I said there was no *evidence in the record* that I was involved. I never commented on what I actually did or didn't do. Even the judge pointed that out."

"Did Rod know you were the Frenchman?"

"Hell, no. Never for a minute. I wanted him to be able to testify truthfully. Mary Morris too. I told you, I don't put witnesses on the stand to lie . . . at least not when I *know* they're lying."

"Who was the driver that got the film? Did Rod arrange that?"

"No, damn it. I told you, Rod's testimony was the truth. The mysterious Frenchman secretly arranged for a driver to go out there and tell that story and get the film. Then it was stored in a safe place, where it still is."

"Where is that?"

"It's better you don't know."

"Christ, you're a smart fucker. But smart as you are, pal, you really took one helluva risk. I see how your plan protected me and Townsend. They couldn't really touch us. But nobody protected *you*, for Christ's sake. If Murphy hadn't named you as a defendant, you'd of had to testify. You could've lost your license to practice, maybe even done time. Why would you do that for me?"

"It wasn't just for you, Joe. I was pissed off at what Consolidated did. I wanted to get back at them. Beat 'em at their own game. I've always been able to use the law to deal with guys like that. This time, they went outside the law—with their phony, lying affidavit and captive judge—and the only way to be effective was to use what we call 'self-help.' I'm not proud of it, but it's worked this far, so let's play out the hand."

"Okay. What happens now?"

"Well, I called Aaron Fernbach from the courthouse. We're meeting at Consolidated in about twenty minutes. We'll talk some turkey to Fernbach and Slutsky, and then settle this thing once and for all. You do want the picture released, don't you?"

Aaron Charles Fernbach was the son of a wealthy New York investment banker. His grandfather had founded the firm, and he was the first Fernbach since that time not to go into the family business. Always fascinated by motion pictures, he had obtained a job as a junior executive at Paramount shortly after his graduation from Princeton. Over the next five years, he'd moved steadily up the corporate ladder. Quickly, he was perceived to be a real "comer," until, eventually, rumors began to circulate that he was a potential head of the company.

At that point, in a surprise move, Yank Slutsky had offered Fernbach an unprecedented contract to come over to Consolidated as the youngest president in its history. Fernbach had accepted with some misgivings, and those misgivings were shared by the entire motion picture community. Would the young Princetonian, with his courtly manners and elegant tastes, be able to coexist with a rough, crude bastard like Yank Slutsky?

Surprisingly, the combination had succeeded. With Slutsky's support, Fernbach had generated a string of Consolidated features that were both critical and financial hits. The studio flourished and the Fernbach-Slutsky partnership was likened to that of Irving Thalberg and L. B. Mayer.

In the process, the urbane and affable Fernbach had become the social darling of the film community. He'd married Dorothy Manning, a charming actress of modest abilities, who, when cast at all, played tall patrician blondes. She had immediately given up her never burgeoning career to concentrate on being Mrs. Aaron Fernbach and serving as the titular head of numerous charitable functions. There was no need for her to continue playing cool blond socialites. Now she was one. Before setting the date for an "A-list" party, any knowledgeable Beverly Hills hostess checked to see if "Aaron and Dot" were available. If they were—and if they'd come—the party was made.

Lately, Fernbach's films had run into a streak of bad luck. But there were ups and downs for everyone in that mercurial business. The popular Fernbach was still considered the best production chief in town, although there were rumors that his relationship with Yank Slutsky was not quite so harmonious as in the past.

The missing film and Harry's win in court had created a special problem—one that could be serious for the company as well as its management. As Harry and Joe Miletti were ushered into his pine-paneled office, Fernbach set about handling the problem with characteristic grace. He stepped from behind an antique pine desk, his right hand extended to greet his "guests." His thinning brown hair was carefully groomed, his left hand stuck casually in the pocket of his brown herringbone-tweed suit. He motioned Harry and Joe to sit on a chintz sofa, then pulled up a Windsor chair and sat beside them, smiling as he looked from one to the other.

"So, it's Robin Hood and Friar Tuck. Where's my forty-million-dollar film, guys? Hidden somewhere in Sherwood Forest?"

Harry smiled too. "Well at least you're taking it in good grace, Aaron. But where's Yank?"

"I recommended that Yank not attend this meeting, Harry. He's so steamed, he would've threatened you, and I wouldn't have wanted that."

"And I suppose your telling me what Yank would do if he were here doesn't constitute a threat in itself? Gracefully put, Aaron, but still a threat."

Fernbach smiled again, polishing his rimless glasses on his white silk handkerchief. "Well, if the law doesn't work for you, I suppose you have to find other ways. Isn't that what you did, Harry?"

"Hey, pal," Miletti boomed, standing up. "Just forget that shit or we've got nothing to talk about."

Harry put a hand on Miletti's arm to calm him. "It's okay, Joe. Let him think what he wants." He turned to Fernbach. "Look, Aaron, I think we can help each other. I think some vigilante who likes Joe or admires his work has that film, and I think he's going to hold it and never give it back until he's absolutely convinced the picture's going to be cut Joe's way."

"Oh, come on, Harry. This is me you're talking to, not a jury. A 'vigilante,' for Christ's sake."

"Look, Aaron, whether you believe me or not makes no difference. Either way, two things should happen. You should get your film back and Joe should have final cut. Am I right?"

"As far as I'm concerned, Harry, Joe should have had final cut all along. I never wanted to take it away, but Yank . . ."

"Oh, fuck Yank!" Miletti interrupted. "Are you running the goddamn studio or is he? I made the deal with you, not him. Where the fuck are your balls?"

Again Harry put out his hand to restrain Miletti. He turned to Fernbach. "Aaron, this is a situation Yank will understand. I'm suggesting an old-fashioned swap . . . good for both sides. Whoever the vigilante is, he'll want Yank's word and yours about the cut of the picture. If that's given, I'd be willing to bet the film turns up the next day. Of course, the guy will want to know there'll be no more claims or lawsuits or anything like that. My guess is he'll feel more secure if there's an announcement in the trade papers. You know, 'Consolidated has reviewed the situation and decided that Joe Miletti's approach to the film is the right one after all,' something like that. Once that kind of story is published, the vigilante, whoever he is, will know that you're not going to go back on your word. It would be too embarrassing."

Fernbach rose and began to pace. Then he stopped and looked at Harry again. "I understand what you're saying; and if you told us you had the film yourself, we could talk. But since you claim you don't have it, how do we know the film will come back, even if we do what you suggest?"

"You don't," Harry replied, "but I'd bet on it once that report appears in the trades. And look at it this way—if the film doesn't come back, Joe doesn't get his final cut anyway. There's no film to cut. That certainly won't make this vigilante guy happy. Whoever he is, it's virtually certain he wants what he thinks is best for Joe. Besides, you haven't got the film now, and you haven't a clue as to where it is; so what have you got to lose?"

Fernbach nodded thoughtfully and resumed his pacing, his hands clasped behind his back. Maintaining his silence, he circled the big antique desk, stopping, staring, deep in thought. Then he came back to stand beside Harry and Miletti. "You know what, counselor? You're right."

"Deal?" Harry said, standing up and extending his hand.

"Deal," said Fernbach, shaking it.

Miletti looked from one to the other, a puzzled expression on his face. "Hey, guys, aren't we forgetting something here? What about Yank Slutsky?"

Harry gave Miletti a tolerant smile and looked directly at Fernbach. "Oh, I think we can assume that Aaron has already cleared the matter with Yank."

Fernbach just stood there smiling. "Gentlemen, I meant what I said. We have a deal. You can count on it. And, Harry, when do you think the 'vigilante' will bring back the film?"

"Well," Harry said, "when will the press release appear?"

"Tomorrow morning."

"Well then I guess, whoever this guy is, he'll bring it back by tomorrow night. . . ."

Riding down in the elevator, Miletti began to speak, but Harry put his finger to his lips, indicating silence. It was not unlikely the elevators in the Consolidated Studios Building would be bugged, if only to hear the thoughts and plans of agents and lawyers as they left their meetings with studio negotiators.

It was still snowing when they reached the ground floor. As they stood in the sheltered doorway of the building awaiting their car, Harry took Miletti by the shoulders. "Well, Joe, it worked. You're going to have your film back and it'll be released your way."

"I don't understand, Harry. Where does Slutsky figure in this?"

"Slutsky calls the shots, Joe, no question about it. But neither he nor Fernbach want it to *look* like he calls the shots, especially not this decision, where they look like they're caving in to blackmail . . . which they are. No, Yank will say this was entirely Fernbach's decision, that he would have fought to the death, if he had his way."

"But how could Fernbach know Slutsky would agree to putting the story in the trade papers like you asked?"

"Because, my naïve friend, Slutsky *did* agree. The room was obviously wired, not just so Yank could hear our discussion, but also because they hoped we'd make a mistake, and they'd catch us admitting we had the film. If that had happened, the leverage would have shifted. We would have had to give it back without any deal at all."

"But why? You'd already been cleared of the contempt charge."

"Yeah, but the civil liability for damages for holding forty million dollars' worth of film would have been huge. Even the lost interest on it would have been a few hundred thousand dollars a month."

"So that's why you used that 'vigilante' bullshit?"

"That's why."

Their limo pulled up to the curb, and the driver came around to open the door for them.

"Okay," said Joe, reaching for a can of cold beer from the tiny refrigerator. "I'm with you so far. But I still don't see how Fernbach could close the deal with us without going out to talk with Slutsky, even if Yank could hear what was going on in the room."

"Easy. You remember when Fernbach put his hands behind his back and walked around the desk like he was pacing and thinking over what I proposed?"

"Sure I do."

"Well," Harry continued, "Aaron's got one of those little digital screens on his desk that his secretaries use to flash short private messages to him without any noise or anyone ever knowing. You know the kind of thing—'Warren Beatty calling from France' or 'your ten-o'clock appointment is here.' Well, they just arranged to flash Yank's instructions to Aaron on that little screen. That's why he circled the desk before he gave us his answer."

"Jesus, you're one smart Jewboy. Well, as they say, 'Set a thief to catch a thief.' "

"Thanks, pal, thanks a lot," said Harry with a wry grin, as the big car moved through the New York traffic.

"No, Harry, I mean it as a compliment. You outsmarted those bastards—beat 'em at their own game. You oughta be very proud."

"Proud? Not really. I did something that's contrary to everything I believe in. I went outside the law because that's what *they* did. But I'm not proud of it."

Harry paused, then went on.

"I've always liked Thomas More's speech in *A Man for All Seasons*. The king wants him to ignore the law, but he won't do it. Someone asks, wouldn't he even cut down the law to get at the devil, and More says something like, 'If I do that, what will I hide behind when the last law is overturned and the devil comes back to get me?' He's right. The law's all that keeps us from living a savage, perilous existence. It was wrong for me to cut it down . . . even to get at the devil."

"Frankly, counselor, that's whakko. After what they did, you did the right thing—the *only* thing. But listen, if you felt the way you do now, why didn't you just give the film back, instead of squeezing the studio into making a deal?"

"Hey, I said I wasn't proud of what I'd done. I never said that, after doing it, I'd throw away the advantage. That *would* be whakko."

Miletti smiled and shook his head. "You're too complicated for me, babe. But you saved my film and my ass, and I'll never forget it."

Harry watched the snow swirling and dancing outside the car window. He wasn't sure how he felt. To do a right, he'd done a wrong. To get justice he'd defied the law, and the law was his religion. Oh well, he thought, leaning back into the plush upholstery, no one said life was simple.

The next morning, Consolidated's press release appeared in both *The Hollywood Reporter* and *Daily Variety*. Harry read them, sipping coffee at La Guardia airport, looking out at the flurries of snow falling on the runways. Both trade papers reported that Consolidated Studio Chief Aaron Fernbach had personally reconsidered the two alternative ways of presenting *The Last Battle* and had decided that, while both were creatively sound, the approach suggested by Academy Award–winning director Joe Miletti was preferable, and that Miletti's cut would be the one the studio would use when work on the film resumed. The rest of the article was devoted to explaining that the $40 million motion picture was temporarily "missing" and how, the preceding day in a New York court, Joe Miletti and his attorney Harry Cain, the legendary "Sunset Bomber," had been cleared of any involvement. It added that all the studio's claims against Miletti and Cain had been dropped.

Later that day, Aaron Fernbach received a call from a man who spoke with a thick French accent. The man told Fernbach the missing film was in a public storage locker near La Cienega and Venice boulevards in Los Angeles, and that the key to the locker could be found at the base of a palm tree outside the entrance to Morton's Restaurant. Fernbach made careful notes and thanked the caller. Just before hanging up, he added "And good night, Harry." His only response was a dial tone.

The Dana-Farber Cancer Clinic is a part of Harvard Medical School. Like the school, it's located in Boston rather than in Cambridge, the university's home. With Harry by her side, Nancy was shown to a room overlooking the low suburban hills of Newton and Brookline, with the Charles River and Cambridge far in the distance. A team of doctors and nurses explained the TNF program and how, each month, Nancy would check into the "Farber" for two days to be given a dose of the new, experimental drug and to be tested for its effect on her tumors and on her general condition.

Harry stayed with Nancy through the day and evening, talking, laughing, encouraging her, telling her that Karen Lloyd and others thought TNF was probably the most likely cure of all, a totally different approach to cancer and one he'd read about for some time. Finally, at nine o'clock, the drug seemed to take effect and Nancy fell into a deep sleep. Harry borrowed a pen from the nurse and left a note on Nancy's pillow saying he loved her. Then he took a cab across town to the Ritz-Carlton.

He sat in a booth in the small bar restaurant, relaxing over a double vodka martini and listening to the romantic piped-in music. The only other customer was a tall, striking-looking woman in a tailored business suit. She seemed in her early forties, but her tanned, intelligent face was surrounded by a dramatic mane of whitish-gray hair. Although she was in the next booth, Harry paid no attention. His mind was on other things. Now he could let down, stop the cheerleading, admit to himself at last that Nancy's chances were not that good, that even Harvard's TNF was a long shot at best and that most likely he was going to lose her. Slowly, he felt the tears begin to flow. He put his head in his arms and began to sob. After a moment, he felt someone slide into the booth beside him and put an arm around his shoulders.

"Hey, are you okay? Can I help?"

It was the attractive gray-haired lady from the next booth.

"Yeah," he said. "I'm okay."

"You're concealing it very well," she said, smiling ruefully.

She began to massage his neck with strong fingers. His pain started to ease. He wiped his face with his napkin and looked at his bene-factor. She was really quite lovely. The whitish-gray hair was obvi-ously premature and an extraordinary intelligence shone from her warm brown eyes. He beckoned the waiter and ordered another round for each of them, a double vodka martini for him, another Rob Roy for her.

She asked his trouble, and he explained about Nancy, feeling odd at telling this stranger about his problems, his fears, and his despair. She told him about herself. She was an advertising executive up from New York to work on a Boston account. She had never married, choosing her career instead. When the drinks came she suggested they have them in her rooms where they could be comfortable. Besides, the bar was closing.

Harry followed her to the elevator, down the hall, and into her suite. The doors closed, she took a long sip of her drink. Harry did the same. He could feel the alcohol hitting him hard, harder than usual. It must be the stress, he thought. His companion removed her suit jacket and shoes. She padded over to Harry and gently, very gently, took him in her arms. He felt her soft body sway against him. It was warm and comforting. She removed his coat and then his tie, opened his shirt and then, suddenly kneeling before him, began unlacing his shoes. Harry stood as if in a trance.

She put his shoes aside and, without hesitation, unzipped his fly and slid her hand in the opening. He was surprised that he was hard. He'd not even thought about sex . . . until then. Slowly, gently she took him in her mouth, tickling and stroking him at the same time. Slowly he began to respond, feeling the waves of erotic sensation take over his body. He pulled away and grasped her by the shoulders, lifted her to her feet. She licked her lips and looked at him questioningly. He quickly unfastened her blouse, removed her bra, her panties. Then sliding out of his own trousers and shorts, he took her hand and led her to the bed, where, swiftly, he moved on her, in her, feeling her surround him, pull on him, holding him, moving, crying, clutching at him as he moved ever slowly and then wildly, crazily, thrusting away at his pain, his fear, making it disappear, swallowed up in this marvelous, comforting woman. Soon he felt the onset of his orgasm and, feeling it, she reached her own climax with a long, low moan.

She held him, comforting him, consoling him. They fell asleep holding each other. Sometime before morning they woke and made love again, this time more quietly and slowly, feeling affection and comfort along with the intensity of the erotic experience. Again they slept, and she was still sleeping at six o'clock, when the gray dawn awakened Harry.

He dressed silently and made his way to his own room. As he showered and prepared to dress for his early trip to the clinic, he thought about this strange and lovely lady. Oddly, he felt no guilt. It was as if this was a cure he had needed . . . needed to give him the strength to deal with Nancy's illness and with the sadness that seemed to be taking over his life. He thought about how this stranger had helped him and comforted him, giving him tenderness he'd badly needed, restoring his spirit and sanity. He hoped he'd given her comfort as well. He doubted that he had, and felt a twinge of guilt that he hadn't shared her troubles as she'd shared his. She must have had pain and sorrow of her own, but he hadn't even asked— hadn't even thought about it. Then it occurred to him that they didn't even know each other's names and probably never would.

Back in California after that first Boston weekend, Nancy tried to seem lighthearted, even joyful. But Harry could see that the laughter came too quickly, was just a bit too loud to be real. He knew the anxiety that lay beneath the smiling façade.

Once again, he asked Nancy if she wanted him to take a leave of absence, to be with her full time. He could carry out his plan for the *Campbell* case, turn over Fumiko Masami's defense to someone else, and spend his time at home. He knew as he spoke that he wanted Nancy to refuse his offer, but he was prepared to go through with it if she didn't. Once again, Nancy rejected the idea.

"Your work is your life, my darling. If I took it away from you, I'd never forgive myself."

He pulled her close and whispered. "It's not my life. You're my life." She was. But he knew he needed the work too, needed it more than ever, and was relieved by her decision. His law practice was the only thing he could cling to, the only thing that would keep him sane and functioning, that would help him avoid the paralyzing effect of the constant pain and fear. He loved her, wanted to help her all he could—to make this horror as easy for her as possible. But he didn't want to give up his work. Of that he was sure.

Harry's idea to save Pat Campbell required a superior court hearing, one unlike any he'd ever heard of. The day of that hearing, Harry awoke refreshed, really excited for the first time in weeks. He'd had enough dark, negative days of late. That morning was different. He even felt positive about Nancy. Somehow, he felt she'd make it. In a few more days they'd be back at the Farber for more TNF, and he knew the stuff would work . . . *knew* it.

He showered and toweled himself dry, singing "Ten Thousand Men of Harvard," starting the process of psyching himself up for the challenge that lay ahead of him in court. The *Campbell* case was more than a challenge. If he could pull it off—save Pat Campbell from Tommy Bowers's extortion, then . . . But could he make the strategy work? Could he sell it to the judge? So far as he knew, no one had ever tried it before. But—he smiled, looking in the mirror—that's what they were paying him for.

He pulled open his dresser drawer, reaching automatically for a pair of green Calvin Klein briefs. He grinned, remembering the cult of the green underwear and how it began.

Francesca Dowling was an Italian actress, a statuesque, six-foot blonde with long legs and warm brown eyes. She was in her early fifties at the time Harry was remembering. She'd grown a little heavy by then, but was aging well. She'd been married for about fifteen years to Iron Mike Dowling, the sole owner of National Cargo, the largest American ship owning company, and the most profitable. Mike had been in his eighties then, five feet two with a full head of slicked-back white hair and a dapper white mustache. He was an orphan who had literally fought his way through life, first as a stevedore, then a professional boxer, then a bootlegger and night-club owner, and finally a shipping magnate, at a time when the term meant just that.

In his day, Iron Mike Dowling was far and away the toughest man in the shipping business, maybe in any business. He had met Francesca in Rome and married her after a two-week courtship. They'd been together ever since. Contrary to what the cynics believed, she'd really grown to love Mike; but his quick temper and baseless jealousy led to childish fights and ultimately to a separation and a highly publicized divorce case. Harry represented Francesca, who was desolate at the situation and, more than anything, wanted to walk out of her bungalow at the Beverly Hills Hotel and go back home to her "Michelangelo." Mike on the other hand, tough, angry, and always a fighter, was unyielding and completely unwilling to talk settlement. Harry had the unhappy job of telling Francesca that there was nothing to do but go to court.

More than $500 million in community property turned on the outcome of the case.

Nancy had become fond of Francesca, and the night before the trial made a last attempt to raise her friend's spirits. Since Francesca was extremely superstitious, Nancy told her that wearing green underwear was absolutely sure to bring good luck. Nancy had made this up on the spur of the moment, but Francesca, clutching at any straw, bought it completely. Nancy insisted that they all dye their underwear green that very night, and they had, using a large box of green Rit. The next day, Harry and Francesca left for court wearing their green underwear. Even Nancy wore green underwear to stay home and await the result.

Two minutes after Harry and Francesca had taken their seats at the counsel table, Mike Dowling entered the courtroom flanked by three determined-looking lawyers, carrying briefcases and blown-up evidentiary exhibits, wrapped in brown paper to conceal them from Harry. They looked as ready for trial as any group Harry had ever seen. But Harry was ready too. He was well prepared, and, even aside from his green underwear, he thought he'd win.

Suddenly, without warning, Iron Mike stepped out from the phalanx of lawyers. He looked in his wife's direction and bellowed "Francesca," in his gravelly stevedore's voice. Francesca turned at the sound. Seeing Mike, she rose, took a hesitant step in his direction, cried out "Michelangelo." They stood for a moment, just staring at each other. Then both rushed across the courtroom to embrace. The tiny old man grasped his amazonian wife and bent her backward in a mid-thirties screen kiss that defied the laws of physics. He looked down at her and grunted "I can't live wit'out cha, Francesca, I surely can't." Looking into his steel gray eyes, now filled with tears, she replied, "I can't live without you either, cara mia, not now, not ever."

Harry notified the judge, and they all went into his chambers. Francesca sat on Iron Mike's lap, her arms affectionately wrapped around the old tyrant, while he patted her bottom and told the delighted judge that they would leave that very day on a second honeymoon. Iron Mike's waggish lawyer whispered to Harry, "Where to, Lourdes?"

Since then, any time they flew or Harry tried a case, any time they faced any challenge or risk, Harry and Nancy wore green underwear. Gradually, their friends had laughingly adopted the practice, and Nancy would prepare a set of green underwear as a gift whenever one was starting a new picture, having a baby, or beginning an election campaign.

Now, of course, he and Nancy were both wearing green underwear every day.

Harry pulled on his jacket, grabbed his briefcase, and started down the stairs. Maybe the luck would work once more. Given the novelty of his idea for the *Campbell* case, he'd need it.

"**Y**our Honor," Leo Hartstein cried, "this is completely without precedent. It's upside down. Mr. Bowers hasn't even filed a lawsuit. Maybe he won't *ever* file a lawsuit. And yet Mr. Cain is in here seeking an order that, if Mr. Bowers ever *does* bring a lawsuit, the file must be sealed, all proceedings must be in a closed courtroom and, in the meantime, he can't even speak to the media. In the history of Anglo-American jurisprudence, nobody has ever obtained an order like that. Aside from all else, it violates Mr. Bowers's right of free speech under the First Amendment. It's a prior restraint of the worst kind. Let Mr. Cain wait until Mr. Bowers sues—if he ever does. *Then* Mr. Cain can start applying for orders like this. And, even then, he can't prevent Mr. Bowers from exercising his right of free speech. Certainly, Mr. Cain can't get orders like this now, *before* Mr. Bowers sues. That's never been done and could never be justified."

Judge Charles Amory's courtroom in the Santa Monica branch of the superior court was empty except for the judge, the two lawyers, Tommy Bowers, and Pat Campbell. Since this was a civil, not a criminal case, the argument was in a closed courtroom. Having given Hartstein notice by telephone, Harry had appeared in Judge Amory's chambers at the small courthouse near the beach. He'd handed the judge a three-inch stack of papers, including his own declaration

spelling out his conversation with Bowers and Hartstein, a civil complaint seeking an injunction against their plan of extortion, and a
proposed order to seal the file in Harry's case and any case Bowers
might file against Pat Campbell and to conduct all proceedings in
either case in a closed courtroom. There was also an application for
a temporary restraining order and preliminary injunction against Bowers and Hartstein filing unsealed papers, releasing the diary, or even
speaking to the press, plus a lengthy brief Harry had prepared in
support of that unusual relief.

Harry had gone on the offensive, had attacked them before they
could attack Pat Campbell. Now he had to make the attack work.

Judge Amory turned to Harry, his long patrician face registering
interest and curiosity as he followed the unique proceedings.

"Any reply, Mr. Cain?"

Harry rose and looked directly at the judge.

"Yes, Your Honor. This may be unusual, but that doesn't make it
wrong. This court is sitting as a court of equity, and it certainly has
sufficient control over any case pending before it to issue the kind of
restraining order we seek. We're not talking about sealing the file in
an ordinary case. This is *not* an 'ordinary case.' This is extortion, Your
Honor, plain and simple. If the file is not sealed and all documents,
including the complaint the defendants threaten to file, are not put
under seal at the moment of filing, and if Mr. Bowers is not enjoined
from holding the press conference he has threatened to call, then the
world will hear these humiliating disclosures, and all the harm will be
done. And it will be irreparable. Mrs. Campbell's marriage will be
destroyed, and this man"—he gestured toward Bowers—"will have
carried out the threat that is at the heart of his plan of extortion. They
do not, they *cannot* deny the element of extortion. My own declaration describing my meeting with Mr. Bowers sets it out clearly. And
look at the exhibit attached to the complaint they threaten to file, the
one made a part of my declaration."

Harry lifted the papers high in the air. "If this isn't extortion, I
don't know what is. Explicit sexual parts of Mrs. Campbell's diary
are attached to their threatened complaint. Those diary entries are
obviously not a necessary part of their pleading. They're completely
irrelevant. This court is sophisticated, experienced, and aware of
what goes on in the world. Surely Your Honor sees why those lurid

diary excerpts are appended to the complaint they threaten to file. There is one reason only . . . to coerce Mrs. Campbell into paying five million dollars, a sum which, in itself, is so out of proportion to any damages they could possibly prove that it is, in itself, further evidence of extortion.

"They assert Mr. Bowers's First Amendment rights. Nonsense! People like Bowers are always wrapping themselves in the Constitution and the flag as a justification for violating someone else's rights. Well, it just won't wash. It's poppycock! We've cited cases in our brief holding that the right of free speech does not protect utterances that are part of a scheme of extortion, any more than it protects against speech that involves the disclosure of a protected trade secret or speech that involves libel or slander. There simply is no constitutional protection here, and every equitable consideration calls for issuance of the orders we seek. In fact, such protection from the court is the only way Mr. Bowers can be stopped from carrying out his vicious scheme and destroying this lady's marriage and her life." He gestured to Pat, who sat pale and sedate beside him at the counsel table.

All the lawyers and parties waited. Judge Amory leafed through parts of the documents Harry had filed. He seemed to be rereading Harry's declaration describing Bowers's threats and the attached draft complaint with its excerpts from Pat Campbell's diary. Pat looked tense and frightened. Tommy Bowers looked angry. He didn't like being caught off balance. He expected to be on the offense, punching, not defending against this sudden crazy attack. Finally the judge looked up.

"Gentlemen, this *is* an unusual case, and Mr. Cain's application for equitable relief before Mr. Bowers's case is even filed is certainly unique, to say the least." Bowers broke into a confident grin and winked at Hartstein. The judge went on.

"But that doesn't make it invalid. Over the centuries, courts of equity have considered new and unique solutions to unusual problems that would remain unsolved if we were to have a rigid, inflexible system of jurisprudence. The problem here is a threat of the disclosure of obviously damaging personal facts, a threat to be carried out by the filing of the lawsuit disclosing those facts and talking about that lawsuit to the press. Mr. Bowers's conduct clearly smacks of extortion." Judge Amory looked over at the surprised actor. "Yes, Mr. Bowers, 'extortion.' And the court finds it reprehensible. I'm satisfied from the evidence in the record that Mr. Bowers's sole interest in being free to make these embarrassing facts public is his ability to wrest five million dollars from Mrs. Campbell. After all, what *legitimate* interest does he have in putting those facts on the public record, airing them before a public gallery, and seeing them printed in the pages of the press throughout the world? The question answers itself. He has none.

"Whatever Mrs. Campbell's personal transgressions may have been, she need not bear this kind of coercion, this threat to destroy her marriage. It is up to a court of equity to fashion an appropriate form of relief, and the form designed by Mr. Cain, while highly unusual, seems appropriate to these facts. I am satisfied that I am violating no First Amendment rights by ordering that, pending a hearing on Mr. Cain's application for a preliminary injunction, all documents in the case Mr. Cain has filed on behalf of Mrs. Campbell and in any other litigation between the parties, including the suit threatened by Mr. Bowers, will be filed under seal, all hearings will be held in closed courtrooms, and no party or lawyer will communicate with the media or any other third party about Mrs. Campbell's diary or any other fact concerning her conduct or these proceedings. It is so ordered." Without another word, Judge Amory rose and left the bench.

Pat Campbell threw her arms around Harry. "My God, Harry, you did it. You really did it."

"So it seems, Pat. We still have to go through a preliminary injunction hearing, but we'll be before Judge Amory again, and there's no doubt in my mind he'll rule the same way. So I think you're going to be okay." He led her out of the courtroom and down the corridor.

Harry could see the Pacific shimmering in the distance beyond the glass courthouse doors. He loved this little courthouse, always had— loved its small-town feeling, its clean ocean air. Moving down the corridor he'd walked so many times before, he felt the extraordinary elation, the incomparable high of winning. He could sense the relief, the joy that Pat Campbell was feeling as she walked beside him, beginning to chatter gaily about the hearing and its participants.

Just then, Harry heard a loud bellow behind them.

"Hey, cunt, wait up." The ugly word seemed to hang embarrassingly in the quiet corridor. Harry turned to see Tommy Bowers walking quickly in their direction. He reached them and rapidly stepped around them, blocking the courthouse door with his square, muscular body. People in the hallway turned to look, including a bus load of fifth graders on a civics field trip.

"Don't think you're gonna get out of this, cunt. Don't think this cocksucker can . . ."

"Hey," said Harry, leaning toward Bowers, "Watch your mouth. You've got a hall full of kids here. And get out of our way."

"Go fuck yourself, counselor. You want to try and get by me?" He stood with his head thrust out toward Harry, his face bright red with rage. Thick cords of muscle bulged in his neck, and his big fists were balled at the end of massive forearms. He was waiting, just hoping Harry would try him.

Harry knew that, on his best day, he was no match for the former Golden Gloves champion. But he also knew he was smarter and maybe even braver. He shifted his weight, assuming a karate-type stance. Calmly, he looked into Bowers's eyes and spoke in a quiet, deadly tone.

"Bowers, if you're not out of our way in ten seconds, I'll snap your spine. If you want to be paralyzed for life, just stay right where you are."

He saw uncertainty replace rage in Bowers's eyes. Seconds passed as the two men faced each other. Harry continued to look calm, totally at ease. As Bowers continued to hesitate, Harry managed a faint smile. Somewhere a clock ticked loudly.

"Aw, fuck it," Bowers said. "I'm not gonna start a fight in a goddamn courthouse." He turned and strode angrily out the door and down the courthouse steps toward the parking lot.

Harry and Pat went outside and stood on the steps, enjoying the clean salt air, still savoring their victory. Pat looked over at Harry admiringly.

"You really are a renaissance man. The best lawyer in America and a martial arts expert to boot."

"Christ, Pat, did you swallow that? I don't know doodly about martial arts."

"But what about that 'snap your spine' business?"

"Absolute horse shit. I'd need three guys helping me to snap his spine and even then I wouldn't know how to go about it. It's just the first thing I thought of that might scare him. I guess it worked."

"It sure did, but I wouldn't try it twice."

"Hey, I may be reckless, but I'm not crazy."

Over the next few days, Harry tried to catch up on the numerous letters and phone calls he'd put aside while in Boston with Nancy. He thought occasionally about the lovely gray-haired woman he'd met there, but only momentarily. There was so much on his mind . . . dealing with Nancy's illness, fighting to keep up her courage and his own. He was trying as best he could to run his law practice and to avoid letting his clients down, to keep on winning despite his preoccupation with Nancy. Although he had over a dozen other pressing matters to deal with, the *Masami* trial was approaching, and it was essential that he look for facts that could help him defend Fumiko Masami.

He bought some Fernet Branca at Greenblatt's Delicatessen. The clerk explained that there was no better remedy for overeating or indigestion, and that many elderly Italians took a glass every night. Noting with some amusement that its contents included such romantic things as frankincense, chamomile, and calumba, Harry poured himself a shot glass of the dark-brown liquid. He sniffed at it carefully—it was strong enough to mask any poison, no doubt about that. He belted it down. "Holy God" he cried, coughing and gagging. He had never tasted anything like this in his life. Plainly no one would notice a little antimony chloride or even sulfuric acid in a glass of Fernet Branca.

Harry followed a number of leads in the Japanese community supplied by the Fujiwara family and by his partner, John Matsuoka, the oldest son of a well-established Japanese-American family. John's father was acquainted with a banker who had handled some local affairs for Hiroko Masami. The banker, a stocky, gray-haired man, joined Harry and John at Tokyo Kaikan for a fine lunch of usuzukari, followed by vegetable tempura and sunomono. The banker carefully explained that he was able to discuss Masami's affairs only because the man was dead and because Harry and John represented his widow. He went on to tell them that Masami had made a number of personal investments in the Southern California area, notably in low-rent apartment houses and, even more frequently, in second mortgages on residential property. He had been extremely tough about refusing to give extensions, believing that foreclosures were in his best economic interest, if efficiently handled. He'd used a local nisei lawyer, Vincent Watanabe, who'd been at UCLA Law School with John.

When John called from the restaurant, Watanabe agreed to see them later that same afternoon. Reluctant to drive back to the west side only to return again to Little Tokyo, Harry and John browsed through the original Contemporary Art Museum just off First Street. The warehouselike structure had been expected to close when the new Contemporary Museum was built on Grand Avenue. But the "Temporary Contemporary" had enjoyed unexpected popularity and remained open despite the success of its handsome new replacement. It featured conceptual artists whose work raised questions that intrigued Harry. Was a man who directed seven friends to paint different versions of the same object acting as an artist? Could he legitimately hang the seven canvases as his own work? And what of the man who went about the city with a photographer telling him to shoot someone buying a newspaper or two people talking in a café? The resulting photos—usually cropped to show only a part of the subject—might be called art, but whose? The photographer or the man who told him what to shoot? Was it art to stencil the words "I am" in black on a raw white canvas, or to place an old sneaker on top of a back issue of *Playboy*? Was *everything* art that its creator *thought* was art? If not, was there a better, more workable definition? Where did you draw the line and who was entitled to draw it—the art establishment? Every viewer? The government?

Harry loved to debate these issues, and he raised them all with his partner as they strolled through the vast building. The time passed quickly, and at three o'clock they left the museum and walked down

First Street to Vincent Watanabe's modern high-rise office. The nisei lawyer was charming and bright. Although he knew little about Hiraiko Masami's personal life and nothing about the circumstances of his death, he'd known the man in business and was willing to help. After an hour's interview, they arranged for Watanabe to testify at Fumiko's trial. She had little enough evidence on her side. Harry would use any help he could get.

"The TNF is definitely having a positive effect. The tests we did yesterday show that the tumors have not only stopped growing, they're significantly reduced in size. We're very pleased."

Harry and Nancy sat beaming in the sunny hospital room as Dr. Kenneth Jackson, the young assistant to the project director, gave them the news. Harry felt a surge of warmth, a sensation of joy and relief he'd never experienced before. He squeezed Nancy's hand and saw that tears were running down her cheeks. He felt his own eyes well up.

They spent the balance of the day talking about everything, wildly, giddily bathing in the glow of the splendid news. They planned a trip to their house in Mexico, discussed adding a third floor and looked through *Vogue* and *Harper's*, selecting a few outfits that would suit Nancy and laughing at most of the rest.

That afternoon, their daughter, Gail, arrived from England. She had flown to California when Nancy was first diagnosed and now she announced that she would try to meet them on each Boston trip. They spent the afternoon listening to the news of Gail's life. She was deputy chief of *Time* magazine's London bureau, and her job was going well. Her longstanding love affair with a married gossip columnist . . . a man Harry hated . . . was going badly, as it had for years. It was a sensitive subject with Gail, and Harry had learned not to push it. They talked of politics, art, and Gail's new mews house in Chelsea.

By nine o'clock, Nancy was almost asleep, having received her new shot of TNF. Kissing her goodnight, Harry and Gail took a cab to Locke-Ober, where Harry reminisced about the old days at Harvard and they enjoyed a grilled venison steak followed by Indian pudding, a classic Boston winter feast. They sat sipping the rest of their wine, continuing to congratulate each other on their amazing good fortune. To have found a cancer treatment that worked just at the critical moment, what a marvelous thing. Momentarily, Harry turned serious.

"You know, Gail, I haven't said this to anyone else, but I feel a little guilty getting your mother in that program ahead of a hundred thousand other patients who were just as entitled to it. It's a sad thing about our system that even medicine, stuff essential to save lives, is doled out on the basis of clout."

Gail put down her glass and took Harry's hand across the table. Her dark eyes were her mother's and so was the sudden warmth of her smile.

"There you go again—the master of self-flagellation. First, on a moral basis, I can't imagine anyone more deserving than Mom. Second, this is an example of the free market working at its best. What you call 'clout' is just one of the rewards, the perks for what you contribute to society. Instead of the government deciding those rewards, the market itself determines them. If society didn't value your contribution highly, you wouldn't have that 'clout.' A poor laborer can't get his wife into the TNF program, because what he contributes to society doesn't command that kind of reward in the marketplace. It doesn't make him a bad man or our society a bad society. It just means his contribution, valued in a free market, is not considered as significant as yours. And, Dad, if you're going to have this system, with all of its obvious benefits, you can't quarrel with the marketplace. It's the *only* objective test. You passed. A hundred thousand others didn't. Don't fight it. Be proud, you've earned it."

He put his arm around her and pulled her to him.

"That argument's just a bit too slick for me, Gail. I can't buy it intellectually. But tonight . . . well, tonight, I'm so completely happy and so grateful, I'm ready to accept any rationalization for getting Mom in that program."

They left the restaurant and walked through the Common and the

Public Garden back to the hotel. A light snow began to fall, and they reveled in the clean fresh feel of it on their faces and in the swirling patterns it made drifting across the street lamps in the ancient park. Captivated by the snow and by the joy they felt, they held hands, laughed, and skipped along the snowy walkway. Their beloved Nancy, wife, mother, friend, was going to live.

The next morning Harry closed himself in the phone booth opposite the nurses' station, ready to return the calls that had come into the hotel the preceding day. He knew these would only be ones his secretary considered vital. That morning there were three such calls, from Dustin Hoffman, Mike Ovitz, and Aaron Fernbach. Dustin was on the set. Harry said he would call back later in the day. He dialed Creative Artists Agency, "CAA" in the language of "the industry," and asked for Ovitz. Whatever the powerful agent wanted was probably significant. Besides, he was a friend.

Harry heard the slightly hoarse, youthful voice: "How ya doin' pal . . . you okay?"

"Yeah, I'm fine."

"And Nancy?"

"Not bad, Mike, not bad. I'll tell her you asked."

"Remember, Harry . . . if there's anything I can do, you've gotta ask. I know you don't like to ask for favors; but, if it's for Nancy, that's different. So ask."

"I will, and thanks." Harry looked at his watch. He wanted to get back to Nancy as soon as he could. He never liked long telephone calls anyway. "I'm returning your call from yesterday, Mike. What's up?"

"You're gonna get a call from Aaron Fernbach. He needs your help, and I told him it was okay to call. You guys've been on opposite sides so much he wasn't sure you'd want to work with him."

"Work with him on what?"

"On *what?* You haven't read the trades?"

"I'm in Boston. We don't really see the trades up here."

"Aaron got fired, Harry. Yank stuck it up his ass—fired him 'for cause,' whatever that means. And he's being investigated."

"Investigated? For what?"

"No one knows. It looks like they've really got something on him, something dirty. Anyway, he's basically a good guy, and he needs your help. If you're going to be where he can't reach you, why don't you call him?"

"Okay, Mike, I will. I'll call him right now."

"Good, I'll have our switchboard connect you. Just hang on. And remember, anytime you need help, you just call."

"I will, Mike, I will."

Harry heard the taped music signifying that he was on hold. Within two minutes, the music stopped and he heard a strong English accent.

"Fernbach residence."

"Mr. Fernbach please. This is Harry Cain."

There was a pause. Harry heard voices in the distance. Then a door closing. Then the familiar voice. Always before, even in the most difficult moments of their conflict, Fernbach had seemed cool, controlled, above the fight. Now his voice contained an unmistakable note of tension.

"Harry . . . thanks for calling. God, I really need your help. I mean, after twelve years of making billions for the scumbag, he fires me without notice—'for cause' he says, and he's 'investigating' me. Jesus! Listen, Harry, I'm still emotional, I know. I'll calm down, but you've got to help me on this."

"I'll be glad to help you, Aaron. But you've already got fine lawyers at Garrett, Small. Tony Mitchum is a very competent guy, and you've been with him for years."

"I know, Harry, but you're the best, and that's what I want . . . what I need. It's not just what *I* think. I've talked to Geffen, to Warren, to Ovitz. They all said that if I could get you, that's what I should do. Tony Mitchum's fine, but you're the best. Listen, I saw what you did to that idiot, Neil Wegman."

"Thanks, Aaron, but you should know that my wife's quite ill, and . . ."

"I know, Harry, and I'm sorry; but I considered that. As Geffen said, 'Harry Cain preoccupied and working part time is better than anyone else full time and paying attention.' So will you help me?"

"Sure I will, Aaron. But you've got to understand. Nancy's my first priority. If something comes up with her, I've got to be available . . . even if we're in trial. Is that understood?"

"It's understood, Harry—absolutely. Now let me tell you what happened."

"Listen, Aaron, I've gotta get back to Nancy now. We'll be back in L.A. tomorrow afternoon. Let's meet at the end of the day, and you can fill me in. Meanwhile, fax your contract to me at the Ritz-Carlton in Boston. I'll read it on the plane."

"That's fine, Harry. How about my place, 1033 Rockingham? Is six okay?"

"Yeah, that's fine. And, Aaron, send along any letters or memos that you think might be significant."

"Okay, Harry. I'll see you tomorrow, and thanks."

"Sure, Aaron. 'Bye."

" 'Bye."

Rockingham Drive in Brentwood is a quiet, tree-lined street in an older neighborhood a few minutes from the sea. Its sumptuous but tasteful homes are sheltered behind massive stone walls and tall hedges. The residents did not always match the charm and grace of their neighborhood, but Aaron Fernbach seemed one who did.

Harry pressed the buzzer in front of the Fernbach estate. He looked into the closed circuit television camera and gave his name. The massive iron gates swung slowly open. Harry drove the Bentley along a winding driveway lined with sycamore trees to a large colonial house subtly floodlit to enhance its dramatic façade. He parked, rang the bell, and was ushered by a young English butler into a handsome library, all cinnamon and brown leather, with floor-to-ceiling bookshelves and a large painting by George Bellows of two tired boxers grappling in a smoke-filled arena.

After a moment, Aaron Fernbach entered the room. He was well dressed as always, in a double-breasted blue blazer, light-blue shirt, and maroon-and-blue paisley ascot. Yet he walked stiffly and seemed heavier and older than when Harry had last seen him only weeks earlier in New York. Harry extended his hand, but Fernbach grabbed him by the shoulders and hugged him.

"Harry, I can't tell you how good it is to have you on my side. My God, what a week."

"Sit down, Aaron, and tell me about it. From the beginning."

Fernbach lowered himself into a massive leather wing chair and began. Three months before Harry's contempt hearing in New York, Yank Slutsky had made himself chairman of the company, a position vacant since the death of Clare Carson two years earlier. Previously, Slutsky had only been the principal stockholder; now he was a corporate officer, senior to Aaron, whose title was president. As a practical matter, he'd always had the power to tell Aaron what to do. Now he had the *right* to do it. Soon he began to exercise that right on a daily basis. "I don't want that cockamamie picture made. Cancel it!" "You'll cast Madonna in that part and no one else. You got it?" "That artsy-fartsy *fagele* uses twenty takes for every scene. Fire him. Now!" Those were the arbitrary, peremptory, stupid orders the man was giving every working day. He was hurting the studio badly and Fernbach, never one to defy power, had finally begun to resist . . . at least subtly. He would delay carrying out Slutsky's most egregious decisions and pretend not to have understood the command. Time after time he would try to show the man how he was missing the point, was hurting the company with his capriciousness. But Slutsky was not one to have his power thwarted or circumvented. As time went on, he had become irritable, then openly angry with Fernbach.

Finally, two days before, Fernbach had returned from a hectic trip to Japan and was summoned to Slutsky's stadium-size office. Slutsky kept him standing and told him bluntly that he was fired . . . "for cause." Fernbach left the office fighting back tears of rage. He went to his own office and found it padlocked and guarded by one of the studio police. A secretary handed him the *Hollywood Reporter*. It announced, in front-page headlines, that he'd been discharged "for cause" and that the studio was conducting "an investigation" into his conduct. It reported that Fernbach "failed to answer the *Reporter*'s calls." Slutsky's PR people had issued the inflammatory press release the day before, while Fernbach was on a plane from Japan. They'd successfully put the studio's story out and prevented any effective reply by Fernbach.

Leaning forward, Harry interrupted. "Aaron, what did Yank say was the 'cause' you were fired for?"

"He never said. I asked, and he said I'd find out from the lawyers. But I still don't know. The story in the trades didn't say, either. Just that it was 'for cause.' And because it says he's 'investigating' me, everybody thinks I stole money or something. Isn't that libel?"

"Not really. He didn't actually *say* you stole anything. He only said they're 'investigating' you, and I'm sure they *are* investigating you. The first thing they do in cases like this is audit your expense account, see if you were charging personal stuff to the company. You've got to level with me, Aaron. Is there anything we've got to worry about on that score?"

"Not a thing, Harry, I promise you. I swear on my kids' lives."

"Good. Then, let's focus on what else 'cause' might be. Did you disobey any orders?"

"Not really disobey. I delayed. I argued. I tried to change his mind. I never just disobeyed. There is no cause. Believe me. There is no cause."

"Okay, Aaron, we'll assume that. But we've got to know what they *claim* is the cause for discharge, especially if we elect to go for a bullet arbitration, rather than a regular court proceeding."

"A bullet arbitration?"

"Yeah. Your contract gives you the right to arbitration by a retired Superior Court judge with a hearing no later than thirty days. We call it an expedited or 'bullet' arbitration, because it's fast. You wait thirty days for your trial instead of three years, which is good, since they owe you lots of money if we win. But its speed is also its disadvantage. There's no provision for an appeal. And there's no discovery—no depositions, no pretrial inspection of documents. Neither side knows who the other side's witnesses are or even the detail of its claims. You go in blind, the old-fashioned way, surprise witnesses and all. Other than that, it's just like a regular trial."

"What's your advice, Harry? What should we do?"

"It's a close one, Aaron, but I'd gamble on keeping them off balance and on our ability to react faster and their not being able to prepare Yank well enough in that short a time. I'd go for the bullet."

"Okay, Harry, that's what we'll do. Will you—" They were interrupted by insistent knocking on the study door. Puzzled, Fernbach threw the door open, revealing the English butler, who was obviously upset.

"Mr. Fernbach, two men are in the driveway preparing to tow away your car."

Fernbach and Harry quickly followed the butler, questioning him as they half walked, half ran through the hallway.

"How'd they get inside the gate?"

"They said they were telephone repairmen. Cook buzzed them in. Oh, I'm so sorry, Mr. Fernbach."

"That's okay, Gregory. We'll solve it."

They arrived in the driveway out of breath, to find two large men in overalls hooking Fernbach's big chocolate-brown Rolls to a tow truck, its lights flashing on and off in the soft Brentwood night.

"Whatta you think you're doing?" bellowed Fernbach. "Get off this property."

"We will," said one of the men, "just as soon as we get this baby hooked up."

Fernbach started for the man, but Harry caught his arm, restraining him. "Let me handle this, Aaron." He walked slowly to the man who had spoken, carefully placing himself in front of the tow truck.

"I'm Harry Cain, Mr. Fernbach's lawyer. Who authorized this?"

"Consolidated Studios. It's their car. Check the registration. We got every right to take it back to them."

Harry turned to his client. "Is that right, Aaron?"

"Well, yes, technically. The car is owned by the company. But our deal was that I get it full time for the life of the contract."

The overalled man grinned. "See, counselor, he admits our customer owns the car. So get out of our way, or we might just drive right over ya."

"I don't think you will," Harry said coolly. "And I don't think you'll take the car either. You gained entrance to this property by false pretenses. That's a criminal trespass, a felony under Section 321 (b) of the Criminal Code. Your threat to drive over me just now is another felony . . . extortion. The maximum sentence is five years for each of those crimes. If you're not out of here with that car unchained in five minutes, you and your boss are going to do no less than eighteen months in a state prison and maybe as much as ten years."

"Oh, bullshit!"

"You think so? Just try me."

Harry folded his arms over his chest and stood blocking the way to the gate. He'd made up the Criminal Code section number and the maximum sentences. But the repo-man didn't know it. There was a long, tense moment of silence. Then the man turned to his partner.

"Okay, George, unchain her. Let's get out of here. This smart-ass lawyer's got some angle, and I don't need to fuck with it." Then he turned to Harry. "We'll be back, counselor, you can bet on it."

When the tow truck had gone, Fernbach walked Harry through the garden to his car. Harry inhaled the fresh breeze from the Pacific and felt a moment of joy. It was a fine evening, and Nancy was going to make it. He forced his mind back to Aaron Fernbach.

"You know, Aaron, I wasn't going to let those bozos get away with that. But it really might get us some sympathy with the judge if they *did* repossess your car. I mean, it's such a childish thing to do. It's got to piss him off."

"You mean you *want* them to repossess my car?"

"Well, it wouldn't be all bad."

"Harry, you don't understand. It's not the money. I can buy another *Rolls*. But this one is different—specially made for me. Park-Muliner chassis. Pigskin seats. My God, I've driven that car for three years now. I take it to every party, every meeting. Everyone associates it with me. Christ, my kids are driven to school in that car every day. He can't take it away. You can't let him. I mean, to take away my *car* . . . You mustn't let him, please."

Harry noticed that Fernbach's eyes were welling up with tears. Tears, Harry thought as he started his engine. Tears over a fucking Rolls? What a town!

The next afternoon, Harry called Greg Morrison, Yank Slutsky's longtime lawyer. He knew Morrison would be representing Consolidated Studios in its battle with Aaron Fernbach. Morrison was a paunchy, balding back-slapper of a man, active in Bar Association politics and the USC Alumni Association. He was also a skilled and experienced trial lawyer. As they spoke, Harry could picture the man's wide smile, his freckled face, and thinning reddish hair. Invariably pleasant, even jovial, Morrison could be stubborn . . . and dangerous.

"Harry, I realize you'd like to know our grounds for discharge; and, if it were up to me, I'd tell you everything. But my client doesn't want me to, and I had to advise them they don't have to . . . not if you choose a bullet arbitration with no discovery."

"But, Greg, if you hope to settle, you've got to show me what you've got. Otherwise, it's gonna look like you've got nothing at all. I can't recommend a settlement on that basis."

Actually, Harry was doubtful there could be any settlement. Too much money was involved—maybe thirty to fifty million dollars in stock options. But studios usually liked to settle their cases to avoid airing their dirty linen in public. Using a possible settlement as bait, Harry thought he might get some badly needed information about the studio's evidence. Greg Morrison surprised him.

"Harry, we don't particularly want to settle with Fernbach. We don't want to pay him anything you'd ever accept, and it would just piss you off if I made you the kind of offer my client would approve. I don't need to mess with a pissed-off Harry Cain, so let's not even get into the subject. Okay? Believe me, we've got plenty of ammunition. Plenty. Mr. Fernbach has done some very foolish things."

Harry tried to free his voice of the anxiety he felt. "Okay, Greg, suit yourself. You and I'll have some fun for a few days. But listen, why fuck around with the guy's car? That's really chickenshit."

"Yank's orders, Harry. 'Grab the car,' he said. 'That asshole worships his fucking car.' And hey, Yank's the boss. But I like Aaron, and I'll do what I can. I'll try to arrange for him to return the car voluntarily. Give him time to buy a new one. How about next week?"

"Well, why not just let him keep the car pending the outcome of the trial? You're only talking about a few days, and if we win, he's entitled to it for three more years."

"*If* you win, Harry, and, looking at the evidence, I really don't see how you can. I'll tell you what: We'll let him *buy* the car. You can add the money to your damage claim."

"Come on, Greg, buy his own car, with the trial only days away?"

"Hey, he doesn't want to buy it, it's okay with me. Let him return it. He doesn't want to return it, we'll tow it away."

"Okay, Greg, but this time you better have a court order to enter the property, and I'm not so sure you can get one."

The clock on Harry's desk softly chimed seven. A moment later the intercom buzzed.

"Mrs. Campbell's here, Mr. Cain."

"Send her in, Clara."

An hour earlier Pat Campbell had called, sounding distraught. She'd asked to see Harry as soon as possible, that evening, if it could be arranged. As she entered the office, he saw that her face was drawn and tense, her expression almost frantic. She was beautifully dressed in a beige knit suit with a light-blue silk blouse. But her handkerchief was balled up in a tightly clenched fist, and Harry guessed she had been crying, more in rage than sorrow. He opened the miniature bar in his cabinet and brought out ice cubes and Scotch. Pouring each of them two fingers of Dewar's, he sat back facing her.

"Okay, Pat, what's the problem?"

"That miserable bastard. I'd like to kill him. I may kill him."

"Hold on. Kill who? What miserable bastard?"

"Tommy Bowers. You'll never believe what that vindictive son of a bitch did. He sent Ewing the diary. Can you believe it? Sent him my diary."

"But that's stupid. If he had any hope of ever getting a settlement from you, it's gone now. Gone forever."

"Yeah, well, so's my marriage."

"Are you sure? Ewing may be more understanding than you think."

"Not a chance. He's already moved to his club to think things out. But I know what he'll do, what he's got to do. He'll divorce me. You read that excerpt yourself. You know he's got no choice."

She swallowed the Scotch in one long gulp and held her glass out for more. Harry poured her another two fingers and began to sip his own drink.

"Harry, you're the only chance I've got. You're a stinking genius. Can you think of anything? There must be a way."

"I'm not sure, Pat. Let me work on it. Go home now and let me think. I'll call you later."

At 8:00 Harry was still thinking. Pacing his office floor, he explored several ideas, running them through his mind, playing out all the possibilities, rejecting one after the other as unworkable.

Finally he sat down, leaned back in his chair and put a Brandenburg Concerto on the tape deck behind his desk. Bach's counterpoint soothed him, made him feel fresh, almost relaxed. He cast his mind about, free associating. Sometimes that worked. A random word, a fragment, a thought would trigger an idea, sometimes a good one. The music made him think of Alla. He pictured her long legs, her green eyes shining with intensity, with desire, her . . . He sat forward, slamming his fist into his open palm. Goddamn it, that's it! Her fantasies!

He sat thinking for five more minutes, developing his plan. Then he reached for the phone, and rapidly punched out Pat Campbell's number.

"Pat?"

"Harry?"

"Yeah, and I've got it—the way to handle this."

"That's fantastic. But how, Harry? What's the plan?"

"Well, you're gonna write another diary."

"*Another* diary?"

"That's right. A current diary, but not a *real* one. I want you to write it tonight or tomorrow at the latest, even if it takes all day. Now, here's what you do. . . ."

Λt nine o'clock that night, Harry had finally made it home and was preparing chicken fajitas, one of Nancy's favorites. He had sautéed the strips of onion, sweet red peppers, and chicken, seasoned with balsamic vinegar, finely chopped jalapeños and Worcestershire sauce. Nancy was preparing to heat the flour tortillas that would be filled with the spicy mixture and eaten by hand. Both of them were relaxed, having already finished most of a bottle of Pinot Noir. Harry noticed they were drinking more these days. But who could blame them? he thought, with death still hanging over their heads. Who could blame them if they used opium?

As Nancy was opening the tortilla package, the telephone rang. Harry picked up the direct line to his exchange to learn who was calling. It was Aaron Fernbach, and it was urgent. Signalling to Nancy to hold up on the tortillas, Harry pressed the button to take Fernbach's call.

"Harry, I'm calling from Morton's. I'm really sorry to bother you at home, but you said to tell you everything. You won't believe what just happened. That fucking Yank! I arrive here, where I've eaten once a week for the last ten years, and Rick seats me in the back of the restaurant. The *back* of the restaurant, Harry, under the Francis Bacon. Now you know that was Yank's doing. Right?"

"Were they crowded?"

"Mobbed, that's the trouble. Everyone saw me sitting there, Diller, Katzenberg, everyone. Like I no longer count. For God's sake, Harry, to seat *me* in the back of the restaurant, *under the Bacon.*

You know what that means. I should've left. But we had out-of-town guests, who wanted to eat here, so . . . They're still there at the table. I excused myself and went to call you."

"Don't jump to conclusions, Aaron. With a big party like yours, they may not have had the room in the front. Rick's not like that, and neither are Peter and Pam Morton. I think it's just coincidence."

"Well, I don't. If it was David Geffen or Marvin Davis or even you, they'd 've carried a big table right up to the front."

Harry couldn't resist a chuckle at the "even you." "Come on, Aaron, lighten up. We've got enough to worry about without getting paranoid about where you sit at Morton's. Go back to your guests and forget it. Don't give Rick a tip if it'll make you feel better. And remember, we're meeting tomorrow, Friday, and Saturday at six, and you've got to give me at least two hours each day. Okay?"

"Okay, Harry. I guess you're right. But under the Bacon, for Christ's sake! That hurts, Harry. That really hurts. Anyway, I'll see you tomorrow."

Harry put down the phone, hugged Nancy, and then turned to reheat the fajita mixture while she warmed the tortillas. He'd calmed Fernbach down that time, but how would this guy behave on the witness stand? If he came across as bitter and paranoid, they were in trouble. Well, it was Harry's job to shore him up, make him appear confident, even-tempered, likable. That was an important part of running a trial, and he'd have to find a way.

They enjoyed their meal, laughing and chattering, something they'd been able to do frequently now that they'd had the good news about Nancy's treatment. As Harry poured them each a small glass of port to take upstairs, the telephone rang. Again, it was Aaron Fernbach.

"Harry, you won't believe it. I'm still at Morton's. Now they've taken my car. Those bastards picked it up right from the parking lot while I was in there eating. The back of the room was bad enough, but this! I know we can't do anything tonight, but first thing in the morning I want a criminal complaint filed, like you said at my house. I'll show that greasy pig!"

"Aaron, hold on. When we stopped 'em at your house, the crime was trespassing on your property, not taking the car. Remember, it's *their* car. It's a breach of contract to take it, but you don't put people in jail for that. Besides, the more I think about it, the more I think this helps us. It makes them look cheap and sleazy."

"You mean there's nothing we can do about it?"

"No, Aaron, there's plenty we can do about it . . . at the trial. But not before that. We'll be in trial in nine more days. It would make us look totally foolish to go to court for some kind of order letting you use the car for nine days. This way, it makes them look bad, not us. Believe me, it's for the best. Now get someone to drive you home, and rent a car tomorrow. We'll hold them for the cost. Okay?"

"Okay . . . and thanks, Harry. I know I'm a pain in the ass; but things like what happened tonight really get to me."

"You're no more a pain in the ass than most clients, Aaron, and I want you to keep calling me when you've got a question or problem. Otherwise, you're apt to do something on your own that could really hurt your case. I think I'll go to bed now, okay?"

"Sure, Harry, g'night."

"Goodnight, Aaron. Sleep well."

Harry put his arm around Nancy and they started up the stairs. He turned to her, grinning. "For this I went to Harvard Law School?"

Just before the Fernbach trial, Harry and Nancy made one more trip to Boston. They got even more encouraging results. The tumors had continued shrinking. They anticipated the day when Dr. Jackson would finally tell them the cancer was gone entirely. Then, of course, there'd be the final five-year wait to see if it returned. If it didn't, Nancy would supposedly be "clean." Harry knew they'd pass the five-year test. After all, what test hadn't he passed? What goal once strived for hadn't been achieved?

Life was pleasant again, livable again. Harry and Nancy were closer than ever before. She was optimistic now, and he was regaining his normal efficiency. They'd battled this thing together and maybe . . . seemingly . . . had won.

Harry left for the Fernbach trial on a clear, sunny morning. The wind from the sea had swept the sky free of haze and left the air fresh and clean. The bougainvillea was a richly brilliant red and orange. The hydrangeas were impossible shades of blue, violet, and purple. He walked through the garden, smiling. It was a good time to be alive.

As he drove down from the hills, he reviewed the situation. Over the course of four evenings, Harry had spent more than ten hours preparing Aaron Fernbach. He continued to feel guilty about taking the time away from Nancy, but it had to be done. He had asked Nancy if he should take the case the first day Fernbach had called him back in Boston. Nancy had insisted that he should. Having taken it, he had to do what was necessary to win it. And that required preparation—hours and hours of it.

Preparation for this case had been different from almost any other. In normal court proceedings, each lawyer could learn about the other's case through pretrial discovery, taking depositions and serving written interrogatories that forced the other side to disclose its contentions and the evidence that supported those contentions. But in a bullet arbitration there was no time for any of that, and the rules did not provide for it.

As a result, Harry had no real idea of the studio's claims. Aaron continued to insist that there could be no problem with his expense account, but they'd spent considerable time on the issue of insubordination, since that seemed a strong possibility. They had also discussed the concept of gross negligence. Aaron's overall management record was exceptionally good. In the past year, Consolidated had released some films that had not done well, but it seemed impossible that the studio could prove the kind of extreme negligence that would permit a discharge under the terms of Aaron's contract. Working in the dark like this was difficult, but it was a trade-off.

They had to sacrifice the usual pretrial discovery if they wanted the immediate hearing that was the principal advantage of a bullet arbitration.

As the plaintiff, Harry put on his case first. That gave him a measure of control over the way the evidence came in. But it also meant that Aaron would testify and be cross-examined by the studio's lawyers before he even knew what he was accused of. They could and would ask him the details of his conduct in numerous transactions that he and Harry had never even discussed or considered. The result could be deadly, no matter how much time they spent trying to anticipate what was coming. It worried Harry, worried him more than he liked to admit and certainly more than he admitted to Aaron Fernbach, whose morale had to be kept high.

The hearing started on a Friday. Opening statements were expected to take most of the morning. Then the actual testimony would begin. When Harry reached the Century City offices of Morrison, Gunsten & Moore, where the arbitration was to take place, he found Aaron waiting in the large, postmodern reception room. Aaron was immaculately dressed in a beautifully tailored gray tweed suit, but he looked pale and nervous as he rose to shake Harry's hand.

Almost immediately, Greg Morrison, the studio's lawyer, came out to meet them and led them into a large paneled boardroom that had been converted into a makeshift court for the hearing. A high desk had been set aside for the judge. A small table served as the witnesses stand, and there was another smaller desk for the court reporter. The lawyers and the parties were to sit on each side of the twenty-foot mahogany table usually reserved for directors of the firm's corporate clients.

Waiting on Morrison's side of the table was a young associate of his law firm. Next to him was Consolidated Studios' general counsel, Lisa Lerner, middle aged, tough as nails, and usually called "the Dragon Lady"—but not to her face. Harry and Aaron nodded to her and took their seats on the opposite side of the table. The proceedings were to start at 8:30 each morning.

At 8:20 Judge Phillip Sandlinger arrived, accompanied by the court reporter. Aaron's contract named ten retired superior court judges who were to be approached in the order they were listed in the contract. The first one available to hear the case within thirty days was to be the designated judge. The ten men listed in the contract were the best of the large pool of retired judges living in Los Angeles County. They were constantly in demand to try cases under California's rent-a-judge system, under which the litigants employed a retired judge at their own expense to try their case in private. Unlike a bullet arbitration, the rent-a-judge system provided a full right of appeal and the ability to conduct depositions and other discovery proceedings. But a rent-a-judge trial, while it came sooner than in an ordinary civil case, was not immediate like the hearing in a bullet arbitration; and, with an appeal, it could take a year or more to get a final decision.

Because the ten judges listed in Aaron's contract were good ones, constantly in demand, Harry had been concerned that none would be available. In that case, the judge was to be picked by the presiding judge of the superior court, and his pick could be any one of the 150 retired judges who had listed themselves as willing to hear such matters. Such an appointee might be very weak, and Harry had feared a weak or vacillating judge or one who might lack sufficient intellectual strength to deal with the difficult issues they could face.

Judge Sandlinger had been second on the contract list. Fortunately, he had just settled a large condemnation case that had been about to go to trial. He was free immediately.

A large, moon-faced man with bushy brown hair and a shambling gait, Phillip Sandlinger was known as hard-working and brilliant. He was impatient with stupidity and quick to sense insincerity. He could be a difficult and sarcastic man, but, all in all, he was an excellent judge.

Sandlinger greeted Harry and Greg Morrison and was introduced to Aaron Fernbach and the others at the massive table. He opened his briefcase and spread several pens and a legal pad before him. He turned to the court reporter, who nodded. Then he announced that the proceedings had begun.

"Opening statement, Mr. Cain?"

"Yes, Your Honor."

Harry got slowly to his feet. Since the studio had refused to make its claims known in advance of the hearing, there was little he could say. He could only try to turn that fact to his advantage and to win some sympathy from the court by emphasizing the unfairness of the studio's tactics.

"Your Honor, I can't really address the proof we'll put on as I usually would. The fact is, I don't know what that proof will be. Not until the defendant puts on its case. That's because Consolidated has consistently chosen to keep us guessing. Despite our repeated requests, they've refused to tell us what they claim to be their grounds for discharging Mr. Fernbach. When Mr. Slutsky, their chairman and principal stockholder, fired Mr. Fernbach without any advance notice, he refused to specify the basis of his action; and counsel for Consolidated has steadfastly refused to tell me why Mr. Fernbach was discharged. That may be their right, Your Honor, but it reeks of game playing, and unfair game playing at that."

Judge Sandlinger looked up from his notes and turned to Consolidated's side of the table.

"Is this true, Mr. Morrison?"

"Yes, Your Honor, but Mr. Fernbach knows full well what he did. There can be no real question in his mind as to why he was fired."

Sandlinger peered over his rimless glasses. "Then why not tell Mr. Cain?"

Harry could see tiny beads of sweat form on Greg Morrison's brow. Morrison's stonewalling tactics would help him enormously during the trial, but there was a price, and he was paying it now.

"Well, Your Honor, we considered that, of course. *Kraft* v. *Robin*, at 230 Cal.App.2d, page 32, holds that an employer may discharge an employee for any legal cause he may actually have at the time, even if he specifies a different reason for the discharge or specifies no reason at all. We feel that Mr. Fernbach has done massive damage to Consolidated Studios, that he is guilty of deliberate wrongdoing as well as gross negligence. We felt it appropriate to use whatever advantages the law gives us. In short, we felt perfectly justified in not doing this man"—he pointed accusingly at Fernbach—"any favors. He certainly didn't do any favors for my client, as the court will hear in detail."

"Very well. You may continue, Mr. Cain."

"In any event, Your Honor, I can't even outline our proof at this point, because, contrary to what Mr. Morrison has said, my client has no idea . . . not the slightest idea . . . as to the supposed cause for which he was fired after twelve years of unquestionably superb performance.

"What you will hear from the plaintiff is that Mr. Fernbach was in the second year of his third successive five-year contract. That is, he had three years to go at two million per year plus additional stock options, which he would lose if he were properly terminated. His contract provides that 'cause' for discharge is only conviction of a felony, disobedience, disloyalty, dishonesty, or gross negligence. Before he was summarily fired, Mr. Fernbach was given no notice, no warning that anything he had done was even considered incorrect, much less cause for discharge. He didn't even know he was being fired until five minutes before he and his family read about it in the newspapers. That's where they also read that he was being 'investigated.' I suppose we'll learn the result of that investigation during this proceeding. We certainly have no idea now what was being investigated. And I know Your Honor can imagine the impact on the community of a statement that the chief executive officer of a major company is being 'investigated.'

"In any event, the night after he was fired and suffered the humiliation of reading about it and about how he was being investigated, Mr. Fernbach had to suffer further humiliation. Agents of Consolidated Studios used false pretenses to enter his property in an attempt to take the car to which he was entitled by contract. They wouldn't even wait ten days for this proceeding. They had to invade his home and take his car away immediately. They . . . "

Morrison jumped to his feet, cutting Harry off. "Your Honor, I object to this attempt to prejudice the court. The matter of the company car that Mr. Fernbach tried to keep even after he was fired has no relevance to this proceeding and certainly the manner in which the defendant repossessed its own car has nothing to do with this case."

Judge Sandlinger looked over at Harry. "What is the relevance of the car, Mr. Cain?"

"Mr. Fernbach is entitled to it by contract, Your Honor. It's repossession is, in itself, an act of breach by the defendant."

"All right, the objection is overruled. But try to be brief on that matter, Mr. Cain. It's certainly not the heart of the case."

"Yes, Your Honor. Actually, given our limited knowledge, I was near the end anyway.

"I just want to add that, in Mr. Fernbach's twelve years at Consolidated, the studio was first in market share among the major studios eight times and was never less than third. He was generally acknowledged in the industry to have done a superb job. He was neither disobedient nor dishonest nor disloyal. If there was a valid reason for his discharge, I have yet to hear it. I'm confident we will not hear it in these proceedings. Thank you." Harry resumed his seat, not really happy with his brief opening; but not discouraged either.

Judge Sandlinger looked over at the defendant's side of the table. "Very well. Mr. Morrison, do you wish to make an opening statement?"

"I'll reserve it until after the plaintiff's case, Your Honor."

"All right. Call your first witness, Mr. Cain."

"We call the plaintiff, Your Honor."

Aaron Fernbach, looking stiff and nervous, made his way to the witness table and was sworn by the court reporter. At that moment, Yank Slutsky quietly entered the room and took a seat at the large table next to his general counsel, Lisa Lerner. His long black hair was slicked back, emphasizing his massive round face and blue-black jowls. An amply cut and expensive black pin-striped suit concealed his strangely wide body. He caught Harry's eye and glared, evidently still incensed at having been forced to relinquish the right of final cut to Joe Miletti.

A new idea occurred to Harry, a possible way to save Aaron from being cross-examined in detail before he could learn the nature of the charges against him. The idea might not work, and he'd have to cut Aaron's direct examination to a few brief questions. But there'd be time to get his story out later. Harry decided to try.

He took Aaron briefly through his educational and business background, then identified his contract with Consolidated Studios and offered it in evidence. Next, he brought out the events of Aaron's discharge and the repossession of his car. At this point, Harry introduced an oversized chart showing the salary and stock options to which Aaron was still entitled by the contract. When Aaron had explained the numbers, Harry stepped back from the table and raised his voice.

"And you have no idea whatsoever what conduct on your part is supposed to be the basis for your discharge?"

"No, sir, I do not."

"That's all I have at this point, Your Honor."

Aaron, who'd been prepared for a longer direct examination, looked at Harry with surprise. Harry winked and quickly turned away.

Judge Sandlinger looked up from his notes. "Mr. Morrison, any cross?"

"Yes, Your Honor."

Morrison also seemed surprised at the brevity of Aaron's direct examination. He turned to his young associate, and, shrugging his shoulders, pointed to a black loose-leaf notebook, obviously the preplanned cross-examination of Aaron Fernbach. The young lawyer slid the book down the table to Morrison, who stood with it open before him. He peered at Aaron for several seconds like a boxer seeking to outpsych his opponent before a fight. Then he began.

"Mr. Fernbach, at any time after March twenty-third of this year did you discharge Terence O'Neil as director of *Carnage*?"

"No, sir, I did not."

"Weren't you ordered to fire Mr. O'Neil?"

Harry rose quickly before Aaron could respond. "Objection, Your Honor. Firstly, the question calls for an improper conclusion, and a legal conclusion at that. We should hear what was said; and the court, not the witness, should decide if those words constituted a legally binding order. But, more important, the question is completely outside the scope of direct examination. All I asked Mr. Fernbach about was his contract, his discharge, and the repossession of his car. I did not go into his conduct, good or bad, before his termination. Nothing I asked went to those issues. I did not offer testimony to show that he did a good job or that he was not disobedient, dishonest, disloyal, or grossly negligent. So, Mr. Morrison can't go into that either. Not with this witness. It's clearly beyond the scope of direct examination."

Judge Sandlinger, peering at Harry over his glasses, looked in-trigued. Greg Morrison's face suffused with red.

"Your Honor," he bellowed, "Mr. Cain established the contract. That opens the door to our showing that the contract was no longer enforceable because of Mr. Fernbach's conduct. Besides, this is just a delaying tactic. Even if the objection were sustained, I would just call Mr. Fernbach later, as a part of the defendant's case, and examine him on all the issues. It makes no sense to preclude me from doing it now, while he's already on the stand. This is just technical nitpicking, Judge, designed to harass. It shouldn't be allowed."

Judge Sandlinger smiled slyly. "I don't think so, Mr. Morrison. I suspect Mr. Cain has some purpose beyond raising a mere techni-cality. The objection is sustained on both grounds."

Harry breathed a sigh of relief. The first part of his plan had worked. If only Yank stayed in the room, the rest might work too. Morrison slipped through the tabs on his loose-leaf, obviously frus-trated by the ruling.

"In light of the court's ruling on the scope of cross-examination, I have nothing further at this time, Your Honor. I will certainly call Mr. Fernbach back to the stand as a part of the defendant's case, and I want Mr. Cain's assurance that he will be here at the time."

"Oh, he'll be here, all right." Harry smiled, beginning to relax a bit.

Judge Sandlinger nodded in Harry's direction. "Very well then, call your next witness, Mr. Cain."

"We call Louis Slutsky, Your Honor, as an adverse witness under C.C.P. Section 2055." Section 2055 of the California Code of Civil Procedure allowed a lawyer to call the opposing party to the stand and question him just as if he were being cross-examined. When the opposing party was a corporation, such as Consolidated, its officers could be called to testify in this way. Now Greg Morrison grasped Harry's plan. He rose to address the court. But Yank Slutsky had moved beside him and was whispering in his ear and gesturing with great agitation. Finally, Morrison whispered for Slutsky to sit down so loudly that Harry and even the judge heard him. Unused to being spoken to in that way, Slutsky resumed his seat, but Harry could see the anger in his face, the crimson in his cheeks.

"Your Honor," Morrison said with evident irritation, "we can now see the purpose of Mr. Cain's maneuver. Before his client is examined about his misconduct, he wants to hear Mr. Slutsky's charges, so they can try to cook up a defense."

Harry leapt to his feet. "Just a minute," he shouted. "We're not 'cooking' up anything. We're . . . "

Judge Sandlinger's gavel slammed down. "Enough! Both of you. If you have an objection to make—either of you—then make it. I won't have these outbursts. Do you understand?"

"Yes, Your Honor," intoned both lawyers in unison.

"Judge," Morrison continued, "what Mr. Cain is trying to do is to cross-examine Mr. Slutsky to get the details of his case, as if this were a deposition. I doubt that he could do that even if he had subpoenaed Mr. Slutsky. And he didn't. Mr. Slutsky is an extremely busy man with a vast corporation to run. He has a critical meeting this morning and, as a matter of law, he is free to leave and attend that meeting, since he has not been subpoenaed." Morrison turned and addressed Slutsky, as if the judge were not present. "You may go, Mr. Slutsky." The corpulent studio head began to lift his heavy body from the chair when Judge Sandlinger's gavel slammed down again.

"Mr. Slutsky, resume your seat . . . now!" Slutsky looked quickly at Morrison and then at the judge. He sat down. "Mr. Morrison, I control this courtroom, not you. I will excuse the participants, not you. Mr. Slutsky may not have been subpoenaed, but he's here, and, as such, he's subject to the orders of this court. He will remain here, and he will testify. If he's got some meeting, we'll take a brief recess, so that he can reschedule it." Harry's plan had worked. They would almost surely get to know the events on which the studio based its claims before Aaron could be cross-examined about them. That could make all the difference.

Ten minutes later, Harry faced a furious Yank Slutsky across the massive table.

"Mr. Slutsky, you personally discharged Mr. Fernbach, didn't you?"

"You know I did, so why waste time?"

Harry ignored the hostile response.

"And you certainly had specific grounds in mind for that discharge, isn't that true?" This was the kind of question Harry liked to ask. Either a yes or a no would be fine. If Slutsky said he had no charge against Aaron in mind, that would lead to the inference that there actually were no grounds for the discharge. If, on the other hand, he answered that he did have specific charges in mind, Harry could go into those charges, so that they would know in advance what was coming before Aaron took the stand again.

Slutsky hesitated. He was reluctant to say yes to anything Harry asked, but he could see that a no answer would make him look irresponsible. He replied impatiently.

"Of course I had grounds in mind."

"And what were those grounds, Mr. Slutsky?"

"Objection, irrelevant," said Morrison, without rising. "It's not this witness's state of mind that counts. It's the actual grounds that exist." Harry started to reply, but the judge cut him off.

"Overruled. You may proceed."

"Mr. Slutsky, what were the grounds on which you discharged Mr. Fernbach?"

Slutsky looked up at the ceiling as if trying to recall the brief preparation Morrison had given him during the recess. "Well, there's disobedience . . . insubordination. I told him to fire Terence O'Neil and he wouldn't do it. I told him not to make a settlement giving that maniac, Joe Miletti, final cut. But he did it anyway. So he was insubordinate. Then there's dishonesty. His expense accounts are full of phony items. And he got us to hire a drug addict, Annie Robinson, when no one else would. He offered her a big contract if she'd go to bed with him."

Harry was quickly taking notes. "All right, Mr. Slutsky, anything else?"

"Sure, there was gross negligence too. He was so negligent he almost cost me the whole studio."

"Anything else?"

Slutsky paused, trying to remember the outline Morrison had given him. "No, I think that's it. But isn't that enough?"

"We'll see, Mr. Slutsky. Let's take the last item first. What were Mr. Fernbach's acts or omissions that you call gross negligence?"

The studio head leaned forward, his dark eyes blazing. "That's easy, counselor. He let a director's drunkenness cost me millions of dollars a day. I already told you he gave a big contract to an addict . . . for a promise of sex. He did all kinds of things like that. He ran the studio so bad I was in bankruptcy. I couldn't meet my payroll. That's what he did to me."

"When was Consolidated Studios in bankruptcy, Mr. Slutsky?"

"Just this last year in November and December and early this year. Right up to when I fired him."

"And when was it that the studio couldn't meet its payroll?"

"Same time, end of last year, beginning of this one. He nearly destroyed me, this man." He pointed to Fernbach. "I didn't even have the funds to pay my poor employees at Christmas." Slutsky gave the judge a mournful look, trying to communicate how deeply he felt for his hard-working employees.

Harry reached into his briefcase for a file he'd collected in anticipation of an attack by the studio on Aaron's management. He hadn't guessed the attack would be this extreme or this specific.

"Mr. Slutsky, did you make an annual report to the shareholders of Consolidated Studios on December fifteenth of this year?"

Slutsky hesitated, unsure of what was coming. "Yes, I think so."

"And did you file that report with the Securities and Exchange Commission?"

"*I* didn't."

"Well, sir, you knew it was filed by your lawyers, didn't you?"

"I suppose so."

Harry waved the document in the air. "And you signed that report, isn't that right?"

"Right."

"Now, did you lie to the SEC in that report?"

"Of course not."

"Did you lie to the shareholders when you made your annual report?"

"Come on, counselor, you know I didn't lie."

"Well, let me read you what you said on December fifteenth on this year, the very time you've just testified the company was 'bankrupt' and 'couldn't meet its payroll.' " Harry looked down at the document he had been waving in the air. "I'm quoting from your own remarks, Mr. Slutsky. Your own remarks. What you said at the time was 'the company has never been in better, sounder financial condition. Cash reserves are more than adequate to meet current needs, and long-term prospects are outstanding.' Did you report that, sir, to the shareholders and to the SEC on December fifteenth of last year?"

Slutsky's face was bright red, his eyes bulging. Harry thought for a moment that he would lunge across the table or rush from the room.

Slutsky looked desperately over at Morrison as if for help. But Morrison just looked down at his loose-leaf. There was no help he could give. Slutsky was on his own.

"I didn't lie to the SEC. I told the truth in my report."

"Then did you lie when you testified here in court that the company was bankrupt at that time and couldn't meet its payroll?"

The studio head squirmed in his chair. "No, I didn't lie here either."

Harry smiled. "Now, Mr. Slutsky, we need a clear record on this, so there's no misunderstanding in the court's mind. You filed a report with the SEC in which you said that, as of the end of last year, just before Mr. Fernbach was fired, the financial situation at Consolidated was rosy and that the company had plenty of money to meet its obligations and to fulfill its plans. You told us that report was true, isn't that correct?"

"Yes, and it *was* true."

"So, when you told the court that, in this same time period, the company was bankrupt and couldn't meet its payroll, that really *wasn't* true, was it?"

Slutsky looked down at his hands as if he'd find the answer there. He said nothing for almost a full minute.

"Can you answer the question?" said Harry, glaring at the witness.

In a small, choked voice, Slutsky finally responded. "Okay, that wasn't completely true."

Harry knew he'd made the point. Further questioning about it was unnecessary and might even be risky. It was a mistake inexperienced lawyers often made in cross-examination. They'd get a helpful or even case-winning answer from a hostile witness. Then, trying to emphasize the point, they'd ask the same question one or two more times, usually in a pompous, stentorian tone. With the repetition, the witness would finally realize the mistake he'd made and correct it, depriving the lawyer of the entire point. Harry had learned long ago that, when he got a particularly useful answer, he should quickly move on to another subject. Having gained a telling admission from this witness, he turned a page of his notes and smiled.

"Okay, Mr. Slutsky, let's move to another item. You said Mr. Fernbach allowed a director's drunkenness to cost you millions. Who was that director?"

"Terence O'Neil."

"And what are the facts upon which you base the claim that Mr. O'Neil's drunkenness cost you millions of dollars a day?"

"I had a thorough investigation done and that was the conclusion."

"Is there a written report of that investigation?"

"There is. I have it here in court." He gestured to Lisa Lerner, who produced a massive loose-leaf binder and handed it to her boss.

"That's the report?"

"Yes."

"Okay, now please show us the part that details where Terence O'Neil's drunkenness cost you millions of dollars a day."

Slutsky put the huge book in his lap and began leafing through the pages. Minutes passed in silence as he continued the process. Finally, he looked up.

"Okay, here it is."

He handed the binder to Harry, who read the page indicated and handed the book back to the witness.

"Would you read aloud where the report says Mr. O'Neil's drunkenness was costing you millions of dollars?"

"Sure. 'At five o'clock P.M. on March eighteenth, Mr. O'Neil was observed on the set with a glass of champagne in his hand.' "

Harry waited, letting the answer sink in. "That's it?" he boomed. "That's the basis of your charge that Mr. O'Neil was guilty of drunkenness that cost you millions of dollars a day?"

"Well, yes. Doesn't that say it all? I mean, there he was right on my set drinking champagne, with millions going out the window."

Harry smiled again. "And that's the entire evidence on Mr. O'Neil's drunkenness, is that correct?"

"I'm sure there's more."

"Well, what is it?"

"Everyone knows he's a drunk . . . always was."

Harry turned quickly to Judge Sandlinger. "Move to strike as hearsay and improper conclusion."

"Granted" came the immediate ruling.

Harry turned back to the witness, who was wiping his forehead with a four-hundred-dollar silk handkerchief from Bijan in Beverly hills.

"In any event, Mr. Slutsky, as a result of your thorough investigation, which filled that entire book, all there was about drunkenness costing you millions is that, one day at five o'clock, Mr. O'Neil was seen with a glass of champagne in his hand."

"I know there's more than that. It may not be in this book, but. . ."

Harry interrupted. "Move to strike as nonresponsive."

"Let him finish," bellowed Greg Morrison. Judge Sandlinger held up his hand to quiet both lawyers.

"The motion is denied. You may complete your answer, Mr. Slutsky."

"Well, that's all that the investigator put in the book. But I'm sure there was a lot more."

Harry pointed his finger at the witness. "I'm asking for what you personally know, aside from what's in your report. Is there any other fact you can personally testify to other than that your report says Mr. O'Neil had a glass of champagne in his hand one day at five o'clock?"

There was a long pause. Finally, grudgingly, Slutsky answered. "No, but other people will. You can bet on it."

"You don't even know whether he *drank* that glass of champagne, do you, Mr. Slutsky?"

The studio head looked at the loose-leaf report in his lap. "Well, it's obvious he drank it."

"It doesn't say in the report that he drank it, does it?"

Slutsky studied the page again, as if hoping the single entry of drinking would magically expand. Finally, he answered.

"No, it doesn't."

"And it doesn't even say that shooting was still going on as opposed to holding a drink after the day's work was over, does it?"

"No, it doesn't."

"Thank you."

At that point, Judge Sandlinger ordered the morning recess. In the men's room, Aaron congratulated Harry enthusiastically.

"You destroyed him, Harry, just destroyed him. As far as I can see, the case is over."

Part of Harry's job was to avoid false optimism when things went well, just as it was to avoid profound depression when things went badly. Either attitude could be disastrous.

"Look, Aaron," he said, "we scored some points, sure, but the game is hardly over. Believe me, they've got something; and they're gonna hit us with it and hurt us before this thing is over."

As they filed back into the hearing room, Harry wondered just what it was they had and just how badly they'd be hurt by it. The judge and the lawyers took their places. Yank Slutsky moved ponderously back to the witness stand, and Harry resumed his cross-examination.

"All right, Mr. Slutsky, what facts indicate that Mr. Fernbach promised Annie Robinson a contract if she'd sleep with him?"

"She told me that's what he did."

Harry turned to Judge Sandlinger. "Hearsay, Your Honor. Move to strike."

As Morrison was about to reply, the judge waved him off. "Overruled. Please proceed."

Harry couldn't fathom the judge's reasoning. The answer was plainly hearsay. But sometimes wrong rulings occurred. There was nothing he could do but move on. He looked down at his notes.

"Are there any other facts that support your claim that Mr. Fernbach promised Ms. Robinson a contract in exchange for sex?"

"No, that's it. But she would certainly know and she told me he did it."

"Mr. Slutsky, you actually wanted to bring Annie Robinson to Consolidated . . . isn't that so?"

"Absolutely not. She was an addict, a no-talent, and a low-life. She was not the image I wanted at my studio."

This was an area that would be difficult. He'd try a different tack. Maybe the old "paper caper" would work. Harry knew that Slutsky loved to talk off the record to the press, loved to feed them self-serving items about himself and destructive gossip about his enemies. He reached into his file and pulled out a typed memo, appearing to scan it carefully while Slutsky waited.

Still holding the memo in his hand, Harry looked up at the witness.

"Mr. Slutsky, on October twenty-second of last year, you had a conversation with Mike Simpson of the L.A. *Times*. Isn't that correct?"

Harry waved the memo dramatically. It was only a report prepared by Milo Putnam showing the annual expenses of Harry's law firm. It had nothing to do with the case. But the witness didn't know that. Convinced that Harry had a statement from the *Times* reporter, Slutsky played it safe.

"Well, that's a while ago. I might've. I'm not sure. Does he say I did?"

Harry ignored the question.

"And did you tell Mr. Simpson . . . " He paused and looked down at the memo, appearing to quote from it, "that 'you were proud to have Annie Robinson directing pictures for Consolidated,' and that 'she was one of the most talented directors in the business.' Did you tell him that?"

"Have you got his statement there? Let me see it."

"Mr. Slutsky, just answer my question if you can." Again Harry looked down at the memo. "Did you tell Mr. Simpson that 'you were proud to have Annie Robinson directing pictures for Consolidated,' and that 'she was one of the most talented directors in the business'?"

Harry could see Slutsky's mind working. He was sure that Harry's piece of paper was a statement from Simpson. He knew he had talked to Simpson frequently. He didn't remember what he told Simpson about Annie Robinson—if anything. But, if he denied it and then Simpson testified that he'd said those things, the judge would certainly think Slutsky was lying . . . again. He hesitated, then plunged.

"Yeah, I think I said something like that. But that was just P.R., you know, to boost the company."

"When you say it was 'just P.R.,' you mean it wasn't true?"

"Well, of course it wasn't true. We do that all the time. It's showmanship. It makes money for the company."

"Are you asking us to believe that, when the company has a few million dollars at stake, you're prepared to create a false impression here and there?"

"Sure. So would any good executive."

"And how many millions does your company have at stake in this lawsuit, Mr. Slutsky?"

Morrison rose, holding out his hand to stop any response. "Objection, Your Honor. That's irrelevant and argumentative!"

"Overruled. It's relevant. But you've made the point, Mr. Cain. Why don't you move on?"

"Thank you, Your Honor. I will."

"All right, Mr. Slutsky. The next ground you specified was dishonesty in Mr. Fernbach's expense account. What facts support that charge?"

"That you'll have to get from the accountants. All I know is his reports were as phony as a two-dollar bill."

"Can you specify any instance of that phoniness—even one?"

"I can't, but, believe me, the accountants can."

"Okay, your last item was disobedience. You said Mr. Fernbach refused to fire Terence O'Neil, right?"

"Right."

Harry had worked hard on how he would cross-examine Slutsky on this issue, the one claim he was sure would be made. To support a charge of insubordination, the studio had to prove that Aaron failed to carry out a firm order, not merely a request or attempt to persuade. Harry's plan was to make Slutsky testify that what he said to Aaron was not an order at all, but only an attempt to persuade him to go along with Slutsky's wishes. He approached the subject obliquely, seeking to make the witness think Harry wanted just the opposite of what he was really after.

"Mr. Slutsky, weren't you generally rude and arbitrary in your dealings with Mr. Fernbach?"

"Objection. His general attitude is irrelevant," intoned Morrison. "Sustained."

Harry had anticipated the objection and the ruling. But Slutsky had heard the question. He'd believe Harry was trying to show that he was rude and arbitrary. At the risk of antagonizing the judge, Harry decided to make it seem even clearer.

"Well, didn't you generally speak to Mr. Fernbach in a curt and peremptory manner?"

"Same objection, Your Honor."

"Sustained." The judge peered over at Harry. "You know better, Mr. Cain. Move along."

"I'm sorry, Your Honor." Harry turned back to Slutsky.

"Well, sir, on the occasion when you spoke to Mr. Fernbach about firing Mr. O'Neil, did you speak harshly or peremptorily?"

Slutsky looked at Greg Morrison, expecting another objection. None came. He paused momentarily, then responded. "I did not."

"Did you peremptorily demand that Mr. Fernbach do your bidding or did you use reason and logic, seeking to persuade him?"

"I used reason and logic. I tried to persuade him. I always did."

"Did you say firing O'Neil made sense and that was what he should do or did you simply make a peremptory demand that the man be fired?"

Morrison was on his feet. "I object, Your Honor, it's just a trick . . . "

Down came the gavel. "Stop, Mr. Morrison! Not in the presence of the witness. Not now. If you have an objection, we'll step outside and discuss it."

Judge Sandlinger was as aware as Morrison and Harry that Morrison's objection was designed to alert Slutsky to the trap Harry had laid for him. That was the reason Sandlinger required the objection to be argued out of the hearing of the witness.

Outside the hearing room, Morrison vehemently protested Harry's tactics. He argued that Harry was tricking the witness, that he'd used improper and disallowed questions to make the witness afraid of appearing to have been "rude" or "peremptory," that Harry was now misleading the witness into giving answers intended to avoid that appearance, and that those answers were creating the erroneous impression that what the witness said to Aaron Fernbach was not an order. Once again, when Harry started to reply, the judge motioned him to remain silent.

"Mr. Morrison, the last two questions, about what was actually said to the plaintiff on the occasion in issue, are proper cross-examination. All the witness has to do is tell the truth. If he tries to guess what Mr. Cain is driving at and twists the truth to avoid that perceived danger, he has only himself to blame. The objection is overruled."

The judge led the two lawyers back into the courtroom and the court reporter reread the question. Slutsky had used the brief interval to think again about the questions Harry had asked. He was absolutely sure what Harry was after. He would not be made to look harsh or "peremptory," whatever that meant. He smiled confidently as he responded.

"I was not at all harsh or peremptory in what I said, counselor. I explained very patiently why O'Neil should be fired, and I told Mr. Fernbach that's what I believed should be done. I said, very politely, that I hoped he agreed."

Harry saw the anger in Greg Morrison's face. The answer made Slutsky's statement to Aaron a suggestion, not an order. Legally, it could not serve as a valid basis for discharge. It was time to move to another point, before Slutsky realized what had happened.

"Now the last item you listed was that you ordered Mr. Fernbach not to make a settlement giving Joe Miletti final cut on *The Last Battle* and that Fernbach did it anyway, right?"

"Right."

"Didn't you expressly approve the making of the settlement with Mr. Miletti?"

"Absolutely not."

"Well, didn't you want that film back very badly?"

"I would've gotten it back anyway. We would have found the film and put both of you in jail. You don't compromise with thieves." Judge Sandlinger looked up, puzzled.

Harry turned to the judge. "Move to strike all that as nonresponsive."

"It will go out. Answer the question, Mr. Slutsky. Then, you may explain if you wish."

Harry's gaze returned to the witness. "Well, didn't you want the film back very badly?"

"Sure. But I could've gotten it without making a deal with gangsters."

"I see. You were not willing to give Mr. Miletti final cut if the film came back?"

"Absolutely not."

"Were you in the New York office of Consolidated Studios with Mr. Fernbach when he agreed to that deal?"

"I was in the building, but I didn't know anything about the deal until after he'd done it. Then I blew up. He just ignored my order. That was pretty much the last straw."

"Thank you, Mr. Slutsky, no more questions." Harry moved back to his chair. It was obvious to him that Morrison desperately wanted the noon recess in which to prepare Slutsky for redirect examination. But that was almost an hour away. He couldn't stall that long without running out of relevant questions and making his stalling obvious.

Morrison plunged ahead, trying to rehabilitate Slutsky as best he could without adequate preparation. But Harry's objections prevented him from asking leading questions, and, without having had the chance to review with Slutsky the questions and answers that might repair the damage Harry had done, there was little Morrison could do. If he wasn't careful, he could make matters worse. He played it conservatively, avoiding the most troublesome points, boring Harry and the judge, but doing what he could. At a quarter to twelve he made a game plea for an early lunch break, but Judge Sandlinger would have none of it. He threw Morrison's own argument back at him.

"Mr. Morrison, you've told us Mr. Slutsky's a very busy man, with a studio to run and a full schedule to meet. We'll take our lunch break when his redirect examination is completed and not sooner."

Harry had to look down and pretend to read a memo in order to conceal his grin.

As he always did in an important case, Harry had arranged for a lunchtime hideaway near the courtroom. This time he had borrowed a friend's townhouse in Century City, a short two blocks from the hearing room. This afforded a place to eat quietly and even shower and lie down during the noon break, and to work in privacy with the witnesses who would testify in the afternoon sessions. Harry's office staff arranged for catered lunches to be delivered to the townhouse every day at noon, and Harry's Guatemalan houseman, Armando, came each day to serve.

This particular lunch hour was devoted to a review of Slutsky's testimony and the preparation of Aaron Fernbach for his reappearance on the stand to rebut Slutsky's claims. Harry refused Armando's offer of wine and turned back to Aaron, jabbing the air with his fork to emphasize the point he was making.

"Damn it, Aaron, they've got something involving your expense account. I sense it. I *know* it. You've got to think. Search your brain. You've got to help me."

"I would if I could, Harry. But there's nothing. It's clean as a hound's tooth. I told you. I swear on my kids' lives . . . and believe me, I love my kids."

"Okay, Aaron, then what's this shit about Annie Robinson?"

"That's all it is . . . just shit. I never touched her, never made a pass at her, and never even suggested that sex would help her get the job. Good God, have you seen her lately? You couldn't pay me to fuck her."

Harry grinned. "That's not exactly the line I'd take in court, Aaron. 'It never happened' will suffice. Can we get Annie to come in and testify on Monday?"

"Absolutely. Annie's got her faults, but she's loyal and honest. You want me to call her right now?"

"Sure."

Aaron dialed Annie Robinson's office and her home. She was at neither place, but he finally located her having lunch at Le Dome. Harry could hear only one side of the conversation.

"Annie dear, I'm sorry to interrupt your lunch, but I really need your help . . .

"Yeah, that's right. In the trial. They're claiming I said you could have the job if you'd fuck me and that they didn't want me to hire you, but I gave you the contract in exchange for sex.

"Well, of course it's bullshit, sweetie. It's an insult to you. But I've got to prove it. Will you come down and testify on Monday? . . . You will? That's great."

Harry quickly scribbled a note and handed it to Aaron.

"Listen, Annie, it'd be great if you could meet with Harry Cain on Sunday night. You know, to go over what he'll ask you. That's great, kid, just great." Aaron read Harry's address over the phone and arranged for a meeting at eight o'clock Sunday evening.

Harry was feeling more and more confident, but there was still much to worry about and prepare for.

"Now what about O'Neil?" he said to Aaron, spearing a piece of grilled chicken. "I'd like to meet him this weekend and have him testify after Annie Robinson. He may refuse, though. I just won a case against him . . . for Fox. We got a big judgment, and I think he's very bitter about it. I doubt he'll even speak to me."

"Well, let's try. Hand me the phone again." Aaron reached Terence O'Neil at his Malibu home. At first the veteran director wanted nothing to do with Harry, but Aaron, an old friend, finally persuaded him to meet on Sunday morning.

Satisfied with what they'd accomplished during the midday break, Harry and Aaron finished their meal and walked back to the hearing room. How free and innocent the lunchtime crowd seemed, the young secretaries and clerks talking, laughing, and enjoying the sun of the plazas and sidewalks of Century City, completely uninterested in the two serious men hurrying past in somber gray suits. For an instant, Harry wondered if he'd ever been like that, or if, all his life, he'd been striving for something—getting grades, winning cases, always something. Then, just as quickly, his thoughts returned to the problems of Aaron Fernbach and of winning one more time.

When the hearing resumed, Harry put Aaron back on the stand. Slowly and carefully he led him through a specific denial of each of the charges made by Yank Slutsky in the morning session. First, Aaron described the healthy state of the company's finances at the time he was fired, and denied that bankruptcy was even a remote possibility or that there had ever been the slightest danger of not meeting a payroll.

Then they turned to the subject of Terence O'Neil. Aaron insisted that he had not disobeyed any order. Slutsky's denial on cross-examination that he had ever said anything "peremptory" with respect to O'Neil made it easy. As Harry had drummed into Aaron in their hours of preparation, he testified that he did not understand Slutsky's statement about Terence O'Neil to be anything but an attempt to persuade him that O'Neil should go and certainly not an "order" to fire the man. Besides, he said, he had never refused to fire O'Neil, but had simply stated his own view: that it would be a tragic mistake.

Aaron also denied that O'Neil was ever drunk during the shooting of the picture or that the director was even over budget, except for added expenditures that Yank Slutsky had personally approved.

As to the Miletti settlement, Aaron described how Slutsky had listened in on the conversation in New York and had personally approved the settlement by sending Aaron a message on his digital receiver.

On the subject of Annie Robinson, he emphatically denied everything Slutsky had said. He had never suggested sex or had sex with her, and certainly never as the price of giving her a directing assignment. He had recommended her for a picture strictly on merit.

Finally, they came to the subject of the expense account. Here there was little Harry could do beyond having Aaron deny generally that he had ever cheated on his expenses in any way whatsoever. "No more questions," he said, turning to Greg Morrison with a smile, radiating confidence he did not entirely feel. The expense account issue scared him. There was something wrong. There had to be.

Morrison rose and began a lengthy cross-examination of Aaron, covering each of the issues on which he had testified. Morrison established that the budget for *Carnage* had been $25 million, but that the picture had actually cost over $27 million, so that it was, in fact, over budget. He got Aaron to admit that he could not really testify that Terence O'Neil had never been drunk on the job, because Aaron had not been there all the time. In fact, Aaron had been on business in Europe for at least three weeks during principal photography. Next, Morrison tried to shake Aaron's testimony about Annie Robinson. Here, he failed. Aaron remained adamant that there had not even been a hint of sex in their conversations or relationship. Frustrated, Morrison tried a different tactic.

"Did you ever have an erection when Ms. Robinson was in the room?"

"I don't remember, but I certainly doubt it."

"But you may have?"

"Your Honor," Harry bellowed, rising from his chair. "That's not just irrelevant, it's a childish waste of everyone's time."

Judge Sandlinger looked over at Morrison. "I agree. If your speech was an objection, Mr. Cain, it's sustained. Move on to something else, Mr. Morrison."

Morrison moved on to the issue of disobedience. But, here again, he had no success in shaking Aaron's testimony that there had never been a direct order to fire Terence O'Neil, only a statement of Yank Slutsky's strongly held point of view.

"Well, you know that Mr. Slutsky wanted the man gone, isn't that true?"

Aaron paused as if considering the question. It was one Harry had asked him repeatedly in preparation, but, as Harry had cautioned, he didn't want to appear preprogrammed.

"Yes, I knew that was what he wanted. He tried to convince me that's what we should do."

"Move to strike the last remark as nonresponsive."

"Denied. It's a proper explanation of the answer."

"Well, Mr. Fernbach, you knew Mr. Slutsky wanted O'Neil fired, and you knew Mr. Slutsky was your superior in the company . . . right?"

"Right."

"And knowing that, you still would not fire him, isn't that correct?"

"No, sir. I *did* not fire him. I was never ordered to fire him. If I had been, I would have done it . . . reluctantly, I admit, but I would have done it."

Morrison looked down at his notes, ready to try another subject.

"Now, before you met with Mr. Cain and Mr. Miletti about *The Last Battle,* you had no idea what they would propose. Correct?"

"Correct."

"So Mr. Slutsky didn't approve the Miletti settlement before the meeting, did he?"

"No."

"And he wasn't in the room during the meeting, was he?"

"No."

"So he couldn't approve the deal during the meeting, could he?"

"Yes, he could. He did. He sent a message on the digital receiver."

"So you say; but you don't really know who sent the message . . . if there really was a message . . . do you?"

"I do. Mr. Slutsky and I discussed beforehand that he would send me a message as to what I should do, and that's just what he did."

"But you don't know that *he* sent the message . . . do you?"

"If you mean did I see him send it? No, I didn't. But he told me he'd send it, and after Mr. Cain and Mr. Miletti left, we discussed that he had sent it."

Still frustrated and having gained little ground by his cross-examination, Morrison turned to his assistant, who handed him a fat manila envelope. He opened it, and pulled out a large bundle of papers stapled to various slips and stubs. He handed the bundle first to Harry and, after Harry had skimmed through it, to Aaron Fernbach.

"Is that your expense report for the first quarter of the year, Mr. Fernbach?"

Aaron leafed quickly through the pages. "Yes, it appears to be."

"Now, do you often eat at Duke's Coffee Shop on Ventura Boulevard?"

Aaron looked puzzled. "No, I think I've driven past it, but I've never been there."

Harry felt his stomach tighten. Here it is—the moment he'd feared. Somehow he'd known from the start it had to come.

"Tell me about the Hi-Hat Tavern on Vanowen Boulevard."

"Never heard of it."

"Well now, Mr. Fernbach, look at your expense report for February eighteenth. Doesn't it show you claimed to have had lunch on that day with Jeff Berg?" Morrison directed Aaron to a specific entry.

"Yes, it does."

"And it claims reimbursement for $123.50, isn't that right?"

"Yes."

"Now turn to the stubs, the receipts stapled to the page. See the one for February eighteenth?" He directed Aaron to a small cardboard tab stapled to the expense account. "Please read us the name of the restaurant, the date, and the amount, identifying for us which entries are printed and which are handwritten."

Aaron looked at the tab and shook his head. He appeared stunned. He flipped back to the expense account and then back again to the cardboard stub. "This is wrong. It's an error . . . I can't explain it, but it's just wrong. How this . . . "

"Just read it to us, Mr. Fernbach, so we all know what's wrong."

In a choked voice, his face paler than Harry had ever seen it, Aaron read the slip. "The printing says 'Duke's Coffee Shop.' Then written in is the figure '123.50' and the date 'February eighteenth' . . . but . . . . "

"You didn't have lunch with Jeff Berg at Duke's Coffee Shop, did you?"

"No . . . and I can't . . . "

"That receipt . . . the one you submitted to Consolidated for reimbursement, it's a phony, isn't it?"

"Well, it's not correct, but I don't know how it got there. I never saw it before."

"Of course." Morrison smiled sarcastically. He handed the bundle of papers back to Aaron, taking a typed memo from his assistant. "Now I'm going to read a list of reimbursement claims from your own expense report for late February and early March, together with the stubs you've attached and I want you to tell me if any of them reflect the truth . . . February twenty-first. Jeffrey Katzenberg, breakfast, $43.70, Duke's Coffee Shop. Is that a true entry?"

Aaron appeared to be at the end of his rope. His jaws were clenched and his forehead beaded with sweat. He seemed on the verge of tears.

"No," he responded in a voice barely audible.

"Speak up, Mr. Fernbach. It's not a true entry, is it?"

"No" came the somewhat louder response.

"And how about lunch on February twenty-third with Joel Silver and on February twenty-fifth with Terry Semel, both at the Hi-Hat Tavern. Is either the truth?"

Aaron looked down at his hands as he spoke. "No, they're not, but I don't know how those entries could be there."

"Well, your expense report shows that you were at the Hi-Hat for breakfast the next day, February twenty-sixth, with Ray Stark and you spent $38.40. Is that one true?"

"No."

"But the studio reimbursed you for the money you claimed, isn't that correct."

"I assume so."

"Now, while we're on the subject of February twenty-sixth, Mr. Fernbach, take a look at your expense report for that date."

Aaron located the correct entry. Morrison checked his own typed memo and then looked back at Aaron.

"Do you see the entry we just referred to, the one that says you had breakfast on February twenty-sixth with Ray Stark at the Hi-Hat Tavern?"

"Yes, I see it."

"Well, look at the entry just above it, it's for the same day. Doesn't that say you had breakfast on the twenty-sixth with David Begelman at Duke's Coffee Shop?"

Harry wanted to slide under the table. Instead, he preserved a look of unruffled calm, trying his best to convey the idea that all this would soon be explained. Aaron seemed beyond caring.

"Yes," he responded woodenly. "That's what it says."

Morrison stepped closer to Aaron and took the expense account from his hands, peering down at him as if he were some sort of repugnant insect.

"So you ate breakfast twice on that day, Mr. Fernbach, once with Mr. Stark at the Hi-Hat Tavern and once with Mr. Begelman at Duke's. Is that your testimony?"

Aaron paused at length and sighed deeply. Then he answered "No, I didn't eat in those two restaurants, but I may have had two breakfast meetings. I sometimes do."

"Of course you do," snapped Morrison sarcastically. "Don't we all." He turned to the judge. "No more questions, Your Honor."

Harry wanted to grab Fernbach by the neck and shake him. Son of a bitch swears on his kids' lives. Jesus! But he sat quietly, looking as calm and confident as he could while deciding on his tactics. It was only 3:30. If he started Aaron's redirect examination now, there would be no way for him to stall for an hour with questions about subjects other than the expense report. Questioning Aaron about that right now, without any idea what he'd say, could be highly dangerous. It could make matters much worse, could even lose the case . . . if it wasn't lost already. Even if they had another brief recess and huddled for a fast five minutes in the men's room, it would be too risky. And the judge would never let him postpone Aaron's redirect examination.

But if there *was* no redirect examination. He considered the possibilities. It would be unfortunate to leave the judge with this terrible impression over the weekend, but it was safer than plunging blindly into the expense account mess that afternoon. There were more witnesses to come and he'd have the weekend in which to find a solution. He could always put Aaron back on the stand as a rebuttal witness if he had to. Harry decided. He rose and addressed Judge Sandlinger with a confident smile.

"As tempting as it is to clear up the matter of the expense report right now, Your Honor, I'm going to reserve that for later. No redirect at this time. And, since it's almost three-thirty and I've scheduled our next witness for Monday morning, I suggest we adjourn until then."

Judge Sandlinger looked puzzled at the absence of redirect examination, but he was too experienced to remark on it. "Very well," he said, "we stand adjourned until nine A.M. Monday."

As they left the hearing room, Harry heard Lisa Lerner congratulating Greg Morrison. "You destroyed him, Greg. Absolutely destroyed him. This one's all over but the shouting."

It occurred to Harry to interrupt with some inanity like "It's not over till it's over" or "it's not over till the fat lady sings." But he didn't really believe it. The fat lady may already have sung. He passed them in silence.

Since the elevator was filled with young lawyers from Greg Morrison's firm, Harry and Aaron rode in silence. Only when they were in the car, leaving the garage, did Harry speak; and, as he spoke, he could feel his anger rising.

"All right now, what the fuck was that about? Why didn't you tell me about the phony receipts?"

"I didn't know, Harry. I swear it. I never ate in those restaurants. But I did eat with Jeff and David and Joel around that time; and, goddamn it, I do have two breakfast meetings every once in a while. I'll have fruit and coffee at one and eggs at the next. It's two breakfasts. It really is. Sometimes, it's the only time I can get to see someone before I start my round of daily meetings."

"Okay, I buy that. Ovitz and Katzenberg do the same thing. But the judge may not buy it, and how do you explain the phony receipts? *That's* what's killing us."

"I can't explain them, Harry, I can only tell you I didn't prepare them. I've never seen them before. I haven't got the foggiest notion how they happened."

"Who prepared your expense report?"

"My secretary, Mona Olinsky."

"Does she still work at Consolidated?"

"No. She was laid off the day I was fired."

"Call her on the car phone. We'll go see her right now."

"We can't. She's in San Francisco."

"Shit!" Harry paused, thinking. Turning quickly, he pulled into the driveway of the Century Plaza Hotel.

"What are you doing?"

"I'm dropping you at the cab stand. Go on home."

"Where are you going?"

"San Francisco. Call my office and leave Mona Olinsky's number. I'll see you Sunday at O'Neil's."

On Sunday morning, Harry drove out the coast highway toward Terence O'Neil's place on Carbon Beach. The Malibu hills were bathed in a soft golden light. The sky was a clear, cerulean blue, and a mild offshore breeze carried the clean smell of the sea. Harry made a U-turn and pulled the silver Bentley in front of O'Neil's two-story neoclassical home. He climbed the wide marble steps and paused between the Doric columns. The place seemed more like a court-house than a beach house. Harry smiled. "De gustibus non est dis-putandum" should have been carved over the portico.

This won't be easy, Harry thought. O'Neil had a nasty temper, and he had reason to be sore. His litigation with Fox had been an angry personal dispute, and O'Neil had lost—badly. He'd been hit with a large money judgment and, to make matters worse, he'd been harshly censured in the court's written opinion. The judge had even adopted the very words Harry had used in closing argument to cas-tigate the director. All things considered, Harry expected O'Neil to be hostile, if not enraged.

The butler opened the massive double doors and led Harry to a sitting room overlooking the sea. Aaron Fernbach was already there, in a tennis sweater and white shorts, drinking coffee with his host. O'Neil, a tall, craggy-faced Irishman, wore a shirt and pants of faded denim and alligator cowboy boots that made him seem even taller than he was. He stood for a moment in silence, his bright green eyes boring into Harry's. Then he moved across the room, covering the distance between them in large, rapid strides. For a moment Harry thought the man intended to start a fight. But O'Neil stopped and threw his arms around Harry, enveloping him in a powerful hug. Just as suddenly, he stepped back, holding Harry at arm's length.

"You sheeny wizard! You're absolutely the best fucking lawyer in the world. You've got a glorious mind and balls of steel. From now on, you're on my side. Right?" He stuck out a big bony hand for

Harry to shake. Relieved, and charmed by the blarney, Harry shook his hand.

"Right." Harry grinned. "Next time you try to do a studio out of a million bucks, a wizard might be advisable, sheeny or otherwise."

"Hey, I told you, babe, it's you from now on. Now let's talk about our friends at Consolidated."

"Will you testify on Monday?"

"You couldn't stop me. I didn't like you much, but I fuckin' hate that scumbag Slutsky."

They spent the next hour reviewing Yank Slutsky's claims and preparing O'Neil for his testimony. Then, with a warm handshake, Harry left and headed for David Begelman's home in Beverly Hills. The veteran producer had been a studio head himself, and he could provide testimony that would support Aaron's position.

Harry hated being away from Nancy this long; but the case was hanging in the balance. Hard work could tip the scales his way. Begelman's testimony would be brief and uncomplicated, but Harry would put *no* witness on the stand—no matter how briefly—without thorough preparation.

Some lawyers considered Harry lucky. He supposed that he was. But Harry felt that luck played a very small part in determining his success. Fortune seemed to smile on the lawyers who were smart and diligent, the guys working nights and weekends, while their slower, lazier colleagues complained about the bad luck they encountered in case after case. Sure, Harry thought, you could draw a good judge or a bad one. But, for the most part, you didn't find your luck, you made it.

Harry liked the way Joe Story put it. Story, a Harvard law professor and former Supreme Court justice, had called the law "a jealous mistress" that "requires constant and careful courtship." It certainly was a jealous mistress, Harry thought, but, these days, it was the only mistress he had. At least *that* was an improvement.

The interview with David Begelman took less than an hour, and Harry was able to spend the rest of the day with Nancy. He made them a late lunch, a chopped salad of arugula, radicchio, chicken and basil, with sautéed piñon nuts and thinly sliced parmigiano. Harry had been cooking more often since Nancy's illness; he'd always enjoyed it, and excelled at it. Now it made him feel he was doing something special for her, as if each meal were a unique personal offering.

They ate on the terrace, accompanied by Vivaldi's *Four Seasons* and surrounded by overgrown ficus, bold red bougainvillea and wild rosemary. They laughed and relaxed, enjoying the music, the meal and a chilled Pinot Grigio. After lunch, they made their way upstairs, flushed with the wine, touching and kissing playfully. Still giggling, they removed each other's clothing. Soon, the giggles turned to sighs and the sighs to moans, as they made slow and voluptuous love in their sun-drenched bedroom.

They spent the rest of the afternoon reading, lying side by side in the huge bed they'd shared for so many years. Nancy had discovered John Fante, and was enjoying *Wait Until Spring, Bandini*. Harry was immersed in Horace Walpole's *Historic Doubts on Richard III*, silently testing and questioning each of Walpole's elegantly phrased arguments in favor of the much-maligned last Plantagenet. He was far more inclined to accept Walpole on this subject than Shakespeare, who, after all, wrote what a Tudor queen wanted to hear.

Every few minutes Harry glanced over to assure himself that Nancy was all right—he'd done that since she was first diagnosed. But his quick looks were less frequent now. She was breathing regularly, and her color was good. She was fighting the disease; and, with the help of the miracle treatment, she was winning.

At eight o'clock that night, Harry drove down to his office to meet his key witness for the next morning. One of the first female directors, Annie Robinson had enjoyed early success, winning an Academy Award for her first film. Then, over a period of two years, she'd grown more and more dependent on massive quantities of cocaine. She'd become unpredictable, then irresponsible, and, finally, unemployable. One of her few defenders had been Aaron Fernbach. First, he'd wheedled, cajoled, and pressured her into a rehabilitation program. Then, when no one else would even consider letting her direct a film, he'd given her a job. His announcement to the press said it all, "I prize talent. It's very hard to find. Annie Robinson has it."

However, the lady always had a reputation for being late or not showing up at all; and, by 8:30, Harry was both concerned and irritable. He tried to concentrate on his trial notes, already starting to prepare an outline for his closing argument. Finally, at 8:45, the doorbell chimed. Harry walked to the reception room and opened the door. It was Annie Robinson. Her appearance was startling. Two years earlier, when Harry had last seen her, she'd been a slim, nervous girl with long dark hair. Now her hair was a harshly bleached platinum, and she'd chopped it unevenly in a punk crew cut. Her face was square and jowly. A faint mustache was visible on her upper lip. She wore a black leather motorcycle jacket and matching leather miniskirt. Her legs were heavy. As she followed Harry down the hall to his office, she smoked an unfiltered Camel in short, staccato puffs, like Bette Davis in a 1930s film. When Harry offered her a chair, she declined.

"I'm not gonna be here that long."

"Oh? I hope you don't have an appointment. We've got a lot of work to do. You'll be on the stand first thing tomorrow morning."

"That's just it. I'm not gonna do it. I'm not gonna testify."

"You've got to be kidding. Your testimony's critical to Aaron's case. He's your friend, the only one who stood by you. Now he needs your help."

"Aaron's a big boy. He can look out for himself. Just like I do. Listen, the man's out of a job. He's history. It's Yank Slutsky who decides if and when I work now; and if you think I'm gonna piss him off to help Aaron Fernbach, you're dreaming."

"That's about the most amoral speech I've ever heard. You always talked about the need for a clear sense of right and wrong. Where did yours go?"

"Don't give me that right-and-wrong crap, you bleeding hypocrite. You've been fucking around on Nancy for years. Nothing could be more amoral than that."

Harry recoiled mentally from the attack. The lady was still quick . . . and she was right . . . but . . .

"I can subpoena you, you know."

"Come on, you're not that dumb. You subpoena me, and I'll drive a fucking stake right into Mr. Fernbach's heart."

"You're talking perjury. You *know* Slutsky's lying. If you testify he isn't, I'll do everything I can to get you prosecuted and convicted and to see that you do time."

"Oh, horse shit! You'll never subpoena me and risk blowing your precious case. So fuck off. I'm leaving. You're lucky I showed up at all."

She turned and abruptly left the room. A moment later, Harry heard the front door slam. He poured himself a double Scotch and stood looking at the city lights. So the lady thinks I won't subpoena her, eh? That I won't put her on the stand? That I won't risk "my precious case"? How great it would be to show her just how wrong she was. She was irritating, amoral, and repulsive. She deserved the kind of life that any fool could see was in store for her. He sighed. The problem was she was right.

On Monday morning, Harry sat gazing out of the windows of the 21st-floor hearing room, awaiting the other participants in the trial. It was foggy, and Harry could barely see the outlines of the neighboring high-rise buildings through the thick morning fog. At 8:20 Judge Sandlinger arrived, and quickly spread out his pads and pens ready for the day's testimony. Next came the court reporter, shrugging off her coat and unpacking her stenotype machine. Just before 8:30, Greg Morrison filed in with Lisa Lerner and two associates. As they took their seats, the judge called the proceedings to order.

Harry stood and addressed the court. "Your Honor, if I may have less than five minutes, our next witness is waiting in the coffee shop downstairs."

"May we know who this witness is?" Greg Morrison asked, still unpacking his briefcase.

"Sure, it's Mona Olinsky."

"Your Honor," snapped Morrison, rising from his chair, "we've had no notice of this witness. She's a former employee of Consolidated Studios. In fact, she's still receiving her separation pay and other benefits from the studio. There's a serious question as to whether it was ethical for Mr. Cain even to contact her; and, certainly, we should be entitled to confer with her before she testifies. I request a brief recess for that purpose."

Judge Sandlinger turned to Harry. "Mr. Cain?"

"Judge, neither side has given the other any notice identifying their witnesses. That's the nature of these expedited proceedings. Ms. Olinsky is no longer an employee of Consolidated and, under the *Boboli* case, I was perfectly entitled to speak with her once she left their employ.

"As to Mr. Morrison's request for a delay to confer with the witness, he's had plenty of opportunity to do that, both before and after she was laid off. She was obviously a potential witness; and, if he elected not to interview her, it's inappropriate to hold up the trial for that purpose now.

"Besides, the practical result of such a conference would be to put express or implied pressure on the witness, since she remains dependent upon Consolidated Studios for her payments. I had no duty even to tell them who our next witness would be. I did it as a matter of courtesy. That courtesy should not be turned to my client's disadvantage and used as an opportunity to harass the witness."

"Very well," the judge intoned. "Mr. Cain, go down and get your witness. We'll hear her testimony as soon as she arrives. Mr. Morrison, you can bring out any matter you like on cross-examination. It's characteristic of this kind of proceeding that there is no discovery and no advance notice of who is going to testify. I see no reason why this particular witness should be an exception."

"Well, Your Honor . . ." Morrison began, but the judge interrupted.

"No, Mr. Morrison, I've ruled. Mr. Cain, you have five minutes, so get going."

Just short of that deadline, Harry returned to the courtroom accompanied by a tall young woman with lank, reddish hair, a broad Slavic face, and a shy demeanor. This was Mona Olinsky, and Harry had spent the weekend worrying about the possibility that Morrison, Lerner, or even Slutsky would get to her before she would testify, that they would pressure her into changing or at least "forgetting" her story. This was why he had concealed her in the coffee shop until the very moment she was to testify.

Hesitantly, she took the stand. When the judge administered the oath she nervously replied "I do" in a voice that was barely audible. Before asking anything, Harry stood silently, trying to calm her with a patient smile. She seemed terrified.

"Did you ever testify before, Ms. Olinsky?"

"No."

He paused and smiled again.

"And you're scared, right?"

The question seemed to relax her a bit. She smiled bravely.

"I sure am," she replied.

Harry thought the judge would like her candor . . . and her smile . . . and that, feeling more relaxed, she would testify more convincingly. That was why he had asked the question. Having accomplished that goal, he went into the substance of her testimony.

"Ms. Olinsky, is it correct that you were Aaron Fernbach's secretary at Consolidated Studios?"

"Yes."

"And did you prepare Mr. Fernbach's expense reports?"

"Yes, I did."

"Was there any policy at Consolidated with regard to submitting receipts in order to claim reimbursement for meals?"

"Yes, we were required to submit either a credit-card receipt or an actual receipt from the restaurant for every meal that was claimed."

"Now, in the case of Mr. Fernbach, were most of his meal claims supported by credit-card receipts or by restaurant stubs?"

"Almost all were supported by credit-card receipts."

"Do you know why some were supported just by restaurant stubs?"

"Yes. In late February, Mr. Fernbach lost his wallet. I immediately stopped all his credit cards, and, in the period before they sent him new ones, he used cash. In that period, we had to send in restaurant receipts for the meals he claimed."

"Now, in that period, did Mr. Fernbach give you restaurant receipts?"

"Objection. Leading," snapped Morrison.

"I'll rephrase it," Harry responded quickly, not wanting the witness upset by lawyers' wrangling.

"What was the procedure you used in late February when Mr. Fernbach used cash for a business meal?"

The former secretary paused, her nervousness seemed to return. Harry saw this and spoke to her in a soothing tone.

"It's okay, Ms. Olinsky, you can tell us."

Morrison jumped to his feet. "Your Honor, I object to that."

Judge Sandlinger responded just as quickly, "Sustained. Let's hear the testimony, Mr. Cain."

Harry repeated the question.

"Well, Mr. Fernbach would give me a note telling me who he had the meal with and the amount he spent. Then I would enter that on the expense report."

"And did you attach Mr. Fernbach's notes to the report?"

"No, we were required to provide receipt stubs from the restaurant. I just threw Mr. Fernbach's notes away."

"Now, Ms. Olinsky, please look at Exhibit twelve there before you, which appears to be the expense report you prepared."

The witness looked briefly at the sheets of paper before her and the stubs that were attached to them.

"Is that an expense report you prepared for Mr. Fernbach?"

"Yes."

"And where did you get the restaurant stubs stapled to the report?"

This time there was less hesitation. "I got those from restaurants where I usually ate."

"Why?"

"Well, Mr. Fernbach just never remembered to get receipts when he paid cash during that period. He'd note down the amount of the check and who he took to breakfast or lunch, but he'd forget to tear off the stub from the bottom of the check."

She looked over at Fernbach, who nodded and smiled. This seemed to reassure her, and she continued.

"Anyway, we had to give them a receipt in order for Mr. Fernbach to be reimbursed. So, when I was at Duke's or at the Hi-Hat, where I ate all the time, I got a few receipt stubs and I just filled them in with the amount Mr. Fernbach had spent and attached them to the report."

"Did you discuss this procedure with Mr. Fernbach?"

"No, I wouldn't bother him with something like that."

"So far as you know, did Mr. Fernbach see the actual expense reports?"

"No. I just prepared them and turned them in to the studio."

Harry paused, letting the testimony sink in. He was delighted with the result of his hurried trip to San Francisco. He hadn't wanted to leave Nancy but it had been necessary . . . and worth the trip. These things could be attempted by telephone, but they never seemed to work out quite so well as sitting down face to face with a witness. At first, Mona Olinsky had been wary and nervous, but dinner at Postrio's on Friday night with half a bottle of Heitz Cabernet had made her relax and develop confidence in Harry, to the point that she'd offered critical information about the case he hadn't even guessed that she would have. Now he would use that additional discovery.

"Ms. Olinsky, do you remember a day in February of this year when Joe Miletti and I met with Mr. Fernbach at Consolidated's New York office?"

"Yes, I do."

"How does it happen that you were in New York at that time?"

"Well, usually Mr. Fernbach used a New York secretary on his trips there. But sometimes he'd ask me to accompany him if something important was going on. This was one of those times."

"And you were in the room during the meeting?"

"No."

"Where were you?"

"I was in the reception room."

"You were alone?"

"Most of the time."

"And the rest of the time?"

"Well, Mr. Slutsky was there and other secretaries came in and out of the reception area."

"Where was Mr. Slutsky?"

"During most of the meeting he was in a small office just off the reception area."

"Do you know what he was doing in that office?"

"He was listening to what was going on in Mr. Fernbach's office."

"How do you know that?"

"I was there when they tested the device and talked about Mr. Slutsky listening in."

"What device?"

"The listening device . . . so he could hear Mr. Fernbach's conversation with you and Mr. Miletti."

"Who talked about doing that?"

"Mr. Fernbach and Mr. Slutsky."

"What did they say?"

"Mr. Slutsky said he'd listen to the meeting and would give instructions to Mr. Fernbach on the digital message machine."

"What's that?"

"It's a machine that lets me type a brief message from my desk in the reception area. Mr. Fernbach can read it on a small screen on his desk."

"And did Mr. Slutsky give you a message to give Mr. Fernbach on that occasion?"

"Yes."

"How long had the meeting with Mr. Miletti been going on when you got this message to pass on to Mr. Fernbach?"

"Oh, I'd say fifteen or twenty minutes."

"And what did Mr. Slutsky do or say?"

"He came out of the little office off the reception area, where he'd been listening, and he said I should send a digital message to Mr. Fernbach."

Harry paused again, this time for dramatic effect.

"What was the message that Mr. Slutsky asked you to send to Mr. Fernbach over the digital screen?"

"The message was 'Okay, make deal.' "

" 'Okay, make deal'?"

"Yes."

"And did you send that message to Mr. Fernbach while he was in with Mr. Miletti and me, just as Mr. Slutsky directed you?"

"Yes, I did."

"And did Mr. Slutsky ask you to send any further message to Mr. Fernbach during that meeting?"

"No. Just 'Okay, make deal.' "

"Now, after Mr. Slutsky sent that message to Mr. Fernbach, did he speak to Mr. Fernbach again while the meeting was going on?"

"No."

"I have no further questions, Your Honor."

"Cross-examination, Mr. Morrison?"

"Yes, Your Honor."

Morrison spent much of the morning challenging Mona Olinsky on each aspect of her testimony, testing her memory for details, insinuating that she was biased and that she'd been coached, all without much effect. On the issue of the restaurant receipts, he was particularly belligerent.

"You realize, Ms. Olinsky, that you were filing false and fraudulent claims for reimbursement, isn't that so?"

"No . . . What do you mean 'fraudulent'?"

"You knew Mr. Fernbach had not, in fact, eaten at those restaurants you put on your expense report, isn't that correct?"

"Yes, that's correct. But he'd eaten at other restaurants with the people I listed, and he spent the money I listed."

"So you say. But you didn't think it was consistent with company policy to list restaurants where he did *not* eat, did you?"

"Well, they said we had to have a receipt, and I didn't think the name of the restaurant made that much difference."

"Did Mr. Fernbach tell you that?"

"Tell me what?"

"Tell you that the name of the restaurant made no difference."

"No, we never talked about any of this."

"Ms. Olinsky, are you admitting that, on your own and with no authority from Mr. Fernbach, you decided to file these false restaurant receipts?"

Mona Olinsky paused, obviously bothered by the question. Harry had warned her that the studio would imply that she had done something wrong, trying to force her to recant. He'd assured her that there was nothing civilly or criminally wrong with what she had done and that she shouldn't let them intimidate her. Now he hoped she remembered what he'd said.

"I had no conversation with Mr. Fernbach about it. That's true. He just told me who he ate with and how much he spent." She took a deep breath and continued. "I did the reports and the receipts on my own."

Looking grave, Morrison turned to the judge. "Your Honor, I want a transcript of this witness's testimony sent to the district attorney of Los Angeles County, and I intend . . ."

Harry leapt to his feet. "That's enough!" he shouted. "This is the worst instance of witness harassment I've ever seen. This lady has done nothing wrong, and counsel is trying to . . ."

Judge Sandlinger's gavel slammed to the table. "That's enough, all right! From *both* of you! Mr. Morrison, you're way out of line. There is no basis in anything I've heard to suggest any possibility of a criminal prosecution, and you know it. Mr. Cain, if you have an objection to make, make it. Don't make speeches. I will not have these colloquies in my court. Now, Mr. Morrison, if you have any further questions, ask them."

Each lawyer looked chastened. Each mumbled an apology. Each felt that what he'd done was worth it. Morrison thought that, despite what the judge had said, the witness might be frightened enough to back away from her story. Harry thought his speech, plus the judge's remarks, would be enough to stiffen Mona Olinsky's resolve. Now they would find out. Morrison's tone and demeanor became softer, more conciliatory.

"Ms. Olinsky, we all have inaccurate memories from time to time. Think back, take your time, try to remember if maybe, just maybe, you did discuss those receipts with Mr. Fernbach. Isn't that possible?"

Harry held his breath. The entire case could turn on the answer.

"No, sir, it's not possible. I never talked to him about those receipts. Whatever happens happens. But that's the truth."

Morrison turned aside with a look of disgust. "No further questions, Your Honor."

"No questions, Your Honor," Harry snapped, trying to emphasize that the cross-examination had failed to shake the witness's story.

During the lunch break, Harry met with Terence O'Neil and David Begelman at the Century City townhouse. Hating Yank Slutsky and anxious to protect his own reputation against Slutsky's charge of drunkenness, O'Neil was firmly on the Fernbach team. With David Begelman it was something else. It was clearly against his interest to oppose Yank Slutsky, but Aaron Fernbach had been a close and loyal friend, and now that he needed help, David was ready to stand up and be counted.

As Armando served them a lunch of ceviche and grilled chicken, Harry went over the testimony he expected from the two men, as well as the cross-examination approaches he anticipated that Greg Morrison would follow.

The point of Begelman's testimony was to prove he'd had breakfast with Aaron. But, while preparing him on Sunday, Harry had learned that he had spoken with both Yank Slutsky and Aaron Fernbach about the settlement between Consolidated and Joe Miletti. Now Harry planned to use that knowledge to set a trap for Morrison. He wouldn't ask Begelman anything about those conversations on direct examination. Instead, when testifying about his breakfast with Aaron Fernbach, Begelman would let it slip that Aaron had talked about the Miletti settlement. Harry would look uncomfortable and would deliberately change the subject. The plan was to make Morrison think Harry was afraid of getting into the conversation about Joe Miletti and to conclude that its contents must be very bad for Aaron's case. If so, Morrison would plunge in, ask about that conversation on cross-examination and get a nasty surprise. Instead of producing something helpful to his side, Morrison's questions would draw a response that strongly supported Aaron's position. The response would be far more effective brought out by Morrison on cross-examination than if it had come out on direct examination by Harry, where it would tend to look planned and rehearsed. It was an old trial lawyer's trick, but it often worked.

Harry finished the last of the raspberry sherbet, wondering aloud when Americans stopped saying "sherbet" and started saying "sorbet." Begelman speculated that it was about the same time *Good Housekeeping* began advising housewives to spread pesto on their meatloaf. O'Neil said it was when good Irish drinkers started asking barkeeps for nouveau Beaujolais.

Harry felt very good about both men. Both were showing guts not always evident in the motion-picture business. Both were going to support Aaron Fernbach against a major studio and a very powerful man. Both could pay for it dearly.

Walking back to the hearing room, Harry explained that, as attorney for the plaintiff, he could control the case, calling all the witnesses—even Slutsky—in the order he wanted, not allowing the defense to develop any momentum or to structure the way the testimony would be presented. He speculated that, when the plaintiff's case was over, the defendant's would probably be over too. There'd simply be no witnesses left to call.

Harry called David Begelman to the stand at two o'clock. Begelman identified himself as the president of an independent motion-picture company. He knew both Aaron Fernbach and Yank Slutsky and frequently did business with each of them. He testified that he had early breakfast meetings most days of the week, that this was a customary way of doing business, and that he knew a number of people in the industry who had two or sometimes even three breakfast meetings in a single morning.

"During the week of February eighteenth of this year, did you have a breakfast meeting with Aaron Fernbach?"

"Yes."

"Where was that?"

"At the Bel Air Hotel."

"Was that a meeting about business?"

Here Begelman gave the response Harry had prepared, the response Harry hoped would lead Morrison into a trap. "Yes, we talked about a picture my company was making for Consolidated." He paused as if uncertain as to whether he should go on. "We also talked about the Miletti settlement."

Harry tried to look nervous. "Yes . . . uh, well . . . what was the name of the picture you were making for Consolidated?"

"The Desperadoes."

Out of the corner of his eye, he saw Greg Morrison make a note. Maybe his plan was working.

"What happened at the *end* of the meal?"

"At the end of the meal, Ray Stark came to the table. He had a meeting with Mr. Fernbach that was to follow mine."

"How do you know that?"

"They both said so. And as I got up, Ray sat down. He and Aaron each took some kind of typed memo out of their briefcases. You know, like they were going to compare notes?"

"Did you have anything to eat during the breakfast meeting?"

"Sure."

"Did Mr. Fernbach eat?"

"Yes, he did."

"As you were leaving, did you see whether or not Mr. Stark ate anything?"

"As he sat down, he picked up a menu and said he was starving. Then he took a piece of Mr. Fernbach's rye toast while he was waiting to give his order."

"No further questions."

The judge turned to the defendant's side of the table. "Mr. Morrison?"

Harry waited to see if his trap would work. Without leaving his chair, Morrison began to examine Begelman.

"Now, you're a social friend of Mr. Fernbach's, isn't that correct?"

"Yes, and of Mr. Slutsky too."

"You've met with Mr. Cain about your testimony here, haven't you?"

"Yes, just as I met with you before I testified for you in the Cannon Films case."

Morrison frowned. He was not having a good day. He looked down at his notes. Again, Harry held his breath.

"Mr. Begelman, you said that, at breakfast, you and Mr. Fernbach talked about the Miletti settlement. Just what was said on that subject?"

Harry leaned forward in his chair. Morrison was going for it.

"Well," Begelman said, looking up at the ceiling. "Let's see. I said I'd seen Yank Slutsky at a party the night before and he'd told me how delighted he was with the settlement they'd made with Mr. Miletti. Mr. Fernbach said that he also was very pleased."

Harry saw Judge Sandlinger make a note—and underline it. Morrison realized too late what had happened to him. He tried to act unconcerned.

"Well, you were a friend of Joe Miletti, isn't that right?"

"Yes."

"And they might have been telling you what you wanted to hear, isn't that correct?"

"Sure, but I don't think so. I think they were very relieved to get the film back, and at that point they didn't care very much about who had final cut. Anyway, both Yank and Aaron told me they were pleased with the deal."

Morrison looked as if he'd had a sudden attack of dyspepsia. "I see," he muttered stiffly. "No further questions, Your Honor."

"No questions," Harry said, smiling sweetly at his opponent.

"Our next witness is Terence O'Neil."

"First we'll take the afternoon recess," said Judge Sandlinger, getting up and stretching. "We'll stand adjourned until three o'clock."

After the recess, Terence O'Neil entered the hearing room, took the oath in a stentorian voice and focused his sparkling green eyes on Harry. After describing his long career as a director, he explained how he had developed and produced *Carnage* for Consolidated Pictures.

"Was there a budget on the film?"

"Yes. Certainly."

"What was it?"

"Twenty-five million and change."

"And what was the actual cost of the picture?"

"Twenty-seven million, more or less."

"You were over budget then?"

"Not technically, because the studio had approved certain 'enhancements,' that is, additions to the film not originally contemplated when the budget was made."

"What were these 'enhancements'?"

"Well. They approved Faye Dunaway, instead of an unknown actress, playing a very small but juicy part. That added quite a bit. She was wonderful, by the way. Then they approved certain special effects that were not originally in. That was a million by itself. And they wanted to reshoot two scenes with Faye and Peter Falk. I said okay, but that cost us a bit more. That's about it, and, with those items, we hit twenty-seven million plus."

"Now who gave those approvals on behalf of the studio?"

"Yank Slutsky. He personally told me he wanted Faye. He thought she would be dynamite in the part, which she was. He said the added special effects made sense in this kind of picture. And reshooting the scenes was his own idea. He thought they should be a lot funnier. He even gave us a joke he wrote out that he wanted included. I just went along. I knew I could edit it out if it didn't work."

"Now, at any time during the making of *Carnage* did you drink any alcoholic beverages?"

"No, sir, I did not."

"Would it be fair or accurate to say you were a drunken director at that time?"

"It most certainly would not."

Harry looked over at Morrison. "Your witness."

Morrison rose to examine O'Neil. He had a large manila file in his hand that seemed to contain news clippings.

"Mr. O'Neil, you've had a long reputation as a heavy drinker, isn't that correct?"

"Unfortunately, yes."

"Over the past twenty years, can you tell me which pictures you drank on and which you did not?"

"I sure can." O'Neil chuckled. Morrison smiled patronizingly.

"That's because you drank on all of them, isn't that right?"

"No, sir, it's not."

Morrison picked up a clipping. "Didn't you drink every day on every picture you ever did?"

"No, sir. I did not."

"Well take *Carnage* for example; after all those years of heavy drinking, you can't recall any specific days on which you didn't drink. Isn't that true?"

"No. I remember quite well."

O'Neil was doing exactly what Harry had counseled. Making Morrison come to him, setting him up. Harry wondered why Morrison didn't grow cautious after what had happened with Begelman's testimony.

"All right, sir," said Morrison, his voice dripping with sarcasm. "Tell me the specific days you drank when you were making *Carnage* and the specific days you didn't."

"Sure. I didn't drink at any time during the making of that picture."

Once again, Morrison seemed slightly flustered, but only for a minute.

"Is that in your datebook? Did you enter each day you didn't drink in your datebook?"

"No, sir, I remember it very well."

"And just how do you remember so well those days on which you didn't drink?"

"Well, I remember because six months before the start of the picture I joined AA, and I've not had a drink since then . . . not one single drink. That's why I really resent Mr. Slutsky saying that I'm still a 'drunken director.' I once was, but not now."

Now Morrison looked pale. He looked back to his notes, flipping pages, apparently stalling for time.

"Okay, Mr. O'Neil, isn't it correct that, on Friday the twenty-sixth, you were seen on the set of *Carnage* drinking champagne?"

"It is not correct."

"Mr. O'Neil, you've seen the report describing your conduct, haven't you?"

"Yes. But it said I had a glass of champagne in my hand, not that I drank it. I didn't."

"Who did?"

"No one. It was for Peter Falk to use in a scene, but he didn't really drink it either. He just took a sip."

"I have no further questions, Your Honor," intoned Morrison, glad to have this behind him.

"Plaintiff rests," Harry said, looking over at Morrison for a hint at what Consolidated might do. Virtually all of the witnesses who could testify on the issues had been called during Harry's case, and there was little ground left to cover. Calling witnesses who could not add measurably to the proceedings would bore the judge and emphasize the fact that Consolidated had nothing to come back with. Harry felt that, if the studio offered testimony at all, it would be very brief. Morrison consulted with Lisa Lerner at some length. Then he turned to the judge.

"Most of the evidence is already in, Your Honor. We may have one or two brief witnesses; but, if we do, I doubt that their testimony will take more than a few minutes, and they would come in first thing in the morning. May we take our break now?"

"All right, we'll stand adjourned until eight-thirty tomorrow morning. Mr. Morrison, I assume you will not be making an opening statement?"

"That's right, Your Honor, I'll sum up at the close of the case."

"Very well, gentlemen, please be prepared to make your closing arguments tomorrow as soon as the defendant rests, unless Mr. Cain has some rebuttal evidence. Immediately after closing argument I'll give you my decision from the bench. I don't usually take cases under submission. I find I'm no more able to decide a case two weeks later than on the last day of the trial."

As they left the room, Harry speculated that, if Morrison had any witnesses at all to call in the morning, they would offer fairly inconclusive testimony and that what Morrison was really doing was stalling, hoping he could find something during the night that might turn the case around.

Trials, like battles, sometimes turn on the element of surprise. This was particularly true of a trial like Aaron Fernbach's, where there was no pretrial discovery and each side's tactics were a surprise to the other. In such cases, victory usually went to the lawyer who could react the fastest and most effectively to his opponent's unexpected moves.

The next session of the Fernbach trial began with Greg Morrison taking an accountant through a lengthy and boring presentation on the issue of damages. Without conceding that Aaron was right on the merits of the case, Morrison wanted evidence that would minimize the award should the judge find that he was.

Harry's cross-examination was brief. When the accountant finally left the stand, Greg Morrison rose and stood beside his chair. Harry waited for him to say that the defendant rested its case. Instead, Morrison turned his face away from the judge and gave Harry a sly

smile. Turning back, he announced, "The defense calls Anne Robinson, Your Honor . . . as its last witness."

As Morrison opened the door for Annie Robinson, Harry felt his
heart pounding, and a dryness in his mouth. He was enraged at the
woman's perfidy and at his own failure to foresee this turn of events.
His surprise, total as it was, was enhanced by her appearance.

Gone was the short leather skirt. She wore a gray tweed suit of
conservative cut and a white silk blouse. Gone was the punk hairdo,
completely covered by a gray jersey turban. Consolidated's wardrobe
department had been busy. Annie Robinson, the aging, drugged-out
hippie, had come to court the complete and cultured lady.

Under Morrison's questioning, she reviewed her background, the
pictures she'd directed, her drug problem, and her attempts at rehabilitation. She testified that after she "kicked the habit," she'd
tried to get directing assignments all over town, but was rejected
everywhere. She hadn't wanted to impose on her few good friends,
but she was desperate. With nowhere else to go, she'd turned to
Aaron Fernbach. She'd felt he'd be sympathetic to her plight.
Whether he'd let her direct a picture was something else. She'd
pleaded with him for the chance to direct a Consolidated film . . .
any film, at any price.

"And what did Mr. Fernbach say?" Morrison asked in a soft,
unctuous voice.

"He said he had a picture for me—that I could sign a contract that
week, but that first . . . and here he used a phrase I'll never forget . . . first we'd have to do some dirty dipping."

"Some 'dirty dipping'? Did you know what that meant?"

"I had no idea. I'd never heard the phrase before."

"Did you ask him what it meant?"

"Yes. I told him I'd never heard it before."

"And what did he say?"

"He laughed. He said 'Where have you been? Living in a tree?'
He said it meant we'd get it on together. That was a phrase I understood. I'd heard it before."

"It meant you'd sleep together?"

"Right."

"And how did you respond?"

"I told him his suggestion was beyond grotesque. But I also said I needed the job desperately and that I had no choice."

"You meant you'd do it?"

She looked down at her hands, as if ashamed.

"Yes," she said in a small, hushed voice.

"Did you, in fact, sleep with Mr. Fernbach in order to get the contract, as he demanded?"

"No, he got fired before it happened."

"Thank you. No more questions."

Harry rose slowly, looked at his watch and addressed the judge.

"Your Honor, I see that it's almost twelve o'clock. May we take the noon recess now?"

"All right, we'll stand adjourned until one-thirty."

Harry jammed his papers into his briefcase and hurried out of the room. Aaron trotted beside him.

As they went down in a crowded elevator, Aaron whispered anxiously to Harry.

"Harry, that's a complete lie. All made up. None of it ever happened. I don't even know the phrase 'dirty dipping,' and I never said anything like that. How could she do that?"

Harry put his finger to his lips, indicating silence. It was never a good idea to talk in an elevator . . . even one that was empty. And this one was full.

When they reached the lobby of Morrison's building, Harry stopped and leaned close to Aaron.

"Look, Aaron, I've got to run. No time to explain. You go on to the town house. Tell Armando I can't come. I'll see you at one-thirty."

He moved away, actually running through the crowd. There was not a moment to lose.

Promptly at one-thirty, the proceedings reconvened. Annie Robinson took the stand, crossed her silk-stockinged legs, primly pulled down her skirt, and looked over at Harry, smiling coolly.

The vicious, lying bitch! How he'd love to wipe that arrogant smirk off her face. He took a deep breath and tried to relax. Anger was something he couldn't afford. He rose slowly and paused before beginning his cross-examination. This was critical, and he had to do it coolly and carefully.

"Ms. Robinson, when you were active as a director, were there pictures you tried to put together that never got made?"

"Yes, that happens to every director."

"Sometimes you'd find a screenplay and submit it to a star and a studio, and the package just didn't come together, right?"

"That's correct."

"Did you work with a particular studio in those days?"

"Yes, I had an exclusive deal at Paramount."

"Did you ever submit any screenplays to Consolidated?"

"No."

"To Mr. Fernbach?"

"No."

"Okay. As I understand it, you remember Mr. Fernbach's precise words when you spoke to him about a job, because they were so unusual. You'd never heard them before—is that right?"

"Yes, that's what makes his exact words stick in my mind. But I'd have remembered the gist of what he said anyway. It was that shocking."

Once more, she gave him her cool, challenging smile.

Harry's face betrayed no expression.

"In any event, that phrase 'dirty dipping,' you're sure that's the very phrase he used?"

"Absolutely. It was such a strange, bizarre phrase and, as I said, it was completely new to me."

"I see. Now when he said you'd have to do some dirty dipping and you asked what that meant . . ." Harry consulted his notes. "Mr. Fernbach said 'Where have you been? Living in a tree?' Is that correct?"

"Yes."

"Those were also his exact words?"

"Yes. There again, it was such an unusual choice of words . . . 'living in a tree.' It just sticks in my mind."

"Okay. And then he told you that 'dirty dipping' meant . . ." again Harry read from his notes ". . . 'getting it on together,' is that correct?"

"That's correct."

"You knew what that one meant?"

"Right."

Harry turned the page of his yellow pad, peering again at his notes. He looked up again.

"And you replied that his suggestion was 'beyond grotesque,' right?"

"Right."

"Were those *your* exact words?"

"Yes."

" 'Beyond grotesque.' That's a somewhat unusual phrase too, isn't it?"

"Well, I suppose so, but it really seemed appropriate here. I mean, this man was supposed to be an old friend, and here he was demanding sex in return for a job I desperately needed. It truly was 'beyond grotesque.' "

"Isn't it possible that this scene you've described so vividly really involved quite different words than those you've related?"

"No, sir. Those were the words. If I've described them vividly, it's because I remember them vividly. I'll never forget them."

Once again, Harry consulted his notes. "So his words 'dirty dipping,' 'Where have you been? Living in a tree?' and 'get it on together' and your words 'beyond grotesque'—each of those specific phrases was used by Mr. Fernbach and by you in this conversation?"

"Exactly."

Harry reached into his briefcase, which was on the floor beside him. He pulled out an inch-thick booklet bound in red vellum. He handed it to the court reporter, who marked it as an exhibit for identification. Then he gave it to Annie Robinson.

"Ms. Robinson, I've handed you a motion-picture screenplay entitled *The Boatman* and bearing the name 'Robinson Productions, Inc.' in the lower left-hand corner and the date September twenty-fourth . . . two years ago. Have you seen that screenplay before?"

Harry watched the color drain from her cheeks. Nervously, she flipped through the pages.

"Yes. It's a screenplay I developed. It never got made."

"Please turn to scene sixty-four which is on page one hundred and eight of the screenplay."

She did.

"Okay. Now I'm going to read you that scene from your screenplay." He looked down and began to read.

" 'ANTHONY: You know what I want to do, Fay? I want to do some *dirty dipping.*' "

Harry paused, looking up at the judge. He continued.

" '. . . some dirty dipping—right here, right now.'

" 'FAY: Do what?'

" 'ANTHONY: Dirty dipping.'

" 'FAY: What's that?'

" 'ANTHONY: *Where have you been? Living in a tree?*' " Harry's voice boomed out the now-familiar words. After a pause he continued reading Anthony's lines in a low, deadly tone.

" 'Dirty dipping, my dear, means *getting it on together.*' "

Harry stopped, looking up at Annie Robinson, whose face was red with anger.

"Would you read us the next line, Ms. Robinson?"

"Read it yourself," she spat.

"All right," Harry said pleasantly. "Where was I? Oh, yes, Anthony says, 'dirty dipping, my dear, means getting it on together' and Fay replies 'If that's what it means, Anthony, the suggestion is *beyond grotesque.*' That's where the scene ends, with Fay saying that Anthony's suggestion of 'dirty dipping' is 'beyond grotesque.' "

Harry couldn't resist a slight smile for Annie Robinson, who gave him a murderous glare in return. Greg Morrison glared with equal fury at his young associate, whose job had obviously been to prepare this witness to testify.

After a moment, Harry continued. "Okay, Ms. Robinson, we're all aware now that you took the scene you described here from that discarded screenplay, isn't that right?"

"Objection . . . argumentative and highly improper!"

"Sustained. You know better, Mr. Cain."

"Sorry, Your Honor. I'll rephrase it. Isn't it true, Ms. Robinson, that you simply made up that conversation with Mr. Fernbach, using the exact scene from your old screenplay?"

"No it's not. That's just what he said to me . . . all of it. He must've gotten hold of my screenplay somehow and used the same language."

"I see . . . and after he used the same exact words as Anthony, you replied in the same exact words as Fay . . . that his suggestion of 'dirty dipping' was *'beyond grotesque.'* Is that what you're asking us to believe?"

Annie Robinson sat there in silence, her face a mask of anger. Greg Morrison was gazing at the ceiling, trying vainly to conceal his disgust. Seconds passed with no reply.

"Ms. Robinson?"

Still no reply.

Harry shrugged and turned away.

"No more questions, Your Honor."

"Re-direct, Mr. Morrison?"

Greg Morrison sat quietly. Harry could virtually read his thought process. They had a good hour before the afternoon recess. He could question Annie, try to repair the damage done by Harry's cross-examination, but with no chance to prepare her, he could make the situation worse. Besides, even if he had time to work with her, what explanation could she give? He made his choice.

"No cross, Your Honor. No need of any."

"Oh, sure," said Harry.

Down came the gavel. "That's enough, both of you. Mr. Morrison, any further witnesses?"

"No, Your Honor. The defense rests."

"Very well. Any rebuttal Mr. Cain?"

"No, Your Honor. Mr. Fernbach has already denied that he had any such conversation with Ms. Robinson. No need to do it again."

"I was looking for an answer, Mr. Cain, not a speech. Are you saying you have no rebuttal?"

"Yes, Your Honor."

"All right then, we'll adjourn now and hear argument in the morning . . . unless, of course, you gentlemen are prepared to argue now." Judge Sandlinger looked at Morrison and then at Harry.

"Okay with me to argue now," said Harry. He wanted a decision as quickly as possible, while the impact of Annie Robinson's cross-examination was still fresh in the judge's mind.

"I'd prefer some more time to prepare," announced Morrison, already pushing documents into his case.

"Very well then, court stands adjourned until nine tomorrow morning, at which time we'll hear argument."

As they left Morrison's office, Aaron could no longer restrain his feelings. "Fantastic! How could you possibly do that? Did you know in advance she was going to use those words? Even so, how could you know about that screenplay? You're a fucking magician."

Harry smiled. "More luck than magic, Aaron. I had no idea they'd get her to testify, and certainly no idea that she'd describe that conversation the way she did. But when she did, I remembered the words. Two years ago, Dustin Hoffman asked me to read that screenplay—wondered what I thought about his doing the picture. I recommended against it. Annie was right about one thing. Those phrases were unusual. When she used them in court, I was sure I'd heard or seen them before; and I thought I knew where. I rushed back to my office at noon and searched through my file of old scripts. It took an hour to find it; but it was right there . . . and so was scene sixty-four, just as she described it in court. Only she'd put Anthony's dialogue in your mouth and Fay's dialogue in hers. As I say, it was mostly luck."

"Not so. And anyway, the way you used it in cross-examination was brilliant . . . just brilliant! It's scary, you know. If you hadn't been able to do that, the judge probably would've believed her."

"Maybe so. But that's litigation. The stakes are high, there's powerful motivation to lie, and it's not easy for a judge to decide who's telling the truth. Besides, much of the time, *both* sides really believe they're telling the truth. People tend to remember things in a way that justifies their own conduct. And after they repeat a story several times, they really begin to believe it. But not Annie. She was just lying."

That night, Harry worked on his closing argument for two hours before dinner. He planned to put in another hour before going to sleep. During his break, he was relaxing, having some wine and preparing capellini with broccoli, pine nuts, and sun-dried tomatoes. He turned off the fire under the broccoli after exactly two-and-a-half minutes of steaming. At just that point, the phone rang. Harry was not pleased. The broccoli would continue steaming even without any fire and even without a cover. The whole damn dinner would be spoiled if the broccoli got overcooked, mushy, and olive drab instead of crisp and bright green. He picked up the direct line to his telephone exchange. The caller was Greg Morrison. Reluctantly, Harry agreed to take the call.

He spoke with thinly disguised impatience. "Greg. What's the matter?"

"Harry, I'm sorry to bother you at home, and I know it's late. But I think our case should be settled. So do my clients."

Harry was immediately wary. This could be a ploy to get him to focus all night on phony settlement negotiations and not prepare adequately for closing argument.

"*Now* they want to settle, Greg? After the whole trial is done?"

"Sure, why not?"

"Well, I suppose there's no law against it, but we all know how this thing's gonna come out, and I'm sure as hell not gonna give you any discount just to avoid having to make my argument tomorrow."

"Harry, I didn't ask you for a discount. We're prepared to pay Aaron the full contract price and to meet your figure for the stock options."

Harry concealed his surprise as well as he could.

"Uh . . . what about attorneys' fees?"

"Come on, Harry, you're not gonna get fees from the judge, even if you win, and you might not even win. You never know."

"This time, I know, Greg. I think you know too, even though you won't admit it."

"Harry, you did a great job. You always do. But any case can be lost. You can never be a hundred percent sure. The judge might not have believed Mona Olinsky. I know I didn't. And he just might believe Annie Robinson, even if she was foolish enough to embellish her story with that phony dialogue. Anyway, why take any chance at all? We're ready to pay you everything you could get from the judge if you win."

"Let me discuss it with Aaron and get back to you."

"Okay, but don't take too long. If we're gonna argue in the morning, I've got work to do."

Harry spent the next fifteen minutes in a tense conversation with Aaron Fernbach. A quick decision had to be made, and the issue was a close one. Harry pointed out that a decision by the judge would give Aaron complete and public vindication, while a settlement, even a 100 percent settlement, would not. Still, the settlement eliminated any risk of losing and would avoid having to go to court to enforce the judgment, a procedure that would be expensive, even though they would ultimately collect. Harry also pointed out that settling would let Yank Slutsky avoid public humiliation and that a humiliated Slutsky—like a wounded tiger—would be a dangerous enemy indeed. Finally, after exploring every aspect of the situation, Aaron decided.

"Okay, Harry, I'll go for the settlement, but on one condition."

"What's that?"

"I get my car back."

Ten minutes later the deal was made. Aaron Fernbach was to receive every dime payable under his contract plus twenty-eight million dollars for his stock options, and, not later than noon the next day, he was to receive possession . . . and ownership . . . of his chocolate-brown Rolls Corniche.

It was over, and suddenly Harry felt let down. Settlements had that effect on him, and a settlement just before the end of a trial was even worse. It was coitus interruptus. All that effort and emotion leading to the final moment and, just before it arrived, withdrawal. Instead of the excitement of making his final argument, the heart-stopping moment before the court announced its decision, and the orgasmic thrill of winning, there'd be just another day and then another and then another. He realized that Aaron was getting a good deal and that it would have been senseless to reject it. Still, if every case settled—even on the most favorable terms—he'd go into another line of work. Sighing, he ripped up the outline of his argument, tossed it in the wastebasket, and poured himself a glass of wine.

He turned to the broccoli. It was seriously overdone. Olive drab, not bright green, and mushy, not crisp. He buzzed Nancy on the intercom. "Say, pardner, how'd you like a bowl of kick-ass chili?

It was raining in Boston when Harry and Nancy arrived for her next TNF treatment. They dined at the Union Oyster House, walked back to the hotel, and then lay in bed in each other's arms, talking for hours and listening to the rain fall on the Public Garden.

In the morning they checked into "the Farber," where Nancy went through the usual scans, examinations, and tests, while Harry analyzed a lengthy contract and made a series of calls.

In the late afternoon Harry sat on Nancy's bed holding her hand, waiting for Dr. Jackson to give them the latest reports on her condition and to administer another dose of TNF. When the young doctor arrived, he smiled shyly as if embarrassed to intrude on their privacy. His right hand played nervously with the stethoscope in the pocket of his white coat.

"Come on, doctor, spit it out," said Nancy, smiling at his reticence. Surprisingly, the nervous smile faded, the young face grew stern, formal.

"I've some rather bad news this time. But, of course, we've known from the beginning that this was strictly an experimental program . . . no guarantees."

"What do you mean, doctor?" Harry said, the dry metallic taste of fear in his mouth.

"Well, I'm afraid the tumors have begun to grow again, and we're concerned about the spinal lesions."

"What spinal lesions?" Harry cried out, dropping the soft polite voice he always used with the doctors who were saving Nancy's life.

"Oh, didn't Dr. Morgenstern tell you?"

"He did not."

"We've spotted some lesions in the spine. Six of them. That kind of migration is rather common with this form of cancer, and that's what's occurred here, I'm afraid."

"Well, shouldn't we increase the dose of TNF?"

"We can't do that, Mr. Cain. This program has to follow strict prespecified guidelines. Besides, we know now, from patients who were in the program before Mrs. Cain, that when a tumor stops shrinking and begins to grow and we get this kind of posttreatment migration, the TNF is not working anymore and won't. We don't know why. It just happens this way, at least with some patients."

"So we just give her the old dose . . . and hope?"

"No, Mr. Cain, we can't do that either. There's no point to it. Besides, there are other protocols Mrs. Cain might try, other programs that seem promising. They'll probably require that Mrs. Cain be free of TNF for at least a two- to four-week period. We don't want to waste time and delay her admission into one of those other programs by giving her a useless dose of TNF."

The unexpected news struck Harry like a blow. He looked over at Nancy; she, too, seemed in a state of shock. Harry had to bolster her courage, had to keep up the fight.

"What's the most promising of those new programs, doctor?"

"Well, you might look into the treatment they're working on at the MD Anderson Clinic in Houston. It's based on a combination of interferon and interleuken. I hear that, so far, the results have been very encouraging." He paused and smiled nervously. "Well, I have to get on with my rounds. I've made arrangements for your release, so you can leave any time you want." He hesitated for a moment, playing again with his stethoscope. Then he extended his hand to Harry. "I'm pleased to have known you both. I'm sorry we couldn't have been more help."

Harry took his hand, feeling that, at any moment, he would burst into tears. Dr. Jackson turned quickly, and, with his white coat flapping, left the room. Harry took a long, deep breath to control his emotions before turning to look at Nancy. Then he slid onto the bed and put his arms around her, holding her tightly to him, rocking her to and fro. He felt her sobbing gently into his shoulder. He had never felt so empty in his life. Finally, Nancy sat back, wiping her eyes.

"My God," she said, "for the first time in all these months I was beginning to let myself make plans."

*　　*　　*

As soon as they got back to their hotel, Harry phoned Karen Lloyd. He explained the situation and asked what she could do to get Nancy into the new program at MD Anderson.

When they arrived in Los Angeles, a message from Karen was already awaiting them at the airport. Harry called her from the limo that drove them home. She told him that the Anderson program was full with a long waiting list, but she had threatened to review their federal grant and to take a hard look at all their future grants unless Nancy was admitted. The chief of the program, entirely dependent upon such funding, had relented. Nancy was to start with a new group of patients in two weeks. But the Anderson program required five days in Houston every other week. Could Harry live with a schedule like that? If not, Karen would organize friends of Nancy's who would take turns staying in Houston with her. Harry told Karen he'd handle it himself, that he was immensely grateful for what she'd done, and that he'd never forget it.

Before leaving for Houston, Harry and Nancy spent a long weekend at their house in Zihuatanejo. They had planned their Mexican home two years before, and a wiry crew of Tolucan Indians had spent over a year building it. It stood on a hill overlooking an emerald bay surrounded by bone-white beaches and thick palm groves that stretched to the base of the rugged Guerrero mountains rising in the distance.

A fresh sea breeze blew through the house, softening the hot tropical sun. Nancy felt weak and had some back pain, but she kept up with Harry's pace, getting intense personal enjoyment, as she always did, from the colorful ambience of the ancient fishing village.

For three days they swam, ate, read, and made love, as if they were on a honeymoon, each striving to make the other forget the paralyzing threat that now hung over them.

Only once did Nancy's bravado fade. Their favorite swimming place was a tiny bay called Contramar, some two hundred feet from the house. Silent and secluded, it seemed to belong to another, more remote age. Pale-green, crystal-clear water lapped against jagged volcanic rocks as the tide flowed in. Then a million pebbles click-clacked softly, pulled by the tide sweeping out. The only other sound was the raucous shriek of jungle birds in the trees beyond the beach.

After a morning of sunbathing and swimming, they hiked up the steep jungle path that led home. The climb was hard for Nancy—she was in considerable pain, and she quickly found herself out of breath. As they reached the crest of the hill, she stopped and looked back at Contramar. The tiny bay was a bright turquoise from that height. Surrounded by craggy black rocks, it was particularly beautiful. She looked up at Harry, and he saw her eyes moisten.

"I was just thinking," she said. "I'll probably never see this again."

The words were like a knife in his heart. He would never forget them.

H arry returned from Mexico determined to throw himself into his work or whatever else could help dull the gut-wrenching fear he felt about Nancy. The *Masami* trial was only a month away, yet he'd spent the last ten days in Boston and Mexico, and now he'd be traveling to Houston for five days more. Nancy came first, of course, and his concern for her dominated his thoughts. But he felt a serious responsibility to his Japanese clients and to Fumiko herself; and he knew he was not prepared for the trial legally or emotionally . . . at least not the way he'd readied himself for major trials in the past.

Well, life was different now, and he'd just have to do what he could. He still wasn't ready to leave the interviewing of witnesses to anyone else; and if the normal amount of time and his usual highly focused attention weren't there, at least he still had the skill and instinct of the ring-wise veteran. Perhaps it would be enough.

On his first day back from Mexico, Harry drove to the Beverly Wilshire Hotel to resume his investigation. Armed with entrée from the hotel's manager, a longtime friend, Harry spent the entire morning interviewing maids, room-service waiters, and security men, making careful notes, forming a detailed picture of Hiroko Masami's last three nights. He noted the addresses of other potential witnesses. He'd see them in the next few days. Some lived far across the city in places very different from the hotel's lavish entrance at the end of Rodeo Drive. He'd be combing patched and peeling bungalows on the side streets of Watts and the Barrio, looking for witnesses who might turn the seemingly impossible case around—somehow give Fumiko Masami a chance. He'd have to find them, get them to talk. There was always danger in that. The places he'd be looking would be mean and tough. The witnesses might not want to be found . . . or other people might not want them to be found—might not want them to talk. Right now though, Harry wasn't even conscious of the danger: He simply wasn't thinking about it.

Returning to his office late that afternoon, Harry found a personal note from Ray Stark, a longtime friend and client.

Sweetheart,
     Your bill sneaks in $45 you're not entitled to. Add it up. If you need the forty-five, I'll lend it to you, but shame on you trying to slip it by.

Your pal,
Ray

Harry smiled at the note. He wasn't surprised that his new computer system would make an error. It often did. Then slowly he recalled Milo Putnam telling him that years ago the firm had made a forty-five-dollar disbursement for Ray Stark, but that another client had been billed for it by mistake and had paid. He wondered if . . .

"Clara, ask Mr. Putnam to come in here, please."

Two minutes later, the pale, long-faced office manager entered Harry's office. He stood at Harry's desk, his thin lips curved in an obsequious smile, his hands clasped together before him. Uriah Heep, Harry thought.

"Mr. Putnam, there's a forty-five-dollar overcharge on Ray Stark's current bill. That wouldn't be the item you mentioned to me sometime ago, where someone else was billed for Mr. Stark's costs . . . would it?"

Putnam blushed slightly. His smile broadened.

"Yes, Mr. Cain. Mr. Stark never paid the forty-five dollars he should have. We have to bring in all that cash. We can't just let others keep our money."

"And did you credit the client who actually paid the forty-five dollars for that amount?"

"No, I didn't. In this case it was Apple Corps. Limited the Beatles' company. They certainly can afford it. Anyway, it's the client's responsibility to raise such matters. For example, Mr. Stark obviously checks his bills carefully. So do others. It was up to the Beatles to check and to ask for an adjustment."

Harry could feel his anger rising. "Did you follow that approach with every client who'd been underbilled or overbilled for costs?"

"Yes, every one."

"But I specifically told you to do just the opposite, to give the clients credit where they'd paid too much and to forget about the times they'd paid too little."

Putnam's hazel eyes took on a pleading look. He raised his clasped hands in a strange supplicating gesture.

"But, Mr. Cain, this is a business. It must be run on businesslike principles. You're too busy a man to make such decisions. It's the responsibility of your chief financial officer to make them for you, to prevent your making foolish choices concerning fiscal matters, to . . ."

"First," Harry interrupted, "this is *not* a business. It's a profession. Second, it's *my* profession, *my* practice, not yours; and, third, Mr. Putnam, you're fired. You can cut yourself a check for two weeks' pay and then leave."

The hazel eyes flared with surprise, then turned hard and angry. The voice was harsh and petulant.

"You can't do that, Mr. Cain, I was only trying to fulfill my responsibilities."

"I've already done it, Mr. Putnam. Now I want you out of here . . . within the hour."

Putnam strode angrily to the door, then turned back, his hand on the knob.

"You'll be sorry about this. There are things going on here that the public should know about; and they will. I'm going to take appropriate action."

"Mr. Putnam, I don't give a flying fuck what you do as long as you do it someplace else. Now get out!"

The door slammed, the wall reverberated, and Harry was alone at his desk. He knew he was upset and irritable because of Nancy. Had that led him to overreact to what Putnam had done? He didn't think so. He'd never overcharged a client in his life. He wasn't going to start now. But what did Putnam mean? What "things" had gone on in the office that the public should know about? What was that prissy idiot talking about? Harry sighed. Most likely he'd find out soon enough.

The Remington Hotel in Houston was lush, sleek, and new. The staff was unusually courteous and attentive as Harry and Nancy checked in and were shown to a large, tastefully furnished suite overlooking the dramatic Houston skyline.

When they'd unpacked, Harry announced that they were going shopping. They weren't due at the hospital until late afternoon, and he insisted that shopping was just what he felt like. Nancy was tired, but went along with the idea, trying to keep his spirits elevated, just as he was trying to elevate hers. Harry arranged for a car and driver, and they started with the Armani collection at Saks. They both loved

Armani's designs, and Harry moved along the racks, picking out dresses, slacks, suits, everything that caught his eye. Cornering a dressing room and a saleslady, he piled his selections on a chair, collapsed in another one himself and ordered Nancy to begin trying things on.

"But Harry," she whispered, as the salesgirl began taking an elegant taupe suit off the hanger, "this is no time to buy clothes. Be realistic."

"Bullshit," Harry whispered back. "You've heard that famous slogan 'When the going gets tough, the tough go shopping.' This is the time to buy. Come on. Do it for me, Nance."

Nancy smiled tolerantly and hugged him, dutifully stepping out of her clothes. If it made Harry feel better, she'd play along. Still, his enthusiasm was contagious, and she did dearly love Armani. Forty minutes later, they had selected two suits, the taupe and a lovely slate blue, a simple but elegant gray dress, three pairs of widely pleated slacks and two blouses. Nancy stood patiently as a seamstress finished pinning the last hem. Suddenly, she grabbed her back and grimaced with pain.

"Wow," she said after a second or two, "that hurt. I think I must have pulled a muscle swimming in Zihuatanejo. Standing and bending here must have aggravated it. Anyway, I'm getting kind of tired. I'm glad we're done."

Harry helped her back into her own clothes and went to sign the charge slip. As they left the store, Nancy slipped her arm through Harry's.

"You're crazy, you know? Buying ten thousand dollars' worth of new clothes is absolutely nuts when we don't even know how long I have."

"Nonsense. I *know* you're gonna make it. We've gone over this. The new treatment is supposed to be dynamite. Yes, things could go bad. Yes, it might not work. But, if it does work, it'll work everywhere, the spine, the lungs, everywhere. So the fact that you've got it more than one place now is irrelevant. That's logical, isn't it?"

That afternoon they checked into the Anderson Clinic, a low, sprawling building, seemingly jammed with doctors, nurses, cancer patients, and their "significant others." Nancy's room was simple but pleasant, and opened onto a broad, empty patio. She unpacked, and within half an hour was led away to begin a battery of scans and other tests that would precede her receiving the clinic's experimental combination of drugs. Harry counted on that treatment to reverse the frightening trend of events that seemed to be shortening her life, to give her the time Harry wanted her so desperately to have.

Toward evening, Harry sat in Nancy's room editing a brief. As always, concentrating on shaping the words and phrases that would define his client's rights made the time pass swiftly. Two hours after Nancy left the room, blowing him a kiss and smiling brightly, the door opened and she was wheeled in on a gurney, deathly pale, soaked in sweat and quite obviously sedated.

A young female resident with black frizzy hair asked if Harry would come down the hall to her office. He followed her to a tiny cubical, large enough only for a cluttered desk and battered metal chair.

"Please sit down, Mr. Cain."

"Thanks. What happened to Nancy?"

"Mrs. Cain had a very bad time getting in position for the spinal X-rays. They're always rough, and given her particular problem, they must have been excruciating. We had to give her quite a bit of Demerol."

"What about her spine? How bad is it?"

"She has at least six spinal lesions, Mr. Cain. Bad ones. And I'm afraid the news is worse than that. She has brain lesions too. I assume they're new. They're not in her records from Dana-Farber. But even that's not the bad part. Her lumbar lesions have worsened, very significantly worsened, to the point that I"—she reached out and took his hand in a gesture so surprising that it startled him—"I don't believe Mrs. Cain can possibly survive more than a few days."

It was as if Harry had been hit by a massive electric charge. His mind went numb. He understood what this child of a doctor had said, but he couldn't assimilate the information. From somewhere he heard himself say "A few more days?"

"At the most" came the soft reply.

Harry looked down at his hands, then looked up at the earnest young doctor. "But maybe tonight's treatment will change things . . . roll the tumors back. I hear the results have been fantastic."

She took hold of his hand again. "No, Mr. Cain, the treatment we're now administering can't deal with this kind of deteriorated condition. Under the terms of our grant, we can't even give her the treatment. And even if we could, it couldn't possibly be of any assistance now. Not given the condition of her lungs. I don't like telling you this, Mr. Cain, but I have to." Again she squeezed his hand, trying to provide comfort where there could be none.

"Well then, I want to take her home. I don't want her to . . . die here." At the word "die" his voice cracked. He felt tears rush to his eyes. He put his head in his arms and began to sob uncontrollably. After a time, he was able to speak.

"Look, she can't know about this. What I'd like you to do is, well . . . give us some medicine in a bottle. I'll tell her we're going to administer the treatment at home, so we don't need to come out here all the time. That way, she won't really know quite how bad it is."

The doctor stood and put her arm around his shoulder. "I'll have to consult with Dr. Levine, Mr. Cain, but I'm sure he'll go along with it. I'm not so sure your wife will believe it, though."

Later that night, while Nancy slept, Harry arranged for a chartered jet to fly them back to California in the morning, a nurse to travel with them, ambulances to take them to the Houston Airport and to pick them up in L.A. and drive them home, as well as round-the-clock special nurses to make it as easy on Nancy as possible once she was there.

Then he called Gail and gave her the news. He kissed Nancy, without disturbing what seemed a peaceful sleep, and walked to a nearby bar, where he ordered and quickly drank two double vodka martinis. Then he went back into the Houston night.

When he returned to the hospital, he found that the nurses had set up a cot for him in Nancy's room. He took off his shoes and walked to the French doors overlooking the dimly lit patio. Harry was not a religious man, but he prayed. He prayed for Nancy. He prayed for

God to let her live and take him instead. That surprised him. It was the kind of empty, melodramatic gesture he'd made so many times in his life, without real meaning or content. This time he meant it. He wanted her to live, even if it meant he would die. Finally, exhausted, beaten, he lay down to wait for a sleep he knew would not come. Just before dawn he heard Nancy's voice, still drugged but not incoherent.

"Harry, is that you? I thought I saw you."

"Yes, Nance, it's me. The nurses set up a cot for me over here."

"Did you eat?"

"Sure," he lied. "I went out for a big steak."

"Harry, am I in trouble?"

He had to make a decision quickly, the truth or . . . He decided.

"No, not in trouble, Nancy. But, given the discomfort in your back, they decided that we can take the treatment just as well at home as here. They've given me the medicine and we'll have nurses give it to you back home. It's silly for us both to be here in Houston when we can do it just as well in California."

"Sure, Harry, that makes sense."

There was silence for a time. Then he heard her again.

"Harry?"

"Yes, hon?"

"I want you to know I could never have gone through any of this without you. You helped me more than I thought one person could ever help another. You made it okay." Her voice trailed off and then came back. "I just wanted you to know."

In the morning they flew home. Nancy's back pain was becoming unbearable. She was sedated. Harry was hung over and numb. Arriving at the house, Nancy was carried upstairs to their bedroom, where a special nurse was waiting for them. She was an enormous, big-breasted black woman, with closely cropped hair and a strikingly beautiful face.

Working gently and efficiently, she put Nancy in a small hospital bed set up at the foot of the large, king-size bed in which she and Harry had slept for twenty-five years. Harry stood beside the bed looking out at the trees and the city stretching far into the distance. He felt empty—just a constant aching emptiness.

Nancy was conscious and seemed pleased to be at home. She hugged Gail, who'd flown out from England. Then she threw her arms around their houseman, Armando, as he struggled to fight back the tears. Finally she reached for Harry's hand and held it until she fell asleep.

That night, as Harry lay alone in the huge bed, he heard Nancy's voice. In a sweet, childlike tone, as if saddened and puzzled by what was happening to her, she murmured "Gee-whiz." Then, after a moment, she slowly repeated those same forlorn words, "Gee-whiz . . ."

As the days went on, Harry continued to pray that he'd be taken and Nancy spared. He continued to mean it. He found it hard to stop the tears from rushing to his eyes when he thought of Nancy dying, of her no longer being there, no longer being part of his life. But as her condition worsened, and the pain and discomfort became constant and unbearable, his sorrow turned to a desperate rage.

Even the increasing dosages of heavy drugs were failing to control the excruciating pain in Nancy's back. Meanwhile, the rampaging tumors destroyed more and more of her lung tissue. Unable to rid themselves of the accumulating fluid, her lungs had to be suctioned by the nurses. Tubes were inserted through Nancy's nostrils and attached to a motor that drained off the viscous liquid. Had this not been done, Nancy would have drowned in her own mucus. The process was painful and humiliating. Nancy, now almost constantly drugged, would fight to pull out of the tubes. One nurse would start the machine while the other held Nancy's wrists. At first the suctioning was needed every two or three hours. Soon it was every half hour, then every fifteen minutes, then every ten.

One night, ten days after they had returned home, the fluid buildup became unstoppable. The big nurse shook her head as she inserted the cruel tube yet another time, deep into Nancy's lungs, gesturing to Harry to hold her wrists. The night became a horror. Suctioning had to be restarted every five minutes, and each time Nancy writhed and moaned and fought. Harry knew she wouldn't want to live that way, knew that nothing could save her now, that there was nothing left but the torturing pain in her back and the grotesque and humiliating discomfort of the constant suctioning. For the first time, he began to pray for her death.

Almost to himself he whispered, "This can't go on."

The huge black nurse nodded gravely. "Too much pain," she said. "Too much."

She pulled the tubes from Nancy's nose as gently as she could. "No more of *that*," she said, speaking softly to no one in particular. She looked at Harry, who nodded, his face a grim mask. Momentarily, Nancy seemed at ease. Then, gradually, she began to cough and choke. Moving deliberately to the intricate system of tubes and valves that dripped the morphine into Nancy's veins, the nurse slowly twisted a knob. At first there was no sound, no change. Then, in a moment, the choking stopped. Slowly Nancy's body relaxed and a faint childlike smile appeared on her lips. Harry thought that, just once more, she might murmur "Gee-whiz." But she didn't. She just stopped breathing. Harry knew his wife was dead.

The big nurse called Gail, who had been asleep in the study, and told Armando to make Harry a stiff drink. While Gail and the nurse were in with Nancy, Harry clutched a double martini and wandered aimlessly from room to room, touching Nancy's things, running his fingers over her robe, her toothbrush. Then Gail came out of the room and, with Armando, tried to comfort him. He was numb. His tears were gone. He simply clung to his daughter and sipped his drink. He tried not to think of Nancy leaving the house . . . tried very hard. Finally, the time came. He heard Armando open the front door and admit two men, brisk, businesslike. Gail, realizing what was happening, led Harry into the study and eased him into a big wing chair, talking, talking, talking to distract him, while the two men went about their strange, morbid work. Finally their voices receded and the front door closed.-

The black nurse came in and took Harry by the arm. Her expression was so caring and tender and her grip so firm that he let himself be led to the bedroom and, once there, to bed. Everything in the room was so familiar, had been such an intimate part of his life with Nancy. As he looked around at the paintings, the books, the soft light from the sconces, the nurse quietly took a syringe from her uniform pocket and, rolling up his sleeve, gave him a shot in the upper arm. In an instant, the pain and anguish seemed to ease and he felt relaxed, almost euphoric. The room started to spin, and its colors and textures to blend into each other. He looked up at the nurse and saw her smile. It was the last thing he remembered that night.

Harry awoke with the first light of dawn. He was alone in his own bed, with the sun streaming in. For a blessed second the day was like any other. Then he remembered. Nancy was dead. He expected to weep. Strangely, the tears didn't come. There was just a hollow, empty feeling that he feared would never leave him. He looked around. The hospital bed was gone and with it the intravenous tubes, the suction machine, everything that had marked Nancy's last days.

Maybe it was all a dream . . . except the part about Nancy. That was real and would be real forever, the most real fact of his life from this point on. He knew that now, knew he was starting a new life, an empty life, one that offered nothing but time stretching endlessly like a vast desert ahead of him. Did he even want to venture into that desert?

He began to wander again from room to room. He moved aimlessly through the upstairs hall, looking at Nancy's portrait and their photographs from years ago. He saw the Fante book in the study, a bookmark two-thirds of the way through. She'd never finish it now—would never know the ending.

He threw himself on the bed again and lay there, staring at the ceiling in a state of vagueness, almost numb, unable to make a decision about anything. Should he go to the office? Why? Why not? There was nothing to do at home. Reading would be impossible. If he stayed, he'd just continue to go from room to room, looking at things that were Nancy's, touching them—remembering. But if he went to the office, he'd have to come home again sometime—home to the empty house, Nancy's house, their home together for twenty-five years.

Maybe work would help. It might be the one thing that *could* help. He rose and dressed, still dazed, selecting clothes at random, buttoning, zipping, knotting his tie by rote, his mind a blank.

At the office, his vagueness continued. He was unsure which paper to pick up, which letter to read, whom to call, what to do next. Clara and the whole staff were kind and solicitous. They tried to be helpful, but there was nothing to be done. In midmorning there was a call from Pat Campbell.

"Oh, Harry, I'm so very sorry. You know I loved Nancy. My God, what a loss. Are you okay? I guess that's a silly question. How could you be okay?"

"No, I'm okay, Pat. A few bad times, but I'm okay. Actually, I'm probably still in shock."

"Well, Harry, please know that I'm here for you. If there's anything you need, please call, and I know Ewing feels the same way."

"Thanks, Pat. How's that going by the way?"

"Well, we're still separated, and Ewing is still planning to divorce me; but I did what you said. I wrote a current diary—the false one—and put it where you said."

"Good."

"What's the next step?"

"Leave that to me."

"Okay, Harry. Listen, I'm sorry even to talk about my problem at a time like this."

"No, Pat. I brought it up and, besides, work is therapy. It's probably the only thing that'll keep me going."

"Well, I think you'll find more than that, Harry, but it'll take time."

"Yeah, it'll take time. Well, so long, Pat."

"So long, Harry. I love you."

Harry put down the receiver and gazed out the window toward Catalina Island far on the horizon. His mind drifted to the lovely weekend he and Nancy had spent on a yacht, anchored at the deserted coves of that startlingly beautiful island, just lazily snorkeling, sunning, and loving. Christ, he said to himself, is everything going to bring it all back? Is there nothing that isn't entwined with memories of Nancy?

Harry crossed the footbridge that led to the gardens of the Bel Air Hotel. The morning sun was beginning to burn away the mist that floated over the small rocky lake. The swans, as cranky as they were graceful, complained angrily to each other as they glided between the giant lily pads.

Harry followed the path through the towering palms and lush tropical ferns that grew beside the pink Spanish buildings of the old hotel. He passed through a small enclosed garden filled with potted plants and entered the quiet dining room.

Ewing Campbell, already seated at a booth across the room, rose to greet him. Harry was always awed by Campbell. Even at his advanced age, his bearing was military, his demeanor forceful, while, at the same time, dignified and courteous. As he peered over his rimless bifocals, intelligence radiated from the dark-brown eyes set in the narrow, heavily wrinkled face. Despite his white hair, the handshake he extended was firm and strong, and he reached out to grasp Harry's forearm with his left hand in a rare gesture of affection.

"I must say, I was surprised at your call yesterday. I gather it was your first day back." Campbell looked straight into Harry's eyes, as if sizing up his condition. "I'm so very sorry for your loss. Are you sure you're ready for a business talk?"

"I am, Ewing. If I don't get to work I'll go crazy, and I still have a responsibility to my clients."

"Well, despite everything, I was pleased when you called. You know, even under these circumstances, Harry, you're always like a transfusion of rich red blood in the thin pinkish fluid that passes for my life these days."

"Oh, come on, Ewing, it's not that bad, I'm sure. Besides, I'm getting to the thin, pinkish age myself."

"Nonsense. When I was your age, I was living with a Spanish opera singer in a fifth-floor walkup overlooking the Seine. About once a month she'd try to kill me. But, by God, there was something to kill. I was alive, really alive."

"You're hardly moribund now, Ewing."

"Maybe not, Harry, but age does take things away, things I always considered vital."

Embarrassed, Harry stirred his coffee, intrigued at the turn of conversation. Maybe now was the time to . . .

"But enough of an old man's self-pity," Campbell said, "especially when your personal loss makes my problems look very small. You came for financial advice and you'll get it. That's one thing I've still got to give. Now, what's the problem?"

Harry had his cover story prepared. He explained that, over the years, he'd come to participate in managing the holdings of a number of his clients, and that he was concerned about whether this was a good time to acquire or even hold stocks or real estate investments, or whether it might be better to anticipate a major economic downturn and get liquid, heavily invested in bonds, money market funds, and the like.

After a twenty-minute analysis of the nation's short-run and long-run economic outlook, Campbell advised Harry that, in his view, Harry's clients would be well advised to err on the side of liquidity, to be ready not only to protect themselves, but to take advantage of a serious and continuing recession or even more significant downturn, by being in the position to make splendid buys at low prices. Even in his continuing state of distraction, Harry was intrigued with the logic and clarity with which Campbell presented his views, and he nodded from time to time to indicate his understanding.

But this was not why Harry had come; and it was difficult to steer the conversation back to where he wanted it. Finally, as Campbell paused to butter his toast, Harry tried.

"I'll tell you one thing, Ewing, it's a pleasure to be dealing in problems like this, rather than my usual run of cases that, all too often, focus on sex and violence."

Campbell looked up, mildly interested.

"Sex cases? Oh yes, I remember that trial you won for Sonny Ball. A film star stroking a policeman's private parts in a public men's room—good God, what bad judgment."

"Well, it's not just that, Ewing—and, by the way, the jury found Sonny *didn't* stroke the cop. But, over the years, a great deal of my practice has involved problems that grew out of sexual conflict, sexual needs." Harry raced on before Campbell could break in. "Why, before the advent of no-fault divorce, I must have tried at least thirty adultery cases and given advice in a hundred others."

"Really," said Campbell, now more than mildly intrigued. "I suppose one develops a certain expertise even in that sordid field."

"You're right, Ewing. I'm not really proud of it—and I wouldn't ever do it—but I could write a book on adultery. How and why it happens, its significance in a relationship, its impact when discovered, how to prove it and how to disprove it."

Campbell was now leaning forward in his chair, keenly interested.

"Listen, Harry," he said, peering over his rimless glasses. "You may be just the man I should consult."

"Oh?"

"Yes. You see I've got this close friend who has a problem in just your area. I mean, what you were just describing." He shied away from the word "adultery." "What happened was he came upon his wife's diary and found that she'd been living a double life, you know, sleeping around outrageously. She recorded every detail, and my friend was devastated. He loves her dearly, but he feels he simply must divorce her, that he can never trust her again, simply could not go on living with such a person, would never . . ." He stopped and, reaching for his handkerchief, dabbed at the corner of his eye. "Damn it, I've had something in my eye all morning," he growled.

Harry felt the time was ripe.

"Listen, Ewing, your friend shouldn't leap to the conclusion that there's really been any adultery."

"What do you mean by that, Harry? How could there be any doubt about it? I mean the diary was explicit. . . . At least that's what my friend said."

"Well, in my experience . . . and I think it's been documented in scholarly works . . . many women record sexual fantasies as if they really happened. Most women have such fantasies—just as most men do, and you'd be surprised how many women record them. You know, in private, unsent letters, diaries, some even on tape recordings."

"Really?"

"Of course. You've never heard of that?"

"Well, I've heard of sexual fantasies, of course. But I was not aware that there was any tendency to write them down in diaries, to keep them in a place where they could easily be found. Is there any way to distinguish recorded fantasy from the real thing?"

"There could be."

"How?" said Campbell eagerly. "I must tell my friend. Maybe what he's dealing with is just recorded fantasy."

"Well, was the diary current or an old one?"

"It was old, written some years ago."

"Then, if your friend doesn't mind being a little bit devious, he might be able to learn the truth."

"What do you mean, devious?"

"Well, most such women continue writing these things. I'd bet anything there's a current diary somewhere. Your friend should read it, check it against the current facts, his wife's whereabouts on the dates in question, the things he *knows* did or didn't occur. If he reads her current diary, he'll know soon enough if she's just recording fantasies or if she's really been doing these things."

"You really think there'll be a current diary?"

"If it's recorded fantasy instead of reality, I'm virtually certain of it."

"Well, where do you think it would be?"

"Oh, that's hard to say. There are certain common hiding places. You know, a jewelry box, lingerie drawer, a high shelf where old hats are stored. Places like that."

Campbell nodded, still listening with interest while Harry paid the check. They stood and shook hands. Again Campbell gripped Harry's arm.

"Harry, I can't tell you how helpful this has been . . . for my friend. I'm going to call him immediately. On his behalf, I'm very,

very grateful; and, again, I want to express my sympathies and tell you that if there's anything I can do, *anything,* please call me."

"Thank you for that, Ewing. It's comforting to have good friends in your corner. And, as to your own good friend," Harry said, preparing to leave, "I wish him the best of luck."

As he drove back to his office, Harry smiled to himself about Ewing Campbell's "good friend." I must tell Nancy, he thought, she'll get a kick out of it. Then, suddenly, he remembered. He'd never be able to tell her . . . anything. Never. For an instant—just an instant—he thought of flooring the accelerator, driving the car at top speed for fifty yards and smashing it into a telephone pole. Then it was gone, that idea, as quickly as it had come. Would it come again? Harry thought it might.

*P*eople v. *Masami* was assigned to department 102 of the superior court, the Honorable William B. Kennedy presiding. A white-haired, charming Irishman, Kennedy was an experienced and efficient criminal judge.

The corridors and the courtroom gallery were packed with reporters and spectators. The exotic nature of the crime, the involvement of sex and alcohol, the presence of Harry Cain, who always made things colorful, created an ideal situation for media coverage. This time, however, the reporters found a different Harry Cain—distant and distracted. There was none of the usual banter, none of the confident charm.

Those who knew Harry and were aware of Nancy's death showed understanding. Seeing his reticence, they moved away, giving Harry a quiet smile, a sympathetic pat. Others, new to the courthouse beat, just thought he was difficult and surly. Harry didn't care.

By contrast, the prosecutor was open and effusive. A dark, striking figure, Bailey Scuneo stood basking in the bright television lights, perfectly tailored, tall, balding, and pockmarked, with a black guardsman's mustache. His fierce black eyes flashing, first with righteous anger, then ironic humor, he fielded every question shouted at him by the clamoring reporters who filled the corridor.

As Harry quietly registered his appearance, the court clerk, an old friend, nodded in the direction of Scuneo, who was still surrounded by the press.

"Scumbag's in rare form today, huh?" Then, remembering Nancy's death, he added, "I'm sorry about your wife, Harry. Been six years since I lost Rose, and I still can't get over it. You okay?"

"Yeah, Todd, I'm okay."

But Harry knew better, knew he was far from okay. He felt anesthetized, numb, present but not a participant. Not at all the way to feel at the start of what was probably his toughest case.

The first two days of the trial were occupied with picking a jury, each lawyer striving, through skillful questioning of the prospective jurors and the judicious use of challenges, to pick the twelve people most likely to favor his side of the case and to exclude those likely to favor his opponent. There were supposed rules about such things, but, like most experienced trial lawyers, Harry considered them silly and stupid. Artists, Jews and fat people were supposed to be sentimental, easily moved, good bets for the defense. Accountants, Scandinavians and thin people were supposed to be tough-minded, harder, the kind of juror the prosecution should want. But, just as often as not, the exact opposite proved true. The tight-lipped Scandinavian accountant was moved to tears by the defendant's plea, and the fat Jewish housewife, outraged by the crime, steadfastly voted to convict. Neither lawyer really knew how any juror was likely to vote. But each, exercising a combination of experience, judgment and instinct, strove to guess, and acted on those guesses in exercising their challenges.

Finally, what seemed a fairly balanced jury was selected. They sat, excited and attentive, in the jury box to the left of the two large counsel tables, one for the prosecution and one for the defense. As Bailey Scuneo rose to begin his opening statement, he removed the tiny rosebud from his lapel and, with a theatrical flourish, handed it to the court reporter. The young woman blushed, and Harry noticed two ladies on the jury smile. He'd seen Scuneo pull that stunt before. It always annoyed him. But, damn it, it did seem to work. He wondered if he could get away with something like that. Probably not—and did he care anyway? Would the time come when he cared about such things again? He wondered.

Then, his mind drifting, Harry began to look around the room—at the walnut paneling, the American flag and the bear flag of California, the court reporter sitting beneath the judge's bench, her fingers flying over the keys of her stenotype machine. He watched the heavy-set, uniformed bailiff put aside his notebook and begin reading a magazine. Then he gazed up at the ceiling, studying the panels of fluorescent light.

Suddenly, Bailey Scuneo's voice captured his attention. Good God, he'd been day-dreaming while his opponent was addressing the jury. That was not just bad, it was malpractice. Scuneo was leaning on the railing of the jury box, moving his eyes from one juror to the next.

"Never . . . I repeat . . . never, at least in a case without a confession or an eyewitness, has there ever been a situation in which the evidence pointed so inextricably, so overwhelmingly in one direction—toward guilt." Scuneo reviewed the case he would present. "The angry, jealous wife carrying poison in her purse, the tired, intoxicated husband feeling ill during the night. He asks for Fernet Branca, an Italian herbal medicine he favored for stomach problems. She brings him a glass. But that glass doesn't contain just the herb drink he requested. It's laced with a fatal dose of antimony chloride. It kills him . . . as planned. And, because of that, we are here, each of us, to do our duty as citizens. Let's work together to do that duty as the evidence will inevitably show it to be. Thank you."

"Mr. Cain?"

"I'll reserve my opening statement, Your Honor."

"All right, Mr. Scuneo, you may call your first witness."

And so the prosecution began its parade of witnesses, weaving a web of evidence inexorably around Fumiko Masami. There was little Harry could do to stop the process. But, despite his vagueness, he was slowly forming a plan.

When Scuneo finished examining most of the prosecution witnesses, Harry simply responded "No questions." Cross-examining a witness with no preconceived design or goal was usually worse than useless. Generally, it bored the jury, shook their confidence in the lawyer, and simply reinforced the witness's original testimony. "No questions" was usually more effective, especially if it could be said with a tone of boredom, implying "I don't even need to cross-examine *that* witness."

Harry did take the hotel personnel through their stories of what Hiraiko Masami's nights had been like, the angry drunkenness, the violence, the hookers and, sometimes, Fumiko herself, standing shyly in the corner, forced to watch, but trying desperately to look away in her pain and embarrassment.

When the crime lab technician testified, Harry roused himself from his lethargy. Cross-examining that witness, he took more time and more care.

"Now, Lieutenant Keough, you testified that what was in the glass by the bed—that is, Exhibit nine—were traces of Fernet Branca and antimony chloride. Right?"

"Yes, sir."

"And you say that what was in the phial found in Mrs. Masami's purse, Exhibit four, was also antimony chloride. Right?"

"Yes, sir."

"By the way, are you absolutely sure that Exhibit four is, in fact, the same phial that was found in Mrs. Masami's purse and not some other phial that just resembles it?"

"I am sure, Mr. Cain. I put my initials and the date in blue indelible pencil on the tag attached to the phial that was found in her purse, and you can still see it right there on Exhibit four." He held up the phial for Harry and the jury to see.

"I see. And can you testify that this was the only phial in the purse or in Mr. Masami's room?"

"I certainly can. A thorough search was made and all items inventoried. There was only one phial, and that's it right there in your hand."

"And you are absolutely sure, lieutenant, that the liquid in this phial as you say, right here in my hand, is the very same liquid that was in Mrs. Masami's purse on the night of her husband's death? Not some other or different liquid?"

The technician looked impatient, as did the judge. "I am absolutely sure, Mr. Cain," he replied with a tone of irritation.

Harry had much more to cover with this witness, especially concerning the lab results, but he wanted to avoid creating any doubt about those results at this point. If he did that while there was still time, the police lab could run the test again and make the lab technician's conclusion seem even stronger to the jury.

"Your Honor, that's all I have of Lieutenant Keough at this time. I may need to recall him later. Can we have Mr. Scuneo's assurance that he'll be available?"

Judge Kennedy looked over at the prosecutor. "One hour's notice, Mr. Scuneo?"

"That's fine with the People, Your Honor," said Scuneo, smiling. He was confident that Harry had made no inroads at all into his well-organized case against Fumiko Masami. If anything, he thought Harry's cross-examination had helped fix her guilt in the jurors' minds.

After two more days, Scuneo rested the People's case. It appeared airtight, and the press was already predicting a quick guilty verdict. But Harry had a plan now, a plan no one else could know . . . no one.

His opening statement was unemotional and extremely brief. He pointed out that a criminal defendant could only be found guilty if there was no reasonable doubt as to her guilt. He said he would show the jury that there was much more than a reasonable doubt here, that others had both the motive and the opportunity to kill Hiraiko Masami, and that the circumstantial evidence pointing to Fumiko fell far short of proving guilt beyond a reasonable doubt, the test on which our criminal justice system was founded. And he would go beyond that, he said. The prosecution had the burden of proof. But he wouldn't just rest on the burden of proof. He would actually prove to them that Fumiko Masami was innocent.

As Harry resumed his seat at the counsel table, the veteran courthouse observers shrugged, whispered, and gave each other knowing looks. This was not the kind of thorough, colorful analysis of the evidence they expected from Harry Cain. Not by a long shot. And his cross-examination of the prosecution witnesses had gone nowhere.

Sure, the guy's just lost his wife. It's understandable he's not at his best. But why not bring in someone else to try the case?

Harry's first witness was Vincent Watanabe, the nisei lawyer he had interviewed with John Matsuoka, on a day that seemed decades ago in another life. Watanabe, a round-faced man conservatively dressed in a dark suit and tie, testified that he was Hiraiko Masami's attorney in certain of his Southern California dealings, especially second mortgage transactions. He explained Masami's views on the desirability of foreclosing to get property back and his total unwillingness to grant extensions of time to pay.

"Just how many times did Mr. Masami foreclose and put people out of their homes in the last five years?"

"Well, I had twenty-two foreclosure files for him and possibly he had some others I didn't know about. He was a very secretive man in his business dealings."

"Were some of those people whose property was foreclosed upset or angry about it?"

"Sure, most of them were. Masami gave them no break at all, no extension. Whether or not they had families or were hardship cases, regardless of what they promised or did, when he could put them out, he simply did it."

"Thank you. That's all I have of this witness, Your Honor."

Harry's next witness was a statuesque black woman in her early twenties. She wore a red pantsuit and white cowboy boots. It had taken Harry two nights of searching the streets of Watts, plus a full afternoon of pleading, to get her to testify. She identified herself as LaVonda Brown.

"Miss Brown, on the night of February fourth, were you in Hiraiko Masami's room at the Beverly Wilshire?"

"Yessir. I was there three nights runnin'. That was one of the nights."

"Now, when you went to Mr. Masami's room, did you have to stop at the desk to announce yourself?"

"Well, we suppose to do that, but we never did. No one ever stop us."

"Did other people to your knowledge go up to the rooms without stopping at the desk?"

"Sure. You can do that. If you look like you know where you goin', nobody try to stop you. Take a man in a suit and tie, he be no problem at all . . . just walk to the elevators and go right on up. Anyway, there's a side door and stairs, so you don' even have to walk by the desk to get up to the rooms."

"Now, when you were in Mr. Masami's room, did you see any other men there?"

"Sure. Three, four guys come to see Rocky . . . Mr. Masami, but I can't remember which night."

"Could it have been February fourth . . . the night Mr. Masami died?"

"Could've been."

"Now these men, did they come alone or were they together?"

"Alone, I think."

"Men in suits and ties, the kind you said could have walked right past the desk without being questioned?"

"Yeah. That's right. That the kind of people."

"Did you hear any of these men talk to Mr. Masami?"

"Talk to him? No. You see, we mostly partying in the big living room. These dudes, they go in the second bedroom with Rocky. There was shoutin', all right—lots of shoutin', but you couldn't really say I heard anybody talkin' to Rocky, so's I could tell you what they said. When he was boozin' he was a mean drunk. You know what I'm sayin'? When he was like that, he didn't really want to hear no talk. He just shout and break things and carry on."

"Did you see all of the men leave who came in?"

"No. I never did see *any* leave that I remember. They surely left though. They was another door out the second bedroom and they was things goin' on all the time in the livin' room and the bedroom. You couldn' keep track of who was there and who wasn't during those three nights."

Harry paused, letting the jury absorb those words.

"Well, what time did you leave on the night of February fourth, the last night you were there?"

"Oh, maybe midnight or so. Rocky wasn't feelin' too good that night, and he was bombed out of his mind. So we lef' more earlier than usual."

"Were any of these other men still there when you left?"

"Could a been. I didn't see none, but they sure could a been there."

"Thank you," said Harry. "Your witness."

Following the afternoon recess, Harry returned to the counsel table, lost in thought. Unlike his highly focused intensity in other trials, his mind wandered frequently. He found himself thinking random thoughts, dreaming . . . a dangerous state for a lawyer in trial. He shook his head like a fighter shaking off the effect of a hard punch and forced his attention back to the courtroom.

He was at the end of the defense case now. He still wanted to attack Lieutenant Keough's poison test, but doing that continued to involve a serious risk. Scuneo could still run another test during the night, then introduce it in rebuttal, after the defense rested. If a second test reconfirmed the finding of antimony chloride, it could do serious harm to Harry's plan. But Scuneo seemed totally confident that Harry had no case at all; and Harry was ready to bet that nothing he'd get out of Keough would change Scuneo's opinion. He was sure that the prosecutor would still think Harry had no chance of creating a reasonable doubt as to Fumiko's guilt and would decline to put on any rebuttal case, wanting to get to the jury as quickly as possible, while he was far ahead. And, at that point, Harry had to concede that Scuneo was *far* ahead.

Harry faced a tough, close decision, with serious risks either way. That decision had to be made *now*. He looked up, and, seeing Lieutenant Keough sitting in the last row of the gallery, he made his choice.

"The defense recalls Lieutenant Keough, Your Honor."

The officer rose in his seat and, carrying his file of lab reports, returned to the stand. Judge Kennedy reminded him he was still under oath.

"Lieutenant Keough, did you personally perform the test for poison? I mean did you do it yourself, by hand?"

"No, sir. It's done by computer."

"By *computer?*" Harry repeated, as if the idea was beneath contempt.

"Yes, sir. We have state-of-the-art technology in the crime lab."

"Well, lieutenant, can your computer tell one batch of antimony chloride from another?"

"I'm afraid I don't follow you, Mr. Cain."

"Well, did the computer tell you whether the antimony chloride in the glass by the bed was from the same batch or vat of poison as you say was in the phial in Mrs. Masami's purse?"

"No, Mr. Cain, it didn't. But, if you've got antimony chloride in the phial in her purse and antimony chloride in the glass by the bed and the accused's fingerprints in both places, isn't it a fair inference that it's the same antimony chloride?"

"Possibly, lieutenant, but if the phial in Fumiko's purse did *not* contain antimony chloride, then your whole inference is blown out of the water, isn't that right?"

"Yes, sir. But it *is* antimony chloride. We tested it ourselves. *That* you *can* tell from a chemical analysis."

"Well, let's talk about those tests, lieutenant. Isn't it true that, *sometimes*, they're erroneous?" Harry reached for a thick blue textbook that was lying beside him on the counsel table. He saw Keough's eyes go to the book, saw him recognize it as the standard text on qualitative analysis, saw him assume that it contained statistics on the range of error inherent in computer testing.

"Well, yes. There's a tiny percentage of error, but it's so infinitesimal as to be de minimus."

"Infinitesimal? . . . *De minimus?*" Harry boomed. "Will you explain to the jury what *that* means?" Harry knew perfectly well what it meant.

"It means that, statistically, the percentage of error is so tiny that it's considered totally insignificant in relying upon such tests."

"It wouldn't be so insignificant to a criminal defendant who goes to the gas chamber because the test was wrong though, would it?"

Scuneo rose quickly to his feet. "Objection, Your Honor. Argumentative and also an improper reference to the death penalty."

Judge Kennedy glared at Harry. "Sustained. The jury is cautioned to ignore any reference to the death penalty or any other form of punishment. Mr. Cain, please restrict yourself to proper cross-examination."

"I'm sorry, Your Honor." Harry continued, not sorry at all.

"Okay, lieutenant, what's the percentage of error in the kind of test used here to tell whether what was in the phial was poison?"

"Oh, maybe one in five thousand, Mr. Cain."

"Every five thousand tests you'd expect one to be in error, is that correct?"

"Perhaps."

"Have you personally seen such erroneous test results here at the L.A.P.D. crime lab?" Either way Keough answered this question Harry would be ahead. If he admitted having seen errors, it made the possibility more real. If he didn't . . .

"No, Mr. Cain. In my entire twenty years with the crime lab, I've never seen an error in any such test."

"Well, perhaps your lab doesn't do that many tests of this kind. Isn't that the most likely explanation—that you're relatively inexperienced in these tests?" Harry wanted Keough to think he was after just the opposite of what he really wanted.

As Harry planned, Keough was annoyed by the question that seemed a slight to his department's experience and competence. "Absolutely not, Mr. Cain. I'd estimate that we've done at least fifteen thousand qualitative analyses of that type while I've been with the department."

Harry was tempted to make his point clear to the jury at once, but quickly decided not to take the risk. He'd make it in argument, when it was too late for the witness to correct what he'd said, and deprive Harry of the point.

"That's all I have of this witness," Harry announced quietly.

"Cross-examination, Mr. Scuneo?"

"No questions, Your Honor."

"The defense rests, Your Honor."

"Any rebuttal, Mr. Scuneo?"

The tall, dark prosecutor stood quietly for a moment, thinking. Harry waited, trying not to look anxious. It could be fatal if Scuneo was sufficiently worried by Harry's cross-examination to run a retest on Fumiko's phial. But Harry had been correct in his assumption that the prosecutor was supremely confident about his case and his chances of winning. Finally, Scuneo answered. "No, Your Honor. The People are satisfied with the record as it is." Harry breathed a long sigh of relief.

"Very well, gentlemen, it's three o'clock, and I'm sure you'd like some time to prepare your summations. We'll stand adjourned until nine tomorrow morning."

As Harry was about to leave the courtroom, Scuneo waved him over.

"Want to change her plea, Harry?"

"What've you got in mind, B.J.?"

"With this evidence, not much. Thirty years. But, of course, she'd have the possibility of parole."

"Come on. That's the worst she'll ever get."

"Don't be too sure, hotshot. She could get gassed. She could certainly get life."

"Come off it, B.J., that'll never happen." Harry wasn't so sure, but he was negotiating.

He saw a nasty grin spread across the pockmarked face, a mean glitter in the jet-black eyes.

"Well then, Mr. Sunset Bomber, I think you should just take your chances or should I say '*her* chances.' "

Harry hated Scuneo, despised the man and his pompous, arrogant style. But if there was a chance to bargain for a light sentence, he had to explore it.

"Hey, I never said I was *sure*, B.J. But thirty years? Come on, that's too tough. How about ten?"

"No way, hotshot," said Scuneo, leaning close to Harry, leering at him. "And guess what? I wouldn't even give you thirty now. My offer's off the table. You had your chance, and you blew it. Just tell your client you could've saved her life, but you fucked it up."

Harry turned away seething, but Scuneo continued. "And one more thing, Mr. Hollywood." Harry continued walking. "Tomorrow I'm going to kick your butt, so get ready for a loss. A very *big* loss. Oh, and by the way"—Harry had his hand on the courtroom door— "I hope you'll attend my press conference after the verdict. The media will certainly want a comment from the loser." Harry pushed open the door, stepping into the glare of the cameras. One thing was certain. If he didn't do something spectacular, Scuneo was right.

The night before closing argument, Harry paid a visit to Fumiko Masami at the county jail. He didn't fully understand why he went. He simply felt a strong need to see the woman again before he finished the case, before he completed his plan.

Fumiko bowed gracefully to Harry as she was led into the small, dimly lit holding cell. Her delicate beauty was moving, unnerving to Harry. She carried two packages wrapped in silver paper. One was small and thick, the other wide and flat. Fumiko turned to Isamu Morita, who was there to translate, speaking quietly to him in Japanese. Morita told Harry that Fumiko had been studying English every day and would try to speak directly to him, but that she apologized in advance for her poor efforts at his language. Looking directly into Harry's eyes, Fumiko began haltingly to speak English.

"I thank Cain-san for all he has done. Domo arigato." She bowed and handed him the small parcels.

"Go ahead and open them, Cain-san," said Morita.

Harry opened the heavier of the two packages and found a beautifully carved netsuke, perhaps the most beautiful he had ever seen. The yellowed ivory had been intricately worked into the form of an old woman, each strand of hair, each wrinkle, each fold of her kimono, as well as its delicate pattern, all carved in amazing detail. It was magnificent. Harry bowed.

"Domo arigato, Fumiko-san, domo arigato."

Fumiko smiled shyly. "Fumiko has another gift for Cain-san," she said, handing him the wide, flat package.

Harry opened it to find a single piece of heavily textured paper bearing graceful Oriental calligraphy.

"It is a writing, Cain-san. It . . ." Fumiko seemed frustrated by her ability to convey her thoughts in English. She turned to Morita and spoke to him briefly in Japanese. Morita listened and turned to Harry.

"It is a poem, Cain-san. A special kind of Japanese poem. Fumiko has written it for you. I'll translate it." He put on his bifocals and quietly read aloud:

> *"Two cranes flying*
> *Along the wind*
> *They are together*
> *They are alone*
> *The sun sets quietly."*

Harry felt his eyes well up with tears. Taking her hands in his, he spoke. "I thank you, Fumiko, for the beauty of your thought." He paused. "Tomorrow, I will do all I can to free you. If I can't, you will know I did my best, and that my heart will be with you."

As Morita translated this, Fumiko looked down at her hands. Then she raised her head meeting Harry's gaze. "Wakarimasu . . . I understand Cain-san, and what . . . whatever may come, domo arigato." She smiled as a single tear started down her cheek. Moved more than he could understand, Harry left.

Harry awoke at 3:00 A.M. Unable to sleep again, he wandered through the darkened house. He passed through Nancy's dressing room, her pictures still there, her personal things untouched, hairbrushes, creams, the mundane objects of her life. It tortured him to look at them, but he couldn't bear to put them away. He wandered into the living room and stood looking through the huge arched window out at the city below, the downtown skyline rising in the distance, the lights still burning in the high-rise towers. His city. His vast, sprawling, rich, and crazy city. The city that had spawned him, taught him, battered him, nurtured him. The city that had come to respond like an adoring woman to the aphrodisiac of his success. Seeing it like this, the miles of shimmering lights spread out beyond the window, used to move him, to fill him with a strange wild joy. Now the feeling was gone. He felt hollow, vacant. It was one thing to feel that savage joy, that fierce pride when Nancy was there to give his life a center—to share it all. Now there was no one, and no joy, no pride—only emptiness, a deep, aching emptiness.

All his life, Harry had been intolerant of suicide. There was always something of value in being alive, he'd argue, even if it was just to sit in the sun and read. When Nancy would ask "And if you were blind?" he'd reply "Then I'd just sit in the sun, feel it on my face, be alive. That's something of value. That's a reason to live."

Now he wasn't so sure. What was ahead that he could conceivably care about? Years of living alone, going to the office, trying cases? Even that—the challenge, the complex game he'd always loved so much—even that seemed hollow now. And what else would there be? Random sexual couplings devoid of feeling? Solitary meals? Drinking himself to sleep?

Would he be upset tonight if a doctor told him he was dying? He doubted it. What did *that* tell him? He stood for a time looking out at the city, considering what lay ahead, pondering his choices.

Then he went into his study and put on the light. There were things he had to arrange.

The morning brought a heavy fog that muffled the sounds of the traffic and gave the freeway an eerie, unfamiliar silence. Harry drove through the mist and stillness lost in thought. Unlike his usual drives to court, there was no whispered rehearsal of his argument, no Sousa marches blaring on the stereo, no attempt to pump himself up for the intense and demanding performance ahead of him. This day was different. The determination was there, but it was mixed with a seriousness, a sadness totally foreign to the excitement Harry normally felt on the day of a final argument.

He arrived at the courthouse earlier than usual. Normally, he took coffee in the cafeteria and sat, gathering his thoughts and gazing out over the downtown skyline to the south or down at Chinatown and Chavez Ravine to the north. Today, after parking, he strolled to the old plaza, the original center of the tiny village that had grown into the huge, sprawling city.

A pale sun was just beginning to burn off the morning fog, its rays glinting on the ironwork of the old bandstand. The deserted structure provided little shelter from the wind, and Harry shivered in his lightweight suit. Nothing was as it used to be. Never would be. He shook himself. Why were these dark thoughts always breaking in, dominating his mind? He should be concentrating, focusing his energy and attention on the argument he was to present, an argument that meant freedom for Fumiko or life in prison, possibly even death.

He stood, breathed deeply of the cool morning air, gave a long sigh, and began walking back toward the courthouse. As he strolled up Main toward Temple Street his pace quickened. There were none of the usual college fight songs, hummed under his breath, to fuel the emotional locomotive that would drive him relentlessly ahead, no urging himself on with emotional symbols, creating a feverish hunger to win. Instead, there was only a quiet, sober determination. He'd made the right decision . . . the only decision. Now he would carry it out.

The reporters spotted him as he entered the courthouse. Pushing his way through the sudden, blinding glare of flash cameras, he made his way to department 102, where the future of Fumiko Masami would soon be decided.

The gallery was filled with representatives of the worldwide media and members of the public who had waited in line for places. Bailey Scuneo was already at the prosecution table, impeccably tailored in a black pinstripe suit, another tiny rose in his lapel. He scowled momentarily as he leafed through the notes for his argument, underlining here and there with a red pen.

Harry took his place at the defense table. His younger partner, John Matsuoka, joined him, gripping Harry's arm in support and affection. Fumiko was led into the courtroom, looking pale and tense, but ready to take what might come. For a moment, it seemed to Harry that only the two of them were in the room. He smiled at her and, for a moment, her face was lit with a smile so warm he had to look away to fight back the tears.

The jury filed in, looking somber, already feeling the weight of the decision they would soon have to make. Their serious demeanor concerned Harry. They certainly didn't look like a jury ready to acquit. But then why should they acquit on the evidence they had? Could he turn them around? Convince them?

The bailiff called the court to order. The crowd quieted as Judge

Kennedy entered and took the bench. He nodded to the prosecutor. "All right, Mr. Scuneo, you may proceed."

Scuneo rose, moved away from the prosecution table and, as on the first day of the trial, took the rose from his lapel and handed it, with another theatrical gesture, to the court reporter. As before, she blushed and smiled. As before, some of the jurors smiled with them. Harry was disgusted.

The prosecutor faced the jury from the counsel table, his hands clasped behind his back. He looked tall and pale in his dark suit, his guardsman's mustache neatly brushed, his black eyes gleaming with intensity. Malachamovis, Harry thought. The angel of death. He remembered the terrifying name from his childhood, uttered in a whisper by his father's immigrant friends. Bailey Scuneo was Malachamovis. He shook himself to clear his head. This was no time for foolish drifting. It was the time for concentration. He must do that—must concentrate—for the little time that was left.

Scuneo had moved slowly to the jury rail, still without a word. Now he began, his voice artificially low, almost a whisper.

"A few weeks ago, Hiraiko Masami was a living person, a live human being, eating, drinking, loving, worrying, arguing . . . living . . . much like the rest of us. Not perfect, not at all. Far from it. None of us are. But he was a living human being, a man." He stopped, looked from juror to juror. His voice rose. "And where is Hiraiko now?" He paused. "Under six feet of wet mud. That's where he is! Dead, cold, gone, finished. Forever. How? Perhaps the worst death of all. Poison. *Hideous*, ladies and gentlemen, I assure you. Unbelievably excruciating and hideous, a ripping knife in the guts . . . unbearable, unimaginable pain, pain, pain!

"Who did this to Hiraiko? Well, ask yourselves, who had the *motive* to kill him? His loving wife, of course. Jealous of his involvement with other women, aware of the fortune she would inherit on his death. Oh yes, she had the motive.

"And ask yourselves who had the *means* to take away Hiraiko Masami's life? Again, the evidence will point to his loving wife. There, in her purse, was the phial of deadly poison, the same poison that killed Hiraiko, the same poison that was found in the glass by his bed. Could someone else have given him the poison? Hardly. Mrs.

Masami's fingerprints were on the phial. No one else's. *No one else's,* ladies and gentlemen, Mrs. Masami's fingerprints were also on the glass and also on the bottle of Fernet Branca. Again, no one else's . . . except, of course, poor Hiraiko's.

"No one else *could* have done it. No one else *did* do it. I know it, you know it." Scuneo gestured toward Harry. "Even Mr. Cain knows it." Then he turned and pointed dramatically at Fumiko. "And, most important, ladies and gentlemen, this woman, who owed her dead husband love and loyalty and, instead, fed him poison . . . *she* knows it!

"There is no need for lengthy argument in this case." He nodded in Harry's direction. "You don't need high-priced Hollywood lawyers to tell you what to do. You can see the facts for yourselves, draw your own conclusions and make your own judgment.

"The evidence clearly points to only one conclusion. I ask only that you carefully consider that evidence, and judge it for yourselves. And, when you do, I'm confident you will find the defendant guilty as charged."

Two or three jurors nodded. Others rapidly made notes.

Short but effective, Harry thought, as he watched the jurors' re-actions. He had only one chance to save Fumiko. He had already decided to take the chance, regardless of the consequences. After all, what did he have to lose?

"All right, Mr. Cain, you may proceed."

Harry rose and walked slowly to the jury box. He stood looking from juror to juror for almost a full minute before he began. The long pause stopped their fidgeting and note taking, focused their attention and brought a return of their serious, concerned mood.

"Ladies and gentlemen, like Mr. Scuneo, I will be brief. Like him, I will let the facts speak for themselves. But facts, ladies and gentlemen, not theories, not possibilities, not even probabilities—just facts. We're talking about a lady's life here; and society, the law, our system, demand factual proof beyond a reasonable doubt. If you have a reasonable doubt, if you believe there is a reasonable possi-bility that Fumiko Masami did not kill her husband, then you must find her not guilty.

"Now, let's look at the facts. Motive? Yes, Fumiko had a motive. Sure she did."

Two jurors looked at each other in surprise at what seemed an unexpected concession from Harry.

"Hiraiko Masami behaved like a brutal animal and treated his wife like dirt, worse than dirt, making her watch his disgusting behavior with common whores, beating her, humiliating her publicly. Yes, Fumiko had a motive. But many of us have such motives . . . and yet we don't kill. After all, she could have divorced him; and, even if she cared about the money, she could have received half his wealth anyway. A good lawyer could have gotten that for her. She didn't need to *kill* him to get her share of the property and certainly not to get away from him. She could have just walked out the door.

"And don't forget, ladies and gentlemen, there were others who had motives too—even stronger motives. What about all those men whose wives and children had been thrown out in the street by Hiraiko Masami, who behaved toward them and their families like the heartless monster he was? What about *them*?

"There were unidentified men present that night . . . angry shouting men, crying out their rage at Mr. Masami behind the closed bedroom door. Were they the men whose families had been torn from their homes—thrown in the street—by Hiraiko Masami? It's a fair inference they were.

"Some say 'don't speak ill of the dead'; but here, we must, because Hiraiko Masami was evil, cruel and disgusting, and his ruthless, heartless conduct gave many people a motive to kill him. They would have had to stand in line and take a number to do it. So, the possibility of a *motive* on the part of Fumiko, and not a very logical one at that, doesn't make her guilty of murder. Not by a long shot."

Harry moved back to the counsel table and stood beside Fumiko, placing his hand lightly on her shoulder, forcing the jury to look at her. "Let's talk about the person herself. Does Fumiko look like a killer? Is there evidence that she was involved in prior acts of violence? That she ever made threats? That she even had a violent temper? Absolutely not." He returned to stand before the jury, again pausing to look from face to face.

"Now let's talk about the means and the opportunity to kill Hiraiko Masami. Sure, you might think Fumiko *could* have killed him, would have killed him, even *might* have killed him. That's not enough. Even if you thought . . . and there's no such evidence . . .

that she *probably* killed him, that's not enough either. You must be convinced by the proven facts beyond a reasonable doubt . . . *beyond a reasonable doubt*. Others had the opportunity too, just as others had the motive. We've already seen that.

"You can't say that, on these facts, there's no reasonable doubt as to Fumiko's guilt. If you'll keep an open mind and reason along with me, then, when we've concluded here today, I'm certain that you will *not* say it.

"First, it would have been surprising if Fumiko's fingerprints were *not* on the glass by the bed. She did, after all, live there. She probably drank from the glass herself sometime earlier and probably brought her husband a drink. Perhaps she even brought him *this* drink." Harry lifted the glass that had been found by the bedside. Again Harry saw the jurors exchange surprised glances at what appeared to be a damaging concession. "Oh, yes, perhaps she even prepared this drink for him *before* someone else added poison to the harmless Fernet Branca she had poured.

"Mr. Scuneo says no one else's prints were on the glass, but what does that prove? Hasn't Mr. Scuneo ever heard about gloves? Besides, the killer didn't have to touch the glass to drop a little poison in the drink when Masami wasn't looking.

"Ladies and gentlemen, we know that there were other men in and out of the suite, men in a rage, shouting men. We know other men had an even stronger motive to kill Hiraiko Masami than his wife, other men who would find it easier to kill him and who had the means to kill him." Harry turned and extended his hand toward Fumiko. "Men who were far more likely to have been the killer than this young, gentle lady.

"Oh, you say, that's all well and good. How come she had poison in her purse? Mr. Scuneo tells you that the phial in her purse is what makes his case, sends this young woman to life in prison or even death. Mr. Scuneo will tell you, I'm sure, that Fumiko stayed in her room that night, so no one else had a chance to plant the phial in her purse, and besides, he says, her prints were on the phial as well, so it had to be hers . . . only hers. Doesn't that establish guilt beyond a reasonable doubt? It may seem so to Mr. Scuneo. For a while it may have seemed so to you. But the fact is, *it does not*!" Harry slammed his palm on the rail of the jury box. He paused, and, taking one step away from the jury, he addressed them in a slow and even tone. "And I will prove it to you, ladies and gentlemen. I will *prove* it to you." The jurors sat forward now, looking puzzled, curious.

"Mr. Scuneo's whole case"—Harry turned and pointed at the prosecution table—"his whole case for putting this lady in prison for life or killing her depends on one exhibit."

Harry paused and walked to the table beside the clerk's desk. He picked up the phial of dark-brown fluid that had been found in Fumiko's purse. He held it up to the light, peering at it silently.

Then he spoke, quietly. "Their whole case depends on this liquid being deadly poison." He walked back to the jury carrying the phial high in front of him, gesturing with it. "If this were poison, there would still be a reasonable doubt that others might have killed Hiraiko Masami. There would still be many possibilities to consider. But the fact is this is *not* poison. If that is so, if I am right and this is not poison, then there is simply no evidence at all from which you could possibly find Fumiko guilty.

"And so, we face the critical question, is it poison? 'Come on,' you will say, 'the expert told us it's poison.' But he didn't, not really. He has no direct and personal knowledge of *what's* in this tube. What he said was that his computer printout indicated to him there was poison in here."

Again, Harry lifted the phial high above him, close to the jury. "Ladies and gentlemen, we live in an age in which we are becoming more and more dependent on computers to govern our lives. We know that sometimes, more often than we would like to imagine, computerized tests and computer printouts are wrong. Has the computer ever made an error on your bank statement? On your telephone bill?"

Harry saw at least three jurors quietly nod.

"I'll bet it has. I had a foolproof computer in my own office. It had state-of-the-art ability to scan my records and send out my firm's bills. Yes, sir, a computer could do that complicated task. The problem was it scanned the wrong line and a client who was supposed to be billed a dollar seventy-five for postage got a bill for twenty-eight thousand dollars. Was he surprised!"

The jury chuckled. Harry thought, at least they *like* me. That's something. They seemed interested, not confused.

"Oh yes, ladies and gentlemen, remember it was a computer that indicated this tube from Fumiko's purse"—he held the phial aloft once again—"was poison. It was not an expert exercising his own judgment, skill, and experience. It was a machine, a computer, just like the one that does your bank statement and your telephone bill and just like the one that scanned the wrong line in my law-firm records.

"Even Lieutenant Keough, the keeper of this particular computer, admitted that it makes errors. Of course, he claimed the errors occur only once every five thousand times. That's what he claimed. But don't you suppose there are hundreds of errors that he never finds out about, that just get filed away, never discovered? Of course there are. If the computer hadn't sent my client that bill for twenty-eight thousand instead of one for a dollar seventy-five for postage, we would never have found the error. If it had just put that number in a file, we would never have known. Perhaps, like Lieutenant Keough, I would have thought my computer doesn't make many errors either.

"But let's even assume that Lieutenant Keough was right when he said his computer only makes an error once every five thousand times. Remember, he also told us they had run at least *fifteen* thousand tests in his office and had not yet found one error. Okay, even if that's so, it wouldn't be surprising at all if we found some errors. We should. In fact, if he's right in his figures, there should be *three* computer errors by this time, and certainly this could be one of them."

Some of the jurors were taking notes. They were following him all right, but he sensed he still hadn't convinced them. He walked to the end of the jury box and pivoted, turning to face the jury again, holding their eyes with his.

"We know that Mr. Masami drank Fernet Branca all the time. Would it be surprising that Fumiko would carry a phial of it in her purse—to give him when they were traveling? Not at all. Couldn't this be a situation like the one in my office, where the computer scanned the recorded data improperly and came up with a printout that said it was poison, when it wasn't really poison at all, but only Fernet Branca? That certainly could be the case. After all, the men in the lab wouldn't know. They wouldn't catch the error. They couldn't. They read the computer printout; and, if *it's* wrong, then naturally *they're* wrong. We know that the two substances, antimony chloride and Fernet Branca, look alike, even smell alike. Those men in the lab couldn't tell by look or smell, even if they tried. And they didn't try. They just relied on the computer—like your bank does, and the phone company, and my office staff.

"So, even if you believe what Lieutenant Keough claimed about the percentage of error, there ought to have been three errors and this could easily be one of the three, and this phial could very well contain Fernet Branca, not poison. If so, then, of course, the case is over, and Fumiko must be acquitted."

Harry looked from face to face. His guess was the jurors appreciated his logic, thought he was making a game try, but weren't sold. And, if they weren't sold, they'd convict. He couldn't let that happen. He wouldn't. He walked back to the center of the jury box, leaned close to the jurors, one hand still holding the phial in the air in front of them, the other pointing to it.

"I say this *'could'* contain only Fernet Branca, ladies and gentlemen, and that should be enough to create a reasonable doubt. But I won't ask you to rely on what *'could'* be so. I told you I would prove it to you, and I will—right here in this courtroom—and from the prosecution's own evidence." Now the jurors looked fascinated, curious. Harry had their complete attention. He turned and pointed at the prosecution table. "Mr. Scuneo there assures you that the computer is right, is infallible—that this is deadly poison, that it will eat through a man's innards and make him die hideously. Those were his words, you remember . . . that the contents of this phial would cause a 'hideous' and 'excruciating' death."

He turned back to the jury, the phial held high before him. "But if, as I tell you—as I am absolutely convinced—Fumiko Masami is *not* guilty and this is *not* poison, not the deadly antimony chloride that will eat hideously through a man's guts, then, of course, you must find her not guilty.

"Is there any way we can know for sure which is the case? There certainly is, ladies and gentlemen. We can know absolutely and *for sure.*"

In one swift movement, Harry pulled the cork from the phial and, before anyone could restrain him or even protest, he drank its entire contents.

A collective gasp arose from the gallery. The jury was stunned, mesmerized. Fumiko looked startled, white with tension. Then she looked down at her clasped fingers. For just a second, Scuneo, the judge, everyone in the courtroom looked on in silence.

Then the prosecutor leapt to his feet. "Your Honor," he cried, "that's evidence. He's destroyed the evidence. He . . ."

Down came Judge Kennedy's gavel. "Mr. Scuneo, sit down! We'll deal with that when the case is concluded . . . as a separate matter. Mr. Cain, have you anything further?"

"Yes, Your Honor."

"Then continue."

Some reporters bolted for the courtroom doors. Others were feverishly making notes or sketches.

Harry turned again to the jury and smiled. "So you see, ladies and gentlemen, the phial in Fumiko's purse did not contain poison after all." He smacked his lips. "It tastes like Fernet Branca to me."

Smiling, obviously savoring the moment, he sauntered back toward the counsel table. He turned and slowly picked up some notes, put them down and looked confidently at the jury, taking his time, making eye contact with each of them. "Ladies and gentlemen," he finally said, "there's really nothing more to say. The matter is clear. There was no poison in the phial, no poison in the purse. Obviously, Fumiko Masami did *not* kill her husband, and, of course, you must find her not guilty. Thank you."

A buzz of conversation swept the gallery. More reporters rushed for the phones. The bailiff stood, raising his arm, signaling for quiet. Judge Kennedy rapped for order. The crowd quieted, settled down. Meanwhile, Harry had returned to his seat. Once again, he felt empty, drained of any feeling. He glanced over at Fumiko and met her eyes. They were wide now, frightened.

"Mr. Scuneo, I assume you have a reply? It's ten-twenty and I would like to finish argument this morning and instruct the jury before lunch. So please proceed. What is your time estimate?"

"Oh, not more than fifteen or twenty minutes, Your Honor. But, first, I would like to comment further on Mr. Cain's conduct. You see . . ."

"No, Mr. Scuneo, not now."

Scuneo got to his feet, obviously in a state of controlled rage. "Your Honor, Mr. Cain's conduct is clearly a contempt of this court. It's . . ."

Again the gavel fell. "Mr. Scuneo, I've already told you not now. If you have a reply argument, make it. Otherwise, we'll proceed to instruct the jury immediately. Mr. Cain's conduct"—he nodded ominously in Harry's direction—"will be dealt with later."

"Very well, Your Honor," said Scuneo as he walked to the jury box. Harry could feel the prosecutor's anger, feel his mind groping to find an effective answer to what Harry had done, an answer to what seemed unanswerable. Harry was fascinated to see if the man could improvise something to deal with this totally unanticipated turn of events.

Scuneo placed his hand on the railing of the jury box. Like Harry, he looked from juror to juror, taking his time before beginning. Artful stalling, Harry thought, while Scuneo searched desperately for an argument to turn the case around, back to the solid prosecution victory that had been there in his grasp only minutes before. Suddenly the prosecutor's voice roared across the courtroom.

"You are a jury! You are not an audience at some amusing sideshow. You are a jury charged with carrying out the sacred function of preserving our society's values.

"Are you going to be fooled by a theatrical trick?" He waited. "Of course you're not. Was that a theatrical trick? Of course it was. You heard Lieutenant Keough. There *was* poison in that phial. It *was* poison when it was tested in the police lab and when it was found in the defendant's purse. We know that errors occur. Things get lost, mislabeled, switched. It's happened to all of us. But we don't let a killer go because of such a mistake. Somehow, in the time between the crime-lab test and the district attorney's office, the phials got switched. Maybe it was erroneously exchanged for a test phial of Fernet Branca. They were around too. Somehow, Mr. Cain found out. Maybe from the smell. So he could pull off his theatrical trick. But that trick shouldn't disguise the fact that there still is more than ample evidence that Fumiko Masami killed her husband.

"We still know the accused had the motive, and, of course, the fact that Hiraiko Masami was, by some standards, a 'bad guy' doesn't give anyone a license to kill him, especially his supposedly loyal wife. Once we start taking upon ourselves the right to judge who should be killed, then our society's in deep trouble and none of us have any personal safety, because somewhere out there"—Scuneo gestured toward the street, "there's probably someone who may think *you*"—now be pointed to the jury—"are a 'bad guy.' No, ladies and gentlemen, the defendant had no right to kill her husband, even though she had a strong motive to do it.

"There is nothing to Mr. Cain's divorce argument—nothing whatsoever. Mr. Cain argues that Fumiko Masami could have divorced her husband and gotten a big property award. First, he's wrong on the law. Second, even if he'd been right, she wouldn't have known it anyway. I doubt that they print the California community property law in Japanese, and that, if they did, Mrs. Masami would have taken time from shopping on Rodeo Drive in order to read it. No, there is nothing at all to the divorce argument, and the classic element of motive is there, clearly and in spades.

"And what about the means and the opportunity, the other elements we must look for. Again, a professional—maybe the best in his field anywhere in the world—has told you that the defendant had the poison in her purse, and it *was* poison when it was found there in her purse, the very poison that killed her husband. She was there in the hotel suite, she prepared his drink—Mr. Cain as much as admitted it—and the drink was poisoned with the same deadly stuff from her purse. Except for poor Hiraiko Masami himself, no one else's prints were on the glass, or on the bottle, or on the phial in the defendant's purse. Only Mrs. Masami's own prints.

"Now Mr. Cain conjures up strange killers wearing gloves. Can't you just picture that? Here's Hiraiko drinking with his guests, and who should stroll through the living room but a sinister-looking guy wearing mittens."

He wheeled and turned to face Harry. "Come on, Mr. Cain, you can do better than that!" Harry tried to look pleasantly confident as he returned the prosecutor's stare.

Scuneo turned again to the jury, his pockmarked skin glowing with the intensity of his effort. "Remember the name of this case is

People v. *Masami*. 'People' means *all* the people. You are each a part of the people. So am I. We all have an interest in seeing that killers do not go free. We can't allow individuals to judge for themselves who's a good guy and who's a bad guy, and execute the bad guys at their own whim. The evidence is there, clearly, overwhelmingly calling for guilt. Don't be thrown off the track because, somehow, somewhere, through a human error, a bottle was mistakenly switched, allowing Mr. Cain to do his dramatic stunt. Don't let such things take your eye off the ball, off the people's case—your case, a case that cries out for conviction. Thank you." Scuneo wheeled again and returned to his chair.

Under the circumstances, Harry thought, not a bad try, not bad at all. The judge took the morning recess, then instructed the jury. At 11:45 the jury retired and began their deliberations. Fumiko looked desperately over her shoulder toward Harry as she was led from the courtroom by a uniformed matron.

Scuneo slammed his briefcase shut and moved toward the door. He stopped and looked back at Harry. "You'll do time for this, Cain. I'll go for your license too. You're finished." He burst through the swinging doors into the glare of the flashbulbs.

John Matsuoka turned quietly to Harry, still seated at the counsel table. "How'd you know that wasn't poison, Harry? Did you get a chance to test it?"

Harry had a strange, almost dreamy look in his face. He glanced over at the court clerk sitting only a few feet away. "Let's not talk about that now, John. I'll fill you in later. Listen, you go on out and get a bite. I'd like to just sit here by myself for a while." Raising his voice, Harry addressed the clerk. "Okay if I stay in the courtroom during the noon recess? I'm a little tired."

"Sure, Mr. Cain. Stay right where you are. I'm going to stay here myself," she said, holding up a brown-paper bag.

"Can I bring you back something to eat, Harry?" Matsuoka said, looking concerned.

"No thanks, John. I really don't feel like eating. I just want to sit here quietly. Okay?"

"Sure, Harry, I'll be back soon . . ."

Thirty minutes later Harry looked nervously at his watch for the fifth or sixth time. He hoped his drinking the contents of the phial had won the jury completely, that it had just blown the case away. If he was right, there should be a very quick verdict. Was too much time passing? Had it already passed? He'd seen the bailiff enter the jury room with trays of sandwiches and drinks, so they were working right through lunch. Then why were they taking so long? He felt queasy, not right. He wanted to avoid talking with the clerk and so pretended to concentrate on the notes before him. She recognized his need to work and sat quietly reading a paperback novel.

At 12:30 John Matsuoka returned to the courtroom. He looked even more concerned. Harry always stayed nearby waiting out the jury. When they left the jury room, he wanted them to see him still sitting there, to know he cared, that he was in this with them. But always before he had paced the floor, made phone calls, remained active. Now he sat quietly, looking pale, somehow unwell. Matsuoka leaned close to Harry, speaking softly.

"You did test that stuff, didn't you, Harry, before you drank it?"

"Later, John. Let me sit here quietly and think. Please."

Matsuoka sat down beside him, nervously moving his papers into neat piles. They both looked up to see Bailey Scuneo and the prosecution team reenter the room. Scuneo would also try to stay nearby. Should the jury have a question or want some evidence reread, he'd also want them to see him there waiting.

At that moment, the buzzer sounded on the bailiff's desk. The bailiff looked over at the clerk and nodded, then got to his feet and strolled to the jury room, knocking and entering in one movement. Two minutes later he emerged.

"Got a verdict," he said, looking to see that all the participants were in the courtroom.

The clerk quickly advised Judge Kennedy, who had remained in his chambers. The bailiff went into the corridor, ostensibly to bring quiet, but actually to let the reporters know that a verdict had been reached. They rushed in to take their seats. The court reporter entered through a side door and took her place at the stenotype machine, punching out the mystifying symbols for "Court reconvened at 12:40."

"Remain seated and come to order," intoned the bailiff as Judge

Kennedy took the bench. Then the jury filed in, their expressions sober, guarded. Every eye was on them as they took their places in the jury box.

"Has the jury reached a verdict?"

A tall cadaverous man, juror number two, was now the foreman. He rose and stood beside his chair, his right hand clutching a folded sheet of paper. "We have, Your Honor."

"Very well, please hand it to the bailiff."

The heavy-set deputy rose ponderously, swung his holster back on his hip and walked across the room to take the folded paper from the jury foreman. He walked to the bench and handed the paper up to Judge Kennedy. Harry, Matsuoka, Scuneo, and the rest of the prosecution staff stood in a posture of rigid attention as Judge Kennedy read the sheet to himself and handed it back to the bailiff, who walked it over to the court clerk.

"Please read the verdict."

The clerk opened the folded paper, cleared his throat and began to read. "We the jury find the defendant, Fumiko Masami, not guilty."

Pandemonium swept the room. Several reporters tried simultaneously to push through the narrow doors to get at the telephones. There was a surge of frenzied commotion and excited conversation in the gallery.

Judge Kennedy rapped for order, and the room grew silent. He formally released the defendant and thanked the jury for its work. Then he turned to Harry.

"Mr. Cain, you will appear in this court at ten tomorrow morning. At that time, we will determine whether or not you will be held in contempt of this court. Thank you." He rose and left the bench.

Fumiko rushed to Harry and took his hands in hers, looking deeply, questioningly into his eyes. He gently freed his hands and moved slowly away from her and out of the courtroom, ignoring the back-slapping and even the attempts of the jury members to shake his hand. In the corridor, dozens of cameras flashed and microphones were thrust in his face. Questions were fired at him from every direction.

"No comment," he muttered, through clenched teeth.

The press corps had never seen Harry Cain like this. Not the

Sunset Bomber, always the source of a colorful quote, something interesting to print, to sell papers, to attract viewers. They certainly never expected to see him this way when he'd just won what might be the biggest, most difficult case of his career. They continued to try, throwing question after question at Harry as he moved slowly down the hall toward the elevators. But he simply repeated the litany, "No comment, not now." As he reached the elevator doors, John Matsuoka caught up with him. Fumiko and Isamu Morita were beside him.

"Harry, are you okay? You look pale. Let me drive you back to the office."

Harry turned facing them all as the elevator arrived. "Please, I'm okay. I just want to be by myself for a while. So stay here. Okay?" He stepped alone into the elevator and turned to face them again, holding up his palm to signal that they should stop, should leave him alone. As the elevator doors closed, he could see their faces tense with surprise and concern.

Minutes later, Harry walked as quickly as he could down Main Street toward the Plaza. Twice he stumbled, catching his foot on the irregular sidewalk. The sun was high now, beating down on his head and shoulders. He needed the warmth. His hands and feet were icy. As he saw the trees of the Plaza and the restored but empty brick buildings of the old city, he felt light-headed, dizzy. He heard a buzzing in his ears that seemed to grow, to become a rushing sound like the sea. He began to feel a sharp pain deep in his gut. He saw the benches surrounding the old iron bandstand, where he had rested so many, many times. He headed toward them, a fitting place for a weary man to have a very long rest.

Then, at the last minute, he turned abruptly, veering, staggering off to his right. Clutching his stomach, doubled over and almost tripping on the curb, he turned into a small deserted street that ran between the gloomily empty Pico House Hotel and an abandoned fire station.

There, parked alone at the curb, stood a large unmarked van. Harry pounded three times on the back doors. Immediately, they swung open. Two white-coated arms pulled him inside, as the doors closed behind him.

"Christ, Mr. Cain, you cut it fine. In ten minutes you'd have entered the critical phase. In twenty more, there'd have been nothing we could do for you." Skilled hands were whisking off his coat, tie, and shirt and pulling a hospital gown around him, helping him onto a surgical table, adjusting equipment, moving it over him.

Half an hour later, Harry still lay on the table, breathing heavily, feeling weak but happy.

"First time you had your stomach pumped, Mr. Cain?"

"First and last," said Harry, managing a wry smile. Somewhat unsteadily, he sat up and reached for his jacket. Pulling out his wallet, he removed two one-thousand-dollar bills.

Harry's sole companion, a gangly black man in his mid-thirties, smiled broadly. "Well, Mr. Cain, that's not bad pay for a morning's work. Not bad at all, and you can be sure there'll never be a peep from me. No, sir, never a peep."

"Thanks, Frank; when Skip Corrigan said I could count on you he was right. Christ, you saved my life."

"Naw," said Frank, as Harry pulled on his clothes. "We had a few more minutes before it was too late . . ."

Weak and utterly exhausted, Harry pushed open his office door. His receptionist looked up from the switchboard and, seeing his pallor, jumped to her feet, pushed down a key on the board and screamed into her headset "Mr. Cain's here." Then she ran to help him.

"Mr. Cain, are you okay?" she said breathlessly, taking him by the arm and leading him toward the sofa.

"Sure, Carol, just a little tired."

The inner door to the reception room burst open, and John Matsuoka entered, breathing heavily, having run the length of the hallway. "Holy Christ, Harry, you scared the hell out of us. We were ready to call the police. I mean first you drink what's supposed to be poison, and then you disappear. Jesus, I was scared; and Fumiko Masami has called four times already. She's out of her mind." He sat down on the couch next to Harry, who turned to his younger partner with a look of amusement.

"Hey, John, I'm okay. Relax, will you. I stopped for a little drink to unwind. That's all, just a little drink."

He picked up the intercom line. "Clara, will you call Mrs. Masami right away and tell her I'm here and I'm perfectly okay."

Matsuoka, relieved, left the reception room to take a call. Two young associates crowded into the room, anxious to hear Harry's version of the trial that, in just a few short hours, had already become an international legend and was the lead story on every television newscast. One associate held up the late edition of the *Times*. Across the front page was the banner headline FUMIKO ACQUITTED followed by LAWYER DRINKS EVIDENCE.

Patiently and consistently lying, Harry answered their questions, trying out the explanation he intended to give the media the following day. He was disappointed at their readiness to accept his story, their failure to find the logical weaknesses and inconsistencies, to probe for a better, more rational explanation.

Finally, Harry stood and, excusing himself, picked up his messages and went to his own office. He sat in the gray corduroy chair and looked out at the lights of the city spreading in every direction as darkness came on. The setting sun still colored the western sky a deep red that faded to purple as Harry's gaze slowly turned eastward toward the downtown skyline.

He switched on Handel's *Water Music* and, opening the cabinet, poured himself two fingers of Scotch. He let the music wash over him as he looked around the room. Everything in it reminded him of Nancy, who had decorated it with such love and tenderness. He felt his eyes fill with tears. Why couldn't he have shown her his love, cherished her when he had the chance? Christ, what a stupid, child-like idiot he was. Would he ever be any different? Did he really care?

What would he have done if the jury *hadn't* come in on time? He didn't know. For years he'd loved his life, relished being Harry Cain, playing that exhilarating role. But now, without Nancy, it wasn't the same. He was surprised. But it was so.

He poured two more fingers of Scotch, bolted it down, and stood up, yawning and stretching. He'd better learn something about the law on destroying evidence before tomorrow's contempt hearing. With that sobering thought, he headed for his library.

That evening, when Harry arrived home, the door was open and music was playing on the CD system. He looked toward the kitchen for Armando and turned to see his daughter coming from the other side of the room. She had to return to London soon and had a story to cover in San Francisco before she left. They were both feeling uneasy about their coming separation, about their return to separate worlds, separate lives. Gail threw her arms around him, and held him to her so fiercely he thought she would hurt herself.

"Congratulations, Dad. I heard about the verdict."

"Thanks, hon, but are you okay?"

She pulled back and looked at him, her eyes red and swollen. "Sure. I've been wandering through the house, and I guess . . . I guess it just got to me. Each time I think I'm all cried out, I . . ." She stopped, hugged him close, and began to sob into his shoulder. Harry began to cry too, and they stood there in the entry hall weeping and clinging to each other.

Later Armando made them dinner, and they sat for hours in the candlelight, sipping their wine and talking. He told her about the trial and how pleased he was at the acquittal. She talked about Robin Milgrim, the married gossip columnist she adored and Harry despised, and about her job in England. In a way, she was anxious to get back to work, but the Milgrim affair just went on and on, painful and powerful. She wasn't so anxious to get back to it. And she wasn't anxious to leave Harry.

Then it was his turn again. This was the time for truth, he thought. Gail should know the truth. He told her about Alla and other earlier women. He said it had been a product of his immaturity, that the women were not really significant and never diminished his love for Nancy, that he would have given up all of them for another hour with Nancy. He told her how he'd prayed to have the cancer himself and for Nancy to be well . . . how much he'd really wanted that. The tears streamed down his cheeks and Gail came around the table to hold him. As she stood with her arms around his shoulders, he was glad he'd been open about this. It was good to tell her everything, to be totally candid. Well, not totally, he thought, realizing that he hadn't mentioned the gray-haired woman in Boston, and that he'd given Gail the same phony version of his trial strategy he'd given to his law firm associates and that he intended to give to the press the next morning. After all, he didn't want his daughter to think of him as disgusting or deceitful.

Harry had a sudden impulse. He put his hands on Gail's shoulders and faced her, gently smiling.

"Look, Sunday's your last day, and I know you've got to be in San Francisco until the weekend. Will you do something with me on Saturday, something I've been wanting to do for years?"

"Sure, Dad, what is it?"

"Walk with me from downtown to the sea—all the way from Number One Wilshire to the Palisades."

"You've been *wanting* to do *that*? Why?"

"It's something your mother and I talked about doing, but never got around to. No one walks in L.A., and we just didn't want to live and die in this city and never walk through it. She never did it, and now I'd like to do it for her."

"Okay then, I'm with you. But don't *you* talk about dying. You've probably got fifty more years."

Harry hugged his daughter to him, leaning her cheek against his. "I guess we never know that, do we, Gail?"

She was silent for a moment. Then he felt another tear run down her cheek.

"I guess not," she whispered.

"Your explanation fails to satisfy me, Mr. Cain." Judge Kennedy leaned forward, fixing Harry with flinty blue-gray eyes. "It may be that you did get carried away with your enthusiasm for your client's case, but, nevertheless, you knowingly destroyed evidence, put it out of the reach of anyone to run another test; and that's inexcusable, Mr. Cain, *inexcusable*! I find you guilty of contempt of this court. You will serve forty-eight hours in the county jail, and you are fined five thousand dollars."

Ninety minutes later, having been fingerprinted and booked, Harry was seated in a small cell wearing fresh county jail fatigues. He smiled through the bars at no less than twenty reporters and cameramen who had received permission to attend his "press conference." Microphones were thrust at him through the bars, strobe lights flashed and illuminated the corridor and nearby cells until the scene resembled a motion-picture premiere.

After a number of questions and answers, a reporter from KTTV made himself heard over the din. "Didn't you take an enormous physical risk . . . drinking from that phial? I mean, what if the prosecution was right? What if it really was poison?" There was a buzz of assent among the others. It was a point that would provide colorful background to the stories they were already shaping in their minds.

Harry raised his hand for quiet.

"No, I never considered myself at risk. First, I had complete faith in my client's innocence and was totally convinced that she did *not* have poison in her purse. But it wasn't only that. I had also trained myself to distinguish the smell of antimony chloride from that of Fernet Branca . . . a subtle difference, it's true, but one that can still be detected. When I was making my closing argument and I raised the phial in front of the jury and pulled the cork, I quickly inhaled the fumes and knew at once that I had been right, that I was dealing with harmless Fernet Branca, and not the deadly poison claimed by Mr. Scuneo. So you can see, I really took no risk at all."

"Well, why didn't you demand another test, Mr. Cain, rather than drinking the material yourself?"

"Well, drinking that fluid seemed the only totally convincing way to show the jury that Mrs. Masami was innocent. If I had simply demanded another test, we would have had two experts testifying against each other and then each side would have hired two more experts and the jury would have been confused and overwhelmed by conflicting expert testimony. There would have been a continuing risk to my client. To me, the safest and soundest way was the one I chose."

"Do you believe the court was justified in holding you in contempt?"

"It wouldn't be proper for me to comment on that. Judge Kennedy did what he thought was proper, just as I did. Each of us followed the dictates of his own conscience. My conscience told me that my duty to my client required me to act as I did, and I believe the jury agreed with me. In any event, Mrs. Masami's innocence has been totally established, and she is a free woman . . . which is certainly what she deserves."

"Bailey Scuneo says that what you did was 'a cheap shyster's trick.' Do you have any comment?"

"Only that you have to consider the source. Mr. Scuneo managed to lose a case everyone considered a slam dunk. Naturally, he's upset and has to blame someone. I feel sorry for him."

At this point, two young Oriental men in black mess jackets pushed their way through the crowd of reporters. They carried large paper bags and a folded tablecloth. The guard opened the cell and allowed the two men to enter.

"From Mon Kee, Mr. Cain. Your lunch," they said, bowing slightly as if they served lunch in the county jail every day.

Harry merely nodded. The two waiters from the Chinese seafood restaurant spread the cloth on the metal table next to Harry's cot and set out chopsticks, a crab cracker and two large porcelain dishes, all taken from one of the bags. Using large serving spoons, they piled one plate high with steaming cracked crab in a black-bean-and-garlic sauce and the other with succulent pieces of lobster sautéed with scallions and ginger. The older waiter turned toward the back of the cell and, opening his jacket, showed Harry a concealed bottle of Trefethen chardonnay, already opened but with the cork replaced. Shielding what he was doing with his body, he poured some of the wine into a plastic cup. He handed the cup to Harry and gestured for him to sit on the stool next to the table. Harry rolled up his sleeves with pleasure, sat down, and taking up the crab cracker began to attack the pungent seafood with relish, continuing to answer questions from the reporters outside his cell.

When he had finished his meal, the younger waiter placed a fortune cookie before him while the older carefully poured a cup of tea. Harry opened the fortune cookie and read it in silence.

"What's it say, Mr. Cain?" asked the reporter from KTTV.

Harry grinned, reading the paper slip aloud in the glaring light of the snapping cameras. "You need more space."

Harry breathed the soft evening air and sighed heavily as he walked down Main Street toward his car. He felt an overwhelming sadness. The contempt hearing, the clamor of the press, the surreal experience of forty-eight hours in jail—all had taken his mind off the fact that he was basically alone in the world. Now, heading toward his car for a long drive to an empty house, he was engulfed by the realization of his loss. The lights of the city were coming on, and the lingering rose-violet of the horizon gave the scene a strange bittersweet quality. Men and women were hurrying through the streets, making their way home to share the day's events. Harry had no one with whom to share. Not any more. The traffic rushed by, the sky slowly darkened, and he was very much alone.

He continued walking along Main toward the old Catholic church, trying to fight off his aching loneliness. Looking ahead, he saw a black limousine with dark tinted glass parked in the church driveway, blocking the sidewalk. As he drew closer, the rear door opened and a woman leaned forward. Through the dusk, he could see her pale skin and lustrous black hair. A moment later, he realized it was Fumiko Masami. She beckoned. "Cain-san, please join me."

Harry stepped to the car, bent down and slid into the rear seat beside her. Fumiko wore western clothing, a black shantung pantsuit and white blouse. Behind her ear was a gardenia. Its exotic fragrance filled the car.

"Cain-san, forgive Fumiko's poor English. We must have a small ceremony. Dozo . . . please."

Harry knew from experience that the Japanese felt that the completion of an important transaction demanded symbolic underlining with a ceremony of some kind—champagne or even tea and cookies, a summation of what had been accomplished and a recitation of gratitude. It was extremely important to them. To refuse was to be rude and insulting. Besides, what else did he have to do? Go back to an empty house? Have a drink or two and then go out to a lonely dinner or sit alone at the big dining-room table while Armando served him in silence?

"Sure, Fumiko, I'd be delighted."

Fumiko signaled the driver, and the limo backed out of the driveway and went north on Main Street, turning right on Sunset. It made two more turns and pulled up in front of the Fuji Bank Building on East First Street. The driver came around to let them out and rushed ahead to open the building's huge glass doors. Fumiko beckoned Harry to follow her to the elevator. As they swept past, a Japanese security guard bowed, but said nothing. Fumiko took a key from her purse and inserted it in a small lock next to the top button of the elevator panel. She pushed the button and the elevator rose swiftly and silently to the top of the building.

The doors slid open, and they stepped directly into the living room of a magnificently furnished penthouse that looked out over the city in every direction. As they moved into the softly lit room, Harry noticed lacquered screens, ivory figurines, stunning Oriental paintings and elegantly displayed ceremonial robes. Everything was opulent and in exquisite taste. Fumiko took Harry's coat and, in an instant, had taken his tie and was kneeling to remove his shoes. She excused herself and returned in a few moments wearing a kimono of lime-green silk with high-heeled slippers of the same material. She brought Harry glove-leather slippers and a wide-sleeved Oriental robe, dark blue printed with bold white figures.

"Is this place yours?"

"Not mine, Cain-san. Family friend."

She led Harry to a carved teak bar and gestured toward a small refrigerator behind it. There, Harry found a bottle of Cristal and two fluted glasses. He opened the champagne and poured them each a glass. Fumiko raised hers, looking earnestly into Harry's eyes.

"Fumiko owes everything to Cain-san. Her life, her pride, every-thing. Fumiko can never repay Cain-san suf . . . sufficiently."

"Your poem is payment enough, Fumiko, as is sharing this mo-ment. . . . Kampai." Harry raised his glass and gently touched it to Fumiko's. "Kampai" she said softly, looking into his eyes. They each took a sip. Then Fumiko took Harry's arm and, smiling up at him, led him on a tour of the penthouse apartment.

Each room was more magnificent than the last. Each had a daz-zling view out over the city in a different direction. Each was fur-nished with what seemed to be priceless art and antiques.

Harry had carried the champagne bottle with them, and they re-filled their glasses as they reached the library, a room stunningly painted with a high-gloss black lacquer, the carved teak desk com-plemented by overstuffed sofas and chairs covered in heavy black silk. They stood in an angled window looking west at the downtown skyline outlined dramatically by the deep-red rays of the setting sun. After a moment, Fumiko broke the silence.

"Will Cain-san stay some time here with Fumiko?"

"I will, Fumiko." He smiled, struck by her extraordinary grace and beauty.

"One more thing. Cain-san hurts inside. Fumiko knows. Can help." Harry started to reply, but Fumiko put a finger to his lips. "Please say nothing. Is not a time for words."

She took his arm again and moved close to him. He felt her warmth. Again they stood in silence, finishing their champagne.

Finally, taking Harry by the hand, Fumiko led him into the larg-est, most lavish bath he had ever seen. The floor was deep-blue tile strewn with white rugs. The walls were lacquered in the same blue and highlighted with tall art-deco mirrors. A huge window faced southwest, and Harry could see planes following each other into the airport in a continuous line, a string of tiny pearls stretched across the sky. In the far distance he could still make out the silhouette of Catalina Island against the purplish-red light on the horizon.

In the corner of the room, placed so as best to enjoy the spectacular view, was a vast sunken tub. Fumiko pressed a switch, and five large porcelain spouts began to fill the tub with steaming water. She turned back to Harry, taking the bottle and glass from him, refilling their glasses and placing them on a blue-lacquered table.

"Cain-san should remove clothing now."

"Fumiko too?" Harry whispered.

"Later," she whispered in return.

She held out her arms, and Harry stood transfixed. Silhouetted against the fading light, she was a vision from seventeenth-century Edo. But she was here now, in the present, standing across from him, looking out at the ten million lights of his city.

Fumiko moved across the room to stand before him. She opened his robe and slid it from his shoulders. She unbuttoned his shirt, looking deeply into his eyes, smiling only slightly. Then, without embarrassment, she undid his trousers, and with one hand on each thigh, slid the trousers to the floor and gently lifted them first from one leg and then the other.

Harry remained silent and motionless, staring at her as if in a trance. Using the same motion, placing a hand delicately on each thigh and slowly moving downward, she removed his shorts. She handed him his glass and again raised her own until it gently clinked with his.

"Kampai again, my Cain-san, kampai."

"Kampai, Fumiko," he replied. Then, standing quietly, facing each other in the darkened room with the lights of the city behind them, they drank their champagne.

As the tub filled, the spouts automatically shut off and Fumiko took Harry by the hand and led him to a stool near the edge of the tub.

"First wash," she said, reaching into a cabinet for a large redwood bucket which she filled from the steaming water in the tub. Taking soap and a rough washcloth, she began to scrub Harry's back, shoulders, and arms. She leaned over him, and he felt an intense shudder of excitement as she began delicately to wash his genitals. She rinsed him all over with clean hot water from the faucet, and then took his hand and led him to the tub. He put in one foot and pulled it out quickly. The water was scalding.

"Slowly, Cain-san. Look at the lights, move quietly, slowly into the water. Think of the lights and not the heat."

He obeyed her, staring at the lights, looking far to the south and west, projecting his mind out into the night. He let his eyes go unfocused, so that the lights swam before him, a vast carpet of flickering golden sparks. Then he lowered his body into the steaming water, willing himself not to break his concentration, not to feel the heat burning his skin.

Amazingly, it worked. Totally relaxed, immersed in the tub, he looked at Fumiko, who was staring out into the hypnotic carpet of lights. She looked over at Harry and, once again, gave him her mysterious half smile.

She pressed a switch near the tub, and gradually he heard soothing Japanese music—a koto and other instruments he could not identify. She reached again for the Cristal, which she had placed near the tub along with their two glasses. Filling them again, she handed one glass to Harry. Slowly he sipped it, luxuriating in the comforting heat of the water, the delicate dissonance of the music, the splendid, emotionally affecting view of the city.

"Won't you join me, Fumiko?" he asked softly.

"Later," she said, "all that Cain-san wishes will be. For now relax—surr . . . surrender to the water."

For twenty minutes he luxuriated in the tub, motionless, silent, letting the music and the heat ease his muscles, lessen his cares. He felt himself sliding into a singular relaxation, overcome by a sense of peace and acceptance unlike anything he had felt since Nancy's death.

Finally, taking him gently by the hand, Fumiko led him from the tub. The room itself was warm, and leaving the heated water, he felt fresh rather than chilled. Fumiko took a huge towel from heated chrome pipes along the wall and dried Harry thoroughly, once again taking great care in toweling down his private parts. When Harry was dry, she threw the cotton robe around his shoulders and pointed to a thin mattress lying on the floor, covered with tatami mats. Nearby was a small teak table bearing a thick fragrant candle that threw flickering shadows across the low bed.

"Harry-san, please lie down now for massage."

As Fumiko slipped the robe from his shoulders, Harry stretched out on his stomach, comfortably relaxed, his head resting on his arm. Through half-closed eyes, he could see the candlelight making faint shadows on the wall. He could hear the soft, strange interweaving of the Oriental woodwinds and strings. The exotic music induced a feeling of calm, a complete removal from the world of turmoil and stress.

Fumiko knelt beside Harry and, leaning close, whispered in his ear.

"Lose self in Fumiko's touch, Harry-san. Drift like boat in gentle sea."

Her fingers were stronger than he expected. She knew just where to press—knew where the sore and aching muscles would respond. She moved up and down his spine, dug deeply into the big muscles of his buttocks, then worked down his legs to his ankles and feet. Gradually, he felt the release of tensions he hadn't realized were there. Time passed, maybe a few moments, maybe a few hours, he was unable to estimate and he didn't care. Finally, she began to use her fingertips like feathers, tracing them lightly over his back and legs. He felt the beginnings of excitement ripple through his body. They'd waited long enough for what was surely going to happen. He rolled over and reached for her swiftly. She moved away from his outstretched fingers, rising and smiling.

"Later. Harry-san must be patient."

But this was not the time for patience. Harry got to his feet. He saw fright and excitement in her dark eyes. She took another step backward, beautiful in the shadowed light. He reached out and took her hand, holding it firmly, pulling her toward him. In an instant, his other hand went to her robe, pulling it back from her shoulders. Shyly, she turned away from him as he drew the robe downward, exposing the golden skin of her back and buttocks. He could hear her breathing, heavy and rapid. He could sense her excitement.

"Fumiko," he called, as the robe fell to the floor at her feet. "Fumiko, come to me."

Slowly, gracefully, she turned to face him, lips parted, eyes shining with desire as he reached to embrace her.

He stopped and heard himself gasp. His arms fell. In that instant that seemed frozen in time, he saw that Fumiko—lithe and lovely Fumiko—was a man.

For a long moment they stood in silence, staring at each other, Harry gaping in amazement, Fumiko, embarrassed at his reaction, pulling on her robe, her eyes already pleading for understanding. Then Fumiko reached out for him, touching his sleeve with outstretched fingers. Instinctively, Harry pulled away as if burned. He saw the look of hurt in Fumiko's eyes. But, overwhelmed with his own emotions, Harry wasn't ready to deal with Fumiko's anguish and silent plea for compassion.

Those fingers reaching now to touch him had soothed him and yes, goddamn it, they'd started to excite him. And they were a *man's* fingers. Christ! Fumiko, the graceful poet for whom he'd felt . . . what? affection? love? desire? . . . for whom he'd damn near killed himself . . . was a man! So many questions raced through Harry's mind he had no idea what to ask first.

"How'd you get away with that in jail?" he asked, surprised at the harshness of his tone.

"When Fumiko first came, asked lady marshal no body search. She thought Fumiko Oriental, so embarrassed. Was very nice. Also Fumiko give . . . gave her one thousand dollars. After that, Fumiko in private cell, so no problem."

Harry shook his head and moved toward his clothes.

"Harry-san, don't go. Nothing has to change—we can . . ."

"Of course it has to change, for Christ's sake, you're a man. That's a fundamental change." He shook his head again. "You fooled the jail. You fooled me. You fooled everyone."

He looked up at her. "My God, did Rocky know?"

"Of course Rocky knew. Knew all along. Found out night we married."

"And he stayed—knowing this?" He gestured toward Fumiko's body.

"He did. Rocky very young then. Full of pride. All Rocky's friends and family at wedding. Wedding highly pub . . . publicized. Rocky couldn't face shame of telling or leaving Fumiko that night or next day. Then time go on, it became our secret—our terrible secret.

"At first Rocky wild with anger. Drink heavily. One night, maybe three months after wedding, Rocky very drunk. Fumiko help to bed. Massaged—like massaged Harry-san tonight. Finally, Rocky let Fumiko make love to him—her way. Rocky respond. Oh yes, respond. Rocky shamed afterward, but respond. After that . . . sex life very good, but Rocky never get over shame and guilt."

"And that's why the drinking, the rage, the violence?"

"Maybe, Harry-san, maybe."

"How could he not know before you were married?"

"Fumiko raised in Shanghai. When Rocky first saw in Tokyo, Fumiko looked like now, like girl. Not sleep together before wedding. Not even kiss. Like you, Harry-san, Rocky not suspect. And, like Rocky, Harry-san would respond. I know this."

Fumiko moved forward, reaching out for him. Again, Harry stepped back.

"I can't, Fumiko."

"Harry-san can. Harry-san re . . . respond before. Harry-san desired Fumiko. Fumiko knows." The graceful hands gestured inward toward the slender body. "This same person."

The point had already occurred to Harry, and had troubled him more than a little. He gave Fumiko the same response he had silently given himself.

"I believed you were a woman then. So much of desire is in the mind; and, in my mind, you were a woman—a very desirable woman. Now that I know you're a man, it's completely different. There isn't any desire for you now. None."

Fumiko turned momentarily to look out at the lights of the city, then turned again to focus on Harry.

"Not *all* in mind. Harry-san knows that, felt it. And even mind can change, can grow, can accept new things. Rocky did, and Harry-san is more sen . . . sensitive man, more ready to grow and change."

"I said I can't, Fumiko. Perhaps it's more accurate to say 'I won't. I don't want to.'"

Again, he saw the pain in Fumiko's eyes. He didn't want to cause that pain. But there was nothing he could do. Nothing he could say. The situation was hopeless.

"I should go," he said, reaching for his clothes, thinking the line was like dialogue from a bad film. But he knew that, in fact, he *should* go. Staying would only inflict more pain.

As Fumiko stood watching him with a look of utter desolation, Harry quickly pulled on his clothes, throwing his jacket over his shoulders and stuffing his tie into his pocket. With Fumiko trailing behind him, he walked to the elevator door through which he had arrived only an hour before, so full of excitement and anticipation.

As he waited for the elevator, Fumiko spoke quietly.

"Please remember some things, Harry-san. Fumiko meant the poem. Meant the gra . . . gratitude. Harry-san saved Fumiko's life with his skill and courage. And Fumiko will always love Harry-san for this . . . and for what he is. Fumiko sorry Harry-san cannot accept this love. But maybe, someday, Harry-san can be her friend." A tear ran down the sculpted cheekbone and fell on the green silk robe.

"Maybe, Fumiko, maybe I can." He stepped into the elevator and, as the doors closed, he looked into those dark, pleading eyes and thought what a strange life this is, what odd, frightened, desperate creatures we are, and how little he had done to assuage the pain he had caused. Then, as the elevator descended, his feelings of guilt began to abate. He passed through the lobby of the building, nodded to the guard, and stepped out into the street. He breathed deeply of the fresh night air, and, more than anything, he felt relief.

Ten minutes later, Harry sat in the cool darkness of the New Otani bar, sipping Stolichnaya on the rocks as he turned the situation over and over in his mind, exploring, analyzing his confused feelings and reactions.

He'd certainly had no desire for Fumiko once he'd discovered the truth. None. That was clear, and it was comforting. But he'd sure as hell expected to end up in bed with her . . . him? . . . when he thought she was a woman. And he wanted to. No denying that. If he hadn't pulled the robe open, they'd have embraced, kissed; and wouldn't he have become fully aroused? Hell, yes. As long as he thought he was kissing a beautiful woman. Who wouldn't have? And that's what Fumiko had counted on—that, fully aroused, drunk on champagne, he, like Rocky, would have gone along, even when he came upon the truth.

No, damn it! He was certain he would have stopped anyway, certain that, no matter how aroused, he would have lost all trace of desire once he saw that the person he was holding and fondling was a man.

Was that really so? Or was he conning himself? He felt it was the truth and was more and more convinced of it as he reviewed the night's events and softened the memory with more and more vodka. After his fourth drink, he felt he'd given the situation quite enough time and energy. Besides, it was beginning to seem funny.

Five minutes later, the driver of a battered pickup truck turned to his wife and pointed out a slim dark man walking north on Main Street. The man's jacket was slung over his shoulder and he was moving erratically up the sidewalk, staring at the night sky and laughing—right out loud. Just laughing like hell as if some private joke was up there, hidden in the mountains of the moon.

"Goddamn town," the driver growled. "Gettin' more fuckin' crazies every day."

Harry spent most of the next day returning calls from reporters throughout the world. *Time* and *Newsweek* were doing feature stories on the trial. Both wanted Harry for their covers. *Newsweek* intended using photos of Harry and Fumiko, but *Time* planned to do a quick oil portrait of Harry, and asked permission to entitle it "California's Legendary Sunset Bomber." Over the years, Harry had taken a child's simple delight in his increasing fame. A *Time* cover seemed the ultimate accolade, and he was thrilled. He paused for a moment, pretending to the *Time* editor that he was seriously considering whether or not to permit his picture on the cover. Then, in a tone as reluctant as he could muster, he gave it his blessing.

Occasionally, Harry thought of Fumiko. He wondered what was going through her mind. He couldn't think of her as "him." What would happen to her now? Poor tortured soul. Would the masquerade go on for her entire life? Of course, what else could happen? After twenty years of living as a woman, she wasn't suddenly going to appear as a man. Probably she'd find someone else—some lonely widower—and try to make it work with him the way she'd made it work with Rocky. In a way he hoped she could. Well, he thought, smiling to himself, she certainly has all the money she'll need. That might help the next guy overlook the one detail about her that's different.

Saturday morning at 7:00 o'clock, Harry and Gail stepped from a cab at Number One Wilshire Boulevard in the heart of downtown Los Angeles. Dressed in shorts, T-shirts, and Reeboks, they stood looking up at the deserted high-rise buildings. "Okay," Harry said pointing westward, "let's move out."

"Yo!" snapped Gail, saluting. And, striding quickly, they moved up Wilshire Boulevard into the incline bordering the downtown Hilton Hotel.

Both were out of breath as they stopped for a signal light at the top of the hill. "Don't be discouraged," Harry puffed, "that was the worst part of the walk."

"Sure, Dad." Gail laughed. "There must be thirty hills bigger than that between here and the ocean."

"Don't confuse me with the facts when I'm trying to psych myself up."

The light changed to green as they began the long, level approach to MacArthur Park.

"There's the Good Samaritan, where I was born." Harry pointed to the massive, faded brown hospital.

"Really, I never knew that."

"Probably lots you don't know about your old man, kid."

"What was my grandmother like?"

"I never really knew her. She died when I was so young. My dad raised me—over that little store I once showed you on Main Street."

"What was *he* like?"

"I remember him as very loving, and with a great ability to turn a commonplace event into an adventure—a wonderful talent. He'd take me to the beach on Sundays on the old red streetcar. We'd swim all the way to the breakwater. Very scary for a little kid. Or he'd rent a boat and fishing stuff and he'd row us so far out I thought he'd never get us back in. Then we'd fish all day. He had the store on Skid Row. He'd take me by the hand, and we'd walk all over the area. He knew everybody down there, hookers, bums, arcade operators, pawnbrokers, everyone. He had damn little money, but I swear that man never passed a beggar without giving him something. But, you know, I don't suppose I ever really knew him in the sense that you learn another person's fears and dreams. I mean, does anyone really know his own father in that way? And mine died so early, in the war—on the beach at Normandy. I never got the chance."

They stopped for the light at the corner of Alvarado. Gail reached over and squeezed Harry's hand.

"I'd like to know my father that way. Will you let me?"

"Sure I will," Harry murmured, indicating that the signal now said "walk."

"If you're going to give me that kind of perfunctory answer I'm quitting right here." She put her hands on her hips and stood staring at him.

Harry laughed. "You'll grab at any excuse to get out of this, won't you? Listen, there'll be no lunch 'til we get to the beach." He put his arm around her and pulled her with him across the street, talking as they crossed.

"Seriously, Gail, I think you know me better than most people know their fathers. I'd like us to know each other completely—if that's ever possible between parent and child. All I can say is I won't hold back."

They walked along the wide boulevard that swept through the park. The day was turning glorious. The Santa Ana winds had blown the air clean during the night, and it was warm and dry. The bright blue sky was reflected in the lake beyond the low railing that separated the curving sidewalk from the old park, once called Westlake Park, but renamed for General Douglas MacArthur after World War II.

Harry nudged Gail. "There's the quintessential California bum." Nearer downtown they had passed three or four winos asleep in doorways, the inevitable bottle of cheap fortified wine clutched to their breasts. Gail looked where Harry was pointing now and saw a shabbily clothed, singularly dirty man asleep on the grass. Instead of wine, he was clutching a large bottle of Evian water. Beside him was a plastic bag of oatbran.

"If he had some tofu, he'd be perfect." She giggled. "But I shouldn't laugh, Dad, they're not bums. They're homeless people, and you should know better."

"Maybe so, but isn't that just a new label for an old phenomenon? I mean what we always called bums are now homeless people. But they're the same guys."

"First of all, they're not all *guys*."

"I realize that, but we always had female bums too. Read William Kennedy. Only now they're called female homeless people. But they're the same people Kennedy wrote about—mostly people who *chose* to live like that."

They had moved into the mid-Wilshire district. They passed Chapman Park and the old Town House and then, crossing Vermont Avenue, stopped to admire the handsome art-deco building that housed Bullocks Wilshire.

"Built about nineteen twenty-six, I'd bet. I love it."

"I'd guess a little later. But don't change the subject, Dad. Homeless people are not bums. There are entire families out there that can't afford a place to live. This government is simply not meeting the basic needs of its people—not even providing housing for millions of its citizens."

"It's interesting you say 'providing' housing. When my dad got off the boat as a kid, he didn't speak English. He had nothing. No one 'provided' him with housing or anything else. When he married and I was born, it was still the Depression, and believe me, they weren't 'providing' any housing. He worked his butt off, and made damn sure his wife and kid had a roof over their heads. And when you were born, do you think we were rich? Hell, no, we had nothing. I worked hard and none of us ever had to sleep in the park. Why are these guys different?"

"Because there are no jobs and, even if they work, there's no affordable housing."

"Look, Gail, housing may seem out of sight, but it always seemed that way. Believe me, when you were born our rent appeared overwhelming compared with what I was earning. We sweated to make it work, and somehow we did it. But these guys *won't*. And I mean *won't*, not *can't*. I don't think economic conditions are that much worse. I think it's just become more socially acceptable to sleep in the goddamn park."

"You're a dinosaur—a lovable dinosaur, I grant you; but still antediluvian."

He took her hand. "No more politics. It's too gorgeous a day."

They passed the round dome of the Wilshire Boulevard Temple, more appropriate to Istanbul than Southern California, and stopped at the carved and decorated walls of the blue-green Wiltern Building.

"That's another deco beauty."

"Sure is. Sim Lee was the architect, S. Charles Lee. Did most of the great L.A. theaters. He was a client of mine once. I loved his architectural drawings. A real loss when he stopped being an architect and became a general contractor."

"Would you consider changing, Dad—doing something else?"

"Well, you know I had the chance to be a judge once. Turned it down; too passive. And I had an offer to run a studio once. Turned that down too. But it was a closer call."

"I didn't know that. What fun!"

"It might have been fun, but still, working for someone else just didn't appeal to me."

Harry pointed up a side street. "See that building—that's the old Wilshire-Ebell Auditorium. My dad and I used to take the bus there to chamber music concerts. What a strange combination of tastes that man had! Just loved chamber music—almost as much as he loved chili verde."

"Chili *verde?*"

"Yeah, green sauce instead of red. He learned the recipe from an old Texas bum—I mean homeless person—he took in and fed. Onions, garlic, jalapeño peppers, pork, and tomatillos—and no beans, of course."

They walked on in silence, passing the faded Miracle Mile, the La Brea Tar Pits and the County Museum of Art with its new glass-tiled façade.

"I wish they'd torn the old one down instead of trying to build around it."

"I agree. The old building's one of those tasteless wonders we produced in the fifties and sixties. Thank God, we've gone back to building with some character and imagination, like they did in the thirties."

At Sweetzer, Harry stopped and pointed to a red-brick, two-story building with white shutters. "That's my first law office. Oh, not overlooking Wilshire. I had a hole in the wall in back, facing the parking lot."

"It looks pretty nice to me."

"It was a new building then, and, being just out of law school, I couldn't begin to afford it. A white-haired New Englander built it, wanted to put up something that reminded him of Harvard Square. Brilliant guy, hugely successful then. I tried a small case for him. His regular lawyers wouldn't handle it. We won, and he gave me other little cases to handle, let me have an office in there for about half the true rent. I learned a lot from that man. Years later, he ran into some hard times and some tough legal problems. I cut his fees just like he'd cut my rent. About half. Never told him, though. With his Yankee pride he wouldn't have stood for it. But it seemed right to me at the time."

Gail stopped and hugged Harry. "You know, I'm proud of you. Did I ever tell you?"

"I'm glad you are, Gail, but it's not going to get you out of the rest of this walk." Laughing, he grabbed her shoulders and headed her in the direction of the sea.

After Beverly Hills and Westwood, the day grew hot; their legs grew heavy and their stops more frequent. As they passed the vast grounds of the Veterans Home, they could finally see the ocean shimmering far in the distance, still a good hour away.

"That's where I went to high school, right down there on West-gate—University High—'Uni' we called it. I lived about a mile farther south in a boarding house—worked afternoons and weekends to pay. Boy, was I poor!"

"Well, now you can make up for all those hard times. You're hardly poor now."

Harry stopped and took Gail's hand, looking straight into her dark, intense eyes.

"Okay, here's another fact about your father. Money doesn't mean that much. It's nice to be able to buy what I want and go where I want. But I'd do what I do even if they paid me in apples or blue ribbons."

As he spoke, he wondered if he really meant that, or just wanted his daughter to think of him that way. He decided he meant it.

"You know, in my days of being poor, I never felt deprived. Sure, I worried; but life was exciting, full of challenge. Especially after your mother and I were together. All those years of struggling together, succeeding at it—I wouldn't trade those times for all the money in the world."

They stood, arms around each other, as the traffic rushed by. Then they started toward the distant sea and the last leg of their trek. Just before the Palisades, Harry took Gail by the arm, steering her around a corner into a quiet old Santa Monica street.

"We're going to see the old apartment aren't we?"

"Yeah, do you mind?"

"Of course not."

They walked three blocks north, each occupied with private thoughts, painful memories. They made a right turn and stopped before a two-story, ivy-covered apartment house.

"There it is. That's where we lived when you were born—when you almost died. I remember the race to St. Johns like it was yesterday. Three in the morning. Ninety miles an hour through the empty streets, praying to a God I'd neglected for a long time, driving with one hand and trying to comfort your mother with the other. My God!"

He pulled her close, feeling the tears run down her face, then felt his own sobs come, racking his body as she held and comforted him. Finally, he stepped back, fished for his handkerchief, and wiped his eyes. He took her arm and they began the two-block walk to the bluff overlooking the ocean.

"I don't think the pain is going to get any less, Gail."

"Sure it will."

"I don't know."

"Look, Dad, I loved Mom. I'll miss her all my life. So will you. But we've both got a long life to live and eventually the pain won't be so intense."

He kept walking in silence. They crossed Ocean Avenue and stood at the railing of the Palisades, looking out at the Pacific gleaming in the afternoon sunlight.

Harry turned to look at his daughter again, so young and vulnerable, profiled against the pale sky and blue-green sea. He wondered if she too felt alone and empty. He decided not to ask.

"Thanks for coming, Gail. It helped me a lot. It reminded me that, no matter what, we have each other."

For a moment, she continued staring out at the water. Then she turned to face him.

"We do, and it helps." She smiled. "I really enjoyed the walk, Dad. Mom would've, too."

"I know—and Gail . . ." he took her hand again. "I love you."

By Monday, Harry was already missing his daughter, wishing that she'd return to live in L.A. Maybe they could live together now that he was alone. No, that was a silly dream. She'd want her own life, her privacy. Someday, he supposed, so would he. But not yet.

That afternoon Harry met with Skip Corrigan about the progress of an ongoing investigation. Skip hugged Harry warmly, patting his back with affection. "I'm sorry about your wife. That's a rough one; but hang in there, my friend. Just hang in there . . . and two more things. Be careful driving. Recent widowers are lousy risks. And don't jump into some new relationship. There's thousands of women out there just waiting to pounce, so don't confuse your dick with your heart."

With those words, the short but formidable detective settled into the gray upholstered chair opposite Harry's desk and began his report. Occasionally taking a sip of ice water, he related in detail the activities of a building contractor who was suing a client of Harry's for $9 million. Harry believed he wasn't entitled to the money; and Skip's work was beginning to show that Harry was right. At least some of the materials charged to Harry's client had been used on other jobs and, in one instance, had gone to build a guest house for the contractor's brother-in-law.

Usually when Skip concluded a report he rose quickly, shook hands, and left. He was not a man to waste time, his or anyone else's. This time, however, he remained seated, giving Harry his characteristic sharklike smile.

"I've got some news for you, counselor."

"Oh?"

"Yeah." Skip took a sip of water. "You remember that Fernbach case, the one you settled the night before closing argument?"

"Of course I do."

"Well, you won it. Congratulations." The sly grin grew even wider. The green eyes twinkled.

"What do you mean, I won it?"

"I mean the judge was going to decide it for you . . . for Fernbach. In fact, he'd already decided it."

"How could you possibly know that?"

"Trade secret. But I can tell you he'd already dictated a draft of his opinion, and you won. You know what else?"

"What?"

"Yank Slutsky knew he'd lost the case. That's why he paid off."

"Come on, Skip, how could Yank possibly know what the judge was going to do before he did it?"

"You know Buck Barringer? Yank's PR guy, big, good-lookin' dude, great cocksman?"

"Yeah, I know him."

"Well, Yank sends Buck in to nail the court reporter. Buck stakes her out, then picks her up in a bar near her apartment. One thing leads to another and they get real close. You know what I'm sayin'? Anyway, she gives Buck the judge's draft opinion. They had it the night they called you and agreed to settle. You got hustled, pal."

"Did Greg Morrison know?"

"I doubt it, Harry. My guess is Yank just called and ordered him to pay you whatever it took." The sharklike grin returned. "So you admit you got taken, huh?"

"Not really. Aaron got every dime that was coming to him."

"Yeah, but the judge was going to give you punitive damages. Another two million."

"You're kidding."

"Would I shit you? I've seen the opinion."

"Come on, Skip. How'd you get all this?"

"I can't tell you, pal. Another case. It just surfaced along with a lot of other facts about your friends Slutsky and Fernbach. You pissed off?"

"Well, in a way. The punitive damages would have been nice, and it would have been better for Aaron to have been publicly vindicated by the judge."

"What do you care?"

"Hey, Skip, you know I care. The guy was getting a raw deal. He works for them for years . . . honest, hard good work. And successful too. They they try to rape and ruin him. And they had nothing on him, nothing! The guy was clean, and they made him look dirty to the whole world. Lots of people still think he's dirty. So sure I care."

"Clean, huh." Again the sharklike grin.

"Of course clean . . . what are you saying?"

"Nothing, never mind," Skip said starting to rise, still smiling.

"Come on, Skip, spit it out. You can't bring up something like that and then clam up."

The detective sat down again, crossed his legs, and took another sip of water.

"Look, Harry, this other case took me into lots of places that turned up stuff about both Fernbach and Slutsky. I really know what went down. Your friend Fernbach lied to you and lied to the judge and he got away with it—'cause he had the best goddamn lawyer in the country."

"You're all wet, Skip. Those restaurant receipts weren't his doing. Mona Olinsky testified he didn't know a thing about it, that she did it all on her own. She told me the same thing when I spoke to her in

San Francisco, and she had nothing to gain and plenty to lose by saying so."

"Boy, are you ever a schmuck. I'm not talking about restaurant receipts. He probably didn't know about 'em. But who do you think Mona's been fucking and living off the last two years?"

"Aaron?"

"But of course Aaron. He's paid for her apartment for two years now. Told her he'd leave his wife and marry her. And do you know who else he fucked . . . your wonderful Princeton prince?"

"You're not going to say Annie Robinson?"

"Yes I am. On his desk, in his private washroom. In the backseat of that fancy car . . . everywhere."

"Come on, Skip. Have you seen her? You'd need pictures to convince me of that."

The detective's smile grew even wider. He slapped his large brief-case. "I thought you'd never ask." He opened the case and took out two photos. One showed Aaron Fernbach on his back with Annie Robinson astride him, her eyes glazed with lust or drugs. They were both nude and at a beach somewhere. Harry thought it might be Malibu. Harry recognized the other picture as Aaron's New York office. Aaron was seated on his big pine desk, his trousers down around his knees. Annie was kneeling in front of him, greedily suck-ing his cock. Aaron's hands clutched the back of her head as if in fear she'd stop.

"How'd you get pictures like this?"

"You know better than to ask that, for Christ's sake. Are you convinced?"

"Hell, yes I am. What a lying scumbag!"

"Hey, I've told you plenty of times you put too much trust in those high and mighty assholes you work for. You kill yourself to save people who don't deserve it and who don't pay you enough. And you go right on doing it, year after year."

Harry sat quietly contemplating what Skip had said. After a mo-ment he rose and walked to his cabinet, poured himself two fingers of Dewar's.

"Some for you, Skip?"

"No thanks. I never touch it."

Harry felt the Scotch burn its way down, felt the easing of his stomach that came with the alcohol. He smiled ruefully.

"Boy, this takes the cake for irony. Aaron lies to me, lies to the judge, and gets a big payoff. Yank tries to ruin Aaron. He trumps up ridiculous grounds, uses every shitty trick, commits perjury, even steals the judge's opinion, and gets away with it all. I defend a guy who's guilty, naïvely accepting his story and believing he's innocent. I fail to grasp the truth, fail to see I'm being conned into a settlement by Slutsky and, after all that fucking up on my part, I get a very big fee, and the world thinks I'm brilliant. It's a win all around, except maybe for truth and justice."

Skip rose and looked at his watch. "I can't spend the whole day bullshitting with you about social philosophy. Do that with your candy-assed Hollywood friends. I've got kids to feed."

Harry was leaving the office early. He had a wedding to attend, his first social event since Nancy's death. He felt uncertain, ambivalent about going. But he had to face people sometime. Might as well be now.

As he was packing his briefcase, the intercom buzzed.

"Mike Simpson from the *Times*, Mr. Cain."

"Okay, Clara."

"Hi, Mike, what's up?"

"Any comment on this case against you?"

"What case?"

"Some guy named Milo Putnam sued you today for breach of contract, wrongful termination, intentional infliction of emotional distress, and sexual harassment."

"Sexual harassment?"

"Yeah. Claims that he was subjected to pornography, and was touched in an erotic manner and that an attempt was made to coerce him into sexual relations."

"By whom?"

"According to the complaint, it was someone named Clara Know-land. But he alleges that you knew about what he calls her proclivity to engage in sexual harassment, so you're liable, too. He also claims you forced him to participate in a scheme to overcharge your clients. Wants ten million bucks and another ten million in punitive damages. Any comment?"

"That greedy little prick!"

The reporter chuckled. "That's your comment?"

"No, that's for background. My comment is 'the lawsuit has no merit and we'll vigorously defend it.' Who's his lawyer?"

"B. J. Scuneo."

"*What?*"

"Didn't you know B.J. left the DA's office the morning after the Masami verdict? Formed a partnership with Herb Simon. I guess you were in jail at the time."

"Christ, what a combination—Scumbag Scuneo and Milo Putnam. Listen, Mike, you've got your quote. If you need more, give me a call later, okay? Oh, and Mike . . . one more thing. Did you read Putnam's claims in the complaint or did Scuneo tell you what they were?"

"Tell me? Scuneo and Putnam held a press conference before they filed."

"Thanks, Mike. We'll talk later."

The moment he hung up, Harry buzzed for Clara. She knocked and hesitantly entered, as always looking shy and frightened.

"Clara, this is difficult and I'm afraid embarrassing." He paused and took a deep breath. "There's been a sexual harassment claim filed against you . . . and against the firm as well."

She paled, and Harry gestured for her take the chair opposite his desk.

"By whom?" she asked, sitting stiffly and pulling down her skirt.

"Milo Putnam."

Clara looked stunned. For what seemed an inordinately long time, she simply sat there, saying nothing.

Finally, Harry broke the silence.

"Did you ever touch Mr. Putnam, Clara?"

She looked up at the ceiling, frowning, trying to remember.

"Once I put my hand on his shoulder when I thanked him for helping me reorganize your time records."

"What did he do?"

"Nothing. He said 'you're welcome'; but he did look over at my hand. I remember being embarrassed and taking it away."

"Any other time?"

"Not that I remember."

"He says you exposed him to pornography. Do you have any idea what he means?"

She turned bright red and nodded. She took a deep breath and then sat forward in the chair.

"Mr. Cain, sometimes I buy *Playgirl*. You know, the magazine with the . . . the nude male centerfold?"

It was difficult for Harry to conceal his surprise. It was impossible to avoid a smile. Clara's face turned an even deeper red as she continued.

"Well, once I had a copy of *Playgirl* on my desk. Mr. Putnam stopped and looked through the pages. I asked if he'd like to borrow it. He kind of snapped 'certainly not!' and went back to his desk. That's all there was to it."

"Clara, I don't really know how to ask you about the last claim. He says you tried to coerce him into having . . . uh . . . sexual relations."

Her hand flew to her mouth and her eyes widened.

"Oh, Mr. Cain, I never . . . I mean . . . I just never . . . that just never happened."

"I knew it didn't, Clara. But I need to find out what he's basing his claim on. Did you suggest any kind of social or personal contact?"

"Oh, *that*" she said, looking down at her hands.

"What, Clara, *what?*" Now Harry was on the edge of his chair.

Clara continued to look down as if studying the hardwood floor.

"I go ballroom dancing every Thursday night. He once asked me what it was like, and I asked him if he'd like to come with me sometime. He said that would be against 'office policy.' I was terribly embarrassed." She looked up at Harry. "Oh, Mr. Cain, I'm *so* sorry. I'd die before I got the firm in trouble."

Harry leaned across the desk and took Clara's nail-bitten hand.

"You didn't do anything wrong, Clara. Not a single thing. This is a phony complaint and we'll beat it. The only thing is . . . you're going to get some rather bad publicity. But, in the end, you'll be publicly cleared. I promise."

He smiled and squeezed her hand. "Would you like to go home now?"

"No, I'd just as soon finish my work."

"Okay. But I think you should warn your family and friends before they read it in the papers."

"The papers?"

"Yes. That's what I meant. Putnam and his lawyer held a press conference. I'm afraid it'll be everywhere."

She squeezed his hand. "It'll be okay, Mr. Cain. I don't have any family and no real friends except at ballroom dancing. And if I have you on my side, I'm not afraid of anything."

She rose and quietly left the room. Harry sat back in his chair, thinking. He could recall no one ever saying anything nicer.

After a moment, Harry dialed his partner.

"John, have you heard about this Milo Putnam case?"

"ESP, Harry. We just got served this minute. I was going to call you."

"You know who the lawyer is?"

There was a pause, while John looked through the papers he'd been handed.

"I do now. I'd heard he left the DA, but taking cases like this?"

"Scuneo would take *any* case against me, John, any case."

"Well, Scuneo or not, you can probably settle the whole thing for a quick ten thousand."

"Settle? I wouldn't pay that lying son of a bitch ten cents, especially after what he's done to poor Clara. 'Sexual harassment' my ass! and claiming we overcharged our clients. He's the guy that tried to do that, to keep the clients' money. I was the one who said 'No, pay it back.' And now that miserable little prick has the gall to reverse the whole thing and say we forced him to overcharge and caused him 'emotional distress.' I'll give him 'emotional distress' all right. I'll sue his tight little ass—and Scuneo's too. I want to file a cross-complaint by the end of the week."

"What's our claim, Harry?"

"First, there's slander. They spread all this horse shit in a press conference before he even filed his lawsuit. He's got an absolute privilege to say what he wants in court, but not in a goddamned press conference. And Scuneo's as liable as Putnam."

"Sounds right. What else?"

Harry paused.

"I don't know yet. I'll think of more when I get time."

Harry took a miniature quesadilla from the silver tray, popped it into his mouth and washed it down with Dom Pérignon. The crowd flowed around him, excited, noisy, waiting for the bride and groom to reenter the room. It was painful not to have Nancy to laugh with about the tiny, senseless, funny things that happened at a gathering like this. But he recognized the need to avoid feeling sorry for himself, the need to regain his old natural buoyancy.

"Harry, can I have a moment of your time?"

He looked around to see Ewing Campbell, dapper in a black pinstriped suit and red polka-dot tie. Pat Campbell, in a gray-green Galanos that softly and subtly clung to her figure, was on his arm, beaming. Ewing turned to Pat with a gracious smile.

"Darling, will you excuse us for a moment? Harry and I have a most confidential matter to discuss."

Pat smiled sweetly, tolerantly.

"Of course, Ewing, I'll be over with the mayor when you're ready."

She moved away through the crowd. When she had gone, Campbell led Harry to a distant corner of the room.

"Remember my good friend, the one with the diary?"

"Sure."

"Well, you were absolutely right. It's amazing. He found his wife's current diary in her lingerie drawer . . . one of the places you suggested. Once he read it, it was obvious from what she'd written about recent events my friend knew *didn't* happen that the entire thing, including the earlier stuff, was fantasy, just a product of her imagination. He was thrilled, because, as I told you, he loves her very much."

"I'm delighted to hear it, Ewing, and I'm glad I could help. Maybe someday I'll meet your friend." Harry couldn't resist this last.

"Oh, I'm sure you will, Harry, but, of course, I could never identify him as the fellow with the diary problem."

"Of course not, Ewing, I understand that. Well, whoever he is, I'm very pleased we could help keep his marriage together."

"Oh, it's more than just keeping a marriage together, Harry, much more than that. Things between them are better than in years." Campbell beamed and, turning, waved to his wife across the room. "Yes, sir," he repeated, "it's certainly more than that."

Harry returned home from the wedding feeling good about what he'd accomplished for Pat Campbell, but curious about Ewing's cryptic remark that he had done more than keeping a marriage together.

Armando met him at the door, took his coat, handed him a glass of Cabernet and disappeared. Harry stood in the softly lit hallway, sipping the dark ruby wine. He noticed a large stack of boxes on the low Spanish bench. Putting down his glass, he turned over one long box. "Saks Fifth Avenue, Houston, Texas." Knowing he shouldn't, he sat on the bench and opened the packages one by one, holding up the contents of each . . . a taupe suit and one of slate blue, a simple gray dress, flannel slacks, and two blouses.

The memory of that afternoon flooded back—the last day Nancy was herself . . . ever—the last day she'd felt some joy, some hope. Here were the clothes he'd picked out and she'd tried on so patiently, so bravely. She'd never wear them now. Would never wear anything again. He slid to the floor amidst the opened packages, smothering his tears in a silk Armani blouse.

On a warm evening later that week, Harry sat reading the trade papers in his office. *The Last Battle* had been released to uniformly bad reviews and was doing no business at all. Harry smiled to himself at the irony of his having risked disbarment, even jail, to protect and preserve what had turned out to be an artistic and financial disaster. Well, he thought, at least it was the film Joe Miletti wanted. That's what they'd fought for. How galling though to think that Yank Slutsky may have been right—happy ending and all.

He put aside the papers and let his thoughts drift in the early evening quiet. No one else was there except Clara, who sat outside the door revising a brief on her word processor.

Harry was expecting a late visitor. His English client, Alan Canning, had called from Zurich, asking Harry to see the widow of a friend. He had described a sad and bizarre situation. Christina Maitland, a top New York model, had married Cesare DeLorenzo, a young Italian banker, the eldest son of an ancient Milanese family. They had been married for some ten years and had a young son. Two months before, Cesare had been murdered, gunned down by two men directly in front of his home. No one knew why or by whom. The family, never enthusiastic about his marrying an American and a model at that, were making trouble about property, about custody of the boy, about everything.

This was all Harry knew, but it was enough to intrigue him. The lady was due in about twenty minutes, and Harry sat back staring at the ceiling, just floating, thinking vaguely of Nancy, of Gail, of so many things.

After a few minutes, the intercom buzzed.

"Letter for you. Just delivered by messenger, Mr. Cain."

"Would you bring it in, Clara?"

"Yes, sir."

Clara came in and handed Harry an envelope, then left, closing the door behind her. The top of the envelope bore the handwritten words "Personal and Confidential," words that kept Clara or anyone else in Harry's office from opening an envelope or package. Harry slit the envelope. It contained a letter from Pat Campbell on thick, creamy bond and what appeared to be a photocopy of a page from her diary.

Dear Harry: How wonderfully right you were about everything. As I told you, I wrote the "current diary" and, as you suggested, I hid it in my lingerie drawer. What I wrote was also what you suggested, as you can see from the enclosed sample.

Harry put aside the letter and began to read the diary entry.

January 25th. Dressing for Nancy Reagan reception. Wearing ankle-length dark green Halston with shoes dyed to match. I stand adjusting earrings. Ewing is (I thought) across the room, slipping into his patent leather pumps. Suddenly I feel my skirt lifted from behind and a hand reach up under my dress, move quickly between my thighs cupping me, massaging me. Marvelous! Thrill runs through my body as I begin to sway, hypnotized by pleasure. Then the hands take me by the hips and spin me around. It's Ewing, of course, but, when I see him, I'm shocked and excited. He's fully dressed in his tuxedo, except his trousers are open, and he's exposed and erect. With a rough whisper, he orders me to lift my skirt. I do and he pulls me onto him. I'm not wearing panties (never do with that kind of dress). I feel him enter me, slide into me, hot and exciting. Absolutely, amazingly marvelous. I'm bowled over with sensation. The earth moves. Wow! Then, he puts strong arms around me, holds me close. We sit like that for quite some time, loving, enjoying each other. Finally, we clean up, re-dress, and go late to reception.

Grinning, Harry put down the diary excerpt and turned again to the letter.

I know he found it, Harry. And, as you planned, he completely bought the idea that, like this current diary, the original one was all fantasy. But you'll never guess *how* I know. When we were dressing to go to the Armbruster wedding (where we saw you) he did *exactly* what I had written in my phony fantasy. He acted it out just as I wrote it . . . except he was sitting down, poor dear. Still, for the first time in six months, *sacré bleu!* It was as good as I described in my "diary." Will it happen again? Maybe. But this once was something to treasure. I'd like to say you're a genius (and you are), but even *you* didn't expect *that* result. I'll thank you forever and so, I'm sure, will Ewing, which was probably what he was doing at the wedding. Anyway, my friend, I had a very bad scare, but you made everything right, and I guess all's well that ends well.

Fondly, Pat.

Harry put down the letter, beaming. So that's what Ewing meant. The old goat. Harry was pleased. He was not really a part of their lives, nor they of his; still, he felt a real pleasure in using his mind, or, more accurately, his wits, to help them. He'd done something right for a change, and it felt good. Also, he was beginning to be himself again. Not fully. That would take a long time. But he was moving in the right direction.

He switched on the stereo, filling the room with the Paganini violin concerto. Leaning back in his chair, he watched the reflected lights from the cars below flash across the ceiling. He began to smile.

The intercom sounded over the music, arousing Harry from his reverie.

"Mrs. DeLorenzo's here, Mr. Cain."

"Send her in."

The office door opened and Harry rose. Hesitantly, a tall, slim woman in her late thirties entered the room. A mass of ebony hair fell to the shoulders of her simple black dress. Her eyes stopped Harry's heart. They were frightened, troubled eyes, bright green and enormous. She looked at Harry and around his office, then, almost shyly, glanced down at her own graceful hands. She was very pale.

"I'm Christina DeLorenzo, Mr. Cain. Alan told me about your wife. I'm very sorry."

She extended her hand. Harry took it, looking deep into those startling emerald eyes. They widened, like the eyes of a cat.

"Thank you. Please sit down," he said, his voice surprisingly hoarse.

She settled easily into a gray corduroy chair, crossing long slender legs. Harry sat down as well and looked at her across the desk. She looked directly back, her eyes locking into his. For a moment, just a moment, it was as if they were staring into each other's souls. Then Harry broke the spell, picking up a pad, ready to take notes.

"Alan told me something of your problem. Let me just get some of the facts. When was your husband killed?"

"April second."

Harry felt the blood drain from his face. He put down the pen and looked up at her.

"That's extraordinary. My wife died the same day." He saw a tremor pass through her body. Her green eyes widened again. There was another long pause. Each sat in silence, wrapped in memory.

"You know," Harry said at last, "it's eight o'clock. Have you had dinner?"

"No, actually I wasn't too hungry."

"Would you join me? We'll go over to Le Dome—get a quiet table off by ourselves where we can talk. It's a little more relaxed than here."

She smiled for the first time, a warm, open smile. "I'd love to, Mr. Cain."

He rose and took her arm. They left the office side by side, beginning to laugh and shyly to examine each other. As they stood in the elevator, he caught the scent of her subtle perfume, felt the impact of her presence. For an instant, it occurred to him to be careful, that he was still raw and vulnerable, that he should go slowly. Then, turning toward her, he saw more clearly the lovely planes of her face and looked again into her amazing green eyes. Careful? he thought. Nonsense. There was a life still to be lived. He might as well get started.